D0062524

Also by Robert Rodi:

Fag Hag

Closet Case

Robert Rodi

What They
Did To
PRINCESS
PARAGON

A PLUME BOOK

PLUME
Published by the Penguin Group
Penguin Books USA Inc., 375 Hudson Street, New York, New York 10014, U.S.A.
Penguin Books Ltd, 27 Wrights Lane, London W8 5TZ, England
Penguin Books Australia Ltd, Ringwood, Victoria, Australia
Penguin Books Canada Ltd, 10 Alcorn Avenue, Toronto, Ontario, Canada M4V 3B2
Penguin Books (N.Z.) Ltd, 182–190 Wairau Road, Auckland 10, New Zealand

Penguin Books Ltd, Registered Offices:
Harmondsworth, Middlesex, England

First published by Plume, an imprint of Dutton Signet, a division
of Penguin Books USA Inc. Previously published in a Dutton edition.

First Plume Printing, May, 1995

10 9 8 7 6 5 4 3 2 1

Ⓟ REGISTERED TRADEMARK—MARCA REGISTRADA

The Library of Congress has catalogued the Dutton edition as follows:
Rodi, Robert.
What they did to Princess Paragon / Robert Rodi.
p.   cm.
ISBN 0-525-93772-2 (hc.)
0-452-27163-0 (pbk.)
1. Comic books, strips, etc.—United States—Authorship—Fiction.
2. Kidnapping—United States—Fiction. 3. Gay men—United States—
Fiction.   I. Title.
PS3568.O34854W43   1994

813'.54—dc20   93-40187
                                                                    CIP

Printed in the United States of America
Original hardcover design by Steven N. Stathakis

BOOKS ARE AVAILABLE AT QUANTITY DISCOUNTS WHEN USED TO PROMOTE PRODUCTS OR SERVICES.
FOR INFORMATION PLEASE WRITE TO PREMIUM MARKETING DIVISION, PENGUIN BOOKS USA INC.,
375 HUDSON STREET, NEW YORK, NY 10014.

For Jeffrey, who is perfect;

and for Christopher Schelling,
whose ideas and guidance
made this a better book.

You boys be nice and share, now.

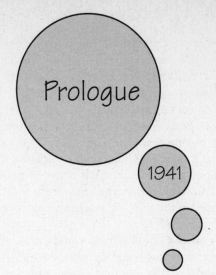

Prologue

1941

All across the country, people clamored for war. On the plains they called for it, and in crowded cities; on the coasts and on the borders. It was a fervent, illicit passion, a welling-up of blood lust. Everywhere, fresh-scrubbed young men and women gathered gleefully to rehearse the politics of hatred. It was exhilarating to have enemies so detestable. It was ennobling to seek them out and make them pay.

Roger Oaklyn was not alone in not wanting war, but he might as well have been. His fellow pacifists had recoiled from the overwhelming militarism of the day; they had holed up in their apartments, with books and music to console them, and now ignored the screams of the hawks, insistent and bullying, that rent the air.

Roger Oaklyn, however, still walked the streets, and walked them boldly, proclaiming his ideological difference with every facet of his appearance. In his floppy sweaters and dungarees, he told his countrymen that he did not think like them by the expedient means of not *dressing* like them. Similarly, he followed none of their other fashions. He wore his hair long and sported a beard. He did not eat meat. He did not touch liquor. He read widely on Classical Greece and considered himself a philosopher.

Yet he had been forced to reside at less lofty a height; for, requiring the common coin to feed his body as well as his mind (books *did* cost money), he had taken a job providing illustrations for grade-school textbooks. But when the infusion into these of racist and nationalist propaganda made his job intolerable, he quit and wandered the city, an anachronism, an anomaly. And as he wandered, he watched.

Roger Oaklyn knew America would go to war. It was inevitable. The country was speeding out of control like a car with too many hands on the steering wheel and too many feet depressing the accelerator; it could not help soon hitting a wall. A year, perhaps. Two at most.

He decided what was wrong with the world was that the masculine principle—force—was in the ascendant, while the feminine principle—persuasion—had all but vanished. When he spoke of these things, he was scorned. People saw only his long hair and longer scarves and called him "professor" and "nature boy" and "maestro."

When his need for food began to nag at him, he reluctantly took the first job he could find—at a publishing company that produced comic books, for which there was an insatiable nationwide demand. In a one-room sweatshop, he worked as a cartoonist on stories that either bored or disgusted him. After two months on the job, one of the editors asked him if he could draw any faster. "Only if I write my own stories," he replied. Go ahead, said the editor.

At home that night, Roger Oaklyn invented a costumed mystery woman who would take her place beside the thuggish mob of mystery men. She stepped out of his soul and into his pen, and when he moved his drawing hand he released her. She wore a cape spangled with stars and stood tall and strong; she was *from* the stars, and had come to Earth to save it. She had come to teach men and women to be forgiving. She had come to teach them to believe only good about their enemies and to bring out the best in those who opposed them. She had come to lead humanity into a new era in which war would be banished and peace revered.

She was the complete and intoxicating reflection of everything Roger Oaklyn believed. She was his feminine principle—all humanity's feminine principle—given form, corporealized as a beautiful figure of power and benevolent authority. She was a perfect woman; she was a perfect human being. Roger called her Princess Paragon.

And then he drew her first story.

PART
ONE

1990

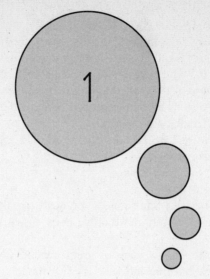

1

Brian Parrish chewed gum when he was nervous. He rolled it around in his mouth. He stuck it up by his gums and then flattened it by sucking in his lips. He bit into it repeatedly so that it became a soggy mass of bite marks that he could probe with his tongue. He grabbed one end of it between his teeth and the tip of his tongue, lifted it with the rest of his tongue so that it stretched and stretched until it was a sticky, fibrous strand, and then snapped it. He hid it under his tongue and pretended for a second that he had no gum at all.

Yet these tricks were nothing compared to what Heloise Freitag could do with cigarette smoke. Even as Brian, who was very nervous at the moment, put his chewing gum through its paces, he marveled at the sight of Heloise sitting at her desk, chewing on a mouthful of cigarette smoke as though it were a hunk of hamburger, then coughing it out in three staccato bursts, each one an almost perfect square.

It was very revealing, all that nervous cigarette smoke. He was grateful she couldn't see what he was doing with his gum.

"So, Brian," she said as she lifted her cigarette to eye level and held it there. Surely she couldn't be comfortable holding her cigarette so high. The smoke oozed around her head and she looked like Mount Saint Helens.

"So, Heloise," he said in non-reply. He giggled anxiously and cracked his gum.

"How's Nico?" she asked.

"Fine. And Tom?"

"Never better." She craned her head to take another drag off the cigarette. Surely it would've been easier simply to lower her hand.

Brian wrapped his chewing gum around his tongue like a lasso, then flicked it free and said, "Well, what's new around here?"

Heloise grinned, leaned back in her chair, and held her cigarette even higher. If she weren't careful, she'd set fire to her hair. "What's *new*, Brian? Everything's new. You know that. If you want specifics, ask specifically."

He smiled. Heloise had been the publisher of Bang Comics for little more than a year, and she'd already begun to turn the moribund company around. After fifty years, the Bang Comics characters were beginning to attract attention again. Heloise had started by taking lots of risks—allowing writers to introduce adult themes, instituting companywide story lines that tied all Bang Comics publications together, inventing new formats with better paper, better color separations, and higher prices.

But then, everyone had expected her to take risks. After all, her ass was on the line. Her last job had been as publisher of another Cooper Communications–owned property, a specifically Jewish-targeted teen magazine called *Sparkle*, and *Sparkle* had failed miserably. Heloise had misunderstood her market; Jewish girls just weren't significantly different from any other group of teenagers. By the laws of the corporate jungle, Cooper should've booted her out the door. But Cooper's CEO, Grant Vander-wheyde, had known Heloise's family since she was a toddler, and so he gave her a second chance. He put her in charge of another

Cooper division: the foundering Bang Comics line. It was Heloise's last chance to make a name for herself in publishing. Of *course* she'd take risks. She was a desperate woman.

Yet nothing had prepared Brian for the risks he'd seen her take lately. She'd hired an angry young British punk, Nigel Cardew, to write the *Moonman* series. In Britain, Cardew had written a roiling, subversive comic book called *Hate-Mongers*, which had actually been denounced in the House of Lords. He was as controversial a figure as this tiny industry had ever seen. When Heloise hired him to write *Moonman*, Brian had thought she'd lost her mind. At one of the monthly inter-company poker parties held at Heloise's house, he'd even seized the opportunity to tell her so. (Of course, having lost a cool hundred to her had helped him descend to such frankness.)

But then the Cardew-written *Moonman* came out. In the first issue, Moonman shot and killed a corrupt cop. In the second, he helped a nun get a secret abortion. In the third, Moonman's kid partner, Comet, was killed by a child pornographer, who filmed the murder for his clients.

Sales went through the roof. Newspapers and magazines, which hadn't covered *Moonman* since the silly 1970s television serial, started to write about the "grim, adult" new series with headlines like "Have You Seen What Your Kids Are Reading Lately?"

As Brian looked at Heloise now, he thought, She's *this* close to doing it. She senses it. Oh, she could still fuck it up; Bang's still going down the toilet and one hot series isn't going to save it. But she's won her first big victory, and she knows it.

He caught Heloise looking at him in turn, expelling smoke through her nose like a comic-book bull. There was a kind of hunger in her eyes—not sexual, for she was not a sexual animal; this hunger was purely mercenary. Brian knew she wanted to make him her *second* big victory.

Well, he couldn't blame her for that. Hadn't he spent the last ten years working for Bang's biggest rival, Electric Comics, single-handedly reviving interest in all of their longest-running titles? When he took over *Quasar Quintet* in 1981, the book was close to being canceled. Soon its sales were soaring into the stratosphere, not unlike the dauntless quintet themselves. Then he revitalized the declining monster title *Sherman Tank*, and made the purple behemoth a first-string star again, a quarter-century after his literally blockbusting debut.

And then, in 1986, he skillfully renegotiated his contract, becoming the wealthiest cartoonist now working in comic books. He assumed complete creative control over Electric's flagship title, *The Centipede*, and had his biggest success to date. His first issue, number 317, actually sold more than a million copies—a feat unmatched since the golden age of comic books, way back during World War II.

Now his contract with Electric was again close to expiration. But this time Electric wasn't so keen to bow to Brian's every whim. During the past several years, they'd hired a slew of teen-age talents who could draw like Brian Parrish and construct a page like Brian Parrish and write dialogue like Brian Parrish. The Electric Comics management, confident in their squad of Brian Parrish clones, began to regard the original as somewhat more expendable than before. Brian found himself faced with the prospect of not being adequately rewarded by the company he'd virtually rescued from bankruptcy.

It appalled him. He'd been an Electric Comics company man for ten years. More than that, he genuinely loved the hip irreverence of the Electric Comics "house style." Its characters talked in slang, argued with each other, had money problems and romantic difficulties—all the attributes of real life that never came within a country mile of a Bang Comics character. Electric Comics had the smart-alecky, vital vulgarity of the early sixties, which is when the company had been founded. Electric Comics were lively in a way that Bang Comics had never been. To Brian, Bang Comics heroes represented grim authority; Electric Comics heroes, joyful anarchy.

Yet as he began to contemplate his possible career moves in the face of an almost certain break with Electric, he discovered that he nursed a secret admiration for the Bang heroes as well. Sure, they were a hoary, square-jawed, stodgy lot. But he loved their bigness, their iconic resonance. Weren't they all indelible figures of Americana? Acme-Man, the atomic knight who performed miraculous feats of daring! Moonman, the veiled vigilante who stalked the darkened city streets in search of evil! Princess Paragon, the beautiful expatriate from a utopian planet who came to Earth to teach enlightened values! Somehow, the Electric Comics heroes seemed petty and venal by comparison.

He was rather surprised by this epiphany; despite the amicable camaraderie between the Electric and Bang cartoonists, there was always that basic ideological difference that separated them. To find himself contemplating defection was startling. You were either Democrat or Republican, Mets or Yankees, Bang or Electric. Some bridges were just not crossed.

Yet money is a powerful incentive for treason, as it is for all things, and Brian had thought, If Electric doesn't meet my terms at signing time, I'll go to Bang and do for them what I did for Electric. I'll revitalize their characters and make them sell again. They know I can do it—I've spent ten years proving it. I bet they'd pay *anything* to get their hands on me.

He had just achieved that level of smugness when Nigel Cardew's *Moonman* came out, and when he saw it, he panicked. Heloise was managing to revitalize the Bang Comics characters *without* him! If he didn't act soon, he'd lose his chance to be part of that—and he'd also lose his only opportunity to remain the top-dollar talent in comics.

That's what had brought him to Heloise's office this morning, a full two months before his Electric Comics contract expired. It was therefore a necessarily clandestine meeting; but Brian felt it urgent that he meet with her at once. If he didn't, in another two months she might have accomplished so much that his time-tested abilities would be wholly irrelevant to her.

Heloise rounded her lips and puffed out a ring of smoke; it hung lazily in the air, and a moment later she shot a little smoky pellet right through it. Then she lifted her cigarette high again and said, "I suppose you know how much you could mean to me."

Brian rolled his gum into a ball and popped it into the pocket of his left cheek. "Well. Nice of you to say that."

"Cut the crap. You sold a million copies of a single issue of *Centipede*. What should I do, insult you? Lie to you and say you're just another wrist?" She tapped her cigarette into an ashtray that was already piled as high as a Shinto funeral pyre. "You know the last time a Bang comic sold a million copies? Nineteen-forty-five, that's when. Nowadays, we're lucky if we sell a hundred thou."

Brian smiled again. He was enjoying the desperation in her voice. He noticed that she was exhaling smoke while sucking in her upper lip. It was precisely the way she exhaled when she had a bad hand at poker. Heloise might be cocky over *Moonman*, but she was still nervous about the rest of Bang. And she obviously wanted Brian so badly that her innate careerist's guile was completely failing her.

He pushed his gum to the roof of his mouth and flattened it there, as if he were making a mold for dentures. "Well," he said, "suppose I were to come on board here. I wouldn't want to have to carry the whole company myself." Beg me to, *beg* me to, he commanded her telepathically.

Instead, she leaned back in her chair and drew hard on her cigarette, as if she were trying to suck a cantaloupe out of it. "You won't have to," she said, smoke seeping out of her mouth like blood. "I've already done a lot of shaking up. You'd just be part of it. An important part, but not the whole show. You've seen *Moonman*."

"Who hasn't?"

She laughed with pleasure. "Well, Nigel's going to be doing quite a lot for me. And, of course, it'll all be like what he's done so far—radical and rough. Quite a rebel, that kid is. Victim of Thatcherism. Got a shaved head and earrings, and he wears these boots the size of import cars. We were going to be on Ted Koppel, him and me, talking about *Moonman*, did you know that?"

"No," said Brian, no longer chewing. He'd never even come *close* to being on TV.

She took a final drag on her cigarette, then stubbed it out.

"Yeah, fell through at the last minute. That Mike Milken jerk had to go and get arrested on my day."

He shook his head. "*Nerve* of him."

She laughed again, then leaned over the desk and said, "We've also got Hector Baez doing *Acme-Man*. He's essentially starting from scratch with the character. Lots of new and fresh ideas. Nothing I can talk about just yet. Not till you're on board, that is. Don't want any leaks to the fan press till all this is firmed up."

Brian actually swallowed his gum. He was stunned. He'd thought he could get *Acme-Man* for himself. But if he was the number-one talent in comics, Hector Baez was definitely number two—and a Bang Comics veteran, to boot. It would be next to impossible to displace him at this late date.

His lips were dry now. Heloise was letting Hector Baez start "from scratch" with *Acme-Man*! Such a thing was impossible at Electric Comics, where if a character had lifted his fork with his left hand in 1964, he'd better not use his right in 1990 or irate fans would write in about the gaffe in "continuity."

Oh, he *had* to be part of this! Suddenly, all his own careerist's guile disappeared as well. "What have you got in mind for me?" he asked, not even caring that excitement colored his voice.

She sat up ramrod straight and tapped another cigarette out of a crumpled carton. "You name it," she said. "Anything you want. *The Blue Bowman. Captain Fathom. The Red Wraith.* Any series you want, it's yours." She stuck the cigarette in the left side of her mouth and spoke out of the right side as she lit it. "As for terms—hell, I'm sure we can agree on something."

He grimaced in distaste. *The Blue Bowman? Captain Fathom? The Red Wraith?* Those were second-string books. The average man in the street didn't even know who those characters were. They had no iconic resonance. Brian felt his forehead sting with anxiety; he was dumbfounded that the internationally famous *Acme-Man* and *Moonman* had already been claimed by slick, nihilist *poseurs* before he'd even had a crack at them.

But there was one other Bang Comics character who was equally famous—as familiar to Americans as Tarzan or Mickey Mouse.

Just a month earlier, he'd heard someone at the Electric offices gloating in the hallway that the last issue of Bang's *Princess
Paragon* had sold only twenty-five thousand copies. A truly pathetic performance; but then, the book had been a dog for years.
It had become an industry joke—the Dan Quayle of the comics
business. And yet *Princess Paragon* was almost fifty years old, had
been a best seller in the 1940s, and was one of the foundation
blocks on which Bang Comics had been built. To cancel the series
was unthinkable. Still, Heloise was going to find it a huge task
keeping it alive, never mind making it into a best seller again.
Virtually no one of any note had worked on *Princess Paragon* in
years—or wanted to touch it now.

Brian took another stick of gum out of his pocket, unwrapped it, and popped it in his mouth. A surge of tangy wintergreen gave him a quick fix of confidence. "If I ask for carte
blanche on a character," he said, examining his cuticles noncha-
lantly, "can I have it?"

Heloise hesitated. "Well—yes. Why not; sure."

"Can I get that in writing?" The wintergreen flavor spread
through his mouth like a bushfire.

Heloise almost choked. "Why on earth do you want that?"
she said, lifting her cigarette even higher. This time it did singe
her hair. She didn't notice.

"I've got a character in mind. And what I want to do with
that character may end up being a little controversial."

She bulged her eyes out at him. "Buster, controversy is what
I *want*. Controversy is the only way I'm gonna *save* this company."

"Well, then—"

"*Okay*, okay. You've got it. I'll put it in writing. You in?"

"I'm in."

"Who's the character?"

"Princess Paragon."

Heloise ran around the corner of the desk, threw her arms
around him, and kissed him on his wintergreen mouth. Later he
would find a cigarette burn on his collar.

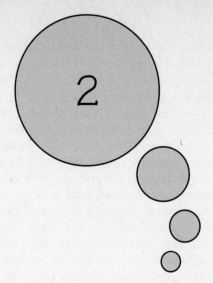

2

It was the kind of day the whole world waits for, but Jerome T. Kornacker didn't notice. The air was moist and sweet and cool, and as it eddied into a breeze and slipped through the blossoming trees like fingers through a head of hair, it picked up the scents of the blossoms and carried them away with it. The sun was brilliant but seemed farther off than usual, less blinding, like a benevolent king glimpsed on a high balcony. Birds were singing merrily, as if delightedly aware that every trilled mating call would be heard by dozens of potential partners.

But Jerome T. Kornacker had the blinds drawn. The sun, after all, would fade the colors of his posters, and his posters were a significant investment. Over his desk was a full-length rendition of Sherman Tank, the Electric Comics hero who was an irradiated purple colossus. He was bellowing in rage and held a truck in one hand, as if readying himself to throw it at someone.

On Jerome's twin closet doors were posters of Speed-

Demon, the Bang Comics hero who caused sonic booms when he ran at top velocity, and Captain Fathom, the valorous king of the undersea world.

On Jerome's ceiling he had managed to affix a gigantic poster of the entire membership of the Freedom Front—fourteen grim but colorful visages who watched over him as he slept every night; and when, as was frequently the case, his grease-compacted intestines kept him awake, he would lie still to ease the pain and recite to himself the trivia he had memorized about each one of those chiseled faces until the sheer, comforting repetition lulled him to sleep. "The Blue Bowman," he would mutter softly. "Secret identity: Lance Stone. Base of operations: Mega City. Sidekick: Jiffy the Archer. Major foes: Lady Lava, Deadeye the Dart King, Emperor Nero. Girlfriend: Joanna Tremayne, also known as Silver Songbird. Joined the Freedom Front in issue number twelve . . ."

And over Jerome's bed there hung another, even more radiant poster, a bold burst of primary colors that coalesced into an image of idealized womanhood, a vision of the kind of wholesome American female that had always managed to be just a few years out of date without ever having been historically realized: Princess Paragon—a thoroughly liberated woman (who wore a costume that showed off her bosom), a heroine devoted to peace (who was in the habit of clobbering her enemies), a national folk icon (who was completely owned by a commercial publishing house). Princess Paragon—lips like raspberries, teeth like sugar cubes, eyelashes like caterpillars, breasts like honeydew melons, waist like an hourglass, legs like an invitation. She gazed out from her poster without lust, without impertinence, almost without sentience; her basic goodness was reflected by the blankness of her expression. She was a tabula rasa with all the empty space filled in. She was the perfect woman; she was no woman. She was impossible; she was here.

It was Princess Paragon, in all her purple, blue, and yellow spandex glory, who concerned Jerome today. For this morning, while other men his age were busy getting their first promotions, fathering children, and worrying about mortgage rates; while outside lawn sprinklers looked like amusement-park rides and children ran down impossibly long streets as though incapable of stopping, laughing with wild and infectious glee; while among his peers sex mattered, and love, and honesty, and ambition; while the world beyond his walls spun with joy and energy and vitality and surprise—Jerome T. Kornacker was pondering the latest issue of *Princess Paragon* to the exclusion of all else.

He was lying on his bed, barefoot, his oily hair in his face, his immense bulk settled in complete repose as he flipped the cheap newsprint pages back and forth, back and forth. Next to his bed were six acid-free cardboard boxes that contained a virtually complete run of *Princess Paragon*, from 1941 on (only four issues were missing). Every comic was snugly packed into a protective Mylar envelope and taped shut, but Jerome thought he might have to open one or more of them for reference as he considered this latest issue, which he found depressingly deficient. For Jerome had decided to write a letter of comment to *Princess Paragon*, and was composing it in his head with admirable concentration, interrupted only by his mother, who every now and then shrieked his name as if wanting nothing more than to give evidence to the world of her existence, like a great ape in the African bush.

There she was again—"Juh-*rome!*" He ignored her and picked up his pen; he was ready to begin his letter. He shifted his great girth and dropped his legs over the side of the bed, then grabbed his note pad and with his pudgy toes grappled the side of one of the boxes and pulled it closer. He would indeed require extensive access to previous issues, he had decided; for his simple letter of comment, inspired by this particularly bland new issue of *Princess Paragon*, was becoming, in his head, a veritable essay on the many faults of the series. He was determined that he should set the writer and artist straight on how the character should be handled.

"Juh-*ROME!*" This time his mother clearly wasn't going to go away. He lifted his head and waited; and soon he heard her footsteps, one by one, pounding their way up to him, as though she were stamping out a cockroach on every stair.

A determined rap on the door; in spite of himself, he jumped at it.

"What is it *now*, Mother?" he said in his world-weariest voice.

"Jerome, haven't I been calling you all morning? It's not like you're your sister or anything, who at least had a record player for an excuse, and besides who had the decency to move out. Will you open this door now?"

"Mother, I *need* my *privacy*."

"What on the earth for? Not to be reading more of those funny books. How stupid do you think I am that I'll keep believing that's all you're doing in there with almost no lights even coming out from under the door? I saw on Jessy Sally Raphael about boys masticating, Jerome. If that's what you're in there doing, you stop it right now! It's not healthy being in the dark all the time playing with your thingie. Go play a ball game! Or something outside and athletic like that."

Jerome was mortified. "*Mother*, I am *not*—masturbating," he said, blushing as he uttered the word; "but if I *did* choose to do so, no idiot-brained talk-show host would be privy to my means of accomplishing it. *Please* understand, I am *writing* now. I need privacy and *quiet* so that I may *concentrate*."

"Writing *what* is what I want to know," his mother continued from the other side of the door. "If it's something to help you get a job, I wish you'd tell me; my heart attack that I'd be sure to have would even be worth it."

"I *have* a job, Mother." He put his pen down on the pad and sighed. It was going to take some doing to get her to go away.

"And how proud am I," she sang out sarcastically, "to tell all my friends how my Jerome is the Carter Foods night watchman. When Mrs. Dickey starts in about how her bank-executive son Donald just got a whole office to himself with a door that even shuts, I get to say, So? My Jerome gets a whole *building* to himself, and how do you bake *them* apples?"

"If you're trying to hurt my feelings, it's not working."

There was a small silence; but, to Jerome's dismay, no corresponding sound of retreating footsteps. "Jerome," said Mrs.

Kornacker, her voice now lowered, "it's seventy-five degrees outside and everyone in the whole world is out in it enjoying themself except you, and me of course who's stupid enough to be in here talking to a door like it's a human person. But this is my last hurrah, now, Jerome. I'm going to go out and catch some suntan, and if you ask me what I think of how you're spending your day inside when outside is like it is right now, I have to be honest and say I blame your father for not being strict enough with you on your bottom when you needed a good whapping, God rest his soul. But even so, you just think of him looking down on you from heaven now and see if you can still go on yanking on that thingie of yours all the time with him watching like he was right there in the room with you." He heard her take a few steps, then stop; and she added, her voice more remote, "I'll give you a penny for my thoughts, Jerome, which are if you don't start getting out of the house sometimes, I'm going to sell it on you, just to think about the fun when you come out to use the rest room and there are new people living here that won't know you're from a hole in the wall."

He listened as she clomped back down the stairs. "*Idiot* woman," he said under his breath. Then he lifted his pen anew and began writing, in careful block letters so that no one would have any trouble deciphering his penmanship, the letter of comment that he was sure would guide Princess Paragon to a new era of greatness—her first in decades.

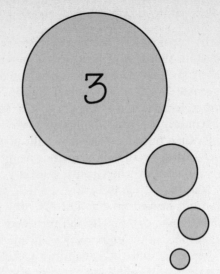

3

Brian met his lover at a sushi bar in midtown. "My God, Nico," he said before he'd even fully sat down, "I hope you've ordered sake. I need a drink like nobody's business."

Nico checked his watch. "Been waiting twenty minutes, hon. I only get an hour for lunch. What's the scoop?"

A slightly built Japanese waiter appeared and said, "This is your other party?"

"That is my *only* party," replied Nico. "Sake."

The waiter repeated "sake" and smiled, then scurried away.

Brian finished hanging his jacket over the back of his chair, then turned to face Nico. "It went better than I ever expected."

"So Heloise'll take you on if Electric doesn—"

"Heloise *has* taken me on. I'm a Bang Comics man now."

Nico's mouth fell open. "But you haven't even given Electric a chance t—"

"Screw 'em," said Brian, popping his gum out of his mouth

and depositing it in the table's ashtray. "Heloise has things really hopping at Bang. *God*, honey, if I'd missed the boat on th—"

"Sake," the waiter announced as he reappeared. He set the little earthen pitcher and cups between Brian and Nico and said, "Are gentlemen ready to order?"

"Yes," said Brian, sweeping the hair from his forehead.

"No," said Nico. "Wait a min—"

"Combination platter," Brian said.

"Very good," said the waiter.

Nico put his hand up. "I'm not ordering till I hear the rest of—"

"*Two* combination platters," Brian interrupted him.

"Very good," said the waiter, and he disappeared again.

"I don't *want* a combination platter," said Nico, coloring. "I hate that hunk of octopus they give you, with a little suction cup pointed at you like it's going to jump on your face and grab hold."

"Give it to me, I'll eat it," said Brian, breaking open his chopsticks. "So anyway, you wouldn't *believe* what's going on at Bang. You know the *Moonman* writer?"

"That British kid you were telling me about?"

"Yeah. Oh, my God, they're really making him into an *event*, honey. They've talked Cooper Books into putting out a *trade paperback* of his first six issues, to sell in all the big book chains! I mean, the mind boggles. Comics usually don't get the trade-paperback treatment until they're a couple decades old, and then it's only because of their historical value. But apparently the books division jumped at the chance to do this, because of all the *Moonman* press. And you know what else? Some independent movie company in Los Angeles wanted to option the new *Moonman*, and Heloise was shrewd enough to let Cooper's film division know about it, so naturally they panicked, and since Cooper owns Bang, they made Heloise say no to the independent guys and started their *own* development deal. And guess who they want to write the script?"

"The British kid," said Nico, putting his hand over his mouth.

"*Bingo*," said Brian, wiping his forehead with his napkin. "I almost got sick when Heloise told me that. I *still* feel a little queasy. That goddamned little punk is only twenty-four years old, and he's got a high-six-figure development deal with Cooper Films just because he wrote a couple of issues of *Moonman* with sex and violence in them. And me, I'm thirty-eight, *barely* making seven figures because I write a bunch of tired old comics that can be merchandised to lunch-box manufacturers." He pressed the bridge of his nose between his thumb and forefinger, and shut his eyes tight. "That should've been *me*, I've been *lazy*, now I'm *paying* for it. I should've been the *first* to have that kind of success."

Nico reached across the table and patted his hand. "My psychotic love-monkey," he said. "You're not going to flagellate yourself, are you?"

"Not here at the restaurant," Brian said glumly, releasing his nose and staring into Nico's eyes. "I feel like puking."

"Sweet-talker."

"No—I mean, you know how it is when you want something so much, it actually kind of makes you physically ill? I want what this Nigel Cardew kid has, only I want it bigger, better, bolder—I want to keep on being the brightest light in this industry. Maybe in the larger perspective I'd still be just a big fish in a small pond, but, Christ, the pond is getting wider and deeper all the time. If Heloise has her way, it'll be a fucking inland *lake* before the turn of the century."

The waiter reappeared with their combination platters. Nico took one look at the hunk of octopus tentacle sitting primly on a bed of rice and averted his eyes. "Get that thing off my plate," he said, "or you won't be the only one who feels like puking."

Brian grabbed it with his chopsticks and popped it in his mouth. "*Mmmm*," he grunted as he chewed it. A moment later he opened his mouth and displayed the masticated octopus-rice mash on his tongue.

Nico wouldn't look at him. "I know what you're doing, and it's disgusting," he said.

Brian smiled and resumed chewing. "So, anyway," he continued, pouring some soy sauce into a dish and mixing a dollop of wasabi into it, "I thought I could get Heloise to give me *Acme-Man* so I could turn it into the same kind of success this Cardew kid's had with *Moonman.* But no, she'd already given *Acme-Man* to Hector Baez."

"Who's that?" Nico asked as he let a tuna cake absorb some soy sauce.

"A big-shot cartoonist I hate," said Brian. He took a swig of sake. "He's this immense geek who always comes to every single one of Heloise's poker parties, I'm sure because he has absolutely no life whatsoever. I mean, all he can talk about is comic books and obscure old TV shows. But Heloise has managed to turn him into some kind of imitation *me* over there—he apes all my moves, and she lets him get away with it. And the kids who read the books don't know any better, so . . ." He poured himself more sake. "Anyway, the upshot is, I don't get *Acme-Man.* And I start to panic. So what do I do? I get this stroke of genius. I ask for the only other character the company's got that has any kind of name recognition. You can probably guess."

Nico paused with his chopsticks in midair. He knit his brow.

"Oh, come *on,* honey," Brian scolded him.

"Don't snap at me, you know I'm bad at this." Nico had never read comics as a kid, and didn't read them now; all he knew about the business was what Brian told him.

Brian slapped his forehead. "Come *on,* Nico. Even *you* must know this character."

Nico grimaced. "The Bug King?"

Brian dropped his head onto his arm theatrically. "*No,* it's not the fucking Bug King! Who the *fuck* knows who the Bug King is aside from a bunch of fucking fanboy *geeks* an—"

"All *right,* Brian," Nico scolded him. "Cut the dramatics. Just tell me who it is."

Brian lifted his head and said, "Princess *Paragon.* Who *else?*"

Nico leaned back and smiled. "Oh, *yeah,*" he said, nodding. "You're right. I *do* know who she is. Oh, God, Brian, you're going to be doing *her?* That's so incredibly camp!"

Brian shook his head. "That's exactly what it *can't* be." He jabbed his chopsticks at Nico to accentuate this point. "Remember, I've got to show the world that I can be as kick-ass cutting-edge as this British punk. If my *Princess Paragon* is going to be the kind of sensation his *Moonman* is, it's got to make people sit up and take notice. It's got to create a goddamned *stir.*"

Nico took a sip of sake. "Good luck. I mean, how on earth are you going to manage that, with that drippy old schoolmarm of a character?"

Brian raised an eyebrow. "Well, for starters, I'm going to turn her into a dyke."

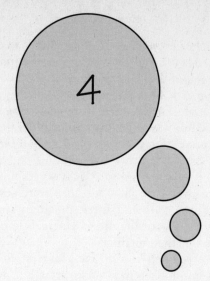

4

Every Thursday afternoon, a new shipment of comics arrived at the specialty shop in Jerome's neighborhood. This provided the only occasion for his getting out of bed before dusk. On his night-watchman's schedule, he wasn't able to retire much before dawn, but in spite of this, on Thursdays he would drag himself out of bed at noon, wolf down a breakfast of sugar-coated cereal, dress in whatever clothing was closest at hand, and set out for the comic shop, which was only a six-block walk.

Those six blocks, however, seemed very long indeed, as they necessarily brought him into the tiny business district of his Midwestern hometown. And as that hometown also housed a liberal-arts college, it was always filled with handsome lettermen and beautiful coeds, usually paired off and smiling wide to reveal rows of big white teeth that looked as though they might bite Jerome's hand if he dared stray too near.

For even though these college students were several years

younger than he, Jerome was deeply intimidated by them. He preferred that his walk to the comic shop be quiet and solitary, but it was seldom either. Today, for example, he turned a corner and espied a group of students walking his way, and he broke into a cold sweat. The students were chattering away in lilting, musical voices, but when they approached him they suddenly fell silent. As he passed them, Jerome had no will but to look at his feet; nevertheless, he felt their eyes on him, and his neck flushed and burned with the intensity of their scrutiny.

And then, worst of all, when they were several yards past him, he heard one of them mutter something—unintelligible to him—and then a few of the others laughed. Jerome heard derision and scorn in that laughter.

When he reached the business district, Jerome passed a store window and looked in it—not through it, but at it; and he could see the street behind him reflected there, and on that street any number of active, attractive students looking at him as though he were some kind of bizarre life form not indigenous to the area. And seeing his own reflection in this context, he couldn't blame them for that; for on these perfectly manicured thoroughfares, where sidewalks were swept and skin was scrubbed—where even the coed sexuality that filled the air with curious scents and signals had a kind of wholesome aspect to it, frisky, like the innocence of puppies at play—in this setting, Jerome's ponderous bulk looked like an aesthetic rebuke, a reminder of the existence of human failure. After years of such dreadful epiphanies, his sense of shame had been numbed almost beyond hope of revival. Oh, it still existed; but it was so swollen and mortified that it enveloped him like a boa constrictor—one so large that even as it strangled him he could see through the gaps between its coils and contrive to forget that it was there. For Jerome, survival meant one thing: hiding, as often and as completely as possible, from anyone who could remind him that his shame was still with him. He had gotten very good at such hiding.

The comic shop offered him a refuge. True, it was frequently invaded by pairs of college freshmen, white-faced and red-lipped, with eyes bright and uncaring, who laughed out loud in the store and remarked wickedly on the breast size of Princess Paragon or Lambent Lady before buying a copy of *Love & Rockets* or *Eightball* and departing. But there were others who haunted the shop on Thursdays, and although Jerome seldom spoke to them, he knew by sight that they were of his ilk. Today he entered the shop and, true to form, found them all in place.

There was the one Jerome secretly called Stickman; he was impossibly tall and frighteningly thin, and his skin was an unnatural shade of gray. His clothes hung off him like wet sheets off a laundry line, and he never failed to carry with him a truly enormous duffel bag of shiny green vinyl. Jerome had no idea what was in that duffel bag.

Then there was Shortman, the diminutive, hyperactive sprite who collected virtually every comic book published; Jerome had often seen him leaving the store, his arms nearly full to the breaking, having just given the cashier more than a hundred dollars in cash. On a few occasions, Jerome had spoken to this strange, wild-eyed dwarf, and had rather enjoyed his conversation, except for the fact that he had a habit of working himself into a fit of excitement over a point he was trying to make, then drooling all over his chin as he made it; sometimes he would even spit. Jerome was usually content simply to nod at him and smile.

Then there was Dirtyman. He frightened Jerome. Every Thursday he appeared in exactly the same clothes, only smellier and more soiled; his hair, a matted mass to begin with, now had patches that looked hard, as though you could tap a pencil on them. The soles of his shoes were falling off, and flapped when he walked; his eyes darted around like he was suspicious of everyone; and—for Jerome, the most repellent thing—he breathed through his mouth. Loudly. As though he were gasping.

The only person in the shop to whom Jerome truly looked forward to talking was its proprietor, Doug, a lanky, long-faced man with a ponytail. Jerome sometimes liked to flatter himself that Doug considered him a friend, but there had been too many occasions when he'd heard Doug banter jovially with some of the truly sociopathic types who occasionally wandered into the shop. Doug, it seemed, was just the kind of guy who would chat with *anyone*.

Jerome was excited by this Thursday's crop of new releases; the long-awaited *Quasar Quintet/Offenders* team-up, by Brian Parrish, had finally been released, as well as the latest installment in the new *Moonman* series, by Nigel Cardew.

Jerome paged through the *Moonman* issue. It was unlike most of the comics he encountered, in that he couldn't instantly determine its plot simply by flipping through its pages; there were so many panels of characters merely standing around talking. This both unsettled and excited him. But one thing was certain: he didn't see Moonman's young partner, Comet, anywhere in the story. A few issues back, Comet had been brutally murdered by a child pornographer; or, rather, Jerome was certain, that's what the reader was *meant* to think. Once the pornographer began attacking Comet, ripping off his clothes and bludgeoning him, the eye of the reader was led away to a wall filled with framed pictures of children in provocative poses. The rest of the supposed murder scene had been handled by superimposing sound effects and word-balloons over still panels of that wall. So in the end, the actual murder was never seen, only heard. "Your sweet lily-white ass is stone cold, chicken," the pornographer said, from off-panel, at the very end.

Well, Jerome had learned that a death in comics doesn't count unless you see the body, and sometimes not even then. He was fully expecting the return of Comet in this issue—after all, this was the story in which Moonman finally tracked down the pornographer and beat him to death in revenge. (Which was pretty severe, even for Moonman.) But there was no sign of him. Jerome felt a flurry of panic and considered for a moment that Comet might really be dead—but no, he couldn't be. He just *couldn't*. He was Moonman's kid partner. He'd been around for *decades*. They were just toying with the readers a little before bringing him back. That *had* to be it.

He flipped through the *Quasar Quintet/Offenders* team-up book and beheld the comforting sight of all his favorite Electric

Comics heroes together in action. His anxiety disappeared. Brian Parrish could always be counted on for a good story. And this issue seemed to resolve the long subplot about Intrepid Girl's pregnancy. A tasty issue; he'd savor it when he got home.

He picked about twenty or so other titles from the racks of new releases, then brought them up to Doug at the front counter.

Doug smiled, said, "Hey, J-man," and started tallying up the purchases on his calculator.

When Doug came to the *Moonman* issue, Jerome pointed his finger at it and said, "Still no Comet."

Doug rang up the dollar-seventy-five price tag for the issue, put it aside, and went on to the next. "Comet's dead, man," he said, without looking up.

Jerome blanched. "You don't really believe that."

Doug looked up and grinned. "Sure. Everyone knew it was gonna happen, J-man. Don't you read the fanzines?"

Jerome grimaced. "Of course I do."

"Well, you get all the news like everybody else."

"I read every one of them," he insisted heatedly. *"Panel Previews, Adventure World*—all of them. I know *all* the news about what's coming up."

"Well, then," said Doug, a little uncomfortably. He went back to his calculator.

"But you know how often they say a character is going to die, and then the death turns out to be *completely* bogus."

"This is true," said Doug, who then punched up the total. "Thirty-six twenty-five, J-man."

Jerome felt his breath coming hard. He pulled his wallet out of his shirt pocket and counted out the bills. "It's *ridiculous* to think that they'd actually kill off Comet."

"Well," said Doug, his hand outstretched to take the money, "I read an interview with Nigel Cardew, and he said, That's it, Comet's dead forever."

Jerome stopped counting the money and looked up. "What? Where did you read that?"

Doug jerked his thumb in the direction of one of the shop's

magazine racks. "The new *Comics Observer*. Came out two weeks ago. You miss it, man?"

"No. I refused to buy it. I hate that magazine. It's elitist."

Doug grinned. "Well. Anyway. Thirty-six twenty-five."

Jerome resumed counting bills from his billfold. A line had formed behind him now.

"Yeah," said Doug, making idle chatter, "bad year for side-kicks all around."

A moment of stunned silence. "What do you mean?" Jerome asked, his counting hand again stilled.

"Well, you heard about Acme-Lad and Acme-Lass, didn't you?"

"No. I didn't. What about them?" He was starting to squeal, like a stuck pig.

"You gotta get the *Observer*, man. They get news tidbits in there that nobody else does."

"I hate that magazine! Their reviewers only like underground comics."

"Yeah, but if you'd read it, you'd know Bang's getting rid of Acme-Lad and Acme-Lass."

"You mean they're killing them, too?"

"No, just dumping them. You know Hector Baez is starting from scratch with *Acme-Man*."

"I knew that. I knew that as soon as anybody did." Jerome's face was scarlet now, like it might burst open. Sweat was trickling down his temples, leaving little rivulets of Noxema flakes.

"Well, he's starting from scratch so he can go in a different direction, man. This time there's not gonna be an Acme-Lad or Acme-Lass."

Jerome was quivering with something akin to fear. The fabric of his reality was unstitching itself. "But Acme-Lad and Acme-Lass are Acme-Man's cousins! They can't just get written out of the series as if they'd never even existed!"

Doug shrugged. "Apparently they can."

Someone in the line behind Jerome coughed, as if to remind Jerome of his presence.

But Jerome was oblivious. "So they're just going to disappear," he said. "Just like that."

Now Doug himself seemed to be growing impatient. "All I know is, in the last *Observer*, Baez says that having Acme-Lad and Acme-Lass around just makes Acme-Man less unique a character. So he's redoing the whole Acme-Man legend without them. And with a bunch of other changes, too."

"That's ridiculous reasoning. I ca—"

"'Scuse me," said the customer directly behind Jerome, as he shoved his purchases onto the counter in front of Doug.

Doug cocked his eyebrows and said, "Thirty-six twenty-five, J-man."

Jerome handed him the bills and a single quarter from his shirt pocket. Then, without a goodbye, he started for the door.

Comet's dead! he thought.

He could hear Doug behind him, now extolling the virtues of a small-press comic to the customer buying it. "Man, this is a *great* story," he was saying. "It's about this married couple that don't get out of bed for a whole month. Really surreal—like Kafka, only funny. Or like R. Crumb crossed with *Ozzie and Harriet.*"

An immediate and intense loathing for Doug surged through Jerome like an electrical charge. It felt purifying.

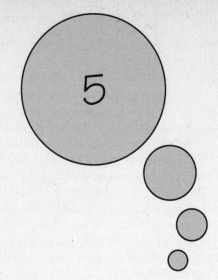

5

Heloise let Brian borrow the dozen bound volumes of *Princess Paragon* from the Bang Comics library. The volumes contained copies of the comic books that had been issued over the preceding five decades. They were, as a result, both priceless and irreplaceable; Heloise was showing her trust in Brian by allowing him to take them out of the office and onto the big, dirty, destructive Manhattan streets.

He brought them home to the nine-room condominium he and Nico owned in Chelsea and spent the next few days hiding out, wearing nothing but boxer shorts and his reading glasses, wading through forty-nine years' worth of Princess Paragon stories. He felt giddy, as though he were getting away with something. He had always worked at home but was usually chained to his drawing board for most of the day; now, however, since Electric had so much of his recent work on backlog, he considered that the remainder of his two months' contractual obligation to them had in fact already been met (and a quick call to his attorney found her in concurrence). He therefore took great joy in shutting the door to his studio and not entering it at all during that week. It felt like a paid vacation.

It was such a pleasure, withdrawing from the world, enjoying the sunlight in the front room, snacking straight out of the refrigerator all day, and taking short breaks to play with his pet parrots (both of whom were named Leonard). And it was especially delightful to listen as the answering machine took the increasingly frantic calls from the Electric Comics management. The rumors must have reached them; for while his visit to Heloise had been unofficial and secret, his presence hadn't gone unnoticed in the Bang Comics hallways. And the Bang/Electric interoffice gossip network was efficient and swift. Pity the poor shmucks at Electric—although they didn't want to give Brian more money, they certainly didn't want to lose him *entirely*.

But he was finished with them. Stretched out on the sofa, the heavy bound volumes perched on his stomach (where, after an extended reading, they left deep red indentations in his abdomen), he flipped through the pages and the years, becoming more and more excited about taking over *Princess Paragon*.

For while Hector Baez was having to reinvent about half the established Acme-Man continuity in order to update it, Brian was amazed to discover that turning Princess Paragon into a lesbian wasn't going to require too severe a break with tradition. After all, she'd come from a matriarchal planet, and her mother, the planet's queen, had never been seen to have a husband or male lover in any of the many recountings of Princess Paragon's origin that had peppered the book's half-century run. For all you could tell, every woman on the *planet* might be a lesbian! There was little to be found that implied the contrary.

The earliest entries in the series were all the work of Roger Oaklyn, the cartoonist who created Princess Paragon in the first place; they were crude and primitive, but Oaklyn's heart was in the right place. In the origin story, the queen of the planet Iri sent her daughter to Earth because, in viewing our world over her "cosmic view-screen" (a glorified television), she'd seen the terrible massing of "angry, destructive men" that threatened "the good women and children of Earth." The faces she had seen were those of Hitler, Mussolini, and Tojo. Well, Brian would have to change that; he'd show Muammar Quaddafi, Deng Xiaoping, and Saddam Hussein. He jotted a reminder to this effect onto a small note pad that lay farther up his stomach.

He also decided to change the title "Queen" to the asexual "Lawgiver," and to replace the "cosmic view-screens" with cosmic telepathic abilities—perhaps achieved as a result of high-level tantric sex?

Back to the original. Princess Paragon traveled to Earth in a rocket ship that looked like a firecracker with Cadillac tail fins and landed in the Nevada desert, where she was found, unconscious, by FBI agent Aaron Marks. (I'll make him CIA, thought Brian.) Marks pulled the beautiful alien from her rocket ship, which then exploded. The explosion awakened the princess, and Agent Marks, captivated by what he called her "otherworldly beauty" (which, thanks to her 1940s spit-curl hairdo, was rather difficult for Brian to see), proposed marriage to her at once. She, having an important agenda on Earth, declined him; and fully half of the stories that followed over the ensuing decades concerned Agent Marks's doomed attempts to become romantically involved with Princess Paragon, who was too busy battling, first Nazis and Japs, then spacemen and monsters, and finally (in the most recent issues) terrorists and supervillains, to pay any attention to him.

But what if she weren't interested in him simply because of his *gender*? Would Princess Paragon swoon before a different lover—a female lover? Would she forsake her mission on Earth in the face of a rarer and more controversial passion—a passion she could not, by nature, deny?

Sure she would, thought Brian. Because I say so!

He trembled in anticipation as he thought of the media circus that would follow his first issue; *he'd* get on Ted Koppel, that's for certain! And then what? A profile in *People*? An interview on "Entertainment Tonight"? A movie deal?

Actually, the movie deal had *better* come, hadn't it? Because once the conservative watchdogs and fundamentalist factions got hold of *Princess Paragon*, his career in comics might end up dead in the water.

Well, let it go, then. He had bigger fish to fry. The young punks like Cardew were snapping at his heels, and if he meant to stay ahead of them he'd better leapfrog into the *next*-biggest pond. And then the next, and the next, and the next . . .

He marveled at how his ambition had flared virtually overnight.

Princess Paragon, he thought, you are my ticket to goddamned *godhood*.

Putting down the bound volume, he saw that his penis was erect, sticking out of the fly of his shorts and pointing up, up, up to the stratosphere!

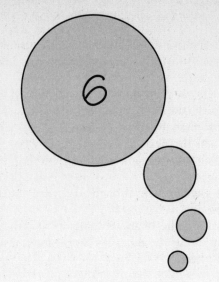

6

A month later, Hector Baez's first issue of *Acme-Man* came out. Jerome went to the comic shop and bought it (at the counter he exchanged only the most perfunctory of pleasantries with Doug); then, as was his custom, he took his purchases to the snack bar in the basement of the office building on Willow Street, where he perused them during his usual lunch of a patty melt, onion rings, and a chocolate milkshake with whipped cream.

The snack bar was almost empty, so he felt no embarrassment in hovering over the new *Acme-Man* as he ate. He flipped through the issue while jamming the onion rings into his mouth, three at a time, as though they had to be eaten quickly lest they suddenly defy gravity and float away. Then he took a noisy sip of the chocolate shake and felt his heart begin to sink.

Oh, this wasn't Acme-Man! This was someone new, someone of the Sylvester Stallone school of manhood—a brute, a braggart, a contemptible thug. The Acme-Man origin story—

once a benign little tale of benevolent science creating an enlightened superhuman—had changed into an ugly morality play about an innocent man abused by ambitious scientists, who enlist him for an experiment knowing full well that it might kill him, only to have it transform him instead into a Hercules. These amoral scientists pay for their blunder with their lives, of course. That was the new way of doing things at Bang Comics.

As he feared, the joyful, exuberant presences of Acme-Lad and Acme-Lass were nowhere in this new version—not even mentioned. Gone for good.

He closed the comic book and sat there, stunned, the mass of soggy onion rings sitting inert in his mouth. He was so demoralized that he was unable to chew.

One of the waitresses approached his table. He looked up; it was Amanda, of course. She smiled at him. He made an effort to smile back, but his mouth was full.

"Ooh, new *comic* books," she trilled. Had anyone else said this to him, he would have considered that he had been mocked. But Amanda was different; she had an endearing habit of speaking on every subject as if she'd only just discovered it, and found it delightful.

"So this must be *Thursday*," she said, overcome by the sheer miracle of it all.

Jerome, his mouth full of onion rings, nodded.

"And here you are, having your usual lunch!" Her tone asked, How can anything be wrong with the world, if this is so?

Jerome smiled, and flakes of fried batter fell from his lips. But Amanda didn't screw up her face in revulsion; she was, after all, plain and rather pudgy, and couldn't afford to make judgments based on appearance—or, at least, this is what Jerome liked to believe about her.

"Well, I hope they're *very* thrilling," she said, smiling again. "You enjoy, now!" She left him and went to clear the debris off a recently vacated table.

Jerome watched her go, painfully aware that he hadn't been able to swallow quickly enough to return even one word of her friendly banter. This caused him some distress, for Amanda was one of the few persons in town who was unfailingly nice to him. He had even developed a habit of thinking about her while he masturbated; it seemed so much more *possible* a fantasy, and therefore a more exciting one, than his usual reveries about starlets, magazine models, and Princess Paragon. He'd even entertained the notion of asking her out on a date.

But strange as it may seem, the new *Acme-Man* had now dashed those hopes. His fantasy world was crumbling, and with it the only workable self-image he'd been able to construct—the only belief system that allowed him to survive.

He sighed and swallowed the onion-ring mass in one painful gulp, then lowered his head and contemplated his expansive waist. His torso was shaped like a pear, but his skin wasn't as appetizing as a pear's. It was milk-white and lumpy, like unpummeled dough. His arms and legs were spindly, seldom used for anything beyond minimal propulsion. On those occasions when he dared look at himself naked in a mirror, he saw what he was; it was impossible not to see it. What he *didn't* see was any possibility of redemption. The heroes of his comic books were not role models for him; how could they be, with their immense chests with colorful emblems sprawled across their pectorals like slogans on vast billboards; their powerful hands, as big as their heads; their square-cut jaws; their steely eyes; their blood running riot with testosterone (even though their genitals caused no actual bulging in their tights)? To be such a figure, such a consummate realization of ultramasculinity, was beyond his ability to imagine. He had no desires or pretensions in that regard. He was, rather, a camp follower. He doted on his heroes, learned the minutiae of their lives, and basked in their reflected glory. When the local telephone company, paying tribute to what they called "a unique and positive American idol," put Acme-Man on the cover of the area phone book a few years earlier, Jerome had beamed as proudly as if he had been on the cover himself.

But after all, when you got right down to it, what was the "message" of Acme-Man but a plea to recognize the value of men like Jerome? In his secret identity of Garrett Trench, unassuming radio personality, Acme-Man was routinely ridiculed by his peers, and most notably by the beautiful news reader Nora Nash, who waxed eloquent on the air about Acme-Man's exploits, but never had the time of day for Garrett. Yet Garrett still embodied all the fine qualities associated with Acme-Man— intelligence, loyalty, honesty, integrity—only without the flashy costume or the tousled hair. Nora Nash was beautiful, gutsy, and desirable, but there was something lacking in her: the ability to see beyond the facade to the inner man. When she began to appreciate the *true* nature of Acme-Man, she would appreciate Garrett as well; and then he could return her love in earnest.

And didn't Jerome share such traits? Weren't intelligence, loyalty, honesty, and integrity (and he wasn't shy about ascribing these to himself) the hallmarks of the superior man? Not the width of his chest; not the length of his hair; not the cut or color of his clothing. For Jerome, the world was one big Nora Nash: it didn't recognize his merit—in fact, it sought to drown him in humiliation—and thus proved itself unworthy of him.

And so to his room he each day retired, accompanied by the fantasies that sustained him—fantasies of a world in which his kind would be accepted; where it was the object of heroes like Acme-Man not to be recognized as handsomer, stronger, and more powerful than other men, but to be recognized as a Jerome T. Kornacker underneath it all. Why then should Jerome endeavor to improve his physical prowess? Why should he seek greater understanding of the world when, as Acme-Man could attest, it was the *world* that needed to understand *him*? Why seek fame and fortune when, by rights, those should be his to begin with?

But now! Now Nora Nash had been turned into a floozy, a bimbo, a bitch in heat. In this first issue of the new *Acme-Man*, she spent her time sexually teasing all the radio station's underlings—all except Garrett Trench, that is, for Garrett was now a big athletic type, as intimidating a slab of machismo as he was in his Acme-Man identity. Nora Nash *liked* this Garrett Trench.

Jerome T. Kornacker did not.

The enemy had won; the Jerome T. Kornackers of the

world had been devalued. What mattered was no longer the interior of a man; it was his biceps, his teeth, his buttocks. What mattered was no longer a man's estimation of himself; it was the effectiveness of his boasting, his swagger.

Jerome watched Amanda diligently clearing off the snack-bar tables and he thought of her, stuck in this overlit basement in this drab office building in a small town in the middle of nowhere, still under the delusion that her life had some merit, not realizing that civilization had fallen and the dinosaurs come back.

What was worse, worse than anything—what made Jerome actually begin to weep—was that even now he couldn't do the proper thing and throw this horrible *Acme-Man* comic into the trash. He knew he'd take it home, slip it into a Mylar envelope, and file it away, giving it the authority it already knew it possessed.

He had never had his weakness so nakedly revealed to him.

He slipped out of the snack bar and got sick in the alley in back.

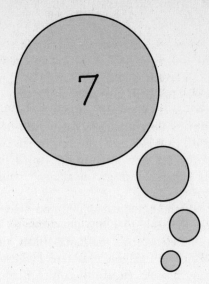

7

After a flurry of desperate counteroffers, Electric Comics finally realized they'd lost Brian Parrish to their competitor and, grudgingly, gave up and left him alone. They did not, as Brian had imagined they might, begin a campaign to sully his name; apparently they nursed a hope of getting him back someday.

Of course, if he failed with *Princess Paragon*, they'd be happily bad-mouthing him all over town.

There were still a few days before the expiration of Brian's contract, and by rights he shouldn't be doing any work at all for Bang. But he was too excited to hold to that; he broke down and began sketching out his plans for *Princess Paragon*. He redesigned the heroine's costume and hairstyle to make her conform to the 1990 ideal of beauty. Then he sketched out new designs for the Lawgiver (formerly Queen) of Iri, CIA agent Aaron Marks, and a new character: Cosmique, the dizzying, dazzling blonde extraterrestrial who was to come from the stars to win Princess Paragon's heart. After creating Cosmique, Brian sat back from his drawing board and thought, Totally, *totally* mega. He could almost *smell* his interview in *People*.

His plan was to begin his reign on *Princess Paragon* with an updated origin issue that would establish Iri as a homosexual planet and Princess Paragon herself as a dyed-in-the-wool Irian. Then he would bring her to Earth, reintroduce Agent Marks as an older mentor for her, and, in the third issue, introduce Cosmique. He got giddy imagining the repercussions in the industry and beyond.

He kept sketching and sketching, and before he knew it, it was the last day of his contractual obligation to Electric, and he was riding up the elevator to the Bang offices, thinking, I'm out of my mind! Princess Paragon a lesbian? Heloise is going to get a lawyer and get herself out of our contract before it's even begun! Everyone in the industry is going to laugh at me, revile me, snub me—the right-wingers will get hold of me and never let go, and—and—

His chewing gum was doing the complete circuit of his mouth in approximately a nanosecond.

The elevator door opened, and he entered the realm of Bang Comics.

Heloise was in the reception area, and whether or not she'd come there to await him, she was now busy excoriating the typing skills of the receptionist in some of the rawest language Brian had ever heard. He could've sworn that the receptionist, who was black, was going positively pale. That was the measure of Heloise's authority.

God help me, he thought; I'm actually afraid of her!

Then she turned and saw him and all at once a brilliant smile lit up her face. "My star talent!" she sang. "Come on in and park it!"

He gave a consoling wink to the receptionist, then followed Heloise past the double doors that were flanked by life-size fiberglass figures of Acme-Man and Moonman. As they strode down the long corridor to her office, some of the Bang Comics employees stopped what they were doing long enough to toss a hello his way. He smiled, though he remembered having met only about half of them.

Heloise had her cigarette lit before she even hit her chair, but her smoking was less manic today. Apparently she had confidence in Brian's ability to resurrect this important but nearly extinct property of hers. And sure enough, as Brian led her through the costume changes and new designs for the series, she actually seemed to become calmer, pleasanter—like a manic-depressive who'd just been given Lithium.

Finally, Brian, his heart pounding, said, "Okay, the *big* change, then. The one that makes all the difference."

Heloise readjusted herself in her seat and raised her eyebrows a couple of times. "Oh-boy-oh-boy," she said, and she sucked in what must have been her body weight in cigarette smoke with a single superhuman breath. She coughed out a few mouthfuls of hieroglyphics-shaped haze and said, "Tell me, tell me."

"Well, first," he said, "let me just say that this is all speculative at this point." Why am I backpedaling? he wondered. He flicked his gum up to the tip of his tongue and ran it along the front of his teeth, then bit sharply into it as if it were alive and he was trying to kill it. "I mean, our contract hasn't actually kicked in yet, and I haven't actually done any real *work* on the series—I mean, I wouldn't, because I'm not getting *paid*." They both laughed. "But I'm here, you know, friend to friend . . ." Get on with it! he admonished himself. "I'm here because, you know, I *have* had these few ideas, and I'm just passing them along as a sort of—you know—a prerelationship kind of flirting." What the hell am I talking about? he wondered. Heloise was looking at him with an increasingly baffled smile. "Now," he continued, "on Monday, when I begin working in earnest, you know—when you've assigned me an editor and everything—I mean, of course, an editor's input will—"

"I get the picture," Heloise interrupted him, exhaling smoke from one side of her mouth.

He laughed entirely too loudly and gave his gum a series of rapid, tiny bites with his front teeth.

"Well, you know, Moonman's been remade as a killer," he said, "and that's been controversial. And Acme-Man's been remade as a demigod, and *that's* been controversial. So I've remade Princess Paragon as a—as a l-le—" Oh, for God's sake! He was stuttering like a fool!

He looped his gum around his tongue and then produced from his portfolio a rough sketch of Cosmique. "Here," he said, shoving it across Heloise's desk.

She leaned over and scrutinized the drawing. "Nice," she said. "Who is it?"

"I call her Cosmique. She's Princess Paragon's female lover."

Heloise sat back and looked at the drawing with the expression she might have worn had Brian vomited on it.

"You lost your mind?" she said, her voice shrill as a rape whistle.

He colored in anger and defiance. "No, Heloise, I have not lost my mind."

She lifted her cigarette so high above her head that she looked like a schoolgirl begging permission to leave the room. "Brian, have you forgotten that this is a *comic-book* series? That we are selling it to *children*?"

"Has Nigel Cardew forgotten it?" he asked, ripping his gum to shreds with his front teeth, then reforming it.

Heloise was so distracted, she was forgetting to smoke. Ashes dribbled from her cigarette and drifted lazily to the floor. Then all at once she waved her hand, and the ashes spun in mad circles in the air, like leaves in a windstorm. "Nigel didn't put any perverted sex in his stuff!" she barked.

"Neither will I," he said, growing really angry now. "And I'm not putting in any perverted *violence*, either, so I should have a leg up on him."

"Oh, God," said Heloise, quickly sucking twice on her cigarette. "Oh, God. What about our merchandising profits? Right now that's almost all the company's surviving on."

"Princess Paragon merchandising brings in pretty close to jack shit," he said. "I checked." He was so angry, his gum actually disintegrated. He reached into his shirt pocket for a new stick.

"It'll bring in *exactly* jack shit if I let you do this," she said, blowing smoke straight at him, as though she were trying to choke him with it.

"What do you mean, *if*? I've got a contract." He waved the smoke away.

She took another drag and blew the smoke in his face yet again. "Brian, Princess Paragon is *not* a lesbian."

"I say she is." He unwrapped the new stick of gum.

"She's never been one before!"

"How do you know? I mean, when has she ever even come *close* to giving in to Aaron Marks? Not once! Maybe she's been holding out for a nice cheerleader." He popped the stick of gum in his mouth and began chewing. An explosion of tart wintergreen followed. "Look," he said, his voice a bit garbled from his chewing, "it doesn't matter if she's fucked the entire membership of the Freedom Front; as of now, she's a dyke. I'm starting from scratch. Like Hector Baez. My contract says I can." Using the muscles of his tongue, he stretched out the stiff new gum, trying to soften it.

Heloise leaned back in her chair and sighed. "I don't know what's gotten into you, Brian. If this is some new gay political thing, I'd appreciate you getting into it on your own time."

"This *is* my own time. I've got a contract that says it is. For twelve issues, Princess Paragon is mine."

"No, she's not. I'm *leasing* her to you, that's all." Heloise stubbed out her cigarette as if she were trying to stab the ashtray to death. "She belongs to me. To *us*, I mean. To *Bang*."

"Fine. Then at the end of my contract, you can change her right back to an asexual virgin. The comic-book industry is about the only place where that can actually happen. But it's my bet that after twelve issues, her sales are going to be so phenomenal that you wouldn't dare."

For a brief moment, he saw her eyes light up. He'd begun speaking her language. But in an instant the light flickered and died. "Look," she said, rummaging through her purse, "I didn't want to tell you this, but just after I shook hands with you on *Princess Paragon*, Nigel Cardew submitted a proposal for the series."

"Good old Nigel. And just what did *he* propose? To turn her into a cannibal?"

She grimaced at him, then found her crumpled pack of cigarettes at the bottom of her purse and dug it out. "No," she said. "He wanted to turn her into a kind of Marxist. Establish Iri as a collectivist planet, and rewrite the origin story to have Princess Paragon coming to Earth to battle Margaret Thatcher." She tried to tap a new cigarette out of the pack, but it was empty.

Brian rolled his eyes. "A *Marxist*? Oh, come *on.*"

"Well, it might be funny," she said, dropping the purse to the floor and frantically searching her desk drawers. "A kind of black comedy. Couldn't you do something like that instead?" In the bottom drawer she found a single, slightly bent cigarette; she sighed in relief.

Brian shook his head. "You think *Newsweek* will write about that?"

She hung the cigarette from her lip and tried to light it. "I'm not sure I want *Newsweek* writing about Princess Paragon being a dyke," she said. Because of the crook in the cigarette, her lighter kept missing the tip; she finally had to cross her eyes to get the proper aim. "Think of the reaction from the fundamentalists," she continued, dropping the lighter back into her purse. "The PTA. *That* whole crowd."

"So what?" said Brian, tossing the now-pliable gum about his mouth as though it were a pinball. "They can't do anything. *We* don't rely on government grants, you know."

"They can still make a big stink. The media can throw a fit."

"The media will throw a fit for a week, maybe two, but all that means is sales for us. Then the reporters will be out looking for the next scandal of the century. That's the beauty of life in the nineties; the country's attention span has been shortened to just under the length of a ratings sweeps period."

She inhaled a lungful of smoke and held it there for so long that Brian thought she must be trying for some kind of world record. Then she exhaled, and it all rushed out like foam from a fire extinguisher. "I don't know, Brian," she said. "I just don't know."

But he had her scent now. "Look," he said, "the last time I checked *Princess Paragon*'s sales figures, it was selling around twenty-five thousand. Well, there are probably half a million dykes in Manhattan alone, and when word gets out, you *know* they're going to start buying the book like crazy." Brian actually had no idea how many lesbians lived in Manhattan, but the number he'd snatched out of the air sounded credible. "And then, when you think of all the other lesbians across the country—not to mention the gay men . . ."

"*God,*" said Heloise, and she started hacking up smoke. "I'm so nervous about this I could just *ralph.*"

"Look, it's almost the millennium," he said. "Someday soon, someone is going to be the first publisher to do a gay superhero. It might as well be you, and it might as well be now. You'll be a villain to a lot of people, sure, but you'll be a hero to a lot more. Look at it this way: all the prudes and fundamentalists and PTA types aren't going to buy *Princess Paragon* even if you *do* turn it into the kind of book they can approve of. But every lesbian and gay man in America will buy it if you let me do it *my* way." He drew a breath and stuck his gum to his molars. "And if I'm wrong—well, the book was headed for cancellation anyway. Look on this as an experiment that has a shot at saving it."

Heloise had one eyebrow cocked; he knew he was getting to her. Could she be seeing herself in *People* as well?

She swiveled in her chair and showed him her profile. It was an almost imperial means of dismissing him; Queen Victoria might have done such a thing.

"I'll have to think it over, Brian. That's all there is to it. We'll talk on Monday."

He got up from his chair and left her sitting there, her cigarette held just about level with her temples. Then he left the Bang Comics offices with a spring in his step and the wintergreen flavor of his gum still intact. He was a happy man. He knew he'd won. He'd vanquished the dragon. Not by impaling it on a sword, but by giving it a whiff of cold, hard cash.

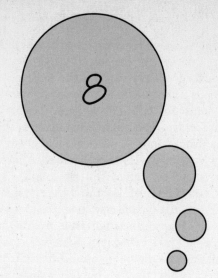

8

A string of identical Thursdays came and went like a single note played repeatedly on a piano. For Jerome, the weekly trip to the comic shop had become a painful duty; he felt like a wartime wife, both desiring and dreading the news from the front. *Moonman* was continuing along its bloodthirsty new path; *Acme-Man* kept distorting itself beyond recognition; and other titles were falling in line. Nigel Cardew was proving extremely prolific; he had taken over *The Red Wraith* and *Speed-Demon* as well as *Moonman*. And, as if that weren't bad enough, other cartoonists had started imitating him. In *The Blue Bowman*, Harlan Peters, once a favorite writer of Jerome's, had produced a grisly story in which Jiffy the Archer was shot in the spine, crippling him for life.

Jerome despised these new violent, sensationalistic comics. Yet he bought them all, read them all, and bagged them all in Mylar for his collection. He felt greater self-loathing than he had ever known.

On this latest Thursday he sat in the little office-building snack bar, consuming his customary patty melt and onion rings and looking over the day's purchases.

As he sipped his chocolate milkshake with whipped cream, he finished flipping through the new Nigel Cardew *Speed-Demon*, which was thoroughly disgusting (what *was* the fascination with seeing a man's head explode?). Then he grabbed a handful of onion rings, stuffed them into his mouth, and picked up the new *Princess Paragon*.

He paged through it as he chewed, being careful not to let any of the grease from his fingers soil the newsprint. He really didn't know why he bothered to take such care. The series was still tripe: the same old silly situations, endlessly replayed, the tiresome repetitions, the—

Oh, God.

On the letters page.

There it was.

His letter.

He wiped his hands on a tiny, flimsy paper napkin that wasn't even close to being up to the job and surveyed the page again.

Oh, *God*.

Me, he thought; it's *me* on the letters page!

He leaned over, readjusted his glasses, and reread his impassioned plea:

Dear Editor,

It's been a long time since I wrote a letter to a comic book, but I feel I must complain about the general decline in this title over the past few years. I am specifically moved to write by *Princess Paragon* #343, in which Miss Anthrope escapes from prison yet again, mines the Statue of Liberty with plastic explosives, and then threatens to blow it up. The only aspect of this story that shows any hint of progress from the old 1940s plots is that Miss Anthrope is now using plastics instead of dynamite. Otherwise, we're asked to bear witness to exactly the same kind of tired heroics we've seen in the series for too many years: Princess Paragon averts the charge into her own body and gets a good teeth-rattling, then throws Miss Anthrope back into jail and bemoans the twisted evil that would attempt to destroy such a monument to freedom.

Did it ever occur to your writer, Herman Cowsill, that it wouldn't matter if Miss Anthrope *did* blow up the Statue of Liberty, because Princess Paragon would just reassemble it in about a minute and a half? That's exactly what she did when the Sphinx of Giza got blown up in #277—which Mr. Cowsill also wrote! In fact, she even found the Sphinx's nose buried deep in the sand and replaced it—which your sister series, *The Freedom Front*, apparently forgot when it featured a scene with the Sphinx in their latest issue (the artist drew it noseless!).

At any rate, there's an even bigger problem with the series than script-rot, and that is the complete loss of what originally made Princess Paragon unique. Do you remember that in the 1940s, when she first came to Earth, her mission was to teach the Nazis love and compassion? Thanks to her creator, Roger Oaklyn, she was the only superhero during the golden age of comics who even *thought* about the possibility of reforming war criminals—and during her heyday she reformed quite a few of them (do you remember her old enemy, Contessa Von Hemlock, who became her best friend?).

Granted, after the war was over and the world found out just what the Nazis had been up to at Auschwitz and Treblinka, it was kind of embarrassing to go back to those old Princess Paragon stories where she talked about reforming them; they were clearly beyond human salvation. But to subsequently drop her lifelong campaign for redemption of the wicked is to throw out the baby with the bath! During the early 1970s, when Frank Cesafsky was writing and drawing the series, we got to see Princess Paragon at her best—emphasizing her *healing* powers over her *destructive* ones, her appeal to *reason* over her dependence on *force*. Of course, this was at the heady height of the feminist movement, when a woman superhero *had* to be different *because* she was a woman; now, in this macho post-Reagan era, we've got to settle for a Princess Paragon who is basically the same character as Acme-Man, only with a different set of chromosomes. I'm really tired of this.

When Princess Paragon's mother, the Queen of Iri, sent her only daughter to Earth in order to help prevent our planet from devouring itself in global warfare, she advised her that her weapons should be these: wisdom, understanding, love, and reason. Mr. Cowsill has been writing *Princess Paragon* for sixteen years now, and I find it interesting that as the character has grown progressively less inclined to use those particular "weapons," her sales figures have dropped steadily lower.

Mr. Cowsill has worked in comics for many decades, and has achieved a fine reputation, but he is killing Princess Paragon. The last time he even *tried* to do something different was in #300, where he had Agent Marks propose marriage to Princess Paragon, and we readers had to wait around till #305 to hear her say no. *Big* surprise. What Mr. Cowsill has forgotten is that in the 1940s, Agent Marks used to propose to Princess Paragon *all the time*. In fact, the first time he met her—when the FBI sent him to the Nevada desert to investigate the meteorite sighted there, and he discovered that the meteorite was really a spaceship with a beautiful alien princess inside—he proposed marriage at once. He said, "You're a vision from heaven—literally! You're like no other woman I've ever seen! Marry me!" And she replied, "I am sorry, but I have a mission on your bright-blue planet that precludes me from beginning any romance here." Don't you remember that scene? (You should; you've reprinted it in enough trade paperbacks.)

The next-issue blurb in #343 informs me that the Banana Republican and his ragtag army are again poised to invade the United States. I wish I had a nickel for every time I've seen the Banana Republican cross our borders only to get pummeled back into his native soil by Princess Paragon. Things do not look as though they're set to improve, do they?

Please! I love Princess Paragon. She was an inspiration to me when I was a kid in the 1960s, and she's much more than that to me now. Plus, I've got a nearly complete run of her issues from 1941 on, which has cost me a small fortune on the collector's market. I certainly don't want to have to give her up now. But she's turned into a ghost of herself, and I really don't think I'm doing her any favor by continuing to support her under these circumstances.

Jerome T. Kornacker
413 Mockingbird Drive
Park Woods, IL

(*Ye Editor replies:* Hey, Jerome—hang on for a few more months, pal! Beginning in the double-sized anniversary is-sue, #350, we're introducing a new direction for our Pulverizin' Princess, with none other than fan-favorite *Brian Parrish* at the helm! And boy, has he got *plans* for our battlin' beauty! If you've seen the gritty new *Moonman* comic, you've got a good idea of just how *radical* the changes are gonna be—and don't say we didn't warn you! In the meantime, be here next ish for the conclusion to Princess Paragon's epochal battle against the ever-unstoppable Willy Nilly!)

Jerome reread the letter and the editor's reply about six more times before he could tear his eyes from the magazine.

Then he placed his hand on his heart and thought, *Thank God!* I wrote that letter in the *nick* of time! Now Brian Parrish is going to take over *Princess Paragon* and do it *right*. I hate to think of what might have happened if I hadn't written when I did!

He imagined the moment in his head: Brian Parrish makes the unprecedented move from Electric Comics to Bang Comics to take over *Princess Paragon*—only to find himself uncertain as to what he should do with the character. He sits, perplexed; he starts to think. Just then, a letter is forwarded to him from the

Bang Comics offices. A note is attached to it: "Brian—this should give you some ideas!" Brian reads the letter—Jerome's, of course—and suddenly his way is clear. He knows exactly what to do!

Might Brian even have written a thank-you note to Jerome, which would arrive in his mother's mailbox any day now?

Oh, happy moment! Perfect world! Princess Paragon was saved! Brian Parrish, the best cartoonist on Earth, was coming to her rescue—armed with the wisdom of Jerome T. Kornacker!

Jerome turned and saw Amanda approaching him, smiling as widely as he.

"Here you *are* again, with new *comic* books," she enthused.

He beamed at her. "Yes, and look at this," he said, swiveling the copy of *Princess Paragon* so that she could see his letter. "That's *me*. Jerome T. Kornacker. I *wrote* that."

She leaned down to look at the page, holding her hair back so that it didn't fall into her face and block her sight; then she stepped back, her mouth slightly agape, and regarded him with so strong a show of emotion that Jerome thought for a second she might cry.

"That's *wonderful*," she said. "Oh, you must be so *proud*."

"You can read it, if you like," he said, handing her the issue.

She looked over her shoulder. "I shouldn't; they'll see me not working. But, oh, Jerome, I *will* buy my own copy and read it at home!"

He turned crimson. "That's not necessary, really, you *may* borrow mi—"

"No, *no*," she insisted, shaking her head. "You won't want to be without it for even a *minute*. You must be too *proud* of it."

Suddenly Jerome thought, as he had never done before, that Amanda was sparklingly pretty. Even the big scar above her left temple—from a childhood bicycling accident, she'd once told him—seemed to have somehow become exotic and alluring.

Before he could realize what he was doing, he said, "Maybe you'd like to come and see my collection sometime."

She actually clasped her hands under her chin. "Oh, yes, I *would* like that, very *much*."

He smiled at her; she smiled at him. Then she was called away to clear the lunch tables.

Perfect day; glorious day! Jerome passed a group of students on his way home, and held his head high. He even managed to meet the eyes of one of them.

Let them scoff if they dared. He was linked in spirit with the great Brian Parrish! The world was *his*.

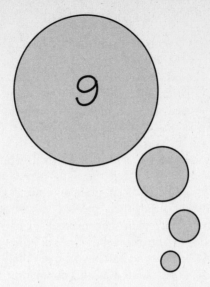

9

The closest to a flush Brian had gotten all night was in Heloise's powder room, and now his hand was worse than ever. He was tired of maintaining a stone face, and at this point in their poker-playing careers everyone here could read everyone else like a book, anyway. He folded and went to get a beer from Heloise's kitchen.

As he left the table, he heard the whispering start, like the buzz of activity around a fresh kill. He consoled himself by noting that jackals always waited until the lions had fed and gone. He wasn't surprised by the attention; Heloise had initiated these poker parties as a means of bringing about a kind of Bang–Electric *détente*, but they'd quickly degenerated into a thriving exchange for industry gossip.

For someone who craved fame so deeply and unabashedly, Brian was strangely uncomfortable being the subject of such talk. But he'd been working on *Princess Paragon* for almost a month now, and there had been nothing *but* gossip since he'd first walked through the Bang Comics door. The "L" word had begun to get around, too, despite all attempts at secrecy. And Heloise, still uncertain that she'd made the right choice in allowing him to proceed with his plans, was smoking so heavily that he suspected she posed as much of a threat to the biosphere as Los Angeles on an average day.

It hadn't helped that Herman Cowsill, who'd been writing *Princess Paragon* for years, left the Bang offices sobbing after his firing; the old guy had been popular among the staff. It also hadn't helped that Brian then waltzed in with a freelance contract giving him more than sixteen times what Cowsill had been making for doing the same book. And it hadn't helped that Cooper's CEO, Grant Vanderwheyde, had called Heloise after he heard the "L" word mentioned in conjunction with one of his subsidiary merchandising properties and breathed fire at her. (She'd managed to calm him down by promising such a wealth of increased revenues that it nearly disarmed his fear of controversy.)

It also hadn't helped that Heloise, in her all-or-nothing-at-all style, had hired him a lesbian editor from an independent comic-book company in Missouri. Her name was Perpetrial Cotton, and she was leaving her popular small-press comic, a black-lesbian anthology titled *Wimmins and Chillens First*, to come to New York and edit *Princess Paragon*. She had yet to arrive in town; she was driving cross-country in her self-described "ancient Impala filled with books, potted herbs, and cats," dashing off excruciating notes to Brian at every rest stop. An example: "Brian: have thoughts on how to decrease patriarchal overtones in project. Anxious to speak on this. Also, must costume reveal so much of breasts? Princess is from enlightened planet; would either cover breasts entirely for protection or reveal them totally for comfort. Would definitely not resort to teasing. Beneath her. Talk soon. Perpetrial." Brian had gone to Heloise and begged her to make this irritating woman in her potty Impala turn around and go back to Missouri, but Heloise was enjoying seeing him squirm: her revenge for all this, he supposed.

As he swung open the door to Heloise's kitchen and strode in, he heard the voices behind him graduate from whispers to open chatter. Then he heard Heloise bark, "Shut up and play cards, you bunch of magpies! If I wanted to sit around a bunch of cackling old hens, I'd invite my mother and her friends over for mahjongg. Christ!"

The door swung shut, and Brian smiled. Heloise was okay.

In the kitchen, he found Nigel Cardew sitting at Heloise's tiny breakfast table, watching the portable TV she kept next to a bowl of decaying fruit. (The blackening bananas had even attracted gnats. Surely she didn't still propose to eat them!) Brian nodded.

Nigel turned his head from the TV and nodded back, then took a long drag off his cigarette. He smoked in so different a manner from Heloise that Brian couldn't resist studying it for a moment. In one fluid motion, Nigel lifted his cigarette to his mouth, inhaled the smoke, lowered his hand, then exhaled through his nose. Then, every few seconds, he would repeat this process. It was comforting to watch him; soothing, like observing a seamstress at work.

Brian pointed to the refrigerator. "Just came for a beer."

Nigel nodded and turned back to the TV. He was watching "Alf."

Brian leaned down to take a Leinenkugel from the refrigerator door; this put him at eye level with a jar of Dijon mustard that must have been purchased during the first Reagan administration; it had hardened into chunks of petrified brown slate. Brian shook his head and stood up; how did Heloise's boyfriend manage to put up with all this? Maybe it was the reason he still maintained an apartment of his own (although Heloise claimed he stayed there only on her poker nights).

He twisted the cap off his beer bottle and a little wisp of condensed brew wafted up from the bottleneck; he sniffed it with pleasure, then took a long, cool swallow.

Nigel Cardew was still watching "Alf"—impassively, as if the constant, insistent hysteria of the laugh track were some alien noise that meant nothing to him. He wore the aspect of a naturalist watching fruit bats mate—a purely academic curiosity.

"So, you don't play poker," Brian said, regretting it as soon as it was out of his mouth. It sounded forced and insipid, as if he were begging Nigel to talk to him. He leaned against the counter and tried to salvage the situation by looking cool.

Nigel turned and took another elegant hit off his cigarette. "Brian Parrish," he said. He stared at Brian as if this demanded a reply, then blew the smoke through his pursed lips in a stream as concentrated as a laser beam.

Brian raised an eyebrow. Nigel's shaved head, crucifix earrings, and huge Doc Marten boots seemed to invite confrontation, not conversation. Suddenly, he wished he hadn't folded. Losing money might be preferable to chatting with this kid. He took another swig of beer and said, "Yeah, that's me. We were introduced earlier."

"Sow Oi recall," said Nigel, his cockney accent thick and off-putting.

Another long silence. Nigel turned back to the television set; he smoked, paused, exhaled. Smoked, paused, exhaled.

Brian tried to nurse his beer, but this silence was uncomfortable. All he could hear was the "Alf" soundtrack, tinny and unbearable.

Finally, the show broke for a block of commercials. Nigel turned to Brian again and said, "You're the one's gowing to mike Princess Paragon turn rug-muncher."

Brian shifted his weight to his other leg. "Well, it's not official yet."

"It's owkay," said Nigel. "Heloise towld me. Oi think it's bloody brilliant."

"You do?" Brian asked, a bit too eagerly.

Nigel smoked, paused, exhaled. "Yes, Oi do. Never been done before, 'as it, an' it's bound to shike up the bloody bourgeoisie."

"Well, thanks. I think so, too."

"You're a poof yourself, then?"

Brian's heart jumped. "I beg your pardon."

"Fancy blokes a bit, Oi mean." He smoked, paused, exhaled.

"Well, yes, I—I mean no, not *actively* anymore, but I—uh—" His answer ground to a halt. He'd been too much taken aback by the question.

Nigel smiled wanly and nodded, then smoked, paused, exhaled. "Oi unnerstend. Heloise towld me you've got a lover. Oi should loike to find meself one as well, someday."

"You're *gay*?"

"That's not what Oi said."

Another long silence. Nigel smoked, paused, exhaled. Brian finished off his beer and tossed his empty bottle into Heloise's trash can, where it hit a pile of other empties and made a frightening, brittle noise. It made Brian think of the Glass Warriors he'd invented as villains for the Centipede. He'd given them up after finding himself unable to devise properly dramatic sound effects for their battles—"clink" didn't quite convey the epic proportions he'd desired.

"Well," Brian said at last, "I'm enjoying your *Moonman* quite a bit."

"Thank you," said Nigel. "Oi'm enjoying wroiting it."

"Still getting poison-pen letters over killing off Comet?" he asked, chuckling. Disparaging obsessive fans was a favorite activity among Brian's circle.

"Every day, mite. But never moind; he's stying dead. Never could stend the little bloighter." Smoke, pause, exhale. "Too fucking cheerful for 'is own good, thet one. Thet's why Oi 'ad to bludgeon 'im up a bit first. Teach 'im a lesson."

Brian raised an eyebrow in surprise; then he half-smiled. So, Nigel Cardew was just another fanboy! He actually took his characters seriously; they existed as real people for him, with inherent personalities and behaviors. Brian, a *true* professional, recognized that his characters were mere constructs, built for the telling of stories and manipulable to an ultimate degree. For all Nigel Cardew's skill, he'd never amount to much if he insisted on treating them as anything more than that.

Brian's chest swelled with superiority. But then, watching this disturbingly quiet young man sitting before him, smoking and exhaling, smoking and exhaling, he wondered to what extreme such a delusion might lead. In Nigel, it had obviously led to a career; but where might it lead someone else—some other deluded fan who actually invested emotional weight in cardboard characters produced solely for commercial gain? The annual comic-industry conventions Brian was obliged to attend were inevitably frequented by a number of sad, shabby young men and women who seemed utterly distraught over the fates of their favorite heroes; he'd been cornered once by a truly terrifying young man with a massive beard and foul breath who begged him, "*Please* don't let Intrepid Girl get pregnant by Ranger Danger! You've got to let her wait till Baron Bravissimo comes back from the planet Amzaxx, so he can win her heart again!" Brian had felt a flurry of fear, but the plea—and the passion behind it—was so ridiculous, in view of its subject, that he couldn't resist mocking the young man to his fellow cartoonists later. And all of them had similar stories to tell.

Now Nigel Cardew—who was undoubtedly a highly intelligent, highly ambitious young man—had found his way into these same cartoonists' ranks; but he was still afflicted with a deranged fan's delusions. Comet must be killed, not because it would make a great story, not because it would sell like crazy, but because Comet *deserved* to be killed.

The commercial break ended and "Alf" reappeared on the minuscule TV screen. Nigel returned his full attention to the show. Brian went to the refrigerator and got another beer; then, thinking how much fun it would be to have some silly story about Nigel to bring back to the poker table, he decided to goad the boy into an embarrassment. He cocked his head and said, "So, you like 'Alf,' do you?"

"Quoite a lot, ectually," Nigel said.

Brian twisted the cap off his beer and grinned. "I see," he said smugly. He had his story; Nigel, the postmodern terror, was an "Alf" fan.

Nigel smoked, paused, exhaled. "Moind you," he said, "Oi'd loik it better if they'd ownly let the monster ripe the little girl."

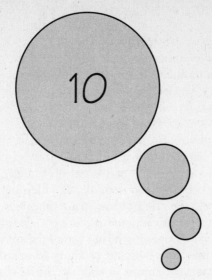

10

Jerome lay on his bed, stricken. He had been felled by such a potent brew of disbelief, anger, and revulsion that he seriously thought he might never rise again.

The sun was spurting through the slits in his blinds and his mother was pounding on the door. It was as if the entire world knew he was at his lowest ebb, and was choosing this moment to rush in and devour him.

"Jerome," his mother harangued him, "I have yet to see you outside this room all day today and even last night. If you're not feeling tip-shape, you have to let your mother in there to take care of you. I am sure that that is some kind of law."

It had all happened yesterday—Thursday—the world erupting as if in a biblical disaster, wiping everything away. He'd gone to the comic shop, and they'd all been there—Stickman, Shortman, Dirtyman, the whole bunch—and they'd been abuzz. When Doug saw him, he'd called out, "Hey, J-man, heard the news?"

What news, Jerome had inquired.

"The news about Princess Paragon!"

Jerome's mother banged on the door again. "Jerome, by not answering me, you only make me convinced that you are not capable of speech, for instance that you are unconscious. Is this the case, Jerome? Answer me yes or no!"

"The rumor's been officially confirmed," said Shortman, spraying his saliva almost a full yard.

What rumor, Jerome had asked delightedly.

His mother tried the door handle. "Jerome, how dare you lock this door!" she cried. "How many times have I told you that I'm a respecter of privacy, and if a door is closed I'd never think of even *thinking* of opening it, not for all the trees in China! Unless I think my baby is dying or short of breath, such as now, when privacy seems almost not important by comparison. Have you been locking your door on your mother's face all these years? I hope you *aren't* in there dying, Jerome, so I can get an answer to that question and then maybe wring your neck."

Doug had smiled and said, "Brian Parrish is turning Princess Paragon into a *lesbian.*"

"She gets a girlfriend in his third issue," said Shortman, a wet sheen on his chin.

"I, for one, hope to see a makeout scene by the fifth issue at *latest,*" said Stickman, shifting his green vinyl duffel bag to the opposite shoulder.

Jerome had felt the floor fall away and the walls spin. You're all lying, he had said.

"I'm on my way to the phone to phone up the doctor," said Mrs. Kornacker. "I guess I'll have to get the fire department over here too, so they can axe down your door, since I lost the key to it in I think it was nineteen-seventy. Jerome, are you hearing this? They'll probably send an ambulance, which we will definitely need because when they break down this door, if you aren't at least almost completely dead, I'm going to elapse into a coma from the embarrassment of it."

Liars, Jerome had said. Liars, liars, *liars*!

"I told you," said Doug, "you've gotta read the *Observer*!

They have a whole Brian Parrish interview in there this month. Bang is putting *Princess Paragon* on hiatus after the next issue, and then in two months the new Brian Parrish series is gonna come out. And this is gonna be a whole new version, where Princess Paragon is a lesbian, and comes from a lesbian planet."

A lesbian planet! Jerome had repeated, appalled.

"It's almost enough to prompt you to buy an industrial-strength telescope," joked Stickman. "Just imagine all those beautiful alien vixens engaged in active sexual congress! The mind boggles."

You're *sick*, Jerome had said.

He listened as his mother's footsteps grew faint; she was on her way downstairs to the telephone.

That would never do. He would have no doctor prodding him now, no fireman bashing down his door.

By a monumental act of will, he summoned the strength to reach over and pick up the receiver of his bedroom extension. He held it to his ear. The hum of the dial tone was all he heard.

A few moments later, however, he detected a barely audible click; this was immediately followed by a deafening cacophony of shrill push-button tones.

"Mother, you imbecile, stop *dialing*!" he howled.

A pause. "Jerome, is that you speaking so disrespectively?"

"Yes, it is I. You need not alert a physician, and certainly not the fire department. I am in no need of any aid they could hope to dispense."

"Then why didn't you answer me when I was by your door going crazy with worrying about my son dying?"

"I—was asleep at the time." He lay back on the bed again and nestled the phone on his pillow above his shoulder.

"If you were asleep, Jerome, then how come you could hear what I said when I said I was calling a doctor and the fire department on you?"

"Well, actually—I, uh, heard you say those things just as I was awakening. It took me a moment to understand what I'd heard. I was still shaking off my slumber."

"Jerome, you didn't go and do your job today. Your boss

called, furious, he inflamed my ear with how he was going to fire you. I had to calm him down and convince him not to do that, and the lies I told him I think God will never forgive me for, even if I spend the rest of my life in a church kneeling down on broken glasses."

"Thank you, Mother, it was kind of you to cover for me."

"Just remember that your grandma died when you go to work tonight."

He rolled over, accidentally dragging the phone's cradle off his nightstand and onto the floor, where it landed with a jarring clatter. "What are you babbling about? Granny's been dead nine years."

"Don't get my gander up, Jerome. I'm only trying to help you. I was forced into telling your boss, so he wouldn't go and fire you, that your grandmother had just passed away to Jesus and that you were too grief-stuck to go to work because of the tragedy of it. I told him I had to give you a shot of a sedative to calm your nerves down."

He shivered at the thought and drew the covers over himself. "I trust, Mother, that I shall never be so woebegone as to allow *you* to approach me wielding a hypodermic needle without protesting in the strongest terms possible."

There was a long pause; then Mrs. Kornacker said, "I can't tell or not if that was an insult to me. I wish you'd just learn to talk like other boys talk."

"I am going to hang up now, Mother."

"Lunch is set on the table, Jerome. That's the whole entire reason I went up to wake you up in the first place."

"I can assure you, I am not even slightly hungry." He curled into the fetal position.

"What do you mean? The day *you're* not hungry, then it's a cold July in hell. I'm calling a doctor."

"Oh, very well, then, have it your way. I'll eat." He rubbed the bridge of his nose. "Just leave a tray outside my door."

"This is not your personal maid you're ordering around here, Jerome. This is not room service at the Buckinghams' Palace."

"*Please*, Mother. Just do it. I would be very grateful."

Another pause. "Okay, then, Jerome. Coming right up. Let me know if I do anything wrong, like not get there quick enough, or make too much noise on the stairs, or accidentally not remember that the whole Earth resolves around you."

"Thank you, Mother. I'm certain you'll carry out this little chore with admirable skill." He hung up the phone.

He lay still as an alligator for some time, until he heard his mother on the stairs again. Within minutes, she was rapping on the door. "Your luncheon, Mr. Trump," she called out in a lamentable attempt at a British accent. Then she retreated.

Jerome threw back the covers, slid out of bed, and tiptoed over to the door. He opened it a crack and peeked out, just to be certain that she had indeed gone; then he pulled in the tray and shut the door again.

He took the tray—which held a greasy hamburger between slices of Wonder Bread, a bowl of Campbell's tomato soup, and an unopened package of frosted cupcakes—and carried it to his desk. Then he sat and, without ceremony, began to eat—with all the Bang and Electric heroes staring at him grimly, watching every morsel pass from his hands to his mouth. They, perhaps alone of those who might regard such a scene, declined to comment on the depressing state of his manners.

From the corner of his eye, he saw the issue of *The Comics Observer* he had bought to confirm the heresies of Stickman and Shortman and Dirtyman and Doug. He had brought the magazine home and made it halfway through the Brian Parrish interview before hurling it against the wall; it now lay on the floor, its pages flung open and curled under its spine, looking like some delicate bird that had plummeted from a great height and died.

He gave in to temptation; he padded over to the magazine and retrieved it. Settled again at his desk, he slurped his soup and picked up reading where he'd left off in anger.

OBSERVER: Isn't it kind of cynical, Brian, that you're turning Princess Paragon gay just because "someone has to be the first" to do a gay superhero?

PARRISH: Not at all. I wouldn't have attempted it if I weren't perfectly in tune with the character. Look, she's always been a pretty radical hero; during the forties, she espoused feminism, pacifism, civil rights—all the ideals that were, back then, pretty loaded and controversial. Fact is, today, all those things are much more respectable—they're part of the political agenda of any number of mainstream groups in the country. Back in the forties, they weren't, and Princess Paragon was on the cutting edge of ideological progressivism; but, of course, since she was a comic-book character, no one took her seriously, so no one took a hard look at her and said, "Hey, I don't want my kids reading this." Which was lucky for us; the series was able to influence an entire generation—a generation that seems to me to have grown up much more enlightened. Well, maybe I'm naive, but I think we can do the same kind of thing now. Sure, comics are in a much brighter media spotlight than ever before, but does that have to mean they're neutered—so scrubbed and sanitized that they have no political charge? That they're the insubstantial crap they've always been in the popular imagination? In *Princess Paragon*, I want to get across to kids the radical idea that *different* doesn't mean *bad* or *wrong* or *evil*. My Princess Paragon is *very* different. She's a lesbian. But she's still a good, decent, brave woman—a woman willing to fight for what she believes. In the face of all the hypocrisy in the world today, I think we *need* her. Just like we needed the original Princess Paragon in the forties: she stood up for people who couldn't stand up for themselves, like American Germans and Japanese.

OBSERVER: Don't you fear a backlash—militant conservative groups mounting some kind of campaign that could result not only in *Princess Paragon* getting canceled but also in the end of your career?

PARRISH: They might try, certainly. But the fact is—and I've said this over and over again—militant conservatives don't buy *Princess Paragon*, never have, and never will. Whereas, if gay men and women buy it, it'll survive the controversy—it'll continue. This is a free market, after all. As long as the book makes money, no one's going to cancel it. So I'd urge you all to go out and buy it.

OBSERVER: Does Bang's parent, Cooper Communications, stand behind the book?

PARRISH: To about the degree you'd expect. They're waiting to see if it makes money. Again, what I said about the free market.

OBSERVER: Some gay groups have criticized you for doing a gay *woman* hero instead of a gay *man*, saying that rather than appeal to actual gay people, you're cynically trying to attract the kind of adolescent male reader who gets off on the woman-on-woman spreads in skin magazines like *Penthouse*.

PARRISH: Oh, brother! I've been hearing some crazy accusations from some fringe gay groups, but that's a new one.

OBSERVER: Is it true?

PARRISH: Of course not—for the reason I've just given you: Princess Paragon is the first gay superhero because it fits the strip's history and character. And, I mean, come on—we're not going to be doing soft-core porn! We probably won't even have sex of any kind, beyond an occasional kiss or embrace. I'm writing about *people*, not bodies. I guess all I can say is, wait till the book comes out, then read it and judge for yourself. That's all—just judge for yourself.

OBSERVER: Do you see yourself as a gay culture hero?

PARRISH: I see myself as a cartoonist striving to grow.

OBSERVER: Are you gay yourself?

PARRISH: Why? Would that make some kind of difference?

OBSERVER: Well—

PARRISH: Look, this is the kind of attitude my *Princess Paragon* is going to be fighting—that you judge people based on their sexuality. Judge me by my work, okay?

OBSERVER: So you don't believe in being open about your sexuality in a public forum.

PARRISH: If this were a *personal* profile, sure. But this is an interview in a trade magazine about my efforts in that trade. My private life is irrelevant. [Pause] Now, if I thought Tom Selleck might read this interview and want to meet me, I might think differently.

OBSERVER: [Laughs] I guess you just answered my question.

PARRISH: [Laughs] Damn, I guess I did!

Jerome closed the magazine.

So.

That explained it.

Brian Parrish was a homosexual.

No *wonder* he was perverting Princess Paragon. He was a pervert himself!

He felt a wave of shame wash over him for having been taken in by Brian Parrish all these years.

He tossed the magazine into the wastepaper basket beneath his desk.

And then he noticed that the sun, still seeping in from behind his blinds, was now illuminating a long, inch-thick strip of his Princess Paragon poster. It was turning one of her eyes incandescent, almost neon—and not only her eye, but the hollow of her throat; the tip of one breast; a pair of ink-slash ribs; her polka-dotted pubic mound.

The strip of sunlight had abstracted her—reduced her to her component parts. It was a kind of pornography. But hadn't Jerome better get used to such treatment? It was all the brave lady had in store for her.

"No, no," he said out loud, chewing frantically on a frosted cupcake he had stuffed whole into his mouth. "I wiw *not* wet vis fing happen!"

Was it his imagination, or did the heroine's eye twinkle in gratitude?

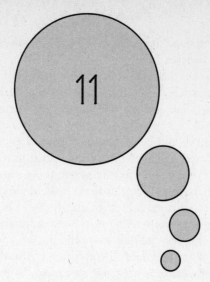

11

"All I'm saying," said Perpetrial Cotton as alfalfa sprouts dribbled from her lower lip, "is that *Lawgiver* is as patriarchal a title as *Queen*." She picked the thready strands from her chin and popped them back into her mouth. "The word *queen* comes from the Old English *cwen*, which means wife, you know—so of course no ruler of a matriarchy could possibly have that title. But Lawgiver is equally bad, because it still represents a hierarchy of authority with one person at the top, which is *strictly* a feature of oppressive male power structures." She smiled beatifically at Brian and Heloise.

Heloise, who had never been to a Middle Eastern restaurant before and had as a result been at a loss as to what to order, was now struggling valiantly with the pita-pocket sandwich she had reluctantly settled on. There was never any doubt how the struggle would end. The sandwich drooped in her hand as she tried to bite it, and a huge glob of curry paste fell onto her white silk

Anne Klein blouse. "Jesus H. Christ in a *shitstorm*," she snarled. "This *would* happen."

Brian pushed his hummus around with his fork. He was not enjoying this lunch. "Well," he said to Perpetrial, a hint of challenge in his voice, "what would *you* call Princess Paragon's mother, then?"

She sat back and cocked an eyebrow. "Let me think a minute." She averted her eyes from him, and it gave him a few moments to study her. She was one of the most startling sights he'd seen in Manhattan in a long time (at least, the most startling he'd seen at such close range). First of all, she wore her hair in a huge Afro—certainly the only Afro he'd seen since the seventies, and possibly the biggest he'd ever seen, period. Second, she was wearing a T-shirt that said "Free Sharon Kowalski," which was alarming not because it virtually screamed "I am a lesbian" but because Sharon Kowalski had in fact *been* free for more than a year. Couldn't Perpetrial have popped for a new T-shirt—especially when meeting her new boss for lunch during her first week of employment?

And third, Perpetrial had the biggest hips of any woman Brian had met since leaving Minneapolis in 1973. And the question he kept asking himself was, How can she have such large hips if she goes around eating stuff like alfalfa sprouts?

Suddenly she turned back to him and smiled brightly. "You know," she said, "on a planet ruled by women—especially dyke women—I don't think there'd *be* a reason to single out one person to serve as the sole authority. I'm sure they'd all rule by consensus; it'd be a perfect collectivist government."

Brian shuddered, thinking, Nigel Cardew back to haunt me. "But if that's the case," he said, coloring with irritation, "then Princess Paragon's mother wouldn't be anyone special; she'd just be another face in the crowd."

Perpetrial shook her head and sighed. "Typical oligarchical thinking," she said. "If someone doesn't have a title, you think she can't be anyone special." She dolloped another forkful of her bean salad into her mouth.

"This crap won't come off," said Heloise, dabbing at the

curry stain on her blouse with a wet napkin. "What the hell do they put in it, anyway? Yak's blood?"

Brian stared into Perpetrial's maddeningly untroubled eyes and felt his forehead crease with anger. "Look, Princess Paragon's mother *is* an authority figure. She has to be—it's an integral part of the story. She's the one who makes the decision about who to send to Earth, and it's a big sacrifice she makes, sending her own daughter. I refuse to give up that angle of the story. It's too good."

"You don't have to give it up," said Perpetrial after taking a gulp of mineral water. "Look, she can be *an* authority figure, but not *the* authority figure, because on a matriarchal planet that kind of person wouldn't exist. But there *would* be women who would be respected and whose judgments would be sought because of their age and experience. The term I like is *crone*. Princess Paragon's mother can be the Elder Crone of Iri."

"*Yuck,*" said Brian.

Heloise caught a waiter by the arm. "Look," she said, "you carry this stuff around all day, you *must* know how to get it out of fine fabrics." She loosened her grip on his arm and felt the shiny, coarse material of his sleeve. "Jeez," she said; "maybe not."

Perpetrial leaned forward and said, "Look, Brian, you've got a lot of unlearning to do before you can write a convincing lesbian book. And the first lesson can be this: terms that apply to old, postmenopausal women are *not* inherently pejorative, because old, postmenopausal women are *not* useless and ugly and frightening. In the pre-Christian era, to be a crone was to be a repository of wisdom; it was to be *respected.* I really *insist* that we consider seriously the implications of dismissing the term on the basis of sexist, patriarchal revisionism alone. Was I correct in understanding that your commitment to doing a lesbian superhero was motivated by a desire to enlighten?"

"Of course, of course."

"Well, then." She sat back. "I mean, I *was* under the impression that this is why I was hired."

Heloise leaned over and said, "Sorry, Perpetrial, I need your mineral water." She grabbed the half-empty bottle from

Perpetrial's place setting. "Carbonated, you see." And then she dumped its contents directly onto the curry stain. Immediately, her entire chest was soaked.

She looked up at Brian and Perpetrial, who were clearly stunned, and said, "Sorry, I'm desperate. This blouse cost four hundred bananas." She dropped her napkin into her chair and said, " 'Scuse me, got to go blow-dry my boobs in the ladies' lounge." With this, she trotted away.

Brian and Perpetrial looked at each other. Brian thought for a moment that they might have a laugh together over Heloise's clumsiness, and in that way forge a bond, but Perpetrial appeared to find the incident not at all amusing. Brian sighed.

"Okay, let's lay our cards on the table," he said, putting down his fork and locking eyes with her. "Yes, you *were* hired because you're a comic-book editor who also happens to be a lesbian. But the book is *mine* to create. You are absolutely right to bring up issues like this crone business—that *is* why you were hired—but the final decisions are mine. *I'm* the one who sells the books, and you have to keep me happy. And toward that end, I really have to insist that you not take such a condescending tone with me."

Her brow furrowed. "Okay, Brian. Fair enough. I'll try."

Christ, she was even patronizing when she was giving in; she made it sound as if it were going to take a superhuman effort not to talk down to him!

But for now, he'd settle for her promise. He extended his hand and said, "Shake."

She shook it, but said, "You know, the practice of shaking hands is almost universally male—it developed as a useful social nicety in that it allowed men to greet one another intimately while reassuring each other that they weren't concealing any weapons. Very few women shake hands, even today; when they do, it's because it's necessary to make an entrée into exclusively male enclaves, like business. I can't say I much like the practice, myself. I'd rather embrace, or kiss." She released Brian's hand and knit her brow. "But I *especially* dislike shaking hands when it's implied that it's got some kind of binding quality, like a signature on a contract. A real woman is as good as her word." She lifted her napkin and wiped her lips.

Brian stared at her, thinking, This is someone I could learn to hate big-time.

"Oh," she said suddenly, "almost forgot. More letters." She opened her vinyl briefcase (she was ideologically opposed to leather, and had announced as much on meeting Brian for the first time) and produced a bulging manila envelope.

Brian took it from her. "The usual assortment?"

"About the same as last time, if that's what you mean." She clamped shut the briefcase and turned back to her bean salad. "A handful of God-botherers, condemning us to eternal hellfire. Lots of lonely lesbians writing their life stories—why, I don't know, but some of them are interesting. A few crackpot funny-book fans who aren't taking the news at all well."

Brian had opened the envelope and was sorting through the missives. "Those are usually the most fun," he said, grinning in anticipation.

"I don't know." She put down her fork and chewed contemplatively. "Some are a little disturbing. There's one in there—you haven't got to it yet, keep going, a little more, there, that one, the one with the Acme-Man stamp on it."

"Oh, for God's sake, I haven't seen one of those in *years*," exclaimed Brian, picking up the letter and gazing at the stamp. "This kid must've bought *sheets* of them when they were issued."

"Open it," Perpetrial urged him. "I mean, it almost made me cry."

Brian arched an eyebrow and grimaced. "Oh, come on. It's not as though—"

"Just *read* it."

He shrugged, then removed the letter from the envelope and unfolded it. It was written on yellow notepaper and printed in block letters. " 'Dear Brian Parrish,' " he began reading loftily, " 'I have just finished your interview in the recent *Comics Observer*, and have no words to describe the utter contempt in which I hold the direction you have chosen for *Princess Parag—*' Perpetrial, do I *really* have to subject myself to—"

"Keep going," she said, finishing the last bite of her salad. "A few paragraphs down."

He scanned the page, then began reading anew. " 'I have loved Princess Paragon for years. She has been more than a character to me, she has been a companion, a friend, a guide, even, on occasion, a lover.' Oh, *man*. 'If you have ever had a fantasy lover yourself, you know how valuable, and yet how tenuous, that relationship can be. Nothing in my ten-year affair with Princess Paragon has been able to disrupt the beauty of my feelings for her.' " Brian lowered the letter to the table and cocked his head at Perpetrial. "I can't believe I am actually reading this."

"Just down to the bottom," she said.

He let his eyes drop to the closing paragraph. " 'You have ruined an American icon. You have altered her, made her monstrous. But, I beg of you—it still isn't too late to reconsider. Don't come out with this new anti–*Princess Paragon*! Cancel it before it has even begun. So many heroes have fallen prey to the prevailing taste for degeneracy; I would hate to see my favorite heroine suffer likewise. Especially because there is so little I can do to save her. That is such a hard thing for me to bear. Cordially yours, Jerome T. Kornacker.' "

Perpetrial shook her head. "Sad, isn't it? To be so *lost* to reality, to have so much love and no place to direct it beyond th—"

"The guy's a *lunatic*," Brian interrupted. "There are hundreds of his kind around, all crazy-eyed and sociopathic. Just wait till your first convention, and see how sympathetic you are then."

"Hey, I've *been* to conventions, Brian. Just because I haven't worked for one of the big, soulless money-machine publishers doesn't mean I'm new to *comics*. And I *know* how reactionary this Jerome person is, but I also know what it's like to be in love with Princess Paragon. Why do you think I sold out, gave up my creative independence and the comic I gave birth to, just to come to this disgusting city and work for an evil corporation? Because when I was a girl, I *loved* Princess Paragon—*romantically*. I *understand* that part of Jerome's letter—about having her as a fantasy lover. I know what he must feel, now that we've as much as announced that we're going to make him disgusting to her."

Brian cocked an eyebrow. "Perpetrial, if you're going to take seriously the whines and moans of every comic-book fanatic who writes in to compl—"

"What'd I miss?" It was Heloise reappearing, her blouse now crinkly and dry and a rather milkier shade of white than it had been before. She scooted back into her chair.

Brian handed her the letter. "We've just been discussing this."

She skimmed it, then handed it back to Brian. "Twilight zone," was all she said before beginning a fresh attack on her pita-pocket.

Brian grinned in triumph at the crestfallen Perpetrial. "A few more months in the big leagues, you'll see we're right," he said, thoroughly enjoying this opportunity to shower her with his own, suddenly Olympic-sized condescension.

Perpetrial opened her mouth to reply, but was forestalled by an eruption of "shits" and "fucks" from Heloise, who had just lost round two of her battle against her lunch order.

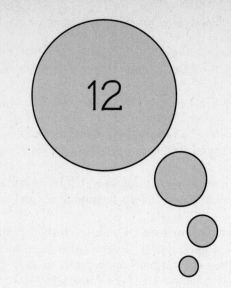

12

Jerome emitted a snort so loud, it woke him up. He propped himself up on his elbows and tried not to be embarrassed about it. His mother often complained about his snoring, how it filtered through the walls to her bedroom and kept her awake. "Sometimes," she would scold him, "I would almost swear that I'm hearing a bleached whale. Is that nice, Jerome?" It was mortifying.

He dragged himself out of bed, pulled a tattered Scotch-plaid robe over his pajamas, and descended the staircase, clutching the rail like a cruise-ship passenger during a typhoon. Then, having managed the stairs and arrived on solid ground again, he lurched toward the kitchen, his head still groggy, thinking only of his first bowl of sugar-encrusted breakfast cereal, and of the rush of giddiness it would afford him.

But as he swung open the kitchen door, he experienced an involuntary burst of adrenaline far beyond the capabilities of even the most heaping helping of Frosty Krunch. For there, tilted back in Jerome's favorite chair, was his appalling young cousin Wilfred, his feet up on the table and the latest issue of *Captain Fathom* in his hands (with, horror of horrors, the cover folded back)!

"What are *you* doing here?" Jerome shrieked. "Let go of that comic!" He stepped forward and snatched it out of Wilfred's hands.

Wilfred immediately jumped to his feet, and through the mountain range of acne that sprawled across his face, Jerome could see that he was smiling.

"I'll thank you to hand that back, *Duh*-rome," he said, utilizing his favorite nickname for his cousin. "As it happens, I purchased it myself. You're not the *only* one in the family who's allowed to rot his brain with this trash, you know."

Jerome looked at Wilfred's gangly, pasty-white arm, outstretched in anticipation of the comic book's return. And he knew then that he had erred; for hadn't he already read this issue of *Captain Fathom*, tucked it into a Mylar bag, and stored it away in a box in his closet? Wilfred couldn't possibly have sneaked into his room and stolen it without waking him—could he?

Wilfred's smug smile convinced him that this was the case. This must be a copy the boy had, for some unimaginable reason, bought on his own. Jerome gritted his teeth and returned it to him. "You shouldn't fold the cover back like that," he said, irritated. "It ruins the spine."

Wilfred sat down and reopened the comic book. "Like I *care* about the spine, *Duh*-rome. I mean, why would I want to preserve this silly compendium of tired clichés, anyway?" He pointed to one of the pages. "Listen to this: the villain—whose name, if I can manage to utter it with a straight face, is Doctor Smash—disappears in a puff of smoke, and as he does so he declaims, 'Captain Fathom! You'll rue the day you first crossed me! Mine shall be the last laugh, and it shall echo down the corridors of *eternity*!' And Captain Fathom raises his fist and cries out— quite heroically, too; look here at the bulging veins in his neck—he cries out, 'I say you *nay*, villain! For wheresoever you seek to thwart Good with Evil, Captain Fathom shall bar the way, with all the might and mastery of the Seven Seas *itself*!' Shouldn't that be *'themselves'*? No, probably not. Anyone who speaks of himself in the third person is undoubtedly incapable of error." He snickered, and flicked the comic book away from him.

Jerome winced. He had enjoyed that story; why, *why*, was Wilfred here ruining it for him?

He decided to ignore his sneering cousin to the fullest extent possible. He went to the pantry and took down the box of Frosty Krunch. But in lifting it, he found it impossibly light. He shook it, and only a few stray kernels danced around inside, making a truly pathetic, lonely sound. How had this happened? The box had been half-full only yesterday!

He stepped back into the kitchen and returned his gaze to the table. There, to Wilfred's left, was a cereal bowl with a half-dozen bloated kernels of Frosty Krunch floating around in a puddle of purple-stained milk.

This was really not to be borne.

"Wilfred," he said, his forehead stinging, "I demand to know why you are tainting this household with your presence. I really see no reason at all for you to be here."

The smug smile again. "I'm here at my Aunt Peachy's invitation, *Duh*-rome. Why else would I risk exposing myself to your putrid aroma?"

"*Mother* invited you?" He put the empty cereal box back on the shelf and took out instead a fresh box of butter cookies. "Would you mind telling me why?" he asked as he broke the cellophane seal with his lengthy thumbnail.

"Only to the extent that I mind speaking to you at all," replied Wilfred, leaning back in his chair again. "It appears to be your birthday, and Aunt Peachy has decided to throw a surprise party for you. She's out now, picking up the cake. I, on the other hand, was sent in search of decorations. According to Aunt Peachy's instructions, I was to negotiate the purchase of any paper tablecloths, napkins, and party favors I could find that reflected the theme of superheroism. This being a reasonably civilized township, I of course found no such thing. So I settled on buying some of these repulsive little periodicals themselves, thinking I could just hang *them* on the walls and cut them up to stick on a plain white tablecloth."

"Oh, *don't* cut them up!" yelped Jerome, shocked by the idea of such heathen disregard for literature.

Wilfred raised an eyebrow and grinned. "Why not, *Duh*-rome? They're just throwaway rags, aren't they?" He grabbed the comic book and rose from his chair. "Now, what do you think about hanging our stalwart Captain Fathom on the wall over he—" He deliberately ripped the comic book in half as he was lifting it. "Oh, dear, *now* look what I've done!" A sinister laugh slithered from between his teeth.

Furious, Jerome turned his back on his cousin and shoved four cookies into his mouth at once. Wilfred was such a *philistine*.

The back door swung open and a woman entered, her face obscured by two large grocery bags. "Oh, hello, Jerome," she said, and when she set the bags on the counter he could see that it was his Aunt Cherry, Wilfred's mother. "We didn't expect you to be rising and shining for another hour or so. Surprise!" She cackled and clapped her hands.

"Thang you, Ann Jerry," he said, his mouth still stuffed with cookies.

Aunt Cherry's hair was dyed the heart-stopping red that even fire engines had long ago abandoned. She swept a wisp of it from her face and started unpacking the grocery bags, her wrists jangling with junk jewelry of every imaginable metallic hue. "Just think," she said, "little Jerome turning twenty-six years of age! Why, I used to bathe your little naked baby body right in this very sink, right here!" She jerked her head in the direction of the kitchen sink. "Wilfred, get over here and help your mother empty these bags out. And Jerome, do you remember the cutest thing you used to do when I bathed you in this sink here?" She pulled a plastic tray of cupcakes from the bag.

"Nuh-uh," he said, trying hard to swallow the fistful of cookies that was lodged rather painfully in his throat now. Wilfred left the room, ignoring his mother's command.

"You used to let a stream of wee-wee flow right up into the

air like someone had gone and turned a garden hose on inside of you, and I'd have to duck my head or get a very unpleasant face full of—*Wilfred!* Get back in here!—face full of baby urinalysis, and, *oh!* How your mother and father used to *laugh* at the comedy of it! But you never did get me, you know," she said, hoisting a liter jug of cola out of a bag and cradling it in her arms as if it were a child. "I was a quick young thing way back then, just a teenager in the first blemish of youth."

Jerome was scandalized by the story, but nodded and smiled. He gulped hard and the half-chewed cookies went down at once, like a wrecking ball being dropped.

Aunt Cherry snapped her fingers and dug into the pocket of her skirt. "I cut something out for you, Jerome, that I saw the other day in the newspaper while I was reading it. I know how you like the funnies so much, so I clipped it out and here it is." She handed him a folded slip of newsprint, which he opened to reveal the headline, "Comic-Book Heroes Flying into Town."

He arched an eyebrow and read the first paragraph:

Not *real* comic-book heroes, of course—those square-jawed superdoers in capes, cowls, and long johns—but the men *behind* Acme-Man and Moonman and their dashing compatriots. You see, these days, cartoonists have cult followings of their own, and when the Seventh Annual Midwest Comic Convention rolls into the O'Hare Grifton Hotel next month, there'll be comics fans galore waiting to meet their epic-shaping idols! And if names like Nigel Cardew, Brian Parrish, and Hector Baez don't set your pulse thrumming with excitement, you obviously haven't made a trip to the five-and-dime lately!

Jerome was accustomed to the patronizing tone adopted by any newspaper feature writer who tackled a story on comic books, so he didn't take offense. Quite the contrary; he felt a kind of gratitude toward this writer for having conveyed such useful information.

Aunt Cherry was putting a vat of ice cream into the freezer.

"Do you know who any of those cartoonists they mentioned are, Jerome?" she asked.

"Of course," he said. "Except that Nigel Cardew isn't really a cartoonist, like the other two. He just *writes* the stories. He has to get someone else to draw them for him. Hector Baez and Brian Parrish both write *and* draw all their stories themselves."

Aunt Cherry closed the freezer and wiped her moist hands on her skirt, causing the junk bracelets to jangle even more unnervingly. "Isn't that nice," she said blankly, as though she were addressing a pet macaw who had just told her for the fifth time in a row what a good boy he was. "Now, where's that rotten little Wilfred? He's supposed to help me put up streamers. *Wilfred!* Get in here right now, or suffer the consequestions!" She flapped her hands at Jerome. "Now, shoo with you, Jerome; vamoose on back up to bed and pretend to be fast in sleep. Your other cousins are going to be here in a little bit of time, and your mother, too; let's let them think they really *are* surprising you."

Jerome sighed at the thought of all those atrocious cousins of his, filling up his kitchen and staring at him with their typical listless disdain. This party was going to be sheer hell. He turned and departed the kitchen, dragging his feet as he climbed the stairs back to his room. Aunt Cherry continued to scream for her truant son, but Jerome knew for a fact that Wilfred would no sooner think of answering her than of slitting his own throat. Jerome had seen him in the TV room, lying on the couch and watching an old episode of "Daktari," utterly oblivious to his mother's window-shattering summons.

In his room, Jerome crawled back into bed, then unfolded the newspaper article and read it over again.

The O'Hare Grifton Hotel. *That's* where they'd be. Nigel Cardew. Hector Baez.

And, of course, Brian Parrish.

He doused the light, tucked the covers under his chin, and settled back. Unable to sleep, he let his eyes travel around the room. Great scoops of shadow swallowed up entire corners, but soon his eyes adjusted to the dimness and he could see the familiar outlines and shapes of his posters. He made out the face of

Comet, and of Acme-Lad and Acme-Lass, and of Princess Paragon. Even in the absence of light, he could clearly see that their lips were moving.

It seemed unremarkable that this should be so. He thought to himself, Now, this really ought to surprise or even frighten me, but it doesn't.

He studied the heroes' mouths, which kept moving and moving and moving; they bit their lower lips, then stuck them out past the upper ones, then shut their lips altogether, then opened them widely, flattening them against their teeth. What could they be trying to say? Jerome tried to move his own lips in the same way, uttering sounds as he did so to help figure out their message.

Ah-ven-juh-me. That was it.

Avenge me. Over and over and over again. Like a mantra.

Comet was begging him. *Avenge me.*

Acme-Lad and Acme-Lass were prostrate before him. *Avenge me. Avenge me.*

And Princess Paragon, her eyes pleading and her hands outstretched in supplication, was beseeching him. *Avenge me!*

He watched her, fascinated, as she drifted out of focus, and the fleshy clouds that had once been her arms floated past his head and engulfed him, like an embrace. He felt something like a wave of warm water wash over him, and then he felt a little jolt.

He opened his eyes.

He looked around him. The lips were silent now, the posters still, the heroes mute.

Had it all been a dream? Had he merely nodded off?

There was a slick path of drool running down the side of his pillow, and when he moved to get away from it he found that he had crushed the newspaper clipping under his shoulder.

He retrieved it from beneath him and checked the article again. "Comic-Book Heroes Flying into Town."

The O'Hare Grifton Hotel.

That's where they'd be.

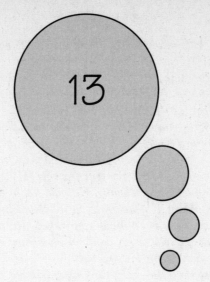

13

"Remember that Woman is part Receptacle," said the Elder Crone of Iri, her blood-hued robes all but enshrouding her withered form. "It is her nature to receive. And yet Woman is also part Creator, in that what she receives, she commingles therewith, and brings forth something greater, something profound." She reached out her hand; her bejeweled fingers grasped her daughter's smoother, naked hand. *"What you have received from me, from my womb, is Possibility; what you must bring forth from that is Realization. What you have received from our sisterhood is Knowledge; what you must bring forth from that is Wisdom. What you have received from your planet is Trust; what you must bring forth from that is Honor."*

"You wouldn't *believe* it," Heloise said, waving her lighted cigarette so that in the darkened stat room it looked like a spastic firefly dive-bombing her face. "Since we broke the news about *Princess Paragon* to the fan press, the book's sales have jumped *five percent!* I mean, people are so excited, they're buying the old series again, even though they know it's a lame duck. Vander-wheyde is *very* pleased. We won't have much trouble from *him* anymore, I guarantee it. No, really, Brian, we *won't.* I *swear.* On my honor as a—as a—well, as *whatever* it is I am." She shrugged. "Who's got time to figure out crap like that?"

*Special Agent Aaron Marks instructed the helicopter pilot to land a half-mile from the point in the Nevada desert at which the agency had detected the brief but powerful magnetic flux. It was dusk, and as he stepped from the chopper, the gust from its blades whipped his hair into his face and set his tie flapping. He could see, in the distance, a human figure, standing as if unafraid, as if—damn it, as if it were cu*rious. *Look at the way its head was cocked. He couldn't read this situation at all. He placed his hand on his holster and felt the pistol resting there, then began his approach.*

As he got closer he could see with increasing certainty that his quarry was a woman—more, a beautiful woman—more, a perfect *woman; tall, strong, clear-eyed, confident. When he was a dozen yards from her, he stopped. He stared at her for nearly two full minutes, uncertain as to how to proceed. Was she American? Soviet? A native of the area? A publicity seeker? How was she connected with the flux that had screwed up every radio and TV and computer within a five-mile radius?*

Finally, she extended her hand and smiled a dazzling, incandescent smile. "I have been awaiting a representative of this world's authority," she said, her voice mellifluous and musical. "I have been transported to your world from another, one unknown to you. I come to teach you, and to learn from you. I offer you peace, and love, and wisdom."

"Since the 'Entertainment Tonight' segment aired, we've been getting about forty calls a day," said Heloise in a low, throaty, pleasure-drenched purr as she soaked up the noon-hour sun with Brian out on the building's landscaped plaza. "There's *tremendous* interest in the new direction we're taking. Problem is, we haven't been able to convince retailers to beef up their orders for issue three fifty, even though most of the specialty-store owners are giving us advance orders *way* beyond our projections. But the average mom-and-pop newsstand isn't going to order twenty copies of *Princess Paragon* three fifty if they've only sold four of each issue prior to that. So what we're doing is canceling the old series with issue three forty-nine and starting your new series with number one. Stop smiling, Brian, I knew you'd be pleased. Just make sure you bring everybody back for issues two, three, four, and five." She undid another button of her blouse and glanced at her chest. "Am I red yet?"

The beautiful alien visitor stood before the assembled representatives of the United Nations, her cape hanging over one shoulder, her purple tunic and yellow leggings standing out from the expanse of three-piece blues and grays like the petals of a brilliant blossom in a patch of dusty gravel. "The impulse to seize power is universal," she said, "and yet, in the context of a civilized community, irrational. Reason has replaced *the power-impulse as the necessary tool of civilized survival, yet many of your race have not recognized as much. Your planet routinely utilizes aggression to promote economic systems, religious beliefs, and even, in some smaller countries, personal self-aggrandizement on the part of the ruling elite. Such goals are meaningless if enforced; any economic system will be embraced by other nations if it is* successful, *and if it is not, no force of arms can change that. Likewise, religious beliefs are only of any value if they undergo constant evaluation; a belief that* may not *be tested or questioned is not a belief that aids spiritual growth. And a ruling class that wields power by oppressing or abusing those in their charge are not leaders, but rather those who must be led; they have earned not authority but enmity, and face a day of reckoning. I do not say they will be brought down; rather, they will* fall *down, as they are passed by—by the legions of the enlightened, the peaceful, and the prosperous."*

By this time, the delegates from China, North Korea, South Africa, Albania, Guatemala, Honduras, and nearly every Islamic state had walked out. But when Princess Paragon thanked her audience for listening, she was confronted by the strange phenomenon of a standing ovation—and, not being a native of Earth, it took her some minutes to ascertain that this was a collective gesture of approval.

"I *told* you, it wasn't my idea," Heloise repeated, clutching Brian's shoulder and leaning close to his ear as they strode down the hall together. "Vanderwheyde's getting cold feet again—I know, I promised he wouldn't. So sue me. He's insisting that we mark the book, in *some* way, as being unsuitable for youngsters. Don't get upset, I know that's who you *want* to read it, but there's nothing I can do. This first issue is going to have a For Mature Readers banner above the logo. I'm sorry. I know the lesbian theme isn't even going to show up till issue three, but my hands are tied. On the *plus* side, I've decided to release two versions of the first issue: one for the regular newsstands, and one a limited-edition collector's item, just for the specialty shops, with gold metallic ink on the cover. It should *double* sales, just from the copies the speculators buy. Feel better?"

The monster stepped from the shadows; it stood nearly eleven feet high. It stank of dried blood, the blood of those it had judged unfit to live. Its skin was flecked with the pulp of books it had shredded with its talons, books by explorers and thinkers and tale-spinners alike. Its face was scorched by the flames it breathed from its cavernous maw, flames that had destroyed countless works of art and architecture. "Alien interloper," it hissed, "know me as Yves of Destruction! I rule this land—and I say you may not have it! And yet I will allow you a small portion of it to call your own: a burial plot. This I will allow." He laughed, and it sounded like the collision of planets.

And Princess Paragon, who had at first reeled in the face of the searing hatred she had felt radiating from Yves of Destruction—hatred like a blast furnace, hatred like a sun—now stood her ground and said, "I do not want this land, beast; I seek no possession of it nor in it, and no power from it nor over it. But I will be free to speak to those who live here, and they will be free to hear me. Do not cross me in that, or forswear me in any way, and I will suffer you to remain ignorant of what power an Irian is possessed!"

But Yves of Destruction, undaunted, stepped forward, his eyes filled with ire and his mien malevolent; he raised high his sinewy arms, and . . . (CONTINUED IN ISSUE #2!)

"Don't touch them," Perpetrial Cotton cautioned him as she spread the oversized Bristol-board pages across the conference-room table. "I brought them in as soon as Jimmy finished inking them, so they're still wet, some of them. But here it is, anyway: the whole first issue, right before our eyes!" She set down the twenty-eighth, and final, page, and turned. "It's beautiful. It makes me want to cry. It's everything I'd hoped it would be. Oh, Brian! Thank you so much for letting me work with you on this. It's just wonderful. I'm so proud of us—of you. You've come so far. I think we've learned a lot from each other, and it's all right here. Goddess! I can't *wait* till we show slides of this issue at the convention. People are just going to *die*."

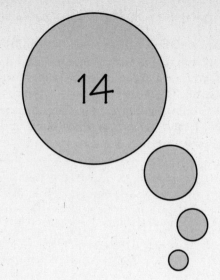

14

"Hello, Jerome. Goodbye, Jerome."

It was two minutes past seven, and as usual Mr. Pinkerton, briefcase in hand and overcoat slung over his arm, was striding toward the front door of the Carter Foods plant with all the determination of a comet entering Earth's atmosphere. He acted as though nothing alive could bar his way.

But then, almost nothing alive possessed the awe-inspiring bulk of Jerome T. Kornacker. In violation of three years' habit, he now stepped into Mr. Pinkerton's path, and Mr. Pinkerton was so astonished by this bizarre new wrinkle in his smoothly run little cosmos that his jaw actually dropped. His momentum, however, was too strong a thing to drop in turn, and a moment later he plowed face-first into Jerome's broad, cushiony chest.

"Oh! Oh! My most earnest apologies, Mr. Pinkerton," cried Jerome, stepping away from his dazed employer.

Mr. Pinkerton, a man not accustomed to changes in his routine or readily accepting of those that occasionally dared occur, shook his head and brushed his shirt front frantically, as if plutonium dust might have spilled on it. "Have you lost your *mind*?" he barked. "You might have *killed* me!"

"Once again, I apologize, deeply and sincerely," Jerome gushed, wringing his hands. "My intention was merely to delay you for long enough to put a question to you."

This was, all in all, a more substantial conversation than the two men had shared in the three years of Jerome's employment, and Mr. Pinkerton was clearly alarmed by its length. He shifted from one foot to the other and kept eyeing the door as if he were Jason and it the Golden Fleece. "Well? Well?" he snapped. "Now that you've nearly dislocated my spine over this question of yours, hadn't you better at least get down to brass tacks and *ask* it?"

Jerome, intimidated by his employer's brusque manner, began to stutter. "Mr. P-P-Pinkerton, what I want, what I want, what I *wanted* t-t-to—"

"I have no fondness for rap music, Jerome," Mr. Pinkerton chided him. Then, seeming rather pleased with his little joke, he visibly relaxed; this allowed Jerome to relax as well.

"What I wanted to ask," Jerome began again, measuring his words, "was whether it would be p-permissible for me to take a few days' vacation."

"Vacation?" Mr. Pinkerton exclaimed. "What? You mean, not come in to work?"

"Y-yes."

"Leave your post unattended for days on end?" He shook his head, as if he had never heard of such unabashed bolshevism. "I had really thought better of you, Jerome."

Jerome withered before this lofty derision and took a step back; he had no confrontational skills whatsoever. Yet he must persist. His voice grew wavery and thin. "B-but when I was g-given this job, I was promised a w-week's vacation each year."

"By God! Were you really?" Mr. Pinkerton put down his briefcase and folded his arms, adopting an I'd-better-get-to-the-bottom-of-this air.

"And I *have* been here for three years without t-taking any of it," Jerome continued, his forehead growing dewy. "And all I'm asking for n-now is just a f-f-f"—he balled his fists and made a little threatening gesture at himself—"*few* days, not even a f-full week."

Mr. Pinkerton lowered his head and glared at him. "I'm surprised at the picture you paint of yourself," he said sternly, "considering that you only recently missed a full night of work and never even called in to explain. I, Jerome, *I* had to investigate your absence *myself*, by calling your home."

"Y-yes, I-I-I-I—"

"Your mother explained to me that a family bereavement had prevented you from pursuing your duties here. And I understood completely. But, Jerome, after almost three years with an unbroken attendance record, to suddenly miss a night without any attempt to notify us, and then not more than a month later to come shoving me around the lobby like a common thug, demanding a vacation—well, it raises some concerns."

"I-I-I-I—"

"Of course, you are, as you so forcefully put it, *entitled* to a few days off." He rolled his shoulders in indignation, then looked away from Jerome, as if the sight of him were suddenly offensive. "I do, however, hope that this is not the beginning of some irresponsible new trend." He picked up his briefcase. "I should perhaps inform you that the controller of this company is questioning whether we require the services of a night watchman *at all*."

Jerome was aghast. He gulped and said, "Wh-wh-what do you m-m-m—"

"Recent technological improvements in the security industry have very nearly rendered you an anachronism, Jerome. The only thing safeguarding your job right now is your salary, which, even with the increasingly attractive prices being offered by competing security vendors, is still far less of an expenditure than the installation of electronic surveillance and alarm equipment. I do suggest, however," he concluded in a righteous wrath, "that you not allow this new cocksure attitude of yours to inspire you to anything so foolhardy as requesting a raise. That would be very unwise, indeed." He nodded good night and strode out the door with his nose in the air, like Louis XIV after a more than routinely trying day.

Jerome wiped his forehead with his sleeve and leaned back against the lobby wall. That had been much more difficult than he'd imagined. But now it was done. He had permission to take a few days off. He made a mental note to leave a memo on the desk of the personnel manager, letting her know which nights he'd be away.

And then he started to shake—not because of the encounter with Mr. Pinkerton, although that had certainly rattled him, but because he had no clear idea what he was doing, or why. He knew he must go to the comic-book convention at the O'Hare Grifton Hotel and confront Brian Parrish and the others; he knew he must somehow make them realize what they were doing to his heroes, and, by extension, to him. And yet the exact manner in which he would accomplish this was far from determined. He was placing his trust in fate, hoping that some plan of action would reveal itself to him when he finally reached that crucial juncture.

But what if the worst happens? he wondered. And by that he meant, What if I fail? What if I am ridiculed? He had made a personal promise to his heroes—and a vow to Princess Paragon was not something to be treated lightly. She herself *embodied* truth.

He shuddered and put it out of his mind. Then he took the key ring from his belt and started on his rounds. He made the circuit of offices, turning out fluorescent lights that had been left burning by the now-departed cleaning lady. He walked through the foul-smelling processing plant, hearing only his lonely footsteps among the vats and pressure cookers that loomed over him—although he imagined they must make a very great deal of noise during the day, when they were cooking up vast quantities of cheese food and cookie mix and the other delicacies that were on display in the lobby in the form of ancient yellowed waxworks.

And then he sat at the receptionist's desk and watched TV for the rest of his shift.

Every night of his three years' employment here had been spent in almost exactly this manner. There had never been anything even remotely resembling a disturbance (although he had originally been hired in the wake of a series of vandalizations by students from nearby dormitories). In spite of this, the Carter Foods management had armed him with a billy club. The only time he had ever used it was one night when, out of boredom, he had experimented at twirling it like a baton, and it had promptly hit him square in the eye, resulting in a spectacular shiner that lingered for weeks. After that, he was content to let the club simply dangle from his belt, like a vestigial tail.

The management had also given him a key to a cabinet in the president's office where a pistol was stored, in case of an emergency. After his first day on the job, when he had been given rudimentary lessons in its firing (and during which his instructor had pronounced him "worse than hopeless"), he had sworn never to handle that pistol again.

Still, this was the perfect job for him, if for no other reason than the solitude. He never actually saw anyone except Mr. Pinkerton going out and old Mr. Ward coming in at four in the morning to prep the machinery for starting time. For the remaining nine, glorious hours, he could pretend that he was the sole survivor of a decimated planet, roaming his little world excavating clues about the lives he had outlasted. And if anyone ever noticed that his or her desk drawers had been rummaged through, no one had yet complained to management about it, for management had certainly never confronted Jerome—who had, as a result, grown rather bold in his foraging.

One night, he found a pornographic magazine in someone's desk, and in an itchy fever of lust he scoured the plant for a suitable place to masturbate over it. He found one at the end of a long corridor that was cluttered with boxes of old personnel records and invoices. Some of the dates on those invoices stretched back to the seventies. Jerome was relatively certain that this corridor had fallen into disuse. The door at the end of the hall was locked, but he, of course, had every key in the place; and when he opened the door, he found a vacated office behind it, caked with dust, windowless, but with a still-functioning overhead light. A perfect, secluded place in which to commit the sin of Onan.

Spilling his seed on the tiled floor of that abandoned office had become part of his regular rounds, especially since the owner of the pornographic magazine was obliging enough to purchase copies of subsequent issues every month and to file them away in the same desk drawer.

Tonight, however, Jerome wasn't up to masturbating. He felt nervous and afraid, as though embarking on some kind of mission of espionage that might ultimately cost him his life. Once again, he couldn't look to his heroes for inspiration, for that was not why he worshiped them. They might jet off to enemy planets at the drop of a hat, but even Jerome, facing the murky prospect of somehow forcing other, unknown, unpredictable human beings to bow to his will and accept his judgment— even Jerome recognized that comic-book heroes could not steer him in that, or guide him, or direct him, or perform any of the other most basic tasks of the heroes of genuine literature.

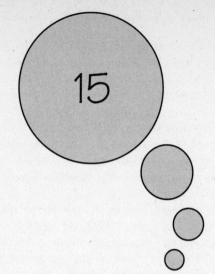

15

All at once, Brian found himself staring into the face of Death.

"That's it," he said, throwing his hands in the air. "Forget it. Forget the whole thing."

Perpetrial, in the window seat to his left, wore a look of guilty embarrassment. "Oh, come on, Brian," she said. "It doesn't mean *you're* going to die, just that death figures into the present condition of your life. Maybe not *even* death. It could be just a transformation or an alteration of some sort. Like taking over *Princess Paragon*. Don't overreact."

"I'm not overreacting," he said, furiously trying to unfasten his seat belt. "I just don't need this voodoo crap scaring the shit out of me when I'm waiting to shoot up into the clouds in a couple tons of sheet metal and gasoline."

"The tarot is not voodoo crap," she protested. She held down the seat tray in front of her, trying to keep the cards from skidding to the floor as Brian lurched to his feet.

"I'm sorry, sir," said a male flight attendant who seemed to appear out of nowhere. "I have to ask you to resume your seat."

"But I have to take a p—"

"We're taxiing for takeoff," the attendant interrupted him in clipped, don't-give-me-any-bullshit syllables. "Seat trays up, too, please," he added to Perpetrial.

Brian wasn't up to a showdown right now. "But we've been sitting on the runway for an *hour,*" he whined.

"Sir, I really must *insist* that you take your seat." The plane lurched forward a little, and he smiled in vindication.

Brian wanted to belt him.

He sat back down, and Perpetrial said, "Brian, I'm sorry if I upset you, but there's no re—"

"No, no," he said, waving his hand. "It's okay. It just got on my nerves, that's all. Sitting here for an hour, trapped in a cramped airplane." He rebuckled his seat belt.

She patted his hand and smiled. "Well, we're moving now."

"I know, but it's too late. I'm already in a bad mood. I've finished off my last stick of gum, and I'm irritable as hell." He sighed. "Know what I need? A drink." He reached up to press the call button, then thought better of it. What if the same flight attendant came back? He decided to take his grumpiness out on Perpetrial. "Plus," he said to her, "when you brought out a deck of cards, I got all excited. I thought we were going to pass the time playing gin rummy."

"You can't play gin rummy with a tarot deck," she said amusedly.

"Well, I didn't *know* it was a tarot deck," he said, mocking her tone. "You may find this hard to believe, Perpetrial, but I know very few women who carry tarot decks in their purses. What's in your backpack—a Ouija board?"

She sat meekly for a moment, then displayed the stack of cards on her still-lowered tray and said, "Sure you don't want to continue?"

He barked a laugh. "What, after the first card I turn over is *Death*? Yes, I'm *quite* sure I don't want to continue."

"Brian, you—" She caught his eye, and the look he gave her

made her swallow the rest of her sentence. She turned away from him and started packing up the cards.

Brian watched her, wondering if he should apologize. He'd actually grown fond of her over the past few weeks. While she was undeniably assertive, she wasn't aggressive in that militant manner he found so off-putting in many of the more activist lesbians he knew. Perpetrial had not the slightest interest in coercion, which, she would tell you proudly, was a "male invention." As for the habitual browbeating to which she subjected all her peers, Brian now came to recognize that as simple bad manners—the result of an excessive enthusiasm for discourse trampling any hint of personal politeness. It was therefore forgivable. And besides, she had endearing qualities, such as her fondness for bad seventies trends like tarot cards, and her habit of wearing hopelessly out-of-date T-shirts, like the one she had on today: "E.R.A. Now!" He'd once teased her that she could donate her collection of T-shirts to the Smithsonian, and she'd smiled at him perplexedly, having no idea what he meant.

As the plane rolled majestically down the runway, the entire cabin seemed to heave an audible sigh of relief. The tension was broken, the long wait over. The pushy flight attendant who had accosted Brian was now reciting instructions over the speaker system, but not one person in ten paid him any attention; everyone was going back to books, or crossword puzzles, or sleep, now that they were no longer called upon to be busy being vexed.

The plane was soon heading down the runway at a dizzying speed, and then, in one miraculous moment, the hum of the wheels on the pavement ceased, and Brian knew that he was airborne. A few seconds later the plane began a forty-degree climb. Brian felt like a spit-wad being shot out of a straw; his stomach dropped into his groin, and his testicles shrank. He wasn't frightened, however; he was, if anything, rather enjoying the sensation. This was one of those thrills he never grew tired of.

He lifted his head and craned his neck to see past Perpetrial, who was staring out the window now, oblivious to him. The sun was shining from the opposite side of the plane, so Brian was able to delight in the sight of the shadow of the plane itself, moving hugely across the bite-sized yards and roofs beneath him. Perpetrial must have gotten the same charge out of it, because she turned her head, caught his eye, and smiled.

Embarrassed at the ease with which she forgave him his rudeness, he sat back in his seat and said, a little unnaturally, "Well, I guess we should get down to work."

"Oh, Brian, just a *minute* more," she pleaded, but almost as soon as she said this the plane climbed into an enormous gob of raggedy, skim-milk-colored cloud. She sighed, sat back, and said, "Okay. What do you want to talk about?" She slipped her unstockinged feet out of her Birkenstock sandals and crossed her ankles.

He settled into his seat in anticipation. "Well, first, there's 'Bella,' " he said, a twinkle of excitement in his eyes. Only a week earlier, Heloise had called him, breathless, to tell him that the company's notorious do-nothing PR firm had at long last come through. To correspond with the Chicago convention, they'd gotten Brian, Nigel, and Hector a guest booking on the Chicago-based "Bella" show. This was without a doubt the most popular daytime talk show in America, and its host, Arabella Martinez, was one of the nation's most visible celebrities—at least among a certain, rather housewifey demographic. Every time she gained a pound or lost a boyfriend, the tabloid newspapers enlarged the story into an event on a par with the stock-market crash or the summit at Yalta. "Bella" wasn't exactly Ted Koppel, but it was a fine first stab at TV for Brian.

Perpetrial, however, appeared indifferent to its possibilities. She shrugged her shoulders and said, "I can't help you there, Brian. I mean, *you're* going to be the guest, not me. And I've never even seen this Bella woman, so I can't help you anticipate what she might say. From what I've heard, though, she's a puffball."

Well, that was true. Brian knew that Bella Martinez was not the kind of interviewer to go on the attack; she knew that her success rested on a stream of happy hype, and that's what she delivered. She was also a big supporter of gay and lesbian politics, so he was confident he had nothing to fear from her.

All the same, he was surprised by Perpetrial's nonchalance. She had practically begged Heloise to let her accompany him on this convention junket; and when Heloise's secretary had booked them adjoining seats on the same flight, Brian had thought, Oh no, two-and-a-half hours of Perpetrial's incessant prattle, with no hope of escape.

But now that the moment had come—now that he was held captive in a place where he couldn't run from her railings—she was close to listless. What was the matter?

He pulled his briefcase from under the seat in front of him. "Well, then," he said, "let's talk about Cosmique." This was an issue of tremendous concern for Perpetrial; he was drafting the third issue now, the one in which Princess Paragon and Cosmique meet for the first time and realize that they are fated to become lovers. The week before, Perpetrial had nearly hyperventilated while giving him advice on how to handle that meeting. "Women are different from men," she'd said. "Men are *visually* stimulated—it comes from having genitals outside the body. You can focus all your sexual energy into that one area; you can be directed—*literally* directed—in a way that women can't be, and your sense of sight has developed in complicity with that. You should know, Brian; you see something that arouses you, and your penis actually *points* to it. Well, *doesn't* it? Whereas a woman's genitals are *hidden*, and what's more, because of the menstrual cycle, a woman's sexuality is not focused in her genitals, either, but dispersed throughout her bloodstream, throughout her body. As a result, women are far less likely to experience instantaneous desire or localized sexual response. There's much more going on—much more involved than just a genital reaction. Instead of instant lust, what Princess Paragon and Cosmique would feel for each other would at first be an almost *emotional* arousal—a sense that here was something, some*one*, different, someone fully realized and capable of great love. The sexual feelings would follow. You have to handle their first meeting carefully, Brian. Strike one wrong note, and dykes everywhere are going to know you're a faker. And another thing: Is there any reason Cosmique can't be a woman of color?"

To that, Brian had said, Certainly not, and suggested green. But the mockery hadn't deterred Perpetrial at all. Subsequent days found her riddling him with so much advice that his head spun like a Hula Hoop around the waist of a particularly hyperactive teenager.

But now, on the plane, she reacted with indifference to the mention of Cosmique. "We just *talked* about her," she said, scratching her neck and wincing. "What's changed since then that calls for discussion?"

"Well, for one thing, I took your advice," he said, opening the briefcase and taking out some sketches. "I redesigned the character so that she's not such a Heather Locklear type, since you say no dyke looks like that. You mentioned a young Vanessa Redgrave, so I rented this movie of hers, *Morgan*, that came out in the mid-sixties, and I did some new sketches based on that. This is what I came up with." He held up the sketch pad for her perusal; it bore a drawing of a woman who had Redgrave's aristocratic cheekbones and unearthly, unfathomable eyes. "The costume's not as skintight as it was before; it's got more of a thirtiesish-aviatrix look to it now, which I'm not sure is quite right either, since Cosmique is supposed to be from another planet. But I'll keep working on it. And as for her superpowers, you suggested that they be nonphysical; well, I was thinking about telekinesis. It's been done before, I know, but this time we'll do it right—not stretch credulity too much, like *Buster Brainpower* does." Perpetrial raised an eyebrow at him, and he said, "I know, I know, I used to write *Buster Brainpower*. Well, that was a long time ago."

Perpetrial sighed and took the pad from him. "It looks good," she said, assessing the sketch. "I always did think Vanessa Redgrave was an archetypal beauty. Sweet of you to take my suggestion, Brian." She handed the pad back to him.

He sat for a moment, stunned. That was it? No criticisms, no assertions, no lectures, no theses? Not even a single parenthetical aside?

"Perpetrial," he said, folding the cover back over the pad and slipping it beneath the seat, "what on *earth* is the matter with you? Is it something I said? I'm sorry I made fun of the tarot. No, wait, I take that back; I'm *not* sorry I made fun of the tarot. But did I say something else to hurt you? Something typically patriarchal and hierarchical and oligarchical and deserving of castration followed by massive injections of estrogen?" She actually smiled at that. "Because if I did, I'm sorry. Although you've never hesitated to tell me when I'd done anything like that before."

She rested her head against the window and sighed again. "Oh, Brian," she said, sounding smaller and more girlish than he'd ever known her. "I'm a little scared, that's all. The main reason I was so determined to come with you to Chicago was to— well, to see someone."

He raised an eyebrow and grinned. "*Oho*. I *see*. Someone special?"

She grimaced. "My ex-wife, as a matter of fact."

He felt a little jolt of surprise. Perpetrial had never before mentioned her personal life to him. In fact, he'd gotten used to thinking of her as being a lesbian in the same way that so many women he knew were Christian: full of passionate rhetoric and fierce belief, but with no actual empirical experience of the heart of the matter to draw on. "Listen," he said, suddenly uneasy, "you don't have to talk about this if you don't w—"

"Oh, Brian, stop being silly and shut up," she said. Apparently she wanted to tell him. "Her name's Regina DePadro," she continued in a whispery voice. "She lives in Columbia, Missouri—where I used to live. Actually, we lived there together." She rubbed the bridge of her nose between her thumb and forefinger. "We had two great years, and then—" She faltered.

"What? What?" he urged her.

"One fight too many. Two days later the rift was still there between us, so I left her. I heard about this job on *Princess Paragon*, so I called Heloise and talked her into hiring me. Two hours later I'd packed all my things, including the cats, into the car, and headed east. I didn't even wait to tell Regina I was going. I just left a note saying goodbye." Tears filled her eyes. "What a coward."

Brian pursed his lips. "Mighty male of you," he said, trying for a bit of levity; but when she turned to him, she wore an expression of acute pain.

"Yes," she said. "Wasn't it." She sighed and lowered her head. "She loves those cats." Then she straightened up and looked severely at the seat back. "Well, now it's time to face the music. She's driven up to Chicago from Columbia, and she's meeting me at the airport. I haven't seen her since the morning of the day I left. Actually, I didn't even see her then. I was pretending to be asleep so I wouldn't have to talk to her."

"My God, Perpetrial, what *happened*? Why'd you—"

"Care for anything to drink?" It was the snotty flight attendant again, behind a big pushcart filled with cartons and cans. Brian turned his head and refused to acknowledge his existence.

Perpetrial looked up and said, "I called ahead about the low-sodium vegetarian menu."

"Oh, right," the attendant replied, waving a finger at her. "You're the one who gets the carrot juice!" He produced a glass of an alarmingly bright orange liquid and handed it to her. "Enjoy!" he said, and he moved on.

Perpetrial took a sip; it left a foamy orange mustache above her ample upper lip. "Mmm," she said. "Just what I needed."

Brian was not to be put off any longer. The romantic in him was in desperate need of an answer. "Perpetrial," he nearly cried, "for *God's* sake, what *happened* between you and Regina? Why'd you *leave* her?"

She rested the glass on her tray, then turned and faced the window, as if too ashamed actually to face him. "It's complicated," she said. "She was wonderful, caring, giving, nurturing. But she was so—so—"

"So *what*?" Brian prompted her.

"—*reactionary!*" she blurted. "*Patriarchal! Essentialist!*"

Brian sat back and looked at her, horrified. "You mean, you actually broke up with someone becau—"

"Yes, that's right," she snapped, turning to meet his eyes, her face streaked with tears and her lower lip quivering. "Go ahead and say it. I ran out on the love of my life, the most wonderful woman in the world, because I couldn't stand that she *wasn't p.c.*"

Brian called back the snotty flight attendant and ordered himself a stiff Manhattan.

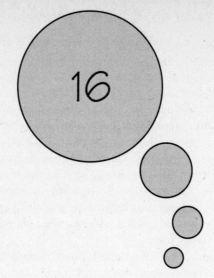

16

Jerome packed four pairs of underwear, each as dingy and gray as the next, into the suitcase his Aunt Cherry had just given him for his birthday. Like Providence, that had been—coming to him at his exact hour of need.

Outside his bedroom door, his mother nagged him. "Jerome, I need for you to tell me, was it something that I said?"

"Mother, go *away*. I'm *packing*." He pulled an armful of flimsy gray socks from his sock drawer and started sorting through them, looking for the pairs with the fewest holes in them.

"We have always traditionally taken our vacations *together*, Jerome," Mrs. Kornacker wailed. Jerome heard her rattle the doorknob; it was a good thing he had locked it. "Jerome, please let me in. We need to discuss this flesh-to-flesh."

"I'm twenty-six years *old*, Mother," he said, stuffing the socks into the suitcase and heading for his closet. "I'm mature enough to go off on my own for a few days. I *will* be back, you know." At least, he added to himself, I *hope* I will.

"But we *always* have taken our vacations *together*," she repeated, more shrilly.

He sorted through his row of drab, ketchup-stained shirts. "We took a vacation together five years ago, Mother," he said. "You dragged me to Chicago, where in three days you managed to lose more than four hundred dollars at the racetrack while I ate chocolate-fudge sundaes for breakfast, lunch, and dinner, until even *I* got sick of them. Or, more accurately, until I was accosted by a deranged prostitute who scratched me on the neck and stole my wallet, and I made you take me home." He took two of the less soiled shirts from their hangers. "That was our first vacation together after Father died. It was also our last vacation together after Father died." He stooped and picked up a shirt that was lying on the floor of the closest. He smelled it, found it rancid, and dropped it back again.

"I've been meaning to plan another one," Mrs. Kornacker bleated from beyond the door. "A nice trip away from here, just the two of us, like in the former years of our family." She was starting to sob.

Jerome rolled up the shirts and stuffed them into his suitcase. "Don't be silly, Mother. I'm not a child anymore."

"So what? Just because of your age, do we have to come to a parting of the waves?" The sound of her blowing her nose shook the door in its frame. "Oh, Jerome! I beseek you, don't leave me like your sister did! I would die from the tragedy of it!"

"Sandra moved to Akron to start a family, Mother. I'm only going to Chicago for a few days. It's *hardly* the same thing." In spite of himself, he felt a lump in his throat. This imbecile woman was actually moving him, and he found the experience both surprising and distasteful.

"*Chicago!*" she cried. "But that's a dangerous city, full of thieves and gangsters and unloosed women. You are only a babe from the woods, Jerome. They'll eat you *alive.*"

He shook his head as he stuffed an extra pair of jeans into his suitcase. "I won't be in the city *proper*, Mother. I'll be miles away, at a hotel near the airport where felons surely find it un-profitable to tread. You needn't worry." He tried to shut the suit-case, but his underwear and socks were sticking out the sides. Not having the patience to repack, he pushed harder on the top half of the suitcase, until he could clamp it to the bottom.

"But how are you getting there, Jerome? There's no bus from here that I—"

"*Driving*, Mother. I am *driving* there."

"Oh, no, you don't! I'm not lending you my car so you can j—"

"I've *rented* a car." He lifted the suitcase from the bed and moved it to the floor. More precisely, he *dropped* it to the floor; it was far heavier than it looked.

"So," Mrs. Kornacker said with a sigh, "there isn't a thing I could say that would make you not go off and leave me?"

"No, there isn't," he said, wiping the sweat from his brow.

"I haven't been feeling at all well, Jerome. In fact, I think I may need to go to a hosp—"

"Not a *thing*," he interrupted her more emphatically. He sat on the bed and awaited her reply. Above him, the poster of Prin-cess Paragon seemed to be exhorting him: *Courage! Courage!*

"Well, fine then," she said at last, her voice small and grav-elly. "I guess I have to submit defeat. You go on off to Chicago and enjoy yourself. But do me a favor and be careful. You just cross your p's and q's, do you hear me? Lock your door at night. Don't get smart with any strangers who might have guns on them. And phone your mother so she doesn't develop the prob-lem of not knowing my son isn't bleeding to death in a gutter somewhere."

"I will," he said. "I promise."

He heard her sigh; then the heavy falling of her feet. He waited a few moments, then dragged his suitcase to the bedroom door and opened it.

She wasn't there.

A minute later he heard the familiar cough of her station wagon's exhaust pipe in the driveway, and he shuffled over to the window just in time to see her drive off.

"How *ridiculously* melodramatic," he said aloud. "Serve her right if she never *did* see me again."

He dragged his suitcase downstairs, its shiny new aluminum frame ripping a hunk of carpeting off each step as he descended.

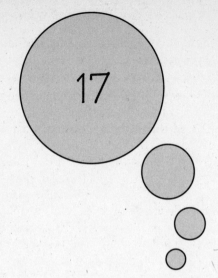

17

The lobby of the Grifton Hotel was an expanse of burnished copper and creamy pastels, and every inch of it was spotless. It was an oasis of waterfalls by open staircases and carefully cultivated beds of flora that showered guests with cool oxygen when they passed. It was soothing but somehow antiseptic.

It was also one of dozens of nearly identical hotels that had sprung up near O'Hare Airport in the early eighties to compete for the booming convention business. Brian decided the competition must have gotten very tough indeed, for why else would the hotel ignore the lessons of the past and consent yet again—for the fifth consecutive year!—to host the Midwest ComiCon, allowing its hermetically sealed, climate-controlled corridors to be overrun by the kind of wild-eyed fanatics that management couldn't help regarding as horrid little viruses contaminating their pristine, hygienic realm? (Brian had seen the pinched faces of the desk clerks and staff.) It was almost funny, the depths to which money could drive people.

Brian had checked into the hotel and was in an elevator now, riding up to his room (which, he was delighted to note, was on the opposite side of the hotel from the one assigned to Perpetrial). He shared the elevator with three shaggy men and one bedraggled woman, all of whom seemed to have been left out in the rain too long, although he knew from reading the paper on the plane that Chicago hadn't had rain in more than a week.

They could only be comics fans. They had that aura about them—the aura of complete obliviousness to anything that wasn't found in full color on newsprint. Brian suspected that they'd come completely unglued if they discovered they were sharing an elevator with The Great Brian Parrish, but he was wearing sunglasses and a baseball cap to avoid being recognized. And anyway, they all had their noses buried in fanzines—cheaply produced, amateur collations of comic-book news, trivia, speculation, rumor, and other such effluvia. Not that Brian considered what he himself did to be literary in the least; but he had the disarming excuse of not taking it at all seriously. He considered himself a kind of pop-culture troubadour, and this convention was just part of his show.

There was a frightening moment when the lights dimmed and the elevator lurched to a halt, and all the fans lifted their shiny noses from their fanzines and began looking at each other with some consternation. But not quite half a minute later the lights came back on and the elevator jolted into motion again. Brian sighed in relief. It would've been a nightmare—to be trapped on a stalled elevator with a gaggle of his hysterical admirers.

When the elevator doors opened he stepped out, leaving the mildewed quartet behind with a sigh of relief. He was glad to get away from them—and yet he'd also been glad of the chance to observe them so closely without their knowledge. After all, he owed his career to such as they, and he was curious about them. He felt a reluctant sort of gratitude toward these fans. Did he *have* to owe so much to people he thought so little of?

What would happen, he wondered, if he stopped catering to them—stopped delivering exactly what he knew they wanted? What if he tried something more adventurous, less married to the clichés and limitations of his peculiar genre? Would they join him for the trip or abandon him as a traitor? And if they abandoned him, would anyone else ever want him?

He often considered this. For, in truth, Brian was growing rather tired of writing and drawing superheroes for the kind of people who obsessed about them almost to the point of sociopathy. But such persons were the ones who enabled him to live like a king in one of the most desirable gay neighborhoods in Manhattan, and that was nothing to sneeze at. (Certainly Nico didn't bring in enough to support them—not with his dime-a-dozen job as a legal secretary.)

And anyway, with *Princess Paragon*, Brian was finding himself more established than ever in the superhero fiction factory, and isn't that what he *really* wanted? Fame, money, power—it was all to be had here. His fans might be an alarming lot, but they seemed to have plenty of discretionary income.

All the same, he was feeling uneasy at being here, and couldn't put his finger on why. And then—as if it weren't bothersome enough to be plagued by his ambiguous ethics and insecurities—no sooner had he put his credit-card-shaped key in the door than he heard his name being called from down the hallway.

He turned and saw Jody Lippmann advancing on him. Jody, a lanky, good-natured sort, was the associate editor of *The Comics Observer*, and one of the few members of that magazine's staff who treated Brian with open friendliness. (Most of the others regarded his work, and, by extension, himself, with thinly veiled contempt; they had consented to running his recent interview only because they knew it would mean big sales for that issue, which also featured a highly touted "Graphic Story Manifesto" by the magazine's iconoclastic editor, Piers Atwood.)

Brian wouldn't have minded chatting for a moment with Jody, but there was someone else with him whose face seemed familiar, and it was only when Jody was standing before him that the identity of his short, emaciated, stubble-chinned, angry-eyed companion came back to him: this was Hiram Krapp, the creator of *For Spacious Skies*, an acerbic, cynical, leftist underground comic that specialized in surrealist takes on American mores and manners. The most recent issue had featured a story, based on an actual argument Krapp had had with his wife, in which the two of them spent an entire month in their expensive new platform bed, so in love with its opulence that they were unwilling to rise out of it for even a moment. The story was praised as a comment on the country's obsession with luxury, which the cartoon versions of Krapp and his wife pronounced "*lug*-zhury"; at its height, the Krapps were shown perching on the edge of the bed, their bare asses hanging off their satin sheets, passing shit and piss into rapidly filling bedpans. *The Comics Observer* had published rave reviews of the book, but Krapp, a combative sort, had written to the magazine saying, in effect, Thanks for the praise, but you morons didn't understand a thing I was trying to say.

Krapp hung back now, his lips curled into a snarl, as Jody patted Brian on the back and said, "Hey, buddy. Here to do the old push-push, huh?"

Brian kept his hand on the door handle. "Oh, yeah," he said with a nervous smile. "Same story every year. You guys have a booth up?"

"As always. Never do much business here, but we make some good connections—pick up a new columnist or two, if we find anyone subversive enough." He laughed. "Hey," he said suddenly, jerking his thumb at his companion, "you know Hiram Krapp? Hiram, Brian Parrish."

Brian managed a nod, released the door handle, and extended his hand.

Hiram Krapp glared at him, then turned his head and left Brian's hand hanging in midair.

Brian was too astonished to take back his hand; he stood stock-still, arm outstretched, as Hiram Krapp stared in the opposite direction and dragged his left foot back and forth across the carpeting.

Jody Lippmann seemed embarrassed by the snub. In a pathetic attempt at saving face, he grabbed Brian's rejected hand and shook it again, as though it had been meant for him all along. "Uh, anyway," he mumbled, "Hiram's doing a new column for us, a kind of ongoing history of European Jewish cartoonists who worked before the Holocaust. Stop by the booth; I'll show you some drafts. Anyway, gotta run." He dropped Brian's hand, then clutched Hiram by the shoulder and led him down the hall.

Brian was sizzling with embarrassment and fury. He'd known that Hiram Krapp had no use for commercial comics in general and superheroes in particular, but to cut someone dead based on a purely aesthetic difference—it was unforgivable.

Sour grapes is what it amounted to, Brian decided, as he turned the door handle and entered his room. After all, his first *Princess Paragon* would sell about ninety times as many copies as even the best-selling *For Spacious Skies*.

He threw his suitcase on the bed, then sat down next to it and scowled for almost twelve full minutes.

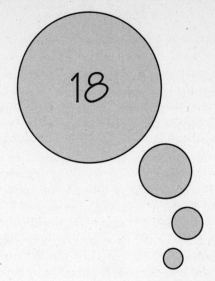

18

Everywhere he looked, Jerome thought he glimpsed Stickman, or Shortman, or Dirtyman, or one of the other comic-book aficionados of his acquaintance; but on closer scrutiny, each turned out to be blonder, or taller, or plumper, or in some other way distinct from his usual comic-shop cronies.

In one sense he wasn't hallucinating, though; nearly *every-where* at the convention there was a misfit of some recognizable type. Jerome had never seen such a number of them, stuffed into ill-fitting clothing, peering out at the world from beneath stringy or pubic-fuzzy hair.

The sight rendered him happy beyond measure.

At long last, he had found a crowd of people among whom he could hold his head high! After so many years of skulking about in the shadows, here was an opportunity to walk where he willed. For no one here would look on *him* with ridicule, any more than he would so look on them. This was his home port, his paradise found—nothing less than geek Valhalla.

As he walked through the enormous exhibition hall the convention staffers called the dealers' room, he saw himself reflected again and again in the form of large, perspiring persons who sifted determinedly through cardboard file boxes filled with musty-smelling antique comic books, searching, no doubt, for the elusive issues they needed to complete their already bloated collections. They could also be seen buying science-fiction movie posters, portfolios of fantasy artwork, old pulp novels, pirated videotapes of Japanese cartoons, and more. It was filled with treasures, this brightly lit, wonderful world, this dealers' room; and, most exciting of all, these outcasts who inhabited it, these gun-shy specimens, these refugees from the caprices of culture and class, were stopping everywhere and *talking to each other.* They had formed a society to replace the one they didn't fit. And as he passed, Jerome could hear that they indeed spoke his language:

". . . much better than the last time Singer was drawing *Señor Samson,* when he was being inked by Caldwell, who hadn't learned to hold a brush yet. . ."

". . . just found a complete run of *Acme-Man Annual* from 1968 to 1972, in mint condition, with the glossy centerfold poster in the 1970 issue intact, for only two hundred dollars . . ."

". . . managed to pick up the original artwork for the page in *Red Wraith* number forty where Dick Petzel drew Diana Rigg as the sultana of the planet Goom . . ."

". . . finally completed my collection of every appearance Moonwoman ever made, including her guest shot in *Freedom Front* number sixty-three, which Moonman himself didn't even appear in . . ."

The words bubbled together in the air, creating a euphoric, almost musical current that nearly lifted Jerome off his feet and wafted him down the aisles. And all at once he thought of the pleasant, tree-lined thoroughfares of his little college town, strolled by young, fresh-scented coeds and tall, handsome frat brothers who wore the kind of faded blue jeans with gaping holes in the knees that implied unconsciousness of the claims of both fashion and function; and he thought of the deli on the corner where these students all convened to eat huge pastrami sandwiches and drink frosted mugs of beer and play rock-and-roll songs that were hits before they'd even been born, and where they laughed with each other and touched each other wherever they wanted and never doubted for a moment that they were golden, that they were blessed, that they were the earth's inheritors.

And for the first time in his life, Jerome wasn't envious. For the first time in his life, he thought of those students and didn't want to trade places with them. For the first time in his life, he experienced the astonishing power of fantasy made reality—of a dream come true.

After a half-hour more of wandering about, enraptured—during which time he found a darkened auditorium where an old kinescope of a 1950s science-fiction TV show was being shown, and an art gallery hung with vibrant, almost fluorescent oil paintings of dramatically posed superheroes done by prominent cartoonists—he happened across another room, much smaller but more crowded, in which artists and writers sat behind folding tables, signing autographs and showing photocopies of their forthcoming work.

It was there that Jerome found Nigel Cardew holding court, and his heart suddenly hardened. All at once he remembered his mission; he remembered what he must do. And now he had the confidence to do it; for wouldn't all these others around him be thankful—wouldn't they all relish seeing the killer of Comet brought to his knees, begging forgiveness, promising restitution?

Trembling, he shoved his way to the front of the crowd that had assembled before Cardew's table.

A heavyset young woman, whose hair had been allowed to grow into the visage-concealing style that even Yoko Ono had long since abandoned, was berating Cardew, who sat with his legs crossed, smoking imperturbably, wearing dark sunglasses, a black T-shirt, black jeans, and black boots. It was exactly what he had worn in the photo accompanying his recent *Comics Update* interview. Jerome leaned forward to hear what the woman was saying to him.

"—clearly stated, in *Exciting Comics* number three nineteen, that he would never take a life," she declared, her voice shrill and insistent.

Nigel Cardew exhaled some smoke, then calmly replied, "Oi haven't enny reason to doubt it."

"And not only that," the woman continued—here she opened her hand and referred to a slip of crumpled paper that had grown soggy sitting in her palm (Jerome noticed that her fingernails were bitten to the quick, too)—"not only that, but Moonman *reiterated* that vow on sixteen succeeding occasions over the next twenty years—and that's just sixteen that I could find, there may be even more. He did so in *Moonman* one ninety-eight, *Moonman* two eleven, *Freedom Front* eighty-three, *Moonm*—"

"Oi'm certain your research is impeccable," Cardew said, interrupting her. He blew a thin stream of smoke in her direction.

She coughed and waved it away, then put the slip of paper in her pocket and said, "Well, if Moonman has repeatedly vowed never to take a life, how can you justify the fact that he's killed three people in your first six issues alone—that Doctor Sleaze villain with his *bare hands*?" She was breathing heavily.

Cardew tapped some ashes from his cigarette onto the floor next to him and said, "Must've lost 'is head, mustn't he?"

The woman was clearly stunned. She faltered for a moment, then said, "I'm not certain you realize what you've done. Moonman's respect for life has always been the backbone of his crusade against crime; now that that's gone—now that he's actually *executed* criminals without due process—what makes him any different from some bloodthirsty vigilante who takes justice into his own hands?"

Cardew's eyes peered out from above his sunglasses. "Hasn't he tyken justice into 'is own 'ands before? Hasn't he always been a *bit* of a vigilante? An' isn't a man allowed the privilege of changing 'is own bloody moind? After all, Doctor Sleaze went and snuffed 'is mite Comet. Oi expect Moonman wouldn't feel quoite spot-on about merely packing 'im off to a cell somewhere, with 'im laughing in 'is fice about 'ow Comet had screamed and begged for mercy. Under those circumstances, Oi imagine even bloody *Gandhi* moight've slammed the bloighter's head against the wall until he joined the 'eavenly choir."

The woman stared at him, speechless, her lower lip hanging stupidly.

Jerome cleared his throat.

"Answered your question, have Oi?" Cardew said. The woman nodded dully in reply.

Jerome cleared his throat again. "Excuse me," he said. "Excuse me, Nigel Cardew."

Cardew turned his way and exhaled another pencil-thin stream of cigarette smoke. He looked Jerome up and down, as if he were considering buying him. "Needn't gow to all the trouble of addressing me as 'Nigel Cardew,' mite," he said at last, a smirk on his face. " 'Your lordship' will be quoite ecceptable."

Some of the crowd laughed.

Jerome blushed, and his voice wavered. "I w-wonder if I m-might have an—an interview with you later? Someplace p-private, like—like a room?"

"Someplace *loike* a room, then! Oi see. Per'aps an elevator, then? Very *loike* a room, that is." More laughter, and Cardew tapped more ashes onto the floor. "You're a scribbler, then? With a magazine, are you?"

"Yes, I am," said Jerome, nodding. "I am with a magazine."

"An' which magazine, friend scribbler, would that be?"

Jerome's eyes went out of focus for a split second; then, in a panic, he said, *"Comics Update."*

"Oh, dear me," said Cardew, and he took another leisurely drag off his cigarette, "but haven't Oi just *given* your little rag a rather exhaustive chat ownly recently? Wouldn't want to do it again so soon, would Oi? Risk you Yanks gowing off me, like Oi was some old fart of an uncle who 'asn't learnt to stop tellin' 'is owld war stories to 'is family, when all they want to do is watch the bloody box."

More giggles from the assembled. Cardew lifted his sunglasses and lowered his head; his eyes seemed to pierce Jerome's layer of deceit. "Oi down't believe Oi caught your nime, friend scribbler."

Jerome took three convulsive gulps of air, then turned and fled in a blind panic. From behind him he could hear the ringing of derisive laughter, merry and violent.

Even here!

Even here!

His memories of cruelty returned, doubled and redoubled in intensity. Everywhere he looked now, he confronted strangeness and fear.

How had he missed it, the first time through the convention's halls? Next to his safe, sanitized little superhero periodicals, there sat racks of underground comics, with bare breasts and erect penises pointing at him from the covers.

There were comic books by and about Africans, Asians, and Hispanics.

Comic books about people stricken by disease and living in poverty.

Comic books about El Salvador and abortion and Ellis Island and drug addicts and Chernobyl and gang warfare and the Kennedy assassination and environmental decay.

Comic books about the real world; comic books untouched by fantasy; comic books sold by clear-eyed young men and women who came from that world, who did not have the look of the hidden, the hopeless, and the hunted.

He crept back to his hotel room, locked himself in the bathroom, and sat next to the toilet, where he mentally commanded the rest of the world, *Don't* come in here, *don't* come in here, *don't* come in here. . . .

And his descent into the maelstrom, which had been slow and halting, now accelerated into a plummet.

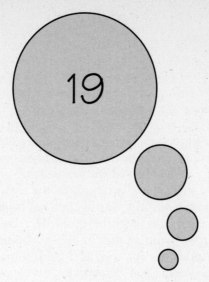

19

"Who the hell—?" Brian wondered aloud as he trotted over to his hotel-room door in response to an authoritative rapping. He opened the door and was surprised to find Regina DePadro standing in the hallway, a suede windbreaker tucked under one arm.

"I've come to give you a lift to the taping," she said, smiling confidently and sailing into his room as if it were her own.

He was still in his bathrobe and wasn't about to strip down and dress in front of her, lesbian or not. "Sweet of you, Regina," he said with gentle insistency, "but I can take a cab."

"Nonsense," she scoffed. She dropped the windbreaker onto the spare bed, then sat at the table by the window and started flipping through the news magazine he'd bought the night before at the hotel gift shop. "I've got a rental car just sitting in the parking lot doing nothing. And besides, I'm curious about you; Perpetrial's been talking about you nonstop, and even though I know she's only doing it so that she doesn't have to talk about *us*, it still makes me a little jealous." She stopped at a certain page, read a few lines, then ripped out the entire page, folded it, and stuck it in her shirt pocket. She looked up, not a trace of guilt on her face. "Better get ready," she said peremptorily, then resumed flipping through the magazine.

He grimaced, grabbed his blue jeans, black T-shirt, and blazer, and slipped into the bathroom. It was cold and cramped in there, and as he dressed he bumped his elbow against the shower door and hit his knee against the toilet. He cursed silently, then wondered why he had bothered being silent about it.

From beyond the door he could hear the sound of more magazine pages being ripped from their spine. He shook his head as he zipped his fly. "Two of a kind," he muttered to himself, meaning Regina and Perpetrial.

In point of fact, while Regina might be as pushy as Perpetrial, the resemblance ended there. Brian had gotten his first amazed look at her when he and Perpetrial had entered the airport after disembarking their plane. Regina had stepped forward, touched Perpetrial on the shoulder, and said a muted hello. Then the two women had hugged rather tentatively. Brian found the physical disparity between them almost startling; Regina looked like someone whose brownstone Perpetrial might picket. She was tall and blond, with aristocratic features and ice-blue eyes. If Perpetrial considered Vanessa Redgrave an archetypal beauty, it was no wonder she'd fallen in love with Regina.

Now fully dressed, he came out of the bathroom and slipped into his loafers. Regina rose from her chair and looked him over. "Very nice," she said. "Wish I knew why gay men are always so good-looking. So Gatsbyish, you know—*gamin*, even when they enter middle age. How old are you, Brian? Forty? Forty-one?"

He reddened. "Thirty-eight, actually."

"Don't look it." She stepped forward and swept a little curl of hair from his forehead; it was a curl he'd just spent a good three minutes moussing into place. This was going to be a *long* drive.

"So thin, too," she said, patting his tush rather suggestively.

If he hadn't known she was a lesbian, he might even have been alarmed. "Maybe you can convince Perpetrial to go on a diet. I can't talk to her about that anymore; she tells me I'm hypnotized by the patriarchy into thinking women are only of any value if they're skinny. She looks at her thighs and thinks, 'Feminist statement.' I look at them and think, 'Heart attack by age fifty.' "

Brian smiled uncomfortably and shrugged. "See what I can do."

She smiled back prettily, grabbed her purse, and strode toward the door. "Better get going."

He checked his pockets for his room key as he followed her. "Perpetrial joining us?"

"No," she answered definitively as she moved out into the hallway and headed for the elevator. "That's another reason I want to drive you this morning: if I don't get away from her for a couple hours, I am *really* going to lose my mind."

The elevator stalled again on the way down, this time for almost five minutes. Brian began to panic, but Regina seemed unfazed. "It's not a live show," she reminded him. "They can hold the taping till you get there." He felt foolish in the face of her almost preternatural calm.

She had rented a Pontiac Sunbird, which, when she got it out on the highway, she proceeded to push to limits it had clearly not been designed to meet. As Brian watched, increasingly alarmed, the speedometer inched closer and closer to eighty-five, while Regina serenely swerved into and out of lanes frequented by pokier, more law-abiding drivers, many of whom saluted her passing with a sustained sounding of their horns. Brian popped a stick of gum into his mouth and began chewing nervously. But Regina seemed oblivious to the chaos she was causing; she had taken up the subject of her ex-lover's many failings, which thoroughly occupied her concentration.

"I'm sorry," she said, shooting past an ancient Cadillac Fleetwood that jumped onto the shoulder to make room for her. "I've got no patience left for Perpetrial and all her hand-wringing feminist sob sisters. They're such moaners, Brian. I mean, what *happened* to the movement? Twenty years ago, there was an emphasis on liberation, on *empowerment*—it was just so intoxicating to go to women's meetings and have your head filled with so many *possibilities.*" At this point, a Dodge Dart had the temerity to move into her lane in front of her; she floored the Sunbird until it was riding the Dart's tail, and after only a few dozen yards, it wisely decided to return to the lane whence it had come. Brian ground his chewing gum between his molars as if it were corn meal.

"Now the only thing any feminist wants to talk about is *victimization,*" Regina continued, "what the horrible old patriarchy has done to us, what the horrible old patriarchy is *doing* to us. It's pathetic, *pathetic.*" She suddenly became aware that the exit she desired was less than a quarter-mile ahead of her; she swung the steering wheel hard to the right and crossed two lanes of morning-rush-hour traffic with a deafening screech of her tires; she made the exit just in time. Brian had gripped his seat and closed his eyes; when he heard no crunch of bone or metal, he slowly opened them and sighed with relief. His gum had popped so far back in his mouth that just a little bit farther and it would have been sucked up into his nasal cavities.

Regina was now steering the car with just three slender fingers of her left hand; her right was busy waving madly in the air to accentuate her points. "These women have completely abdicated responsibility for their lives," she said. "In the seventies, that was the whole *point*—taking *charge*. But this new generation—Perpetrial's generation; she's thirteen years younger than I am, did you know that?—they act as though they're helpless in the face of patriarchal whim, which is just *bullshit*. They get together and instead of inspiring each other to go out and remake the world, they hold hands and whine about how *oppressed* they are." She suddenly swerved into the left lane, passing a rusted-out Impala, then just as quickly dodged back into the middle lane, then over to the right, passing a Honda Accord driven by a shirtless teenager who was too busy singing along with his radio to notice that he was in Regina's way. She swerved back into the middle lane mere inches in front of him, as though to teach him a lesson; Brian turned around and saw that, sure enough, the incident had brought his performance to an almost literal dead halt.

"You see it all the *time* in work situations now," Regina continued as though nothing had happened. "I work in PR at the University of Missouri, so I *know*. These women come in to take professional jobs, and they say—as they *should*—that they insist on total equality for themselves in the workplace. But then, just let one of the men make a suggestive comment or tell an off-color joke, and suddenly these same women are screaming harassment."

A huge pothole gaped at them from the road just ahead. Brian waited for Regina to change lanes to avoid it, but instead she not only approached it, she actually sped up. He braced his arms against the dashboard and his tongue against his chewing gum; and then, with a CH-THUNK, the Sunbird sailed over the hole with only a token jolt. There was something to be said, it appeared, for breakneck speed.

Regina continued her diatribe without missing a beat. "First they say they want total equality with men, then they say they want special treatment *from* men—and they never understand that there's a contradiction there. *That's* the problem in a nutshell. Perpetrial, of course, doesn't see it that way. She's done it with you, I'll bet. Hasn't she? Demanded equal footing with you but also demanded that you tiptoe around her. As if she could ever have it both ways. Mind if I turn on the radio?"

"No, no," said Brian, startled by the request, which came as something of a non sequitur.

"I just have to calm down about this or I may end up driving recklessly," she said, switching the dial to a station that was playing the new single by U2. "*God*, I love this song," she said. "Seen the video?"

"Nuh-uh," gasped Brian as they careened past a swerving semi. He regained his composure and said, "My musical tastes don't get much more modern than Patsy Cline."

She grunted, then drove in silence for some time—still at great speed, for despite the sweet blandishments of U2, she hadn't seemed to calm down at all—until she zoomed onto another exit ramp, this one taking them into the crowded streets of downtown Chicago. Brian became aware that he had been holding his breath for most of the ride; he let it go with an audible sigh of relief. Regina pulled up to a stoplight, and, incredibly, *stopped.*

She rolled down her window and hung her elbow outside the car. "And I'll tell you something else, Brian," she said, switching off the radio and turning to face him. "The fact that Perpetrial just packed up her things and left me—ran off like a coward, and that's *not* too strong a word—that just convinces me I won our last argument about all this. You know what the argument was about? I called her an essentialist! That's *it*! Can you believe she left me for *that*? She acted like I'd called her a fascist or something! See, she'd been going on and on about how different women's sexual responses are from men's—something about desire in men being localized in the penis and in women being distributed throughout the body—and I said, 'Ha! Got you! Essentialism!' Which I thought was kind of funny, because of course *I'm* an essentialist. But Perpetrial—I mean, it's such a dirty word to her and all her social-constructionist friends, who *insist* that the only differences between men and women are the ones they're taught to have. Well, she just flipped out."

Regina ran her hands through her hair and then rolled up her window as a bum with a squeegee approached, eyeing her windshield. "Wouldn't admit that I'd caught her," she continued as the bum sprayed the glass with a viscous yellow liquid and started scraping it off, leaving dirty streaks the size of fettucine. "Kept insisting that she saw no contradiction to constructionist dogma in what she'd said, which is like looking straight up at the sky and saying you don't see blue. But then, she wouldn't *dare* admit that there's an inherent difference between the sexes, because that'd mean women are wholly responsible for their social condition, and she'd rather *die* than admit that we're all not tragic victims of 'the system.' So because I had her cornered, she ran away! Do you believe it?"

The bum, having completed his task, was now tapping on the window; Regina couldn't have been more oblivious if he were a housefly. "Rather than face me and learn to think like a rational human being, rather than let the woman she loves help her grow into intellectual independence, she runs off to another city where she can sit huddled with her friends in the shade of her shaggy old p.c. willow tree, and never have to step out into the clear, illuminating light of the truth. I love Perpetrial, I *swear* I do, but till she grows up and stops trying to pass the buck for her failures onto 'patriarchy'—I hate that term!—there's no way we can go on together. I've traveled a long way to see her here, but that doesn't mean I'm giving in to her that easily. She's a fool if she thinks that."

"Fitty cent for th' winda, man," the bum was yelling through the glass.

Brian didn't want to find himself wedged between embattled lovers, and he certainly didn't want to acknowledge the bum, so he steered the conversation back to more abstract matters. "What are you saying—that women should put up with rudeness in the workplace? I mean, men don't come on to other *men* in the office—not as a rule, anyway. Believe me, I'd have noticed. I mean, aren't women just talking about simple *respect* here?"

"*Twenny-five* cent," the bum hollered. "Half-price! C'mon!"

Regina grinned. "But what form does that respect *take*, Brian? Among male co-workers, I've always noticed a kind of loose, flippant camaraderie that often has an obscene side to it. Like, when your boss sticks his head in your office and says, 'Hey, cocksucker, you up for lunch?' isn't that really a sign of his *approval*?" The light changed to green. She rolled down the window, turned to face the bum, and said, "When work is performed without being explicitly contracted, there is no legal or moral obligation to provide payment. Welcome to America." Then she slammed her foot on the accelerator and careened through the intersection. "Of course," she said, resuming her conversation with Brian as though nothing had happened, "there are always going to be creeps who *do* try to play sexual mind-games with female co-workers, but that doesn't mean women have to get all bent out of shape anytime someone makes a lewd remark to them. It's par for the *course*, for God's sake." She gave him a quick smile, then returned her eyes to the road. "That was a good question, though; you're pretty sharp for a cartoonist. I *like* you, Brian. Maybe you'll be good for Princess Paragon." She paused. "Used to read her as a girl, myself."

Brian was about to remark on this coincidence when he realized with a chill that it might not be so very coincidental; that it might, in fact, be Regina's ulterior motive in getting him alone and away from Perpetrial. Was she now going to launch into *her* vision of how Princess Paragon should be handled? Was there no one in the world who'd just trust him to do it *his* way?

Fortunately, a moment later the car screeched to a halt in front of the studio where "Bella" was taped. As Brian stumbled out of the car and suppressed the urge to kiss the pavement, Regina promised to bide her time by shopping downtown until he was ready to be picked up again.

"That's okay," he insisted, perhaps a bit too strongly. Between Regina's driving and his suspicion of her real interest in him, he'd decided he'd rather *crawl* back to the hotel than let her chauffeur him. "I mean, I don't even know how long I'll be. It's not fair to you. Really, go on back. I'll hop a cab. Bang'll pay for it."

Having finally convinced her, he watched her speed away, slipping through a yellow light at the exact moment it turned red. He spat out his gum; it lay limply on the sidewalk, looking as if it had been through the Vietnam war. Then he took a deep breath and entered the building.

At the security desk, a guard called the set to confirm that he was expected; then he was allowed to take the elevator to the third-floor "Bella" studio. When the elevator doors opened, a perky assistant producer with three pigtails was already there to meet him. She introduced herself and shook his hand, then took him into a makeup room for some rudimentary touching-up.

While Brian was in the chair, being shaped and highlighted to conform to minimal television standards, in walked Arabella Martinez herself, followed by another assistant, who was clutching a clipboard as though she were in the process of breastfeeding it.

"*Hi,*" said Bella, her smile wide and dazzling. "I'm Bella Martinez. You must be Brian Parrish." She extended her hand.

"Yes. It is. I mean, I am," he said, giggling, feeling a little starstruck in spite of himself. He took her hand and shook it. "Good to see you! You're looking well! I mean, uh—actually, I don't know *what* I mean."

She laughed. "Thanks, anyway. I get the point." Her rich, black hair was impeccably coiffed, and she wore a tight-fitting red suit with a black collar, cuffs, and buttons. Chanel, unless Brian missed his guess. He thought her exquisitely put together.

She finished shaking his hand and then, still smiling, said, "Did—uh—" She checked the assistant's board. "Did Hector Baez or Nigel Cardew happen to arrive with you?"

He shook his head. " 'Fraid not. I arranged for my own ride."

"Well," she said, shrugging, "they're not *very* late yet. And Roger Oaklyn is already here, so we're—"

"Who?" Brian asked, suddenly on full alert.

"Hold still," the makeup man admonished him. He gripped Brian's shoulder and sprayed his hair with something foul-smelling from an atomizer.

"Roger Oaklyn," Bella repeated, smiling brilliantly. "He's the creator of Princess Paragon. Surely you knew that."

He nodded. "Of course. But what's he *doing* here?"

Her smile grew forced. "He's appearing on the show with you. Weren't you told that? You and your friends are sharing the stage with the creators of your characters. It took some time to round them up, believe me! The Acme-Man originator even turned out to be *dead.*"

Brian sighed in exasperation and shook his head slowly. "No way," he said. "No *way* is this really happening."

"I beg your pardon?" said Bella.

"I said, *no way.* This won't do at all."

The makeup man suddenly chirped, "All set, dear," packed up his things, and scooted out of the room. He'd wound up his work rather abruptly, however; Brian suspected that he was beating a hasty retreat before the storm broke.

But that didn't deter Brian. He got out of the chair and faced Bella, who was, after all, quite a bit shorter than he, and said, "Having Roger Oaklyn on the show gives the interview a totally different perspective than the one I want. This is supposed to be about the *new* comics, what's happening *now*. I absolutely *will not* appear with him. This is my moment to be in the spotlight, and I'm not sharing it with some has-been from the forties."

Bella's eyes narrowed to slits. She was still smiling, but now her smile was something terrible to behold. "Mr. Parrish," she said, "the format for your interview was arranged by your publisher's public-relations agency in New York. They have even issued press releases about the show, which your publisher's management approved. We've gotten a lot of press pickup, too. And we've sent out station promos about this show. I *myself* taped the on-air spots. 'The old cartoonists confront the new. Friday on "Bella." ' That's what I've been saying on the air all across the country, for two days now. Do not, Mr. Parrish, do *not* fuck with me on this."

The epithet sounded like the report from a gun. Bella's assistant was visibly trembling; she was staring at her shoes, unable to look up. The pencil in her hand clattered against her clipboard as though it might bolt from the room if she let go of it.

Brian balled his fists, then relaxed them. "I'm sorry, but I refuse to share the stage with Roger Oaklyn." He felt his upper lip start to sweat. Why had he spit out his gum so soon? "Bad enough I've got to share it with Hector and Nigel, but I'm not having anyone else up there talking about *my* character—even if he did originate her. Christ! *Especially* because he originated her. Comics are advancing, Ms. Martinez—marching out of pulp obscurity and into the big time. They *matter* now—because people like me are *making* them matter. I'm not going to allow you to hold me back by putting the focus on the past. It's embarrassing." He was so nervous, his voice was wavering; he hoped she didn't notice. "So it's up to you. You can have me, or you can have Oaklyn, but not both. And if you choose Oaklyn—well, I hope your audience can handle a whole half-hour of endless stories about how lousy the comics business was fifty years ago, because I'm sure that's all you'll get from him."

They faced each other for what seemed a small ice age. Brian felt his tongue swell up in his mouth, and he developed a quiver in his left hand that he could still only by pressing it against his thigh. Bella was staring at him as though she might at any moment emit laser beams from her eyes and burn away his resistance, like that villain he'd created, the Pyro-Technician.

But finally she turned to her by-now ash-white assistant and said, "Send Mr. Oaklyn home, Donna. With our thanks." At which command the girl fairly flew down the hallway.

Bella took a step toward the door, then nodded her head at Brian and said, "See you on the set in ten minutes, Mr. Parrish."

But her eyes were clearly telling him, You Will Be Sorry.

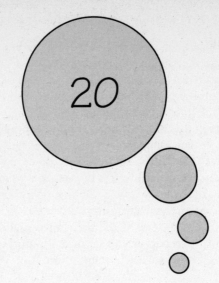

20

It was an indication of the severity of Jerome's desperation that in his need to calm his roiling, ravaged mind, he actually called his mother. But, alas, her answering machine kicked in after the third ring.

"This is Peachy Kornacker," the greeting began. "Since my son Jerome has disbandoned me, I have decided to go to the city of Akron to visit my daughter Sandra, who also left me several years ago but who at least has some grandchildren to show for it. Please leave a message after the bleep for me to call you back whenever I get home, which I don't even know when that will be."

Jerome hung up without saying a word.

Dizzy with hunger now, he was forced to leave his room and head for the only restaurant in the hotel, a dark, fern-dotted place that pumped cottony New Age music across its expansive length, which would've been enough to drive Jerome insane if he hadn't been driven there already. He ordered a hamburger and fries, which disappointed him by turning out to be almost grease-free, as though they'd been fried in some kind of weightless vegetable oil.

All around him, comic-book fans were clustered at tables gossiping about who was going to be on the "Breaking into Comics" panel, and ogling two stupefyingly chesty models who had been hired to stroll the convention dressed as Vampirella and Wonder Woman. Jerome eavesdropped, hanging on every word, but inside he seethed with hatred that his fellow diners—his fellow fans!—could be so merry and larky while Comet lay dead, while Acme-Lad and Acme-Lass remained trapped in limbo, and while poor Princess Paragon was even now being readied for a descent into rank perversion.

After he finished eating, he decided to go back to his room and try to work up the courage to confront Hector Baez or Brian Parrish. He'd never have the nerve to face Nigel Cardew again, but at least he'd learned something from that encounter: it was imperative that his initial approach to the cartoonists be made when no one else was around. In picking on him, Nigel Cardew had obviously been playing to an audience. Jerome wasn't going to let that happen again.

He contemplated the difficulty of finding either Brian Parrish or Hector Baez alone in a hotel filled with their fawning admirers. He'd already asked the clerk at the front desk for their room numbers, but had been turned down; the hotel wasn't in the habit of giving out such information to just anyone who happened to ask. But if not in or just outside their rooms, how would Jerome ever manage to talk to them one-on-one?

He returned to his wing, dashed for the elevator, and lunged through the doors just as they were shutting. Inside, he grunted and gasped from the effort of having achieved such velocity, then was embarrassed to find himself accompanied by two other riders, witnesses to his clumsy careening—a tall, blond, long-haired youth and a short, scowling, middle-aged man. The latter was staring at Jerome with naked scorn; Jerome, his own mind a whirl of derangement, dared to stare back. The man was wearing a ComiCon badge imprinted "Guest," and beneath that, in Magic Marker, was scrawled "Hiram Krapp." The name was vaguely familiar to Jerome—some awful, misanthropic underground cartoonist, he seemed to recall.

Jerome's clumsy entry had caused the elevator doors to slide open again, and now another pair of riders took advantage of this to dart inside. The first was a tall, startling-looking middle-aged woman dressed entirely in black, with a long salt-and-pepper ponytail hanging heavily down her back. Her companion was a nubile young redhead who'd been practically poured into a filmy Intrepid Girl costume. She was holding up one of her shoulder straps, which had snapped from her cape.

The elevator began its slow ascent. The sixth-floor button was illuminated. Jerome extended a pudgy finger and depressed nine. The tall woman reached out a taloned hand and pressed seven.

"I *tole* youse dis costume was fer shit," said the obviously distraught redhead in a horrifically flat Chicago accent. "Big suhprise it broke on me! Dis crappy material's about as sturdy as a fuggin' Baggie. Plus it's chafin' me in places I din't even know could chafe!"

The older woman rubbed her lined forehead and sighed. "This is what the Jennifer Jerrold Talent Agency has come to!" she lamented in a voice drenched with melodrama. "Once, I represented the finest lights in Chicago theatre. Now I am reduced to squeezing part-time courtesans into petrochemical-based burlesque costumes for the amusement of an illiterate horde."

"How many times I gotta tell youse, Miz Jerrold, I ain't *never* been a whoor?" snapped Intrepid Girl. "Enny special *langwich* I gotta say it in? Hah?"

The blond man exchanged glances with Hiram Krapp, then said to him in a low voice, "I'll come get you at a quarter to four and bring you down to the self-publishers panel."

Hiram Krapp nodded, but refused to take his eyes off Intrepid Girl's attractively round rear end. "Just don't stop to introduce me to any fuckin' superhero hacks along the way," he growled.

The tall man blushed. "Christ's sake, Hiram, he's harmless. You could've at least shaken his hand."

"Brian Fucking Parrish? *Harmless?*" he barked. "Fucker's a millionaire from shovin' subgenre crap down adolescents' throats!"

"Jesus, *I* know that." The tall man glanced at Jerome, who quickly turned his head to watch the floor numbers light up overhead. Three, four, five . . . "*I* think his influence is pernicious, too. But incivility isn't going to solve anything."

The elevator lurched to a halt.

Jerome looked at his fellow riders. They all looked back.

Then the elevator dropped a full foot and a half.

The blond man grabbed the railing and yelled, "*Whoa!*"

Jerome and Intrepid Girl emitted nearly identical shrieks.

Hiram Krapp bellowed, "*I'LL SUE! I'LL SUE THE FUCKERS!*"

Everyone held his breath for a few seconds; the elevator seemed to have steadied itself.

Jerome exhaled voluminously.

"Miz Jerrold!" wailed the redhead. In the excitement, she'd let go of her shoulder strap, and her creamy left breast was now bobbing up and down in naked splendor. "Whadda we gonna do, whadda we gonna *do?*"

Jennifer Jerrold refused to release the railing. "*You* think of something!" she snapped. "You're the daring and dauntless Insipid Girl!"

"Dat's *Intrepid* Girl!"

Hiram Krapp said, "This is great. Just fuckin' *great*. Told my old lady I'd call her at one. Five after *already*. I'm in here for another five, I might as well call my lawyer first."

"Hiram, calm down," said his companion. "Everything's going to be o—"

"Five more minutes, this thing just *better* drop, you unnerstand what I'm sayin'? 'Cause I ain't callin' my old lady ten minutes late without a least a couple broken ribs for an excuse. I—"

With a mechanical grunt, the elevator started moving upward again, agonizingly slowly; it took eighty-four seconds to finish reaching the sixth floor. Then the doors opened.

Ungallantly, Hiram Krapp tumbled out ahead of the women. His blond friend held the door open until Jennifer Jerrold and the model had exited. Then he turned to Jerome and said, "I'd get the hell out of that thing, if I were you."

"But I'm on *nine*," Jerome protested.

"Hey, you might never *make* it that far. I'd get out of there and take the stairs, pal." He turned and started down the hallway.

Jerome suddenly saw the sense in this, so he scooted out of the elevator just before the doors slid shut again.

He followed the blond man, Hiram Krapp, Jennifer Jerrold, and the redhead (who'd now re-covered her breast) down the corridor of the sixth floor.

"We only have to walk up one flight of stairs," said Jennifer Jerrold. "Then we'll go to my room and get my sewing kit, and fix that strap." She shook her head, sending her ponytail swaying. "Then God help anyone who stands between me and the bar. I'd kill my own mother for just *one* vermouth-soaked olive."

"Dis is the most imbarrassing day of my life," Intrepid Girl said in a stage whisper. "Did'ja see dat fattie on the elevator? Got a look at my boob an' I swear to Gahd he started *droolin'*! If we gotta do dis shit nex' year, I wanna be She-Ninja or Damsel Death. *Dey* get to wear body stockings."

"If we have to do this next year, may I be dead in time to miss it," said Jennifer Jerrold.

As they passed room 614, Hiram Krapp waved a hand and sang, "*Yoo*-hoo, *Briii*-an! Brian *Paaarrish!* Come on out and sign my autograph, you meshuggana fruitcake!"

The tall man shook his head. "*Christ's* sake, Hiram. Give it a rest."

At room 622, the tall man stopped, inserted a key, said "Ten to four" to Hiram Krapp, and disappeared inside.

At room 626, Hiram Krapp unlocked the door and entered.

The door to the stairwell was at the end of the corridor, but as Jennifer Jerrold and Intrepid Girl passed through it and headed up to the seventh floor, Jerome doubled back and stood before room 614. After a moment's hesitation, he knocked on the door. "Yoo-hoo, Brian Parrish," he cooed under his breath.

He stared at the door, awaiting an answer for a very long time, then retraced his steps to the stairwell. On the way, he called out a little thank-you to Hiram Krapp.

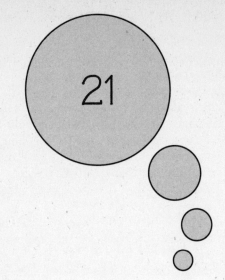

21

"How's the sexiest, hottest, most desirable man on seven continents?"

There was a stunned pause at the other end of the line. Then Nico said, "What's the matter?"

"What do you mean, what's the matter? Can't I just call up my spouse to tell him he's the sexiest, hottest, most desirable man on seven continents?"

"After four years together? Right. What's the matter?"

Brian sighed and let his head drop into the pillow. "I taped 'Bella' today," he said.

"And?"

"And it didn't go so well." He kicked off his loafers and let them fall beside the bed. "Bitch came after me like a pit bull on amphetamines."

"Really? I'm a little surprised by that. Doesn't seem the type."

"Well," he said, grimacing and scratching the top of his head, "I *sort* of brought it on. I had a—well, a kind of altercation with her before the show."

"Oh, for God's sake. About *what*?"

"Nothing, really," he insisted, embarrassed at having to make his confession. "It's just that she'd brought in the old guy who created Princess Paragon, and wanted him to be on the show with me. I put my foot down, said no way."

Nico sighed audibly. "Brian, Brian, Brian."

"Well, I was thinking about my career." He examined his fingernails.

"And did it do your career any good? Kicking an old man while he's down—and pissing off a national heroine in the process? Any good *at all*?"

Brian curled up in the fetal position. "Oh, *come* on, honey. Give me a break. I need a little support here."

"You need to be taken down a peg, is what you need. Sounds like Bella did that."

"Christ, Nico—*thanks*. What is this? You still punishing me for that incident with the hand lotion at Jimmy and Mark's?"

"I'm hardly that petty, Brian. No, I just think you've turned into a primo schmuck since this whole Princess Paragon thing started."

Brian reddened and sat bolt upright. *"What? What?* I have *not,"* he said, his hands on his chest. "I can't believe you said that. This is sour grapes, isn't it? I'm finally getting the attention I deserve, and you can't *stand* it!"

"You're right, I can't stand it. You're wrong about the reason."

Brian rolled over on his back and started pulling off his socks. "Look, that 'Bella' show airs at one o'clock today. At three, I've got to give a slide presentation on my first *Princess Paragon* issue to an auditorium packed with five hundred people, every one of whom will have just seen Bella-fucking-Martinez grind me into paste like a Cuisinart going at a clove of garlic. Do you know how nervous that makes me?"

"Come on, honey. They're *comics* fans. How bad can it be?"

"*Bad.*" Brian dropped the socks on the floor and lay back on the bed again. "You haven't seen the show yet. It was a *disaster*. First, I made Bella drop Roger Oaklyn. Then, at the last minute, Hector—Hector Baez, you remember, I told you about him, the guy who does *Acme-Man*—well, he gets stage fright and can't go on. Turns into a heap of jelly. So it's just me, Nigel Cardew—who suddenly decides to go national with his I'm-inscrutable-and-answer-questions-in-one-syllable-or-less routine—and these two old cartoonists, one of whom can't shut up about how he got screwed by Bang Comics and the other of whom looks like he's going to let loose and wet himself at any second. And Bella is just *furious* about all this—I mean, as if she weren't pissed off enough to begin with—so she decides to go after me, big-time." He reached for his foot and started scratching between his toes. "And, I mean, I'm ready for any question she can ask about the sexuality issue—which I don't figure she'll ask anyway, because she's always been gay-friendly—but she takes me completely by surprise by harping on Roger Oaklyn."

"That's the old guy," said Nico. "The one who made up Princess Paragon."

"Yes, yes." Brian was scratching his ankle now. "Did I consult Roger Oaklyn before making Princess Paragon a lesbian? she asks. Well, no, I say. And do I know if Roger Oaklyn gets any royalties from Princess Paragon?" He switched to the other ankle. "I say I don't, and, what do you know, *she's* got the answer: he doesn't get a red cent."

"He *doesn't*?" said Nico, appalled.

"Apparently not. Then she asks, How does Roger Oaklyn feel about the new direction I'm taking with Princess Paragon? And I say, How should I know? I never asked him. And she just keeps *coming* at me, Nico." He released his foot, reached underneath the waistband of his pants, and started scratching at his pubic patch. "I mean, at one point she tried to do the same thing with Nigel, because the old Moonman creators were right there on the set with us. She kept asking them, Doesn't it bother you that this man has turned your creation into a cold-blooded killer? But the old guys just kept saying, Hell, no, we just wish they'd do the right thing and pay us about one-tenth of what they're making off it. And Nigel sat there staring at molecules, like Andy Warhol on Prozac. So Bella kept coming back to me and harping on the Roger Oaklyn issue, until the audience was looking at me like—like I was some kind of *corporate raider* or something."

"How very unfair of them," said Nico with more than a trace of sarcasm.

Brian grimaced. "What's that supposed to mean?" he snapped. He got up and started pacing the bedroom. "Look, are you on my side or not?"

"I'm not," said Nico firmly. "What you did to that old guy was wrong. I think you got what you deserved. I only hope you learn a lesson from it."

Brian felt a flash of intense anger. "Fine. Thanks so much, honey. What a wonderful lover you are. Now I'm all set to go hear the same shit from an auditorium of five hundred sociopaths with problem skin. How thoughtful of you to prepare me for that."

"It's always 'me, me, me' with you lately, Brian. Think about how that must make the rest of us feel."

Brian rubbed the back of his neck. "Listen, Nico, I don't want to fight. Let's stop this."

"Fine. Let's stop it," Nico agreed, still sounding a little defensive.

"This 'Bella' thing has really shaken me up. I feel scummy; I feel like a villain. And since you feel the way *you* do about it, maybe we should—I don't know, give it a rest between us for a while. Just a week or two." He paused, his face flushed with emotion. "It's not you. It's me. You're right about that. The pace of all this has been—I don't know how to put it. Over my head. The fact that you honestly think I'm wrong—it's—it's—well, I have to think about that. Plus, I really feel like keeping a low profile after this whole fiasco." He brushed his hair away from his forehead and sat on the bed. "Maybe I'll even get Perpetrial to do the panel for me, so I don't have to appear."

"Brian, take my advice: face your fear. Otherwise it'll jus—"

"No platitudes, honey—*please*. I need some time to think—

time for this thing to die down. Maybe I'll stay in Chicago for a week or two after the convention's over. I've got to finish writing this third issue—you know, the one where Princess Paragon meets Cosmique—and I need concentration for that. I need *total* solitude. This will all work out for the best."

Nico sighed again. "Well, this is all highly theatrical of you, but—okay. Fine. Do what you think is best."

"Thanks for understanding, honey. I love you."

"I love you, too."

"Feed the Leonards. Change their water every day."

"I will. I have been."

"I'll call."

"I'll be here."

"Well." He paused, then shrugged his shoulders. "*Bye*, sweetheart."

An even longer pause from Nico's end; then a hushed "Bye."

Brian waited until he heard the dial tone before he hung up the phone himself. Then he sat on the edge of the bed, his mouth agape, feeling as if he'd been hit by some kind of cosmic bus. Everything was happening so quickly—so much to analyze, so much to sort out.

He slipped out of his jeans and T-shirt and put on the terrycloth bathrobe he'd swiped from Nico's closet. He sniffed the collar; it smelled like Nico's atrocious cheap cologne. He sat down at the desk and had a little crying jag.

It was almost 12:30. He was determined to avoid that hideous "Bella" broadcast; if he stayed in the room, he knew he'd be compelled to tune in. So he had a quick shower, pulled on his jeans, his loafers, a rugby shirt, and a baseball cap, and left for a long, solitary walk around the hotel grounds to gather his wits before the Princess Paragon panel.

As he headed down the corridor, he felt edgy, panicky, anxious. He'd believed himself to be on the verge of something wonderful, and now—overnight, it seemed—it was all going up in smoke. And true to form, he'd opted out—ducked for cover. Nico was right; he should be facing his fear. But he couldn't do that; he'd never been able to do that. No, Perpetrial would just have to do the panel for him. He knew he'd end up asking her.

Still, he had to do *something* to rescue his self-esteem—not to mention his career. Something drastic. But what? *What?*

When he got to the elevator, he found it blocked by a large cardboard sign reading "Out of Order—Sorry for the Inconvenience."

"*Shit,*" he muttered. But he wasn't surprised—not after the way the elevator had been behaving.

He turned back and trekked all the way down the hall to the stairwell.

He opened the door and started down the stairs.

He couldn't see more than half a flight before or behind him. Despite the claustrophobic setting, his footsteps echoed loudly, as though he were in a chasm. He sounded almost like an army descending.

I'd be the perfect prey in a mad-slasher film, he thought, giggling uneasily.

Then he turned on the first landing and almost bumped into an extremely weighty young man with dark, greasy hair, wearing a Princess Paragon T-shirt that was about two sizes too small for him.

Brian forced a smile and said, "Bitch about the elevator, huh?" He tried to pass him.

But the young man moved into his path, barring his way. "Bitch about Princess *Paragon!*" he hissed.

Brian was instantly on alert. "Don't know what you're talking about, buddy," he said, trying again to pass him.

"Yes you *do!*" the hefty stranger howled, throwing himself into Brian's path. "I know who you are! You have to *stop* it!" He was almost hyperventilating now.

Brian began to feel real fear.

"You have to leave her alone! She's not like you say she is!"

Brian shook his head slowly and said, "You've got the wrong guy, pal. Be a sport and step aside, huh?" He tried to dart past the quivering, wild-eyed fanatic, but the man grabbed him by the arm and held fast.

And then his assailant started shaking him.

"*Christ*," Brian yelped in fright. "*Jesus.*"

He started to fight back, and an awkward scuffle ensued.

He managed to break away, panting, and started to run; but from behind him, his attacker cried, "*You can't lie to me! I know who you are!*" and pushed him.

And Brian went rolling down a full flight of stairs, coming to a sudden and sickening halt on the next landing.

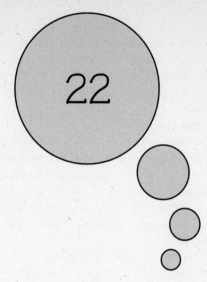

22

Jerome was gasping so hard, he had to hang on to the railing and hold his hand over his heart.

It was safe to do so now; Brian Parrish was clearly unconscious. He was lying very still, in a bad, twisted position; one of his arms was extended from his body in an odd, unsettling manner. Had it been broken? Jerome fervently hoped not.

Gasp—gasp—gasp—gasp—

He couldn't seem to regain his breath. He felt dizzy and faint.

He kept staring at his victim. It was really *him*, wasn't it? Brian Parrish, the world-famous cartoonist. Brian Parrish, the homosexual pervert. Brian Parrish, author of *The Centipede* and *Captain Ashram* and *Buster Brainpower* and *Doctor Dirge* and *The Offenders* and *Major Muscle* and *Galaxy Girl & the Go-Getters*. Brian Parrish, who had taken Princess Paragon away from him. Brian Parrish, who had written the six-issue "Interstellar

Odyssey" story line in *Quasar Quintet*, which Jerome had virtually committed to memory, panel by glorious panel. Brian Parrish, whose face was now beginning to swell with welts and bruises, and whose arm was twisted into a bad, odd position—so still, so *still* . . .

Gasp—gasp—gasp—

It was frightening, not being able to breathe. And the fright chased away the clouds of madness that had gripped him. The insane, uncaring, overwhelming hurt and anger that had spurred him on to this stairwell—now it was dissipating, departing him, like a demon vacating a host body, leaving him to confront the carnage he had wrought, unable to believe that it was really he who had wrought it.

Oh—gasp—gasp—*my God*—gasp—

He descended to the landing and crouched over Brian Parrish; he put his face next to the cartoonist's and, despite himself, felt a little flurry of excitement at his proximity to so renowned an artist.

He reached out his hand and shook the cartoonist gently.

No response.

This was unbe*liev*able. What was he going to do? How had he *ever* let himself lose control to this degree?

As if to answer that, he let the image of Princess Paragon in the arms of another woman enter his mind, then just as quickly he banished it. Mustn't even *think* of that, he admonished himself; it leads to a dark, scary place.

He tried to lift Brian Parrish and couldn't.

Dismayed, he put his hands to his face, then turned around, as if he might spot something in this cramped little concrete chute that could help him.

And then he heard the hum of other voices on the stairs below—voices that got louder the longer he listened.

Well, of course—the elevator was still out of commission. There'd be a *lot* of traffic on these stairs; and the longer he stayed here, the likelier it was that someone would climb to this floor.

A rush of adrenaline gave him new strength. He reached

down and grabbed Brian Parrish under the armpits (the damaged arm didn't seem to be broken, thank God; it hung limp, but not unnaturally), and dragged him as gently as he could (which wasn't very gently) up the stairs and down the hallway to the door of Brian's room. Then he fished through Brian's jacket pocket for the key, unlocked and swung open the door, and hauled him over to the bed, onto which, after a herculean effort that found him grunting and groaning like an orangutan in the throes of orgasm, he managed to drag the unconscious cartoonist.

A little more maneuvering and he had his victim under the covers and facing away from the door. He looked for all the world as though he were merely dozing.

Gasp—gasp—gasp—

So far, so good. Now all he had to do was slip away without being seen, head back to his own room, pack up his things, and check out.

He stopped in the bathroom first, to get a washcloth to remove his fingerprints from the doorknobs. No one would *ever* be able to trace this crime to him. Brian Parrish might provide a detailed description of his assailant, but with so many heavyset comics fans in the hotel, the police wouldn't know where to begin a search. It wasn't as though Jerome would stand out!

He plucked a washcloth from the towel rack and started to tiptoe toward the door, which was still propped open. One of Brian Parrish's shoes had fallen off and become wedged between the door and its frame. Jerome bent down to pick it up.

Then, from the hallway, someone knocked.

His head almost flew off his neck in alarm. He vibrated in terror and indecision for a moment, then darted back into the now-darkened bathroom and slipped behind the shower curtain, trying desperately to control his harsh-sounding breath.

Gasp—no, no, stop it—gasp, gasp—*stop* that—

"Brian? You in?" came a voice from beyond the door. A woman's voice.

What would Brian Parrish be doing with a *woman*? Jerome wondered with a sneer.

The door swung open, and through the slit in the shower curtain he saw not one woman, but two, enter; the first was an imposing, steely-eyed blonde; the other was shorter, and black. The black one was wearing a "Ferraro for Veep" T-shirt.

They weren't more than a few feet away from him. He could hear the tall blonde whisper, "He's sleeping."

"No, he's not," said the black one, more loudly. "It's the middle of the day. I'm sure he's just sulking." She turned in the direction of Brian Parrish's bed, and called out gently, "Brian, it's us. We ran into Hector. He told us what happened at the taping."

Hector? thought Jerome. He felt a surge of excitement. They must mean Hector Baez!

"Brian, it's not the end of the world," the black woman continued. "We came to watch the show with you. We figured you'd need us here, as objective observers, to tell you it wasn't so bad." She lowered her head to await a response, then said, "Goddess, Brian, this is so *childish*."

"I wish you'd cut that 'goddess' stuff, Pet," said the blonde. "Unless, of course, you're trying to *irritate* him into talking to us."

"Leave my religion alone," the one called Pet snapped.

"If it *were* a religion, I would, but it's just a set of attitudes you trot out whenev—"

"Regina, don't start this here—"

"If you're going to be a pagan, at least do it right. Don't give me this watered-down New Age—"

"*Aargh!*" Pet growled, holding her head in both hands. "We're here for *Brian*, remember?"

Regina sighed, and both women fell silent for a moment. Jerome held his breath lest they hear him.

Finally, Regina said, "Well, then, I suggest we respect his privacy."

"If he wanted privacy, why'd he prop the door open?"

"He's sleeping, Pet. Let's leave him alone."

"No, no, not with the *door* open; he wouldn't have gone to sleep with the *door* open. *Think* about it."

"I don't see wh—"

"It's a cry for help," she stage-whispered. "He can't face us, so he's pretending to be asleep; but by sticking his shoe in the door, he's *inviting* us to *force* him to face us."

"Or he might've just been too upset to realize where he was throwing his clothes when he came in," said Regina.

Pet sighed. She reached into her back pocket and produced a sheaf of paper. "Brian, if you *are* awake—well, I've read your first draft for issue three, and I think it's beautiful."

"She wouldn't let me see it, Brian," Regina called out.

"I thought you were so sure he was asleep," said Pet.

She busily examined a thread on her blouse. "Well, just in case he's not," she said airily.

Pet padded into the room, and suddenly she was out of Jerome's range of sight; he felt his heart lurch—what if she tried to awaken Brian Parrish?

But then he heard a papery flutter, as though she'd dropped the sheaf onto the desk. "I've made some suggestions in the margins," he heard her say. "Don't get too upset over them, I basically *love* what you've done; it's just fine-tuning. Look it over when you get up." A short pause. "We're going to get ready to watch 'Bella' now. We'll call you afterward. We're sure it's not as bad as Hector said. You know how he exaggerates."

Then she padded back into Jerome's field of vision; he saw her motion Regina into the hallway.

But Regina said, "Just a moment, I need to make a pit stop." She stepped over to the bathroom, reached her hand inside, and started to probe the wall for the light switch. Jerome backed into the shower and cowered in terror.

Pet reached over and grabbed Regina's arm. "Come on, you can use *our* loo."

"With the elevator busted?" she protested. "We won't get back to our room for twenty minutes! Just stop being so silly, I'm right here—it won't take a moment."

Pet gave her another tug. "I don't want to be alone in a bedroom with a man."

Regina removed her hand from the bathroom wall and

turned, her jaw on her chest in disbelief. "You *what*?" She shook her head. "Pet! This is a *gay* man in a *hotel* room with your *lover* in the adjoining *john.*"

Lover! thought Jerome with a jolt of revulsion.

"It's the principle of the thing," Pet explained.

Regina grunted. "I have more respect for principle when my bladder is empty," she snapped. "Sorry, Pet. You're on your own."

The overhead light flickered to life.

"Well, then, I'm coming in with you," said Pet insistently.

"Oh, for God's sake. This is so ridiculous." Regina's voice was now barreling around the naked walls of the bathroom, sounding much louder and much nearer than before; and when the Pet woman answered, so did hers.

"Well, I have to pee too," she said. "Swear to God." The door clicked shut.

"Oh, right," said Regina. "Fine. Long as I go first."

Jerome didn't dare to breathe. And while he stood there, his heart racing, listening to Regina fumble with her zipper and her pants, he realized that he'd backed right into the bath spout, which was pressing into his leg with enough pressure to cut off its circulation. But it had to be endured. He *couldn't* be discovered.

Pet started humming; Jerome didn't recognize the tune.

"Mind looking the other way?" asked Regina, her voice low.

Pet cackled. "Oho! So the fearless feminist firebrand actually *does* have an inhibition! What's the matter, Regina? Something shameful about urination?"

"Course not. Hell, you've seen me pee in bushes lots of times. But this place is so—I don't know. *Clinical.* Like a doctor's office."

"Fine, I'll turn away. But then you owe me one."

A pause. "Very funny, Pet. Turning into the mirror is not what I had in mind."

Another cackle. Then, "How's this?"

"Perfect. Just stay there."

And then Jerome heard the full-throttle flow of Regina's

urine pouring into the bowl. His leg was growing numb with pain; he clutched his mouth so that he wouldn't cry out.

Eventually, Regina said, "Okay, your turn," and Jerome could hear the flapping of her blue jeans as she dressed herself.

"Don't flush!" Pet cried.

"Wh—what do you mean, *don't flush?* You get kinky or something since you left me?"

"If you must know, I was just considering the biosphere. Know how much water Americans waste every day by flushing unnecessarily?"

"No." Regina's voice was coming from the opposite side of the bathroom. "How much?"

"Well, I don't know *exactly*. But a lot." A long pause. "You can go now."

"What?"

"You're done, Regina. Scoot."

"Like hell! You stood here listening to me; now I'm going to stand here and listen to *you*."

"That's ridiculous. You can go back to the bedroom. *You're* not afraid of Brian."

"Not in the dark with my fucking *hands* tied am I scared of Brian. But that's got nothing to do with it."

"Regina, *go*."

She chuckled. "I just went."

"*Goddess!* You're driving me crazy! Get *out* of here!"

"Nuh-uh. It's the *principle* of the thing, Pet. You know about *principles*, don't you?"

A small, tense silence. "You're childish and unevolved," snapped Pet. "Turn your head, then!"

As Jerome listened to the Pet woman fumble with her belt and zipper and settle down with a little sigh, he reflected, in the sheerest despair, that he was a celebrity assailant hiding out in a hotel shower with a leg about to give way from lack of blood, and eight inches away from him a pair of lesbian lovers were relieving themselves. The situation could not be any worse.

And then he felt a quiver in his own bladder.

It started as nothing more than an urge—his kidneys demanding a bit of attention. But before his mind could register alarm, the urge became stronger—the various excitements of the day combining with his two Classic Cokes over lunch to create a gushy imperative, growing more expansive and dizzying with each passing second. His eyes rolled back in his head; his loins felt like a water balloon being held out a twelfth-story window. His face knotted up into the exact shape of a cinnamon roll. At any second the dam might burst.

The room whirled around his head. I am going to die, he thought, pressing his thighs together and digging his already blood-starved leg farther into the bath spout; I am going to drop dead in the tub, and it's no less than I deserve.

Through ears plugged with stress and tension, he could barely hear the tinkling and trickling of the Pet woman getting down to business. It was worse than a tease; it was agony.

As if that weren't enough, Regina started crooning, "I'm *siiiing*-ing in the rain, just *siiiing*-ing in the rain. . . ."

"You are so crude," Pet hissed. "You belong in a men's locker room! Stop that this *second*!"

Jerome was now holding his breath—holding it for longer than any Olympic swimmer he'd ever heard tell of. He was listening with inexpressible relief to the rustle of Pet dressing herself again.

"This was a mistake, coming here," she was muttering. "I should've known better."

"Yes, you should've." Some unidentifiable noises. "Come on. Quit pouting. Come here. Give us a kiss."

Jerome fought off faintness. He felt vivisected.

"You're despicable. No." The toilet flushed. At the sound, his agony doubled and redoubled.

"All right, then, give us a lick."

"Ugh! Get your hands off me. Get out of my way."

"Pet—"

Jerome bade his mother a telepathic goodbye. His knees started to buckle.

"Oh, Regina. What's the use of th—"

"Pet." Softer now. "My Pet. My only Perpetrial."

"Regina, why does everything have to be so—" A tiny gasp. "Oh, hell. I'm so sor—"

"No, no." Softer now. "Hush. Don't want to hear that."

Lip noises, mouth noises. Jerome was blind now; he couldn't even see the tiles of the shower that surrounded him. His crotch was an alien presence—virulent, radioactive.

Cooing, then; billing and cooing. Tears streamed from Jerome's eyes. He sank, lower and lower, into the tub. It was inching out of him now. Any second . . .

Then, miraculously, "Let's go, okay?" A breathy, girlish Regina.

A sniffle. "Let me wash my hands."

Jerome's face quaked; a spasm—an almost erotically pleasant spasm. A small patch of warm dampness spread between his thighs. He managed to hold back the rest, during the nine million years Pet spent at the faucet. Then the bathroom door opened noisily. A second later, the light went out.

A few more seconds and he'd have *made* it.

Still trembling, he peeked out from behind the shower curtain. The women were hand in hand, heading toward the door.

"Later, Brian," called Regina. "And, listen, about 'Bella'— take it like a man, okay? Better yet, take it like a *woman*."

Jerome heard the Pet woman hoot; then the door clicked shut.

He ripped aside the shower curtain and stumbled out of the tub. In the tiny bathroom, his heartbeat sounded like cannon fire. He fumbled with his zipper as though he'd never operated one before. It was so frustrating, he actually hacked out a few sobs. Then he stood by the toilet and released his long-pent-up flow, feeling somehow unburdened, as though he might at any moment float away.

His breathing was now somewhat restored as well. With renewed confidence, he crept back into the bedroom and headed for the desk; there he found the script that Premenstrual—or whatever her name was—had dropped on Brian Parrish's desk.

He picked it up, pulled the chair out from the desk, and sat down. Then he made a quick check of Brian Parrish—still out like a light—and began reading:

PAGE FOUR, PANEL ONE: Cosmique stands before P.P. Her eyes are ringed with sadness and exhaustion. Her hands are open in supplication to P.P. She says, "I know that you have but lately come to this planet, to spare it the ravages of male aggression."

PANEL TWO: We see P.P.'s face as Cosmique continues, "But my planet faces a graver danger, by far—and is in greater need of a champion."

PANEL THREE: A mid-shot of the two of them standing, facing each other. There should be tension evident in their postures. Cosmique continues: "Will you come to my world, Princess Paragon, and join us—save us? Any reward you name will be yours. Anything I can do to persuade you, I will do with gladness."

PANEL FOUR: Closeup of Cosmique; she continues: "Including the giving of my body. I know that this is what you desire. I am from a race of telepaths—I can see it written in your thoughts."

PANEL FIVE: Similar closeup of P.P.'s face—a stunned expression on it. P.P. says, "Very well, then, I will be your champion—and here is what you must give me in return:"

PANEL SIX: Mid-shot of the two of them (perhaps in silhouette?). P.P. says, "You must give me your vow that you will never again dishonor yourself by offering your body against your will to those who desire it."

PANEL SEVEN: Cosmique replies: "I did not say it was against my will."

PANEL EIGHT: Extreme closeup of P.P.'s eyes as she realizes what has been said.

PANEL NINE: Extreme closeup of P.P.'s hand, extended in the air.

PAGE FIVE, PANEL ONE: Mid-shot of Cosmique's hand meeting P.P.'s in midair; the second, third, and fifth fingers of each hand touch; the fourth finger of each hangs in empty air.

PANEL TWO: Extreme long shot of the two, still touching hands, against a limbo backdrop; the world has fallen away for them—they alone define existence for each other at this moment.

In the margin, someone—that Preposterous woman, Jerome presumed (and suddenly he recalled having read that the editor of the new *Princess Paragon* was a woman whose name was an odd concoction of syllables beginning with P)—had written, *"Beautiful, Brian! I have tears in my eyes. But what exactly is the nature of the danger Cosmique's planet faces? It's going to have to be something if it's greater than the dangers that face ours."*

Jerome shook his head in disgust and relief. How close they'd come! They were almost ready to inflict this upon an unready world! He'd gotten here just in time.

Without bothering to read the rest of it, he ripped the entire script in half, then dumped it into the wastebasket, where, as far as he was concerned, it belonged.

He sighed and sat for a while, feeling that in spite of the difficulties and doubts, his mission had been successful.

Then he heard a groan of pain erupt from the body behind him. He turned.

Brian Parrish was propped up on one elbow and rubbing his temples with his free hand. His eyes were teary and his jaw swollen. He seemed woozy for a moment; then he got his bearings, sat up straight, and looked about him. His gaze settled instantly on Jerome.

Something in his eyes made Jerome jump out of his chair. As soon as he'd done so, he knew he shouldn't have; he'd revealed his weakness to Brian Parrish—and the look the cartoonist was now wearing was one of instant comprehension.

"You," he said balefully, his voice cracking. He held his head and rocked himself back and forth. "You lousy little filthy fat-boy *criminal,"* he howled. "I'm going to sue you for everything you're

worth, you pathetic piece of shit, you fucking moron, you scum, you leech, you *geek*."

Still hurling invective at Jerome, he carefully got to his feet and headed for the bathroom. Jerome did his best to flatten himself against a wall as he passed.

A moment later, Jerome heard him scream. Then came a new avalanche of terrifying profanity. "Look at what you've done to my *face*, you goddamned psychopathic insect! I'll see you strung up by the *balls* for this! If my profile's ruined, you'll rot in jail till the crack of goddamned *doom*, I swear to Almighty fucking *God*."

Jerome nearly swooned in horror; his face and forehead were slick with sweat.

He heard the water running, and more wild ranting and raving. He had a terrible feeling that he had lost control of this situation, but had no idea what to do to regain it. He could, of course, attack Brian Parrish anew; but without the morning's madness to spur him on, he really wasn't capable—that had been some other Jerome, some berserk beast created by derision and disappointment and humiliation. He couldn't just summon up that terrifying alter ego out of thin air. His fear was like a great wet blanket over his shoulders, preventing the ignition of his fury.

And so he stood against the wall, paralyzed by indecision.

Brian Parrish reappeared, using a wet washcloth to daub his badly battered jaw and nose. "I'm going to have hotel security up here so fast, it'll make your flabby *head* swim," he snarled, approaching the phone.

Completely defeated, Jerome sank into the chair next to the dresser and stared at his feet. The only thing he could think of—the most frightening thing he could conjure—was what his mother would have to say when she heard about this.

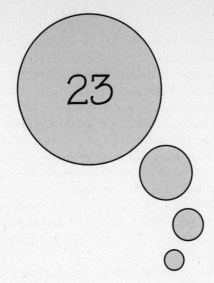

23

Brian started dialing. It caused him wrenching spasms of discomfort; he was holding the washcloth to his swollen chin with his good arm and, as a result, had to handle the telephone with his bad one, which felt now as if it had been yanked from his body and then reattached with Scotch tape.

His mind was moving at lightning-swift speed, spurred on, he supposed, by the rush of excitement and pain that electrified all his nerve endings like a cattle prod at full charge. As he pushed the first digit of the number for hotel security, he thought: This is the last straw! After all the *shit* I've had to take the past two days, I get attacked in the fucking stairwell by a paranoid schizophrenic the size of a Volkswagen Rabbit, who first nearly kills me, then tucks me into bed and sits next to me like some creepy kind of *nanny!* I'm going to hang this lunatic fat-boy out to dry, I don't care what *anyone* says.

And as he pushed the second digit, he thought: Wait'll that

bitch Bella hears! When this news gets out, she's going to look like the one who *inspired* this slob to come at me like a World Wrestling Federation wannabe. And wait'll *Nico* hears. *He'll* be sorry he was such a jerk to me.

As he pushed the third and final digit, he thought: But then, I'm not really in *such* bad shape—just banged up a little, maybe concussed. The guy took me by surprise; no one will ever believe he was really any match for me. In fact, I can see this news not even reaching Bella at all—and Nico might even make fun of me! I can just hear him: "So you got into a shoving match with a customer. Big deal. You expect me to believe you were in any kind of *danger* from that out-of-shape *kid*? He's a fan, not a fanatic."

The hotel-security line rang once, and Brian slammed down the receiver.

He's a *fan*, he repeated to himself, rolling the words around in his head, not a fanatic.

A Brian Parrish *fan*.

He turned and looked closely at his quivering, simpering attacker.

And suddenly he realized what had incited this poor schmuck to such passion. It had been his own work—Brian's work, his plans for Princess Paragon—that had driven this hopeless drudge to lurk in a stairwell waiting for him to appear, then launch into a hysterical tirade that had whipped him into a frenzy of—well, *look* at him, the big, fat jellyfish; he obviously never intended to get violent. That he did was just a measure of how seriously he took this thing.

Against all odds, Brian found himself feeling rather flattered.

After all, Nico didn't take him this seriously. Despite the fact that he earned about thirty times Nico's salary, he had to endure his patronizing little asides and feigned interest in the comics business. And Heloise! She wasn't any better than the smarmy management drones at Electric, who viewed him only as an investment. Perpetrial, too, saw him as an unfortunately necessary tool for fulfilling her feminist agenda. Even that yellow-media queen Bella had treated him with contempt.

But to this kid—to this poor, mewling, overweight, twenty-something geek—what Brian did *mattered*. To him, Brian *was* something. Something to fawn over, something to obsess about, maybe even something to attack—but *something*.

It was a kind of attraction-repulsion—a mysterious mixed reaction that almost exactly mirrored what Brian felt for his fans in return. That moment when he'd thought he might be trapped in an elevator with four such fans—it *had* been frightening, but hadn't there also been a slight thrill in knowing that if they *were* stuck, he'd be at the top of their little isolated crisis hierarchy? That not one of them would question his authority, that they would accept him as their superior without even a whimper of dissent?

Brian now realized that what he felt in the presence of his fans was the disturbingly enjoyable sensation of power. He felt it now, over his attacker: power absolute and irrevocable. The fact that the poor slob had lashed out at him, hurt him—who *could* pass up an opportunity to lash out at a supreme authority? Children rebelled against parents. Prisoners taunted their jailers. But nothing changed because of it. Wasn't his attacker here awaiting Brian's punishment?

Brian had been taught to regard the enjoyment of power—and the desire for it—as morally suspect. But he recognized now that it was probably the sole reason he'd stayed in superhero comics. He needed this—to counteract all the frustrating, complex, egalitarian relationships in his life. He *needed* this passionate, potentially turbulent reverence—needed to know that somewhere lives were lived in thrall to him. And in the aftermath of all that had gone wrong in his life recently—culminating in the unmitigated disaster of "Bella"—he decided that he needed *this kid*.

Slowly, deliciously, he formed an idea. It was the perfect solution to his present predicament. He wouldn't be worrying Nico at all; they'd already agreed to be apart for a few weeks. And if he disappeared from the convention, everyone—including Perpetrial—would simply assume he'd stormed off in a snit after the "Bella" fiasco to sulk in private.

And best of all, he was already a month ahead of the *Princess Paragon* production schedule, so he could afford to drop out of sight for a while, then reappear and pick up exactly where he'd left off.

It was perfect, *perfect*. Hadn't he told himself that he needed to do something drastic to salvage his pride? This was it. It was karma; it was kismet.

He studied his attacker. The large young man was still sitting quietly; he was drenched with sweat and stank like a cattle car in high August. Not quite the vestal virgin he would've chosen, but gods have to take the worshipers they can get. And for the next month or so, this kid was it for Brian.

"You realize I could send you to jail," he said in a low voice. The young man nodded.

Brian pressed the wet towel to his jaw. "I'd have every right to send you there, after what you did to me."

The kid gulped, and Brian thought, Come on, *plead* with me.

A moment passed maddeningly, and Brian continued, "I'm not a bad guy. I could be merciful, but you—hell, you're obviously remorseless." He reached for the phone again, then cocked an eyebrow at the stranger. "I could have pity on someone who at least expressed remorse."

Sweat seemed to spurt from his assailant's brow. The color bleached out of him again.

Brian sighed. Was this guy dense, or what? "Yep," he said, placing his hand on the receiver, "I'd better just have security come up here and get you. Too bad, really. I don't get any pleasure out of this. But there doesn't seem to be any other way. . . ."

He deliberately allowed his voice to trail off, then picked up the receiver and propped it between his shoulder and chin and started dialing again, this time very slowly; each button he pressed still caused him a shrill flourish of pain.

Two buttons down. One more to go. Come *on*, he commanded mentally.

Then, a sound like a sheep bleating: "I—I—I—"

Brian turned, his dialing finger poised above the third button. "Yes?" he said. "You have something to say?"

"I—I—I—"

Oh, for *Christ's* sake. "Relax. Don't be afraid. Just tell me what you're trying to say."

Nothing; only a look of abject terror. Then the poor slob

must have had a nervous muscle spasm, because his arm lashed out and knocked over a lamp; it clattered to the floor, and its ceramic base broke clean in two.

"*Forget* it. Just ignore it. *Look* at me," Brian ordered, waving the receiver at his assailant, who was with great difficulty bending over to pick up the lamp. At Brian's command, he straightened up again, a terrified grin on his face. "Are you trying to tell me," Brian said through gritted teeth, "that you *are*, in fact, suffering from remorse?"

Frantic nodding.

At *last*, Brian thought. Climbing *Everest* would've been easier.

He hung up the phone and faced him. "Well, then. I suppose I should at least hear your side of the story."

Just a glassy stare in reply.

Brian sighed and thought, This may take a while, then sat on the bed, still holding the washcloth to his face. "I can probably guess what you're going to tell me. You've been reading *Princess Paragon* for years, and you feel like you have some—I suppose you'd call it a kind of *proprietary* interest in her, right? Some kind of emotional stake that should be acknowledged. Am I right?"

The attacker's head bobbed up and down like an epileptic pigeon's in fast-forward.

"And along I come, with my big plans to change the character in ways you don't approve of and might even find unsavory. And it just *gets* to you. You feel—" He gestured as if searching for the proper turn of phrase. "Inside of you, there's this welling-up of—of you don't even *know* what. Isn't that it?"

A little sob burbled from the young man's lips, and he nodded again.

Brian lowered his head and in a humble voice said, "But don't you like my work?"

Frantic, insistent nodding.

Brian looked at his hands and pretended not to have seen this. "Is it so repulsive to you?"

Almost spastic head-shaking. "No, no," the fan blurted, speaking at last. "I think you're a genius! I swear it!"

"Well, then," said Brian, looking him in the eye, "why don't you trust me? Haven't I *earned* a little trust?"

The fan pulled back; a look of suspicion and fear came over his face.

"You see there? You *don't* trust me! You *aren't* a fan of mine. This is just a sham; you've been lying all along!"

Positively demonic head-shaking.

Brian shook his own head. "I don't believe you. You're making all this up just so I won't call security. Listen, I'm at a difficult place in my career right now. I'm writing the script to the third issue of the new *Princess Paragon* series—the issue where she meets the woman who's going to become her lover. It's probably the most difficult and important piece of writing I've ever had to do, and I can't do it if I don't have my readers behind me. I've taken heat from my publisher, my editor, the dealers, a goddamned TV talk-show moron—hell, if I haven't earned the goodwill of my *fans*, then I might as well just give up and retire." He actually managed to choke off this last word, as if he really were terribly upset.

Brian was astonished to see actual tears brimming from his attacker's eyes.

"I mean," he continued, "if you *were* one of my people, if you *did* trust me, why'd you push me down a staircase, for God's sake? If you were really on my side, you'd be helping me, not hurting me." He shrugged. "This is ridiculous. I'm calling security."

"NO!" the fan yelped. "No, Brian Parrish—please! I didn't mean it. I—it was just like you said! Something came over me! Oh, please. I'd do *anything* for you—*anything* to prove I'm really your fan. Just don't call security, please. I'll do anything you ask."

Brian smiled. "You know, I almost believe you."

He was so upset he actually stamped his foot. "*Believe* me! Go ahead and ask! Anything!"

Brian got to his feet with a little wince of pain. "Ow! Damn. Okay, listen. Here's the deal. There *is* something. And if you do it for me, I'll know you're really a fan of mine. And if you don't, well ..." He looked tellingly toward the telephone again. "In that case, I'll know you're not. So listen up: here it is."

PART
TWO

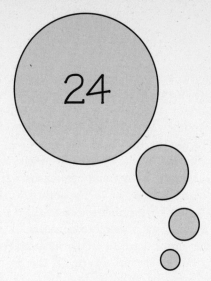

24

Jerome thought, I have *definitely* lost control of this situation.

He was driving his rented Buick back to Park Woods with Brian Parrish stretched out in the back seat—Brian Parrish, his former idol, the man he was now shepherding to an artist's retreat beneath his mother's roof.

"I need *absolute* solitude and *complete* support during the writing of this issue," he'd said, "and only you can give it to me. Get me away from all my detractors, to someplace I can hole up in and feel at home. We'll just leave this hotel, not tell anyone." He'd been in the bathroom when he'd said this, gathering up more men's toiletries and cosmetics than Jerome had ever dreamed existed. "Don't worry about checking out; Bang's paying for the room. Let *them* do it. We'll go to wherever it is you live. Pass me that jar there—the Lancôme Après-Raser—that's right. Anyway, that's where I'll write the issue. You'll see what I'm doing every step of the way. That way, if you have any objections or fears, you'll tell me. That's fair, isn't it?"

It was more than fair! Jerome was so relieved at not being arrested—not to mention at having his longtime idol actually confer this great honor on him—that he fairly shouted his agreement. And with his mother away for an indefinite period of time, there was nothing to hinder him from bringing Brian Parrish home.

It was only now, in the harsh light of day, as he drove down the interstate, getting farther and farther away from the O'Hare Grifton and closer and closer to his hometown, that he realized that this might not be the delirious idyll he'd thought. For one thing, Brian Parrish was proving to be extremely trying company. He'd spent the entire drive so far barking orders: "Get into the left lane; you can go faster." "Turn off the air conditioner; I'm freezing." "Change the radio station, for *God's* sake." An endless litany of peremptory commands.

"Say, how's your gas?" the troublesome cartoonist blurted now, popping his head over the seat to check the fuel gauge. "Still half-full, huh? Well, let's stop and fill up anyway. I mean, why wait till you're on empty? Plus, I need to pick up some gauze or something for my arm; it's swelling. And I'm almost out of gum. I've *got* to have gum. Look, that sign says there's an exit just two miles up." He stuck his good arm past Jerome's face, momentarily obscuring the road; Jerome, startled, inadvertently swerved the car to the left and then fought to regain control of it. "Get off there, okay?" Brian Parrish continued, withdrawing his arm, completely oblivious to the trouble he'd just caused. "See if you can find a gas station with one of those minimarts attached to it." Jerome must have looked at him with naked irritation, because he grew visibly angry and said, "Well, come *on*. I'm going to *need* things if you're going to put me up for any length of time. Just humor me, okay?"

Jerome almost remarked that humoring self-obsessed cartoonists was getting to be rather a specialty of his, but he held his tongue. It would be too absurd to start whining to the man he was supposed to be joyously welcoming into his home as an honored guest. He no longer *wanted* so much to have him as a guest, but as long as he was, he'd better at least maintain the illusion of control. The alternative was simply too disgraceful to consider.

Later, after they'd made the stop, Brian Parrish sat in the back seat and contentedly bandaged his arm with a roll of white medical gauze. Every once in a while, he'd wince in pain and let a blistering "son of a *bitch*" slip out, but he didn't verbally abuse Jerome directly. He appeared to be too happy with his lot to require any of the scalding profanity he'd flung about so maniacally in the hotel room.

After fifty minutes, they were deep in the heart of Park Woods. It was almost four o'clock. The students were all out in the streets, holding hands, laughing, strolling, playing grab-ass in the park. Brian Parrish had rolled down his window, and he hung his uninjured elbow outside the car. The wind tousled his hair as he took in the town's sights. Jerome thought, *He's* in charge here. Why did I let him do this? Why am *I* doing this? He's walking all over me and I have to allow it, just because I got a *little* upset and accidentally pushed him down a couple of stairs. God, isn't there *any* way out of this?

But he couldn't exactly back out—not now. If he did, Brian Parrish would just march to the nearest police station and say, "This man came to my hotel, threatened me, and threw me down a stairwell." And before he could stutter out a denial, Jerome would be in prison getting raped or cleaning toilet bowls with his tongue.

Back when he'd been filling up the car with gas, and Brian Parrish had been in the minimart buying gauze and Dentyne, Jerome had gotten the idea of simply hopping in the car and driving away. Typically self-centered, Brian hadn't even gotten around to asking Jerome's name yet, and Jerome himself hadn't mentioned it. If he just got in the car and drove away, the cartoonist would be stranded off the interstate with no solid evidence as to Jerome's identity. The idea had electrified him with its simplicity, and his heart had begun to pound with excitement—until he remembered what had happened in the hotel parking lot, when he'd been packing the suitcases in the trunk of the car, and Brian Parrish had said, "Hey, look at your license-plate number—QQ 1281! That's a good-luck sign; it's the initials and date of the first

Electric Comic I ever did: the December 1981 issue of *Quasar Quintet.*" So Brian Parrish couldn't possibly forget that license plate, and if Jerome abandoned him, he'd simply use that information to track him right to his lair, for Jerome had filled out the rental papers with his name, address, and driver's-license number.

So he was stuck with Brian Parrish, and stuck good. And yet part of him still managed to be excited by that. Brian Parrish might be an egomaniac, he might be condescending and pushy and demanding—not to mention queer!—but he was *still* Brian Parrish. And the idea of having him as a guest in his house was thrilling beyond belief.

But then he thought of Princess Paragon becoming a depraved libertine right under his own roof. And what if Brian made advances of his own? His head began to spin and his gorge to rise, and suddenly it seemed again that he was trapped in a pit in hell.

"Pretty town," said Brian Parrish, his chin resting on his elbow. He blew a bubble and popped it, then continued to watch in droopy-lidded pleasure as the succession of quaint little vistas drifted by.

Jerome shook his head. He was a bundle of nerves, a quivering mass of anxieties, and Brian Parrish was as relaxed as a kitten. There was no way out of this. Oh, Lord, he prayed; end it now! Let a Mack truck come barreling down the street and roll right over us!

But none did. And Jerome resigned himself to his fate and turned the corner that would take him to his mother's house. He had nowhere else to go.

Brian Parrish sighed and ran his fingers through his hair. "I'm hungry," he said. "Where are we going, when do we get there, and what's in the fridge we can munch on?"

Jerome shook his head. Dear God, he thought; forget everything else I've asked you today. Heavenly Father, grant me but one wish instead, and I will never petition you again. Ever. Not for health, not for happiness, not for wealth or women or work, not for release from my suffering, nor escape from my demise.

Dear God, grant me only this one small thing, this trifling, insignificant favor: *that I get rid of this man before my mother comes back!*

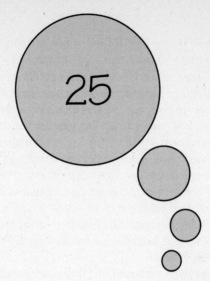

25

His fan turned a corner, and by the way the gravel on the road crunched beneath the wheels of the car, Brian knew that this was not a corner turned very often; those who turned it at all must be those who lived just beyond it.

He realized this but rebelled against the realization, for it was such a squat, ugly little street, bereft of shade or shrubbery, bordered on either side by a row of virtually indistinguishable blond boxes in various stages of disrepair. It was in marked contrast to the resplendent neighborhoods on the opposite side of the campus.

This, Brian deduced, was one of those instant developments that had swept like a plague across the country during the first big baby boom, paving over perfectly charming rural areas with little split-level temples to conformity. Civilization's low point, no mistake. With all the emphasis on speed that the people of that era placed on getting married, having kids, and throwing up houses to move into, you'd think they actually had something pressing to *do* with their lives—some urgent matter that awaited them as soon as they'd established themselves as presto-change-o suburbanites. Brian's parents had been the same way—as a matter of fact, they still were; they rushed out to buy every new convenience, every new timesaving device on the market, and for what? An extra hour or two each night of the television's bluish phosphor haze dulling their skin and clouding their eyes.

Brian had escaped that kind of life; being gay, he'd had to. In the early seventies, gay culture had been a strictly urban phenomenon, so it had been necessary to move to a city. Brian had, characteristically, chosen the largest city in the world, and he was proud to reflect that he'd found fame, fortune, and true love in its dog-eat-dog environs.

Now, as the car turned into the driveway of one of the street's indistinguishable cubes, Brian took a hard look at his host, who was swinging his pudgy arms over the steering wheel, attempting to right it so that he could inch the additional five feet to the garage door. Once this was accomplished, he pushed his glasses up his nose, snorted, and shifted the car into park. Then he turned to Brian and said, "This is it. You can get out now."

Brian nodded and cracked his gum, and as he slipped out of the car and stretched his legs on the pavement he continued to regard his host, who waddled up the adjacent walk to the front door. And, strangely, Brian found himself feeling something close to pity; this blighted corner of a faraway suburb was very close in spirit to the one he himself had fled; but this young man hadn't been so lucky—this young man had not escaped.

A little breeze swept through Brian's hair and tickled his face. He looked around, but there were only a few stray and scraggly trees that he might watch with pleasure as they reacted to that breeze. He turned to his right; there were lawn chairs in the front yard, their legs dug deep into the brown grass. Did his host actually sit out here? And with whom? There were two chairs. Might he be married? Brian hadn't considered that.

Then he turned and saw him fumbling with his keys at the

front door, as though unaccustomed to having to use them. And suddenly Brian knew the truth: it was even worse than he'd thought—he lived here with his *parents*. Not only had this poor, awkward loser not escaped this prefab hell; he hadn't even escaped parental subjugation!

Brian was too stunned to be fully alert, so when he reached the front door and saw the name "Kornacker" above the mailbox—punched out in bas-relief letters on a thin, colored-plastic strip made by one of those ubiquitous 1960s letter-guns—the name had no immediate resonance for him.

Dumbly, he followed his host into the house, letting the ill-fitting screen door slam shut behind him.

The decor was true to the architecture; the house that looked from the outside as though it had been built in a day looked on the inside as though it had been furnished in a day. And Brian was reasonably certain he could pick the day, too: it must have been near the end of the summer of 1964, that period when the country had gone temporarily mad for vinyl. So cheap! So convenient! Just wipes clean! It was exactly the same kind of furniture that filled every nook and cranny of his parents' house, with its easy-care, petroleum-derived splendor. What no one could have guessed then was how the gloss of vinyl would wear down over the years to a dull, dirty smudge; how its color would mutate into something science-fictionally hideous; how it would begin to give off elusive and unsettling odors that didn't remotely correspond to anything in nature.

There was even a bowl of plastic fruit on the coffee table, and a row of plastic flowers planted in real sand along the bottom of the picture window. Oh, Mrs. Kornacker, Brian thought, I know you *so* well.

For it was certain now that this was a mother's house, wherein the son was but a lesser entity. Brian's fan on his own would certainly not possess a curio cabinet filled with cheap porcelain madonnas; and the presence of a yellowing lace coverlet draped across the top of an upright piano (Brian bet himself it was out of tune) argued against the existence of a *Mr.* Kornacker.

As did the calendar over the television, displaying pictures of adorable puppies and kittens at play.

Instead of being repelled, Brian was feeling strangely at home; this was the kind of environment in which he himself had grown up. The one unfamiliar aspect was the proliferation of yellow adhesive notes, which were posted all over the walls of the house. Brian stepped up to the nearest one, which had been stuck above an umbrella stand, and read it. In a jerky, nervous hand, someone had written

Jerome, as you may know, I've decided to go and visit your sister in Akron. Take your shoes off here when you come in.

Brian suppressed a chuckle, then looked down to see that Jerome had, in fact, taken his shoes off at the appointed place.

He entered the living room and found Jerome busy reading the remaining adhesive notes to himself. Brian couldn't resist; he sneaked a glance at another. It said

I do not know when I will return. Weeks maybe. Put the mail here.

He dropped his gaze to the area below the note; there was a small writing desk and on it a letter opener emblazoned with the logo of Sea World.

Poor Jerome, Brian thought, and then he realized that he had inadvertently learned his fan's first name as well. Funny, he hadn't thought to ask before now. Almost reflexively, he put the two halves together. Jerome Kornacker.

Jerome Kornacker.

Now wait a minute, he thought. I've *heard* that before.

He looked over at Jerome, who was reading a note stuck on a mirror by a low doorway. His lips were moving as he read. And Brian had to suppress a sudden shudder.

He *knew* Jerome Kornacker's name. But how? From where? In what context? It was vital that he find this out. He'd thought he had the upper hand in this relationship, but the fact that

Jerome had some as-yet-unrevealed connection with him disturbed him greatly; it threw him off. He'd thought he had Jerome all figured out. Now he wasn't so certain. But he *needed* that certainty. That was the whole point of *being* here.

At that moment, Jerome turned and grinned sheepishly. "This is my mother's house," he said.

Brian nodded. "Gathered that."

"She's left me notes on what to do while she's away." He gave Brian a radiant smile. "She may not be back for weeks."

"*Well*," said Brian, at a loss as to how to respond.

Jerome kept smiling, smiling, smiling, like an actor who's just read his last line but hasn't yet had his cue to leave the stage.

This, more than anything Jerome had done up to now, unnerved Brian. What have I got myself into? he asked himself. I'm in a strange house with a comic-book fanatic who's already demonstrated his capacity for violence. And even though I *think* I've got him under my thumb, what's to prevent him from turning on me while I'm asleep or something?

A little spidery surge of fear scampered up his spine, and he wanted to be safely locked away from Jerome as soon as possible. He rolled his gum into a pellet the size of a ball bearing, then knocked it around his mouth—a sure sign that he was losing his cool. He shifted from one foot to the other and said, "Well, uh, why don't you show me my room now, or something?"

Jerome raised his eyebrows and scratched his belly. "I thought you wanted something to snack on."

Brian was, in fact, desperately hungry, but Jerome was suddenly giving him the creeps, and he wanted to be left alone to think all this through. "Could you just bring something up to me?" he asked. That met with a blank stare, so he added, "It'd help me concentrate on my work."

Jerome shrugged. "Okay." He paused, then began to wring his fingers. "I don't cook," he said, smiling nervously. "Is a bag of Ruffles okay?"

"A bag of *what*?" Brian asked.

"Ruffles," Jerome repeated, his glasses almost fogging with

what Brian guessed was embarrassment. "Potato chips. You know, '*Ruf*-fles have *rid*-ges.' "

Brian flattened his gum into a thin film and then pierced it with his tongue. "I have no idea what you're talking about."

Jerome turned his head; he was blushing so hard he resembled the Red Wraith. "Well, you'll like them. I'll bring them up with a root beer."

"Don't you have any diet dri—" The question died in Brian's throat. All you had to do was look at Jerome Kornacker to know he didn't have any diet drinks in the house. "Forget it. Forget the whole thing."

Jerome shrugged and turned toward the staircase. He led Brian upstairs, and Brian felt uncomfortable at being led farther and farther into the recesses of a house in which he had no place. At the first landing, he actually had to conjure up the image of his future profile in *People* to keep him going.

The second floor of the house was awash in great pools of murky gray dimness; it was obvious that the halls were navigable only by someone who'd spent a lifetime walking them. Brian found himself feeling the walls, like someone nearly blind, as Jerome led him down a seemingly interminable corridor.

Finally, Jerome stopped and opened a door in the left wall. "This is my sister Sandra's room," he said. "She lives in Akron now, so she won't be needing it."

Brian slid past Jerome and into the room, which was dark and quiet. The curtains were drawn and the floor and dressers bare. There was a twin bed in the middle of the room with an enormous poster of a sweaty and shirtless Sting hung over it. Not the most unpleasant of hideaways. Brian began to feel sleepy. He sat down at the vanity next to the bed and looked at his face in the mirror; the bruises around his head and face were unpleasant to behold now—purple and blue and black, like a family of barnacles attached to his face. He shook his head, aghast at his reflection. "Any writing paper in here?" he asked. He should begin working on *Princess Paragon* number three soon; that's why he was here, wasn't it? Away from Perpetrial, away from Nico, away from everyone who had seen "Bella."

"There may be some in the dresser," replied Jerome, the sound of his voice receding.

Brian swiveled in his seat just in time to catch him shutting the door.

"Wait a minute," he yelped, holding out a hand to summon him back. "Where are you going?"

Jerome stood in the hallway, the door open barely six inches. "Why do you want to know that?"

"In case I need to call you," said Brian. "In case I need something."

He could barely see Jerome through the gap in the door; all that was visible were the bottle-thick lenses of his glasses, reflecting the minimal light that spilled from the room. "I'm just going across the hall to my room."

"What about my snack? My 'Ruf-fles have rid-ges'?"

"I thought you said forget it."

Brian rubbed his forehead. "Oh, yeah," he said hoarsely.

Jerome pursed his lips and started to shut the door behind him.

Brian rubbed his forehead again. Fatigue was washing over him. "Wait. Jerome. What's your middle name?"

A long pause. "What?"

"I said, *what's your middle name?*"

"Don't laugh." He blushed. "It's Titus. Why?"

Jerome Titus Kornacker. Jerome *T.* Kornacker. Bells went off. That was even *more* familiar.

"Ever been to New York?" Brian asked, eyeing him in the mirror.

He guffawed. "Oh, my God, no!"

"Jerome, be honest. Have we ever met before?"

"No. I would've remembered. Why?"

Brian put his head in his hands. "I don't know yet. Listen, forget it. You're getting me the *Ruf*-fles with *rid*-ges? I'll wait here."

The door swung open again and Jerome re-entered. His face was scarlet.

"First," he asked, gritting his teeth, "you say you're hungry, then you say you're not. Then you say you are. Which is it?"

Brian felt the need for sleep overtake him. He took his gum from his mouth and stuck it on the vanity mirror, then got up, went to the bed, and lay down. "I'm not," he said as he punched the lumpy pillow twice to soften it. "Stop being such a prick."

"I'm not being a—prick." He whispered the word.

"Fine, you're not," Brian said, resting his head in the pockets he'd made with his fists. "Forget the Ruffles, okay? Just let me sleep for a while." He remembered that he was probably concussed; the excitement of the day was doubtless taking its toll on him. He shut his eyes.

The last thing he heard was, "You are a very strange man. I don't understand you. And I'm not sure I like you."

Oh, *fine*, thought Brian. And then he was asleep. But he wasn't aware that he was asleep; he dreamed that he was where he was, in Sandra's bed, and that Jerome was still there before him, and then Jerome was pushing the bed out the door and toward the flight of stairs and Brian said no don't and Jerome said shut up and then when they got to the top of the stairs Jerome gave the bed a push and—

He woke up. It seemed as though he'd been asleep only moments, but the room was black as ink now. His breath was coming hard; he was like an engine idling too high.

He lay back on the bed and all at once remembered where he'd heard the name Jerome T. Kornacker before. That was the name of the fan who'd sent that loony letter, wasn't it? The one who was romantically in love with Princess Paragon. The one Perpetrial had felt sorry for, back at that Middle Eastern restaurant where Heloise had threatened to sue the manager for the replacement cost of her blouse.

Well, wait till Perpetrial heard about *this*.

He tried to picture her expression, but couldn't. He tried to laugh at the idea of her reaction, but failed. His face hurt, his arm hurt. He'd had no idea this morning that he'd be in so strange a bed tonight, and the whirl of events that had brought him here now seemed confusing and terrifying. He was faintly aware that if he weren't concussed, he might not have allowed his rage and fear such dangerous sway—might not have allowed himself to run away from everything that threatened him into such a strange, unsettling place. As career decisions go, it wasn't just unorthodox, it wasn't just unethical; it was also not entirely safe. Then he remembered the Death card that he'd turned over on the airplane, and for the first time since this entire affair began he felt the full effects of real fear.

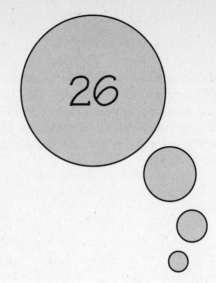

26

Guilt and glee did battle in Jerome's breast as he made his way back downstairs and into the kitchen.

Guilt, because he'd agreed to take his idol, Brian Parrish, under his wing and to give him the privacy he required to finish *Princess Paragon* number three—without ever telling him that he had, in fact, ripped up the first draft of that immoral issue and thrown it in the wastebasket of the cartoonist's hotel room.

Glee, because this gave him the opportunity to delay and maybe even halt the ruination of his beloved Princess. He'd destroyed the Precipitous woman's copy of the script, and he presumed that the only other copy was now upstairs with Brian Parrish, waiting to be refined and polished on pale-blue sheets of Sandra's Kids from "Fame" notepaper. As long as he could prevent that revised script from reaching a mailbox, Princess Paragon would remain a chaste, demure heterosexual. And in the meantime, he'd have time to try and persuade Brian Parrish to see things his way.

In fact, he thought, opening the refrigerator door to find the Entenmann's Louisiana Crunch Cake he'd left half-eaten before going on vacation, as long as he was in this position of power, he could theoretically pass along a *fake* script to that Persnickity woman—one that bypassed the lesbian angle entirely, and thus save his heroine forever!

Suddenly, his hand went still on the refrigerator-door handle; his eyes fogged, and his mouth went dry. Glee began to edge out guilt, and before long had it down for the count.

An idle idea—but so tempting! Who was to know? While Brian Parrish toiled away in Sandra's bedroom, Jerome could be down here at his mother's desk, working on his *own* script for *Princess Paragon* number three. And if he worked quickly enough, that could be the script that appeared in the Bang Comics offices—under Brian Parrish's own name, of course! And once the editors saw how superior it was to Brian Parrish's proposed direction, that would be that. The Princess would be spared— her honor restored before it even had a chance to be lost!

Of course, when Brian Parrish found out, he'd be furious beyond Jerome's ability to imagine. His wrath back in the hotel room over a simple accident on the stairs had been enough to freeze Jerome's blood in his veins. How much worse might his anger be when he discovered this treachery on the part of someone whom he had entreated to prove his devotion to him— someone who had agreed to demonstrate his loyalty as a fan?

This was treachery—sheer treachery.

And, accordingly, Jerome decided against it. Would Acme-Man sneak about behind an opponent's back, subverting his plans like a weasel while outwardly pretending friendship? Would Moonman? Would Captain Fathom, or Speed-Demon, or the Blue Bowman? No, of course not; those heroes would boldly confront the enemy and face him down, man to man! No lurking for them; no subterfuge or crawling, no secrecy, no lies and smiles.

His ethics having been tested and found worthy, he relaxed

his shoulders and sighed. And suddenly he could almost hear his mother at his back, scolding him. "Jerome, for heavens to Pete, stop standing so long with the door open to the icebox! Cold air doesn't grow on trees!"

He removed the Louisiana Crunch Cake and shut the refrigerator, then took the entire box to the sink, opened it, and began clawing up handfuls of the cake, which he unceremoniously stuffed into his mouth. Crumbs tumbled from his lips and fell into the sink. Every few seconds he turned on the faucet and washed them down the drain.

He felt himself bathed in a kind of moral superiority—a halo of a sort, like the one that magically appeared above the Scarlet Seraph whenever he put on his costume and wings. It would've been so *simple* to deceive Brian Parrish—so easy a thing to secretly produce his own, far superior script. The restraint he'd demonstrated in choosing the more difficult path was evidence of his advanced ethical fortitude. After all, he'd chosen to overlook the undeniable righteousness of his cause, not to mention the siren call of intimacy with the one and only Princess Paragon.

He wiped his lips, turned on the faucet, and again sent crumbs whirling into oblivion. Then he crammed another fistful of cake into his maw.

He wondered, How would I have done it, anyway? And purely for the sake of satisfying his intellectual curiosity, he tried to imagine how he would have altered Princess Paragon's destiny, had he been the kind of sneak thief who'd stoop to doing so. After only a few minutes of thought, his chewing became slower, his fingers fell limp over the Louisiana Crunch Cake box, and his eyes began fogging over.

And then he was running a dishrag over his hands and making his way out of the kitchen and over to his mother's desk.

"Just for fun," he muttered, suppressing a burp and moving aside a paperweight that read "World's Greatest Grandma." "Just to *see.*"

And as the hazy gray of dusk crept into the house and sullied the interior light, leaving Jerome squinting increasingly harder at the pages, he hunched over a yellow legal pad and wrote and wrote and wrote, until finally he sat up and decided to have a look at what he'd written, and found to his surprise that he had to turn on a light just to locate it.

In the heat of his creative passion, he'd been flinging paper all over the desk as he ripped the pages from the pad. He picked up one at random and read it.

PANEL FOUR: Cosmique stands before P.P., arms akimbo, her eyes lit with depraved desire. She says, "At last I have found you, Princess Paragon, champion of Earth! Now you will bow to the power of *Cosmique*! I will make you my slave and return you to my planet, where you shall kneel before me and fulfill my every carnal whim!"

PANEL FIVE: P.P. stands, legs wide apart, fists clenched, her look steely and determined. She says, "Never! Never will a princess of Iri allow herself to be bound in servitude to an interstellar wanton!"

PANEL SIX: Closeup of Cosmique pressing her fingers to her forehead. Weird rays emerge from her brow. She says, "Do not be so sure, O proud one! For Cosmique is a Mistress of the Mind, and whomsoever I bid do my will must needs do it!"

PANEL SEVEN: P.P. in agony, collapsed in a crouch, her hands tearing at her hair. She cries, "No! No! What foul perfidy is this? Some sinister force *saps* the fabled Irian will that has heretofore been my most profound power! It cannot be! *It cannot be!*"

PANEL EIGHT: Cosmique stands triumphant over the fallen P.P. and says, "*Oh yes it can! OH YES IT CAN!*"

Jerome shuddered with delight. This was *thrilling*.

He gathered together all the pages he had written and arranged them in order and read them through in one orgiastic sitting. Then he leaned back and actually giggled. This was *much* more exciting than he'd imagined. He decided to keep it up— just for fun, of course.

He looked at the clock: seven minutes to midnight! Tomorrow, he'd figure out exactly how Princess Paragon would beat the evil Cosmique. For tonight, however, his labors were ended. He patted the pages into a nice, neat sheaf and started searching his mother's tchotchke-laden desk top for a paper clip.

In doing so, he accidentally knocked over a pile of mail that had been propped against a Hummel figurine of a raincoat-clad girl under an umbrella. As he reached to the floor to pick up the strewn letters, he froze in alarm. For there, in the midst of them, was an envelope addressed to him, from Carter Foods!

Leaving the others where they lay, he picked up the envelope and tore it open. Then, trembling so violently that he almost ripped it, he unfolded the letter and read it. It was on Carter Foods letterhead, of course, and it was distressingly short and to-the-point:

Dear Jerome:
　　After due consideration of our recent conversation, I have changed my mind and decided that it is indeed high time for Carter to join the 1990s by installing an electronic security system. Accordingly, your employment is to be terminated one week and two days from the date of this letter.
　　I wish you well in your future endeavors.

Sincerely,
Linus B. Pinkerton

The letter was dated Wednesday. Just two days earlier.

Something flickered and smoldered inside him, giving off both heat and smoke. It was the ember of madness, never fully doused by his disastrous confrontation with Brian Parrish. Now it threatened to spark and ignite anew.

So *this* was to be his reward for maintaining his moral beauty? *This* was how the world responded to his self-denial, his humility, his self-sacrifice?

He leaned back in his chair and exhaled. And as he did so he expelled every wisp of the ethicality with which he'd so puffed himself up not three hours before.

Well, *fine*, then, he thought with a sneer. He'd play by the world's rules. He *would* send this script, under Brian Parrish's name, to Bang Comics. Hell, it was too good *not* to! And after all, didn't he have his oath to the Princess to honor? He *must* send it. Let Brian Parrish rage! His editors would force him to adhere to this new direction—Jerome's direction, in which Cosmique was a villainous lesbian mastermind out to test Princess Paragon's character as never before.

And he went up to bed, wondering if Cosmique might not enjoy having a scrawny, sniveling, scampering little henchman named Linus.

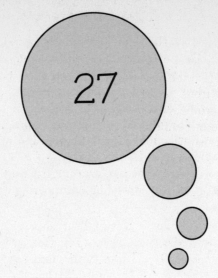

27

On Brian's fourth day in the Kornacker house, he realized he'd spent more time there sleeping than writing. In fact, according to the digital Snoopy alarm clock on Sandra's bedside table, he'd racked up twelve hours of slumber his first night, fourteen the second night, and thirteen-and-a-half the third. He suspected this was due to his concussion; his head still felt jarred, and he had trouble focusing on objects across a room. Well, if what he remembered about concussions was correct, all he could do was wait for his brain to recover on its own. In the meantime, sleeping a lot was probably more helpful than harmful.

Yet in spite of all the time he spent wrapped in the arms of Morpheus, he'd managed to honor his muse as well—so much so that in the late afternoon of the fourth day of his stay, he actually completed the painstakingly difficult final draft of *Princess Paragon* number three. He'd surprised himself by being so incredibly *focused* on the work; the words had just come streaming out of him, deliberately and effortlessly. This was almost certainly the result of being away from all the detrimental, interruptive influences in his life: the panicky phone calls from Heloise, the six-page memos from Perpetrial, the hurtful indifference of Nico.

True, Jerome was sometimes surly or skittish, but he'd largely stayed out of Brian's way—had even given him a little bell to ring if he happened to need anything, which Brian thought was an incredibly submissive, almost feudal thing to do. Which of course made the pleasure of ringing it all the greater.

For a while, Brian had wondered if Jerome's aloofness might be due to a fear of Brian coming on to him sexually—as if he had anything to worry about there! But he showed no reticence in entering Sandra's room when Brian rang for him, and he would even sit on the bed while he took Brian's lunch order or scribbled down the brand names of the ibuprofen tablets Brian required. No, he was clearly staying out of Brian's way because of his sheer awe of him, which was really rather touching. On more than one occasion, though, Brian had caught him eyeing the script-in-progress sitting on Sandra's nightstand, and so Brian knew he was curious about it; but not a word was said. Well, now that he'd finished it, he'd give it to Jerome and ask his opinion. That ought to flatter him. Not that Brian was being totally altruistic in this; he was mad with pride in his work, and wanted to hear it praised. And if his handling of the Princess Paragon–Cosmique love affair could win over a homophobe like Jerome, he'd know it could win over anyone.

Pleased with his benevolent condescension, he packed the script under his arm, crept over to the doorway, and peeked out. Through the perpetual dimness of the hallway he saw that the door to Jerome's own room, which was just a few yards down the hall, was closed.

Feeling somewhat giddy, he crept down the stairs to the kitchen, where he took from the refrigerator one of the six-packs of Samuel Adams lager he'd had Jerome buy for him. Then he slipped back up the stairs and headed down the corridor to Jerome's room, where he stopped, hid the beer behind his back, and rapped soundly on the door.

At once, he heard a flurrying of papers and a shrill "Just a minute," then more flurrying and fluttering and shuffling, and drawers opening and shutting, until Jerome finally opened the door, his face flushed and dewy, and shrieked at him, *"What are you doing out of your room?"*

Brian was surprised by this vehemence, and more than a little put off by it. It was a far cry from the worshipful tone he'd expected.

He refused, however, to let it intimidate him. *"Sorry,* Jerome," he said in a basically pleasant but pointedly strained voice. "I just thought you might like to celebrate with me. I finished the issue." Here he held up both the script and the six-pack, and smiled.

Jerome was so flustered that his glasses fogged up, making him look uncannily like an old Moonman villain, Blind-Man Biff. "I *told* you if you *wanted* me to *ring the bell*!" he snapped.

Brian had had this scene already staged in his head, and he wasn't about to allow Jerome to ruin it by not knowing his lines. He clicked his tongue, said, "Take a pill, Jerome," and boldly shoved his way past him into the bedroom.

"Now *just* a minute," Jerome said from behind him.

"Jesus," said Brian, surveying the room for the first time. "This looks like every poster Bang or Electric ever *produced.*"

A slight pause. "So what if it is?"

Brian turned slowly, taking in the garish gallery that screamed from the barely lit walls. A number of the posters were his own work, and he hadn't seen them in years. There, in fact, to the right of Jerome's creepy unmade bed, was the first poster he'd ever done, of the Quasar Quintet in their Quint-Jet, barreling out of the ozone and speeding straight toward the viewer. Brian winced. Looking at it now, with older and wiser eyes, he could see that Galaxy Man's arm was extended from his body in a way that would be possible only if it were yanked from its socket, and that Intrepid Girl was proportioned so that if she actually got up from her seat she'd be at least two heads taller than any of her massive male teammates. He grimaced in distaste and turned away. It wasn't pleasant having his old work turn up to haunt him.

Jerome was still standing at the door. "I believe you have inadvertently entered my room without having been invited," he said, his nostrils flaring.

Brian dropped the six-pack and the script onto a desk littered with fanzines, food crumbs, and, fortuitously, a pocketknife. "Give me a break, Jerome," he said, pulling the chair from the desk and dropping into it. "Stop talking like a Victorian lady and get over here." He grabbed the pocketknife, located a bottle opener from among its tools, then slipped a Sam Adams from the six-pack and pried off its cap. "Good thing you've got this," he said. "I *hate* twist-off caps." He handed the beer to Jerome. "Give me calluses on my fingers. Here."

Jerome inched toward him. "I'm not accustomed to having my private space invaded like this," he said, his chest heaving in indignation. Apparently Brian's presence was well and truly bothering him.

"No one ever been in the old sanctum sanctorum before, eh?" Brian said merrily as Jerome gingerly took the beer from him. He looked around the shambles of the room. "Certainly no cleaning lady, that's for damn sure." He grabbed another bottle, removed the cap, and took a swig. "No need to be embarrassed, Jerome. I'm a slob myself." He wiped his mouth with the back of his hand. "But when exactly was the last time you had some fresh air in here?" He put down the beer and headed for the window, which he tried in vain to open; a closer examination revealed that it had been painted shut.

"Feels like fucking King Tut's tomb," he said, unbuttoning his cuffs and rolling up his shirtsleeves. "At least let's have some *light.*" He gave the shade a quick tug and released it; it went flapping up to the top of the window. White light surged into the room and immediately filled up every corner, as though it had been anxiously awaiting entry all year. When Brian turned, he saw that Jerome was covering his eyes with his hand.

"Seen too many Dracula movies?" Brian asked.

"The—light," said Jerome, through clenched teeth, "will

fade—the colors—on the posters." He appeared to be shaking with fury.

Brian put his hand on his host's shoulder. *"Chill,* for Christ's sake. If that happens, I'll draw you a new one. Promise. A Brian Parrish original. No cheap-shit reproduction." He gave Jerome a squeeze, then went and sat down again and lifted his bottle. "Okay, then. A toast! Jerome, lift your head up. Jerome! Your head! That's better. All right. Now hold your bottle in the air. Higher. *Higher,* for God's sake. It only weighs twelve fucking ounces! *Okay,* then. A toast to me! For successfully writing one hell-of-a-difficult story that's going to make me both the most notorious and most notoriously *rich* man in comics!"

He waited, but Jerome just sat there, beer in the air.

"You're supposed to echo the sentiment, Jerome."

Something flashed across Jerome's face, too quickly for Brian to pin down; then it was gone.

"To *Princess Paragon* number three," Jerome murmured at last.

"All *right,*" said Brian, and he took a long, sweet gulp. He sighed in pleasure and looked at Jerome. "You're supposed to drink too, Jerome."

He wrinkled his nose. "I don't like beer."

"Jesus! *Humor* me. I'm feeling godlike today. And I don't often."

Jerome looked as though he were going to say something sarcastic, but apparently thought better of it. He sighed, then took a swig of beer and made a face like he'd just been gelded.

"Now, that wasn't so bad, was it?"

Jerome gasped in reply.

Brian sat back in the chair and crossed his legs. "Listen, Jerome, I'm leaving the script here for you to read. You've been—well, I can't say I couldn't have done it without you, because I could, but the fact is, I *didn't* do it without you. You took me in, you gave me privacy, you waited on me hand and foot—I just think I owe you this."

"Oh, thank you, *thank* you. My very great *pleasure.*"

This sounded faintly sarcastic to Brian, but he decided to ignore it. "Plus, I have to tell you. I'm interested in hearing your reaction. I know you're against my making Princess Paragon a dyke"—here another inscrutable flash across Jerome's face—"and so I figure, if I can win *you* over, it's clear sailing with the rest of the world." He took the script from the desk and presented it to Jerome. "Just promise me you'll read it with an open mind, okay, guy?"

Jerome put down his beer and idly flipped through the first few pages. "Of course I will," he said listlessly. Suddenly he stopped and looked up. "Who, may I ask, is the Elder Crone of Iri?"

"Oh, *her*," Brian said, embarrassed that the first thing to catch Jerome's attention was one of Perpetrial's lamebrained additions. "That's the new name for the old Queen of Iri. See, in this new series, there's no hierarchy on the planet, so there's no queen or any kind of—"

"If she's not the Queen of Iri," Jerome interrupted, "then how can Princess Paragon be a princess?"

Brian felt blood rush to his face in alarm. "What?"

"I said, if the Queen of Iri isn't the Queen of Iri anymore, then how can her daughter be called Princess Paragon? If she's not the daughter of a queen, she can't be a princess." He looked up from the script. "You'll have to retitle the series *Ms. Paragon* or something." Jerome seemed almost tickled by this.

Brian was trying to avoid panic. "Not necessarily," he said, his mind racing. "I mean, look at Major Domo and Captain Attack; neither one of those heroes can honestly claim his title, because neither one has ever had any connection to the military. It's just the way they *style* themselves. Same with Princess Paragon." A brainstorm hit him. "Kind of like, in the real world, Elvis was called the King of Rock-and-Roll. Or Bessie Smith, the Queen of the Blues."

"Bessie who?"

"Never mind. Prince, then. Prince isn't royalty, is he?"

"I hate Prince."

"Not the point, Jerome." He took another swallow of beer. "Duke Ellington, too. There are probably a million examples."

Jerome closed the script and tossed it onto his bed (which

Brian thought a shocking show of *lèse majesté*), then sat with his hands folded primly in his lap.

Brian laughed. "Jerome, I wish you'd *relax*. Everything's fine! I'm not judging you."

Jerome became immediately defensive. "That's not what I was thinking! How dare you think I was thinking that? Why would I ever think you *should* judge me?"

Brian shrugged. "Hell, *I* don't know. This dingy room. Comics and fanzines all over the place. Clothes on the floor." He had another gulp of beer, which emboldened him. "Plus, you know, your whole—your *size.*"

All the color drained from Jerome's face. He was beyond white. He was almost translucent.

"You see?" said Brian, pointing at him with the hand that still held the bottle. "Your reaction right now—that tells me everything, right there, pal. *Jesus*, Jerome, you think I haven't been there? *I* was a fat kid, too. *I* had a room like this, too."

Jerome was breathing hard. He pursed his lips and said nothing.

"I mean, yeah," Brian continued, after finishing off the bottle. "I was a little younger than you are—well, a *lot* younger—but, you know, I made my own opportunities. You can do the same thing. I know what you're going through, buddy; *fear* is what it amounts to." He placed the empty bottle on the floor and went for a new one.

"I *am* making my own opportunities," Jerome said, his voice not much louder than a whisper. "You wait and see. You wait and see. Should be a big surprise for you." He trembled. "How *dare* you judge me! You, of all people! A *sodomite*, judging me!"

"You're judging *yourself*," Brian said as he pried the cap off his new bottle. "*I* never said being fat is bad. I just said you *are* fat. *You* made the inference of a value judgment in that." He took a quick gulp of beer and said, "Hell, you should see Hector Baez!"

"What about Hector Baez?" said Jerome with telling eagerness. He would, apparently, respond more positively to the invocation of his idols.

"Guy weighs three hundred pounds if he weighs an ounce,"

said Brian. "Doesn't hold *him* back. Everybody around the office *loves* him." Except me, of course, he added to himself. "Goes in to Bang once or twice a month and every secretary in the place jumps up to hug and kiss him. I was there once; I saw it. No one goes around sneering, 'Oh, Hector's *fat*.' Hector's *Hector*. Know what I mean?" Another mouthful of beer.

Jerome was shaking now; Brian realized with terror that the poor slob was on the verge of a squall of tears. He decided to change the subject as quickly as possible.

"Anyway," Brian said, "I *don't* judge you, because I *like* you. You're okay, Jerome. I mean, who better to go to with a new Princess Paragon script? From what I can pick up, you're the Princess Paragon *expert*." Oh, hell. He hoped that didn't sound as condescending to Jerome as it did to him.

Jerome straightened up. "I am! I have an almost complete set of the series, from number one all the way up to now. Only four issues missing."

"No *kidding*," Brian said carefully, and he emitted a slow whistle.

"No kidding," said Jerome, and, his self-esteem apparently revived by this exchange, he actually picked up his beer again.

"I read through the entire run a couple months ago," said Brian. "Took me more than a week. Gotta admit, most of the issues kind of blend together in my head now. Especially the ones from the fifties, which have this kind of enervating sameness to them." He slugged down another mouthful and belched. "First one I ever read, though—as a kid, I mean—I'll never forget that one. Number one sixty-four."

"March–April, nineteen sixty-six," said Jerome, and he took a tentative second sip of his beer. He grimaced. "Princess Paragon's first battle with Willy Nilly."

Brian slapped his thigh. "*Yes!*" he yelped. He was starting to feel the first hints of drunkenness. "God*damn*, you're *right*! How'd you know that?"

Jerome held his head a little higher. "Like you said, I'm an expert on Princess Paragon." He actually took a full-bore swallow of his beer. He winced a little, but got it down without incident.

Brian laughed and finished off his second bottle. "That's the story," he said, reaching for his third, "that starts out with Willy as a skinny loser getting fired from his job and then rejected by his girlfriend, and then—then something else happens—"

"His car gets towed," said Jerome, who burped as he said it.

"*Right,*" cried Brian. He opened his third bottle. "And then, just as he's standing there cursing the world, he gets hit by mysterious rays from outer space and is suddenly surrounded by an entropy field, right?" He resumed drinking.

"Right," said Jerome, who'd by now finished three-quarters of his own bottle and was appearing more and more relaxed. "He discovers that everywhere he goes, anything within half a block of him just sort of falls apart. Because of his entropy aura. So he becomes a supervillain, and he calls himself Willy Nilly because he can go anywhere he wants and nothing can stop him."

"And then," said Brian enthusiastically, "do you remember the next scene? He goes to his girlfriend's house—"

"—and it just falls apart, all the boards just rot and fall apart," Jerome interjected gleefully.

"And his girlfriend is in the shower, so there she is standing in a towel among the wreckage of her house, and she's demanding to know what Willy did—"

"—*and then the towel rots and falls apart!*" Jerome howled.

They rocked with laughter together. Brian leaned back and actually tipped over in his chair, which inspired them to even wilder heights of hilarity.

He righted himself and sat down again. Wiping the tears from his eyes, he said, "That scene just cracked me up when I was a kid," he said, his voice still wavering with mirth. "Pretty risqué for the mid-sixties, too."

Jerome chuckled. "I agree," he said. He'd finished his beer. "But, I mean, you couldn't really *see* anything. She was naked, but you couldn't—well, not that *you'd* care." He gulped. "Can I—I mean"—he snickered—"*may* I have another one?"

"You *may,*" said Brian with a giggle. He passed a second

bottle over, then said, "Where's mine? Where'd I—I thought I put it—oh, *no!*" He started laughing again, and pointed down to where his upended bottle was gushing beer all over the floor. "Who did *that?*" he shrieked.

Jerome, who was unsuccessfully trying to twist off his bottle cap, went white again. "Uh-oh," he said woozily. "If my mother ever comes in here, she's going to *kill* me."

"She won't," Brian scoffed.

"She *will*," Jerome insisted. "You don't know her!"

Brian crooked his finger and commanded Jerome to come closer. "C'mere," he said. "I got an idea."

"What?" said Jerome, leaning closer.

"C'mere." He crooked his finger until he and Jerome were nearly touching heads. Then he whispered, "Let's kill *her.*"

Jerome turned red, and his face looked as if it would explode; and then it *did* explode, with a sustained whoop of laughter that sounded uncannily like an air raid. *"We'd have to drive a can of Pledge through her heart,"* he squealed when he caught his breath for a moment, and then he and Brian buckled over and gagged with laughter on this positively Wildean surfeit of wit.

A few minutes later, each was sitting limply in his chair, exhausted by merriment. "You know, though," said Jerome, his eyes heavy-lidded, "sheriously—I mean *seriously*—that story, that Willy Nilly story."

"I know it well," said Brian loftily. "March–April, nineteen sixty-six." He giggled, then looked at the empty six-pack. "We've got more of this stuff downstairs, you know."

"No, *seriously*," said Jerome, waving his bottle at him. "It is *not* a perfect story."

"No fucking kidding!" said Brian in mock surprise.

"Really, I mean it." He took a last swig of beer, then dropped the empty bottle to the floor. "Remember the scenes where Princess Paragon attacks Willy, and she's beating him up an' everything, an' all of a sudden she realizes that she's growing really old?" He tried to rest his arm on the back of the chair, but missed.

"Oh, *yeah*," said Brian. "Her hair turns all white and starts to fall out, and then her skin gets all wrinkly. From the entropy aura, right?"

"Right." Jerome's head lolled on his shoulder. "So Aaron Marks yells at her to get away from Willy before she completely decomposes, so she takes this big one-mile leap and lands *waaay* outside the vicinity of the entropy aura, and by the time she lands her skin is all fresh again and her hair is back and all shiny an' everything."

"I remember."

"Well," said Jerome with something close to outrage, *"this would not happen.* Entropy cannot be reversed. It's shilly." He furrowed his brow and shook his head. *"Silly,* I mean."

Brian shrugged. "Well, that's the way comics *were* in the sixties. I mean, none of the guys who wrote and drew those stories back then would've dreamed that grown men would be sitting around discussing them a quarter-century later. They thought they were just producing crap that was gonna be thrown away. But now we *know* better. That's why I'm taking such care, Jerome. I mean, that's why I worked so hard on *Princess Paragon* number three. I *know* these things make a difference. I *know* they can be a positive agent for change. I mean, sure, I'm cynical about it. I'm in it for the money, but Jesus Christ, who isn't? And why shouldn't I be? But I'm not a hack, Jerome. My *name* goes on this. I *care.* And you can trust Princess Paragon to me, I swear. She's my ticket to the top, Jerome. I wouldn't misuse her. I'd be crazy to. You believe me, don't you?"

Jerome's body jumped a little and he grunted like a pig. Snoring.

He was *asleep.*

Brian shook his head and sighed. It was pathetic: the beer virgin and the concussion victim, getting drunk off a single six-pack.

He got up and headed for the door. Then, feeling a kind of fraternal—if not paternal—affection for Jerome, he doubled back and pulled the shade over the window again.

Then he went back to Sandra's room and fell onto the bed, his shoes on the pillow and his head at the foot, and contemplated the sweaty nipples of Sting until he fell fast asleep himself.

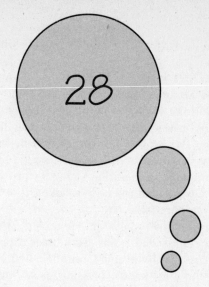

28

Thursday was the penultimate night of Jerome's employment at Carter Foods. As of Saturday, the new security system would be activated, and he would become more of an anachronism than ever.

To soothe his ego during this last week, he'd decided to treat himself by forgoing the bus and driving to work in the rental car he'd hired for his trip to Chicago. He hadn't yet returned it, even though it was costing him a fortune, because he hoped that at any moment he might need it to drive Brian Parrish to the airport. After all, the cartoonist had been here for almost a week, and had long since finished his stupid script, so there was absolutely no reason for him to prolong his stay.

Yet prolong it he did. He said he wasn't leaving till Jerome had read the script and given him his opinion of it. Jerome, who didn't know if he could stomach reading it, had made excuses about being too tired when he got home; but Brian Parrish, sticking his nose where it certainly didn't belong, soon discovered the letter from Carter Foods. (Granted, Jerome had made no attempt to hide it, but had left it lying open on his mother's desk.) So now he knew that Jerome was a night watchman who had exactly nothing to do during his long hours of duty (Jerome had previously maintained that he worked a night shift at a steel mill, but Brian Parrish had never really seemed to believe that); worse, he also now knew that Jerome was soon to be laid off. All of which was potent ammunition to use against Jerome's protestations that he was much too busy to take a look at the script for *Princess Paragon* number three.

So Jerome had had to give in. He took the thing to the plant with him and read it, and it was every bit as depraved as he'd expected: Princess Paragon and Cosmique flying around in the stratosphere, holding hands, praising each other's beauty and valor, vowing eternal love, and at one point even falling into an embrace and kissing.

Even so, the menace facing Cosmique's planet was classic Brian Parrish. Industrial pollution had corrupted the planet's computers, somehow turning its vast network of sentient electronic brains into a single, malevolent artificial intelligence that could "possess" any electronic device, just as a demon can possess a human being. This mad electronic entity, which called itself Lectronn the Conqueror, had tried at first to fulfill its longing to be human by performing the one human function for which it was never designed: reproduction. Failing that, it was now bent on the opposite course: self-destruction, which it could achieve only by entering and destroying every electronic device on the planet, since each one was an integral part of Lectronn's communal intelligence.

Jerome was so impressed by this menace that he stole it for his own Princess Paragon script. He changed the focus so that rather than industrial pollution, it was the villainous Cosmique who created Lectronn the Conqueror, and it was she who had driven it mad with a lust that it could, by virtue of its nature, do nothing to sate.

So Jerome kept hold of Brian Parrish's script until he'd

managed to sift through it for everything remotely worth pil-
fering, which had taken some time. In fact, he'd only just given
it back to the cartoonist tonight, with the comment that it was
wonderful and "very humane." The look of sincere pleasure that
crossed Brian Parrish's face at this was almost more than Jerome
could bear; for ever since their little beer binge, Brian Parrish
had been so unwaveringly *nice* to him—friendly and warm and
appreciative, and even a good listener when Jerome had something to say (which wasn't often).

And it was this that made Jerome want to shout with pride
at the comic shop this afternoon, when Doug and Stickman bent
over the counter and began excitedly analyzing the gossip sur-
rounding Brian Parrish's mysterious disappearance from the convention. Rumor had it that he might have quit *Princess Paragon*,
but nobody knew where to reach him for confirmation or denial,
and there was frantic, hushed conjecture that he might even have
been murdered or something. Jerome had had to bite his tongue
to keep from blurting, HE'S WITH ME! HE'S AT MY HOUSE! HE'S MY
FRIEND! HE LETS ME READ HIS SCRIPTS AND HE ASKS FOR MY *AD-
VICE*!

But, no; he must overcome his pride, quell his hero worship
of Brian Parrish, in view of his larger, more important task. Brian
Parrish, however great his genius, was a mere mortal—and,
Jerome now knew, an erratic and disturbed mortal, at that. Princess Paragon, however, was eternal. Fifty years old and still
young, still radiant, still bursting with everything that was fine
and good in humanity. And that's how she'd be fifty years
hence—a *hundred* and fifty years hence.

Unless, of course, Jerome failed in his task.

Wordlessly, he'd handed over $42.75 for the week's new
purchases. Then he skipped his usual patty-melt-and-onion-rings
lunch because he'd promised to go to the gaudy Thai Palace restaurant on Larch Street and get some takeout food for Brian
Parrish. He wasn't looking forward to this errand; he'd had to
write down the order on a sheet of notepaper while the cartoonist rattled it off to him, and he wasn't sure he'd gotten all the odd
and somewhat frightening names right; there was, for instance,

one dish that sounded an awful lot like Gang Bang Some Young Guy, which was all the more alarming coming from Brian Parrish.

But he'd managed to survive the experience, and was now arriving for work, swinging open the glass door to the Carter Foods lobby and finding it deserted and desolate as usual. As he crossed the tiled reception area, his shoes squeaked like ducklings in the quiet. One more night, he thought; just one more night at the receptionist's typewriter, and *my* script will be finished.

And then he could use the Carter Foods fax machine to send it directly to Bang Comics, with a cover note directing it to Heloise Freitag herself. And not a moment too soon, either. For at the comic shop this afternoon, Doug and Stickman had been singing the praises of that Percipient Cotton woman, who had apparently handled the Princess Paragon slide presentation solo after Brian Parrish didn't show up. She had, so they'd said, handled all the hostility with aplomb, answering every argument with a counterargument that revealed its folly, and everyone in the audience had come to appreciate her enthusiasm and her conviction. This woman, Jerome sensed, could still ruin *Princess Paragon;* that's why it was imperative to sneak his script past her to the publisher's desk.

He fetched his belt and billy club from the utility room and was just fastening it around his waist when Mr. Pinkerton appeared in the doorway, wearing his remarkably crease-free trench coat and carrying his briefcase. "Oh, Jerome," he said jovially. "Hello!"

Jerome hadn't run into Mr. Pinkerton since getting his letter; it was almost as if the man had been avoiding him, which would've been fine. Jerome had no desire to see the smug, oval, unlined face of the traitorous wretch who had fired him. "H-h-h-hello, Mr. P-P-P—"

"No hard feelings," Mr. Pinkerton said, interrupting him, and he extended his hand and smiled one of his eerie, underwaterlike smiles. Jerome took his hand and gave it a limp shake, and after he released it, Mr. Pinkerton astonished him by using it to clasp his shoulder in an almost friendly manner.

"Come on," he said, "I'll show you the new system. That is, if you don't mind—which of course you don't! You're a man, right? You can take it! Progress marches on, eh? This way, out here in the lobby. Watch it, there, watch the billy club, Jero— *Oh!* Never mind; we can replace the vase. Leave it, Jerome, the cleaning lady will—Jerome, I said leave it. Jerome, *leave* it. Now, come over here. See this panel on the wall? This is your rival, Jerome; yes, this tiny thing! Imagine that! Looks like the panel of a push-button telephone in a way, doesn't it? Well, it's much more than that. It's connected to a system of sensors that are set up in every corri— Jerome, are you paying attention? Look over here, then. And stop apologizing, for God's sake. Where was I? Oh, yes. The sensors are set up in every corridor in the building, and they also run through most of the doors and windows. Look here, this is a layout of where we've pl— Don't be afraid of it, Jerome, it's just a sheet of paper. It's not going to bite you. Come and take a look. See those red marks? Those denote the sensor-protected areas. As you can see, virtually every window and door and every stretch of hallway is protected. More than *you* could keep track of at a time, am I right? Now, if there's even the *slightest* movement anywhere in the plant or offices, the sensors will relay that information to a nerve center in Chicago that will then instantly notify the local authorities. The system will even be able to pinpoint the exact location within the building that the intruder is to be found, and direct the police there. All right, you can get let go of the layout now, Jerome, we're finished looking at it. Jerome, let go of it now, pl— You really are something, aren't you, Jerome? Don't apologize, it can be Scotch-taped. I said *don't apologize.* Anyway, what I was about to— Oh, yes. The system will sound a rather deafening alarm at the same time it's alerting Chicago. Would you like to hear it? Of course you would! Hold on, now; I think I've got the code memorized. . . ."

Mr. Pinkerton reached up and began punching in a series of numbers on the panel. Jerome made a mental note of them—3-4-3-4-5-6—after which Mr. Pinkerton depressed a button marked "on."

He waited a few moments, then trotted across the lobby and

opened the front door. Immediately, a whooping, ear-shattering siren filled the air. Jerome jumped almost four inches and tried to stuff his hands into his ears. It felt like some shrieking animal was trying to claw its way into his brain.

Mr. Pinkerton gleefully trotted back, depressed 3-4-3-4-5-6-Off, and the siren stopped.

Jerome took his hands from his ears and gulped.

Mr. Pinkerton grinned and said, "Well, that's really *something*, isn't it? I'm sure you see now why we decided to let you go." He picked up his briefcase and tucked it under his arm. "After the first year, this system will actually cost us far less each month than you do now, believe it or not. No offense intended. Well, in case I don't see you tomorrow, best of luck to you, Jerome." He tipped his hat as he donned it, then turned on his heels and strode out the door like a man who had a date with destiny.

Jerome stood there watching him go, feeling besmeared with humiliation; it seemed to be sticking to him in great clumps, as though it were mud, or chocolate pudding. He took a deep breath and forced himself to think of Princess Paragon—of her shining beauty, her inviolate integrity, her cleanness of spirit—and then he shook himself and set himself to his task. Ignoring his rounds, he went directly to the couch in the reception area, where he lifted one of the cushions and retrieved a sheaf of papers. It was his *Princess Paragon* script, which he'd hidden here at the plant to prevent a nosy Brian Parrish from "accidentally" stumbling across it at the house.

Then, after a few minutes spent cleaning up the vase he'd broken, he sat himself at the reception desk, turned on the typewriter, and in a matter of hours finished his script of *Princess Paragon* number three. He was interrupted only once, by the departure of Irena, the cleaning lady, who since hearing that he'd been let go had developed the distressing habit of bursting into tears and hugging him every time she saw him.

He carried the finished script to the Carter Foods fax machine, prepared a cover sheet, and signed Brian Parrish's name to it, then sent all twenty-seven pages to Bang Comics' office in

New York, which took eleven minutes and forty seconds. (He'd gotten both the fax number and a copy of Brian's signature from Brian's Filofax while the cartoonist was in the shower one morning.) "Thank you, Carter Foods," he muttered appreciatively, feeling deliciously evil.

Then he gathered up the script, took it back to the couch, and stuffed it back under the sighing Naugahyde cushion. It wasn't yet safe to bring it home—not while Brian Parrish was still around.

At the thought of Brian Parrish, he remembered one last task he needed to perform tonight. He left the building and returned to his car in the parking lot, and from the front seat he retrieved a manila envelope addressed to Perpetrial Cotton at Bang Comics in New York, New York. Brian Parrish had asked Jerome if he'd be so kind as to take it to the post office and have it sent Express Mail. Then he'd given Jerome fifteen dollars to cover the cost.

Jerome took the envelope to the back of the plant and tossed it into a container filled with used cooking grease. It caused a little burp in the surface, then slowly disappeared from sight.

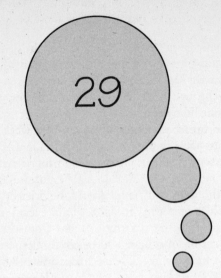

29

Brian belched and tasted curry. Then he got a whiff of it, too, as his expelled breath hovered in front of his face. It was sort of half-appetizing, half-disgusting, and it brought him out of the aimless reverie into which he'd fallen. It was then that he realized he had next to no interest in the public-affairs show he was ostensibly watching on the Kornackers' resplendent forty-inch TV; but even so, he couldn't summon up the energy to reach for the remote and turn it off. Instead, he settled deeper into the pillows on the green vinyl couch, and rested his head dreamily on one crooked arm.

He was feeling wonderfully content. His dinner had been terrific—spicy and alive and hot—and Jerome had even gotten nearly the entire order right (Brian had had fears about this). But more important, Jerome had delivered the food to him with a little ego-stroke appetizer: he'd read the script, he said, and loved it. "Wonderfully humane," he'd called it.

More than ever, Brian was convinced he'd done the right thing by coming here. Jerome's adulation and slavish devotion had been exactly the tonic—and the stimulus—he'd needed. Maybe, once he was back in Manhattan, he ought to look into hiring someone like Jerome as his private secretary—someone who lived and breathed comic books, and for whom Brian would be nothing less than royalty, if not divinity. It would drive Nico crazy, of course, but Nico's attitude was part of the problem that made such a move necessary, wasn't it? And until Nico's income matched Brian's, which it never would, he'd just have to grit his teeth and endure it. Not that Brian would ever be so crude as to put it that way to him.

In fact, despite the sternness of his thoughts, Brian was actually feeling rather lonely for Nico now. His task here was completed; he'd finished the script to *Princess Paragon* number three and even had Jerome send it off to Bang via Express Mail. There was really nothing to keep him here. He could fly home tomorrow morning, and be in Nico's arms by midafternoon.

He toyed with the idea of just showing up at Nico's office and surprising him; but then he remembered the bruises on his face, and decided Nico would keel over in shock if he appeared without warning looking like the receiving end of a battering ram. Better to call him first and tell him what to expect. Actually, it would be a good idea in general to call him, considering how long it had been since they'd last talked: almost a week—ever since that day in the hotel room, just before Brian had run into Jerome and had had that unfortunate (or perhaps, in hindsight, fortunate) scuffle in the stairwell. Before this, the longest he'd gone without talking to Nico had been two days. All the more reason to call him before popping up in his life again. He might well be nursing a whopper of a grudge against Brian.

But then, Brian couldn't blame him. Why *had* he let so much time slip by without calling? Probably the concussion, he reasoned; it's easy to not miss your lover when you're spending more than half of every day sleeping. Well, he'd call him tonight, and that was that. Especially since the public-affairs show he was half-watching appeared to be about ACT-UP, which only served to revive Brian's anxiety about Nico's health. Nico was HIV-positive, and while he'd spent the three years since his diagnosis without a single problem, this could very well be the week that something bad flared up. It was a morbid thought, Brian knew, but a persistent and troubling one. Might Nico even now be in a hospital bed, with tubes running through him, gasping for breath, and with no way of contacting Brian; all alone and in pain and—

Brian sat bolt upright. Okay, he admonished himself; don't get all paranoid or panicky. Just go to the phone and call. He'll be fine. And you'll tell him you love him and that you'll be home tomorrow.

He scampered across the room and dialed hastily. After seven interminable rings, he got the answering machine. "Hi, this is Nico," said the recording merrily. "Brian's off on business, and while the cat's away, the mouse will go to plays! You'll find me on Broadway, wherever an Andrew Lloyd Webber tune can be heard; but if you'd rather not go looking for me there, just leave a message at the tone. And Brian, if it's you calling"—and here he started singing—"Think of me, think of me fondly, when we say GOOOOD-bye. . . ." *Beep.*

Wordlessly, Brian hung up and thought, *Ugh.* Nico had reverted to his old show-queen identity. It had taken Brian months to knock that out of him after they'd met, and *now* look. Out of his sight for only a few days, and he'd snapped back like a rubber band. And the tone of that message—as though Brian were some kind of ogre who had barred him from the Great White Way! Why, Brian *gladly* consented to step out for Sondheim; it was only beyond that that Nico was on his own.

He checked his watch. It was almost midnight in Manhattan. No musical, however bombastic and spectacular, went on this late! Where *was* Nico?

Well, the hell with him. Here was Brian, worrying about his lover lying at death's door, while said lover was undoubtedly out at some crystal-chandeliered piano bar, drunk on Pimm's Cup and singing the entire score to *Mack and Mabel* at the top of his lungs. And God help the rest of the bar's patrons if there happened to be an Ethel Merman wig on the premises.

Who needed this kind of grief? It was exactly what he'd come here to escape.

He returned to the sofa and once again assumed the supine. Then he grabbed the remote from the coffee table, turned off the TV, and settled into a sulk. Suddenly, he wasn't in such a hurry to go home. Nico was apparently doing just fine without him.

And anyway, wouldn't it be kind of rude to just walk out on Jerome after all his hospitality? The more he considered it, the more he thought he really ought to stay and do something nice for the kid—return the favor, as it were. Not that bestowing his celebrated presence hadn't been favor enough, but, well, Brian had become rather fond of Jerome, and believed he understood him.

More than anything, he knew Jerome was lonely. That much had been obvious from the start. But Jerome had surprised Brian by increasingly revealing himself to be, beneath the slabs of fat and insecurity, a potentially engaging human being. The little beer binge they'd shared in Jerome's room had been the first glimpse he'd had of the less inhibited, more likable Jerome. So Brian had spent the ensuing days trying to bolster his host's confidence—much the way that Jerome had bolstered his, by providing this haven of worshipful privacy. Brian had begun treating him as an equal, asking his opinion—on more than just the script—and, most of all, *listening* to him when he spoke. He'd found Jerome's defenses melting away; he was acting happier and more self-assured lately. But he was still secretive; there seemed to be a pocket of his life that he just wouldn't empty for Brian—a little dark, secret space that stalled their conversations into silence whenever they got too near it.

Well, never mind; Brian would think of something to do to repay Jerome before he flew home. And in the meantime, as long as he was going to be here a while longer, why not use the time to his advantage and get a jump on *Princess Paragon* number four? Excited by this idea, he got up from the couch and took the stairs two at a time up to Sandra's room—he was getting quite good at navigating the gloomy hallways now—where he plopped down on the bed and grabbed some Kids from "Fame" notepaper.

Princess Paragon number four, he'd decided, would be a change-of-pace issue, told mainly from the viewpoint of CIA agent Aaron Marks. Since Princess Paragon would soon be leaving Earth for Cosmique's home planet, the issue would open with her saying goodbye to all her Earth friends. But when she flew to Washington to bid farewell to Agent Marks, she'd be told by his CIA superiors that he was missing in action in South America, where it was believed he was being held captive by the head of the cocaine cartel he was investigating: a nine-hundred-pound drug lord called El Humongo. The Princess would then race across two continents to rescue him, and in the meantime the reader would be given a series of harrowing, wrenching entries from the prison diary Agent Marks was secretly keeping on toilet paper in his cell.

The tone of these entries must be exactly right, Brian decided, or they'd sound either too hysterical or too depressing. So he began experimenting with a few practice entries, to find the right balance. Lifting his pen, he wrote:

Again today, El Humongo denied me food and drink until I was weak with hunger; then, at the end of the day, he gave me moldy bread and brackish water. I ate and drank greedily, then threw up. El Humongo laughed at my discomfort. He never questions me, never asks for information, has not to my knowledge demanded a ransom for my release. He seems to want nothing from me but the perverse pleasure of watching me suffer. I dread hearing the floorboards outside the door creak beneath his appalling weight. If only I could find an opportunity to escape—if only there were some disguise I might don and so slip away unnoticed when h

He was interrupted by a shrill summons from the telephone. This surprised him, because it hadn't rung once in all the time he'd been here. Thinking it might be Jerome calling him, he reached over, snatched the receiver from Snoopy's grasp, and brought it to his ear. "Hello?" he said.

A slight pause. "Hi, I—I'm calling for Jerome Kornacker." A woman's voice, of all things!

Intrigued, Brian dropped the notepaper and sat upright. "I'm sorry, Jerome's not here right now. Can I take a message?"

"He's all right, though?"

Brian knit his brow. "He's fine. May I tell him who called?"

"Oh, he probably doesn't remember me; my name's Amanda, and I'm—well, actually, I'm just a waitress at a place he usually has lunch at on Thursday. Sometimes we talk. That's all. It was silly of me to call. Only he didn't show up for his regular lunch today, and I thought—this really is *too* silly." Some nervous laughter. "Please, don't tell him anything. Just so long as he's okay. It was just—nothing. Never mind. Thank you." She hung up.

Brian pursed his lips and listened to the dial tone for exactly eight seconds before hanging up himself.

Then he sat back and smiled. He knew *exactly* what kind of favor he could do for Jerome.

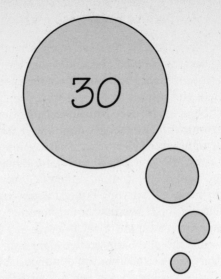

30

Jerome got home from work at 4:30 a.m. and went straight to bed, intent on a good long sleep. But just a few hours later, the unmistakable aroma of frying link sausage wafted into his room and roused him from his slumber.

He pulled on his tattered bathrobe and groggily descended to the kitchen, where he found Brian Parrish at the stove, a spatula in his hand and a miasma of smoke hanging around his head. "What in the world are you doing?" Jerome asked.

The cartoonist turned and grinned at him, and Jerome could see that he was wearing one of Jerome's mother's aprons—the blue one that said "Kiss Me, I'm Lithuanian." "Good morning, sleepyhead!" he trilled. "Pancakes?"

Jerome approached the stove, intrigued. "Where'd you get the makings for pancakes?"

"What do you mean?" Brian Parrish said with a mock pout. He flipped the pancakes, then rolled the link sausages to brown them evenly. "*Every* kitchen has them: eggs, butter, milk, sugar . . ." He cocked his head and winked at Jerome. "Just kidding. I like you, but not *that* much. I went to the market last night and bought a box of the instant stuff. Add water, and *voilà! La pièce de résistance!*" He slipped the spatula beneath the pancakes and slapped them onto a platter containing an already precariously balanced pile of their predecessors. "This enough, or do you think you'll want more?" he asked, dumping the sausages onto a separate plate.

"You left the *house*?" Jerome asked, astonished.

"Well, yeah," he replied. "Christ, Jerome, I'm not Elvis Presley! I may be in hiding, but Joe Average at the U-Tote-Em grocery isn't going to go apeshit at the sight of me. In fact, the only reason anyone gave me a second glance was that my face still looks a little too much like hamburger." He held up the empty, grease-stained pan. "Last chance. More?"

Jerome shook his head, and Brian Parrish plunked the pan into a sink already filled with soapy water. "But how'd you *get* to the market? *I* had the car!"

"I hailed a cab," said the cartoonist. He gave his hands a quick rinse and then dried them.

"A *cab*?" exclaimed Jerome. "In Park Woods?"

Brian Parrish nodded as he undid his apron. "Cabs are like queers, Jerome: whether you know it or not, they're lurking everywhere." He picked up the platter of pancakes and the plate of sausages and gingerly carried them to the table. "Grab the orange juice from the fridge and bring it over, okay?"

Jerome opened the refrigerator and found a tall plastic container of murky orange liquid. "You're obviously feeling better," he said.

Brian Parrish had seated himself and was spreading his napkin across his lap. "Maple syrup, too, if you please; it's right there on the counter. Yes, I'm feeling *much* better. How about you?"

For a moment, Jerome considered saying something sarcastic, like, I'll feel much better when I have a certain cartoonist out of my hair, but then he remembered who this was, and suddenly he realized that *Brian Parrish* had made him *breakfast*. His face flushed. The world's greatest comic-book artist, waiting on *him*? Had someone rewritten the rules of reality while he was asleep, or what?

"Let's tuck in, shall we?" Brian Parrish said gaily as Jerome took his seat.

Jerome twisted the cap off the orange-juice container and poured himself a glass. Then he took a sip and grimaced in disgust. "Ugh! This has *pulp* in it!"

"It's fresh-squeezed, yes," said Brian Parrish as he gnawed on a sausage.

"My mom only buys the kind that doesn't have pulp."

"You mean the kind that's pasteurized?" He shook his head. "Jerome, this is a perfect summation of everything that's wrong with your life. You shouldn't be so *afraid* of the world! Dare to confront things at their full potency. Don't insist that everything be neutered or blanderized beforehand." He nodded in exclamation, then cut into his pancakes like a man possessed.

Jerome frowned, reconciling his longtime awe of the name "Brian Parrish" with what he knew of the actual man. He was getting more than a little tired of that man's incessant advice. He decided to rise above it and say nothing.

"And now," Brian Parrish said after a few minutes had passed in silent chewing, "why don't you tell me about Amanda?"

For a split second, Jerome felt the carnival-ride, floor-drop-away disorientation that he experienced only when some thread of his life inexplicably crisscrossed some other completely incongruous one. How in the *world* did Brian Parrish know about Amanda? Could he have seen her at the U-Tote-Em? Unlikely; and even if he had, what would have inspired him to *approach* her? It's not as though he could've known just by looking at her that she was an acquaintance of Jerome's.

Brian Parrish was smiling like a game-show host. "You should see yourself," he said, laughter bubbling up in his voice. "You've gone white as the Ivory Avenger. And your jaw's hanging open."

He shut his mouth and put down his fork. "How do you know Amanda?"

The cartoonist was busy masticating a cheekful of pancakes. He made a motion for Jerome to wait a moment, then, after he'd swallowed, said, "What's it to you?"

Jerome had absolutely no idea how to answer this.

Brian Parrish gulped down some orange juice and said, "Your jaw's dropped again."

Jerome clamped it shut. He was starting to get angry. "Would you *please* be so kind as to tell me *how you know Amanda*?" he bleated.

Brian wiped a smear of maple syrup from his mouth, then said, "Jesus, don't get so *testy*." He shrugged. "She called here last night."

"She called—*here*?"

"Yeah. Said you'd missed your usual Thursday lunch and was concerned you might be sick or something." He leaned across the table and said in a low, throaty voice, "She was *concerned*, Jerome."

Jerome panicked. "I b-b-barely know her!"

"I never said otherwise."

"You had no business talking to her!"

"So sue me."

"What did you say to her?"

"I lied. I said you'd told me all about her, and then I asked if she was really as beautiful as you said she was."

Jerome felt the world go quite white for a moment; and the next thing he knew, Brian Parrish was beside him, pounding him on the back and saying, "Jerome! I was kidding! Come on! Snap out of it!"

Feeling faint, he grabbed his glass of orange juice and took a large swallow, then started to choke when he tasted the pulp.

Brian Parrish dared to laugh. "Have you got it *bad*, or *what*," he said, returning to his seat.

"What's—that—you said?" Jerome sputtered.

The cartoonist cut himself another wedge of pancake. "I could tell from Amanda's tone of voice that she had some kind of thing for you, and I was wondering if you had some kind of thing for her, too." He popped the pancakes into his mouth. "I guess you do."

"I do *not*."

"Trust me, Jerome," he said, casually waving his fork at him, "I have more experience in these matters than you do."

"Yeah, with *men*," Jerome said with a sneer. "With other *sodomites*. What do you know about *normal* people?"

Brian Parrish reddened for a moment. "Don't let's get talking about 'normal' people, Jerome," he said, not a trace of humor in his voice. "I somehow don't think that'd make either one of us very happy."

Jerome snorted and pushed away his plate.

"Now, then," Brian Parrish continued, seeming to regain his spirits, "the question is, what are we going to do about this little romantic stalemate?"

"Stalemate?" yelped Jerome. *"We?"*

"You're hot for her," Brian said, swinging an impaled sausage to his right, "she's hot for you," he continued, swinging it to the left, "but somehow no one's willing to come right out and say, '*Do* me, baby.'" He sucked the sausage into his mouth, whole.

"This is *really* the last straw!" Jerome cried, shoving his chair away from the table.

Brian Parrish leapt to his feet as Jerome stormed out the door. "Give me *one* good reason why you shouldn't ask her out," he called after him.

Jerome whirled his head and snarled, "It's none of your *fucking* business."

"I said a *good* reason," Brian Parrish countered, following him out of the kitchen. "And listen, don't say 'fucking' anymore. You don't say it right. You say it like the Queen Mother."

"God—*damn*—you," Jerome choked as he started up the stairs.

Brian lifted the receiver from a phone on a table near the bottom of the stairs and held it toward Jerome. "Shall I dial for you?"

Jerome looked down at him and laughed. "You don't even have her number!"

"Do *you*?"

His face must have given him away, because the cartoonist smiled in triumph. It was true; Jerome had looked up Amanda's number some months ago, and committed it to memory. Just in case—

"Jerome, I'm still waiting for one good reason. Just *one.*"

He sensed himself on a precipice. After all, he still nourished hope for his future: someday he'd strike out on his own, someday he'd find a wife, start a family. But now Brian Parrish was forcing his hand on this particular hope, and Jerome somehow realized that if he refused, he could never have it back; it was now or never. God damn it! God damn Brian Parrish!

Trembling with fear and a weird kind of euphoria, he came back downstairs and grabbed the receiver from Brian Parrish's hand.

"Ask her out for tonight," the cartoonist said. "Don't give yourself a few days to change your mind and cancel."

"I can't," Jerome said, aghast. "I have to work tonight!"

"So you miss it, or show up late." He shrugged. "What are they going to do—*fire* you?"

Jerome took a deep breath and began dialing. "If she says no, I am going to kill you," he growled ferociously.

Brian Parrish laughed. "Oh, I wouldn't do that," he said. "You'd never find out how Princess Paragon defeats Lectronn the Conqueror, then, would you?"

Amanda's line started ringing. Jerome squinted and shook his head. "You fatuous egotist," he said. "What makes you thi—"

"Hello?" It was Amanda's sleep-drenched voice, sounding just a touch alarmed.

"Oh, I'm sorry," said Jerome, realizing for the first time that it was only a quarter past seven in the morning. "Did I wake you?"

"A little. Who is this, please?"

Brian Parrish grinned, then ambled back into the kitchen.

"It's Jerome. Jerome T. Kornacker."

A slight pause; the sound of rustling sheets. Jerome pictured her checking her clock in disbelief. "Hello, Jerome," she said, sounding puzzled, but not displeased. "What a surprise!"

"Listen," he said, his tongue suddenly feeling thick in his head. "Um—Amanda—I—I was wondering if maybe—um . . ."

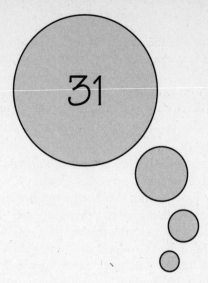

31

Getting Jerome off on his date had been hard work, and Brian was feeling it. He lowered himself onto his bed (funny, he no longer thought of it as Sandra's) and wondered how it was possible for someone to have a closet full of shirts without having at least one that a Third World refugee wouldn't turn up his nose at. And pants! All of Jerome's had worn perilously thin and had horrid little balls of polyester clinging like spider eggs to the areas where his inner thighs chafed against each other. Plus, no decent shoes, no ties that weren't stained or clip-on, and no suitcoat that could be buttoned without putting the unsuspecting Amanda at risk of getting hit by a tiny plastic projectile should Jerome accidentally inhale too deeply. In the end, all Brian could do was make Jerome promise to take her someplace dark, and hope for the best.

He felt the room spin as his head settled onto the pillow, but not nearly so vertiginously as yesterday; he must be recovering, if slowly, from his concussion. Well, never mind, he'd be home tomorrow night, and in Nico's care—if Nico could bring himself to resist the siren call of the cast of *Cats*, that is—and he'd have the Leonards to play with, and his own bed to sleep in, and his medicine chest and video collection to dig through, and all his mail to answer, and everything would be all right again.

Still, it had been worth staying the extra day; Jerome's gratitude had been more sincere and more touching than Brian had ever expected. He'd been nervous and silent throughout most of the preparation for his big night out, until Brian was brushing off his jacket and heading him out the door; then he'd turned and blurted that he wasn't worthy of this, he wasn't worthy of Brian's friendship, and if Brian only *knew*—but Brian had shushed him and said don't be silly and sent him on his way. It was the perfect way to end his visit; he felt like a character in a Vincente Minnelli movie, someone glamorous and important who sweeps into a nonentity's life and redeems him. Not without being somewhat redeemed himself, of course, but that was just a grace note in the overall theme, wasn't it?

Filled with contentment and self-love, Brian let the waves of exhaustion tug at his thoughts until they dragged him easily into sleep, and his dreams were soothing and colorful.

He awoke with a start sometime later, feeling something warm and moist and alien lying on his face. He tried in vain to slap it away from him, but found himself strangely disabled; his right arm wouldn't work. So he sat up and scooted over to the edge of the bed, and the thing that had been on his face fell onto the pillow where his head had been. Brian, breathing hard, stared at it until his eyes adjusted and he could see that he was looking at his own right hand. Obviously, his arm had fallen asleep—he must have been lying on it—and when he rolled over, his meaty, dead hand had flopped onto his face like the hand of Doctor Zombie or Ursula Undead.

Relieved, he started to laugh; he wished he had someone with whom to share this comical moment. He looked at the clock: it was just a few minutes shy of midnight. He got up, shak-

ing his arm back to life, and padded down the hallway to
Jerome's room. He knocked softly, but got no answer.

"Jerome," he called out in a low voice. "Home yet, buddy?"

He waited a moment for a reply, then turned the knob and
opened the door. Peeking in, he could see that Jerome's bed was
empty. He smiled. The date was continuing later than he'd expected; that could only mean it was going well.

He felt a slight headache coming on—no doubt from all the
excitement of the day—and so returned to his room for a couple
of Advil. But to his dismay, the tiny plastic bottle held only one
caplet, which was scarcely enough to do the job. He swallowed
it anyway, then wondered if there might be an additional supply
somewhere else in the house.

He went back to the hallway and started down its length.
The first bathroom he came to was Jerome's, but Brian was reluctant to enter it; he felt certain Jerome wouldn't approve of yet
a further erosion of his privacy. So he continued to the next
bathroom, which was connected to the bedroom used by
Jerome's mother.

Brian switched on the light and gazed at the expanse of
peach tiles and peach floor mats and peach bath towels. He
noted a pill dispenser with seven drawers marked with the days
of the week; dusty flower-shaped soaps sitting in a gold dish, as
if they were being held in reserve for a special occasion that
would never come; a bathroom scale with almost the exact shape
of a pair of bare feet worn away from its ancient surface. It reminded Brian of his own mother's bathroom: an inner sanctum
where private female anxiety could be given full vent.

He sat down at the vanity and opened the top drawer. To his
surprise, he discovered a treasure trove of lipstick tubes—more
than he'd ever seen in one place before.

"There must be a *hundred* here," he muttered in awe, running his fingers through them as though they were coins. "She
can't possibly *wear* all these!"

And sure enough, he opened a few and found them untouched by human lips, boasting the same smooth contours and
glossy surfaces they'd had since their manufacture. Brian won-

dered if maybe Mrs. Kornacker was just an obsessive collector of lipsticks, the way that Jerome was an obsessive collector of comic books.

An urge welled up in him, and not only was it irresistible, he saw no reason even to attempt to resist it; it wasn't as though Mrs. Kornacker would ever know the difference. So he swiveled her makeup mirror to show his face to best advantage, then puckered his lips and artfully applied a lipstick shade called Evening Pomegranate.

He smacked his lips and studied his reflection. He hadn't looked this fey in years—not since he'd gone to a Fire Island drag party dressed as Susan Hayward. How long ago had that been? Fifteen years, probably; almost everyone he remembered as having been there was now dead. Suddenly he felt silly and lonely and depressed, so he gave in to his worst impulses and started digging through Mrs. Kornacker's vanity drawers. Within a half-hour, he'd completely made up his face.

"God, am I *aging*," he moaned as he finally lay down the eyebrow pencil and examined his handiwork. "Last time I did this I looked like a whore. Now I look like a madam."

Emboldened by his new face, he strode into Mrs. Kornacker's bedroom, switched on the overhead light, and threw open her closet. His eyes fell immediately on a glorious peacock-pattern kimono that looked as though it had never even been worn. And sure enough, the store's tag was still on the sleeve. Gleefully he took it from the closet and slipped its cool silkiness over his hairy, naked body.

He shut the closet to see how he looked in the full-length mirror that hung on the door. He'd thought he might look like a geisha girl, or at the very least a particularly *gamin* geisha boy; instead he resembled a dowager empress of Japan. He decided it must be the lighting, which allowed his bruises to show even through the heavy makeup. He returned to the far kinder illumination of the bathroom.

He *did* look better here; so he brushed his hair a little and admired himself. Then he seemed to realize for the first time who he was and where he was, and the surreality of the situation startled him. He sighed, and said aloud, "What the hell am I doing here?"

He made up his mind that it was long since time for him to go home. And since he was now awake, he'd go back to his room and start packing his bags.

But first, he must answer the call of nature. He stood before the toilet and lifted the lid; then he hiked up the kimono with one hand, grabbed hold of his penis with the other, and directed a noisy stream of urine into the bowl.

He was still at it when a voice behind him cried, *"What in the name of Sam Hill is going on here?"*

He whirled, so startled by this intrusion that he didn't think to stop pissing, with the result that he found himself drenching the shoes of a tiny middle-aged woman with puffy peach hair, who wore a peach pants suit and stood next to two peach suit-cases, and who stared at him with furious, steely-gray, unforgiving eyes.

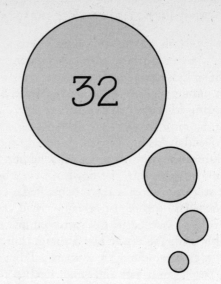

32

The Amanda who dashed out to Jerome's rented car from the door of her squat little apartment building was a very different Amanda from the one he thought he knew. Her hair was piled on top of her head in a half-chic, half-haphazard fashion, and she was wearing a very short dress with a kind of floppy halter top held up by very, *very* thin straps. She wore what Jerome considered dangerously high heels, and carried a black purse that didn't look big enough to hold more than a credit card.

As she drew nearer the car, Jerome could see her breasts flopping beneath the loose dress, like sentient beings trying to escape it. He felt his penis start to come alive, and put his hand on it to keep it at bay. Amanda's heels click-clicked down the pavement, and Jerome was certain that this was some kind of Morse-code message along the lines of "Danger—Woman Seeking Sex!"

She flung open the car door, provocatively slid herself inside, and gave Jerome a dazzling smile. Then she slammed the door and immediately flipped down the passenger sun visor so she could check herself in its mirror.

"Perfect timing," she said, using her little finger to rub a fleck of mascara from the corner of her eye. "Sitter just got here."

"Sitter?" said Jerome. "What sitter?"

She flipped up the sun visor and buckled her seat belt. "The babysitter. For the kids."

"You have *kids*?" he asked, dumbfounded.

She pulled her dress down a bit—it had ridden up when she'd buckled the seat belt—and then sat primly, her hands folded over her purse, ready for the evening. "Uh-huh," she said. "I never mentioned them? They're why I first noticed you, Jerome. My kids love comics, too, so when I saw you in the snack bar so wrapped up in reading yours, I kind of felt all maternal toward you." She smiled and looked at the steering wheel, as if to say, Anytime you're ready.

Jerome pushed his glasses up the bridge of his nose. "You never said you had kids before."

She shrugged. "Well, I do." She arched an eyebrow slightly. "Does it matter?"

Of course it matters, he thought; but he couldn't tell her that. He looked at her, and instead of seeing a kindred spirit—a lonely soul, a virgin soul, a trapped houseplant craning its stem toward the sun—he saw her as she really was: someone who had gotten farther down life's path than he had. He was no longer her rescuer from the despair of solitude. Quite the contrary; she was *his*. He still lived with his mother; she *was* a mother. It was mortifying.

He shifted the car into gear. "No, it doesn't matter," he said in a voice that clearly implied that it did.

They drove in silence for a few minutes, until Amanda said, "This is a *very* nice car, Jerome. How long have you had it?"

"A few days."

"Oh," she trilled. "It's new? How exciting for you!"

"No, no, I'm just renting it."

A pause. She readjusted her purse in her lap. "Well, all the same. How exciting to have a car!"

He signaled left, then took the turn rather too abruptly; Amanda's body slammed against the passenger door. When he straightened out the wheel he said, "Don't you have a car?"

She shrugged off the jolt, patted her hair, and attempted a smile. "Well, yes, actually, I do." Jerome grimaced, and she hastily added, "A very *old* one. More of a deathtrap on wheels, actually. I hate letting the kids into it." She laughed nervously.

"Where's their father?" He'd blurted out the question before he could stop himself, sounding like a prosecuting attorney.

Amanda stared at the road ahead. "I'm not quite sure," she said. "Wherever he is, he can stay there." Another pause. "He'd *better* stay there."

Jerome was stunned by her tone. He'd never heard her speak with anything less than delight in her voice. This quiet anger—it was something new. It shocked him into silence.

The silence lasted until they reached the restaurant, and even then ended only with trivial exchanges of the I-think-I-see-a-parking-space variety.

The restaurant bore an Italian name, so Jerome, whose experience of restaurants was lamentably scant, had thought it must be fancy; he saw his error immediately upon entering. It was nothing but an elaborate, multilevel pizza parlor and was infested with college students of the type that made him cringe in fear. An old Doors song was playing at just a few decibels short of blowing off the roof, and the whole place smelled of beer. Jerome's shoes were sticking to the floor.

Instead of a well-groomed maître d', like he'd seen in the movies, they were approached by a diminutive Asian woman with an astonishing patchwork haircut, wearing blue jeans and a Megadeth T-shirt and carrying a walkie-talkie. "Two?" she shouted.

Jerome nodded.

She switched on the walkie-talkie. "Calling Ass-Wipe; come in, Ass-Wipe."

A crackle of static, then a scratchy response: "No Ass-Wipe here, and fuck you, too."

The Asian woman laughed. "How's it look on three for two?"

"Three for two—copacetic, Red Leader."

"Coming up, then. Smoking or non?" This last to Jerome.

Jerome looked around the restaurant. Was it *possible* to find a place without smoke hanging over it? "Non, please," he shouted.

"Actually, if you wouldn't mind," Amanda said, pulling out a nearly crumpled pack of Winstons from her purse and tapping one out. Jerome's eyes bulged out of his head.

"Make it smoking, Ass-Wipe," the Asian woman bellowed. "Red Leader out." She switched off the walkie-talkie and hung it on her belt. "They'll seat you up on the third floor," she said. "Stairs are over on your left."

"Isn't there an elevator?" Jerome asked mournfully, faced with the prospect of hauling his great bulk up three entire flights.

"Sorry, pal," the woman said. She jerked her thumb toward the staircase. "It's that way or the highway."

Amanda went tripping lightly up the stairs while behind her Jerome struggled to keep up. Soon she was so far ahead of him that he was sweating in embarrassment. If only she'd just *wait* a second . . .

And at that moment he got his wish, for someone coming down the stairs did indeed stop Amanda, by grabbing her arm. It was another woman, a redhead, with snaky tendrils of coiled hair; Jerome thought she looked exactly like Baron Bravissimo's mortal enemy, Mistress Medusa.

"Aman-*daaa!*" she shrieked, and Amanda shrieked back, and they fell upon each other with hugs and kisses. Jerome, huffing and puffing, had almost caught up by now.

The woman held Amanda at arm's length and said, "You look great, just *great*. God, I haven't seen you in—it must be since graduation!"

"Well, you know," said Amanda, shrugging, "work, kids—it

takes a lot out of you. Now, a big night for me is when there's a miniseries on TV."

Mistress Medusa shook her serpentine head sadly. "And you were such a party *fiend*. I idolized you my freshman year!"

"I remember. You were such a kid then! It was like having a sidekick."

Jerome was standing on the stair below Amanda now, but Mistress Medusa hadn't even looked his way. Instead, she leaned close to Amanda and stage-whispered, "And what about El Hunko Supremo? What was his name—Craig?"

"Yes, Craig," said Amanda, color draining from her face.

"Heard you up and married him!"

She looked at her feet. "Well, yeah."

"And how's that?"

Amanda sighed and met her friend's eyes. "Didn't work out." She switched her purse to her other shoulder; a nervous gesture, Jerome guessed. "Had two terrific kids together, but— eventually, I just had to walk."

"Oh my *God*," said Mistress Medusa, placing a hand on her heart. "What was the problem?"

"*You* know," said Amanda.

"I do? *Me? What?*" She stared pleadingly at Amanda, who returned a meaningful gaze, until she grabbed Amanda's wrist and said, "Oh, no. He was still *hitting* you?"

"*Beating* me," Amanda corrected her. Then she pointed to the scar above her temple. "One of his little mementos," she explained with an unconvincing laugh.

Mistress Medusa gasped. "*Jesus*," she said. "I thought he'd stopped that!"

"Yeah, well, so did I."

Jerome's face was now filled with all the color Amanda's had lost. She'd told him that scar was from a childhood bicycling accident! Amanda had *lied*.

"Well," said Mistress Medusa with a sigh, as if to say, At least you're out of it. "You seeing anyone now?"

Amanda turned and, for the first time since mounting the staircase, acknowledged Jerome's presence. "Actually," she said,

"I'm being squired by Jerome here tonight. Jerome Kornacker, Wendy Felman."

"Hello," said Jerome timidly. He extended his hand.

Wendy shook it weakly, her smile visibly wilting as she gave him the once-over. "Oh. *Hi.*"

Amanda put her hand on Jerome's shoulder. "It's nice to be out with someone considerate and gentle and kind," she said. Jerome realized that this statement was meant to perform double duty: it was to tell Wendy Felman that Amanda was dating Jerome precisely *because* of his lack of machismo, which he personally found offensive; and it was also to tell Jerome that Amanda expected him to rise above his disappointment at discovering she had children, which he didn't like much better.

Wendy was clearly put off by Jerome; she turned away from him, leaned in close to Amanda, and said, "Listen, *call* me. I *mean* it." Her unspoken but implicit message was, I can set you up with better guys. "I'm in the book. Look me up. I'm *serious*, Amanda."

Amanda laughed. "Okay, I promise." She kissed Wendy goodbye and continued climbing to the third floor, where she and Jerome were seated at a small table in the middle of what must have been an all-out frat-brother binge. At one point a lanky, bleary-eyed boy in a rugby shirt actually passed out while walking and plummeted to the floor not six inches from Jerome's lap. Jerome found it difficult to be quite comfortable after that.

Dinner was a strange experience. Amanda was still Amanda; she delighted in everything ("This pizza is *delicious*! Do you come here often, Jerome? If I had the budget, I would!"). But she smoked and crossed her legs like a sexually experienced woman, and when she leaned forward to hear what he was saying, her breasts hit the table and flattened there just as they would if he pressed them with his hands.

Whenever he began to feel aroused, however, he would look at Amanda's scar and think, Liar, liar, *liar.*

Amanda must have caught him looking at it, however, because at one point she self-consciously touched it and said, "Oh, Jerome. I never did tell you how I *really* got this, did I?"

"No," he said, a little sneer in his voice. "You certainly did not."

She grimaced and lit a new cigarette. "I'm sorry you had to hear the truth on the stairs like that. It's just that when a woman gets beaten up by her husband, people tend to think it's her own fault. They think she must've brought it on herself. If I went around telling people my husband gave me this scar, they'd think, Well, she probably deserved it." She took a drag off the cigarette.

"You didn't mind telling your friend Wendy," he said accusingly.

She blew the smoke out of the side of her mouth. "Not the same thing. First, she's a woman; second, she knew me when I'd just started dating Craig. He slapped me around a few times back then, and Wendy always gave me a hard time when I made excuses for him." She sighed and her eyes grew distant. "Maybe I *did* bring it on myself. By not having the courage to walk away at the beginning."

Jerome had no experience with this kind of talk and found himself unable to respond. He looked down at his pizza, bewildered; and then, after a pause, he resumed eating it.

As Jerome chewed on a gratifyingly big chunk of pepperoni, Amanda snapped out of her funk and said, "But, listen, I really did mean what I said on the stairs. Your kindness, your gentleness—they're special. The sight of you in the snack bar with your comics always touches me. There's a kind of honest simplicity about you that I admire. I'm *very* grateful that you think enough of me to take me to dinner!"

This was almost exactly what Jerome had always longed to hear from a woman—what Garrett Trench had always longed to hear from Nora Nash—but now that he was finally hearing it, it repelled him. Amanda was making him sound like some kind of docile sheepdog! He felt like telling her that only a week before, he'd personally thrown a perverted cartoonist down a hotel stairwell, and what did she think of *that*?

But instead he said, "Thank you very much," then licked his lips and took another slice of pizza from the gooey, fibrous pie.

When he lifted his eyes, he found Amanda looking at him in a funny manner, a manner that made him nervous. He cleared his throat and said, "So, what comics in particular do your kids like?"

After dinner, all he could think was, I want to go home, I want to go home. Amanda, however, said, "It's still early. Want to go to a bar or something?"

A *bar*! Lord Jesus Christ in heaven! What *next*?

"Actually," he said, "I'm a little tired. May I take you home?"

She sighed, and her eyes darkened a little; it was as if she were thinking, Well, I gave it a shot. "Sure," she said, attempting a smile. "Long day tomorrow, after all!"

The ride passed in silence, and when he pulled up in front of her apartment building, she turned and said, "I had a *wonderful* time, Jerome!"

"Thank you," he said. "I mean, you're welcome. I mean, um—"

She leaned over and kissed him on the cheek. His penis sprang to attention, as though a kind of biochemical reveille had been played.

Then she opened the car door and slid out. On the sidewalk, she yanked her skirt down again, then turned and said, "You don't have to see me in, I'll be okay. Thanks again, Jerome, and good night!"

Jerome watched her clickety-clack up the sidewalk, slip her key in the door, and disappear. She never even turned back.

He drove the car around the corner, stilled the engine, and sat there, his mind a whirl of lust and envy and self-recrimination.

All he knew for certain was that he couldn't go home this early; Brian Parrish would only make fun of him.

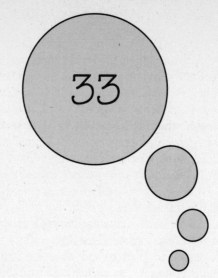

33

It was ridiculous, and Brian knew it; but all the same, as he lugged his hastily packed suitcase and cosmetic kit down the gravel road (one shoe flopping annoyingly because he'd been in too much of a hurry to tuck in his heel), all he could think of was the "Interstellar Odyssey" serial he'd written for *Quasar Quintet.* That had begun with the much-misunderstood fivesome being chased off Earth by a massing of the world's great air powers, leaving them wandering through space in their Quint-Jet, their hearts heavy and their futures uncertain. "Where do we go now?" Intrepid Girl had asked plaintively, leaving Galaxy Man to gnash his teeth and reply, "God help us—I just don't *know....*"

Well, that was a position with which Brian could now sympathize. Having been chased from the Kornacker house by a peach whirlwind of righteous anger and mangled syntax ("You'd better take that kimono off and get amscraying because I'm right now calling the police up! And don't even *think* of trying to rape me because I learned Joe Jitsu at the community center!"), he had no idea at all where to turn. He lowered the suitcase for a moment, pulled his handkerchief from his pants pocket, and wiped frantically at his face; he hadn't even had time to wash off his makeup, and knew what he must look like.

At the corner, where the gravel road intersected the wider, paved thoroughfare, he stopped to consider his next move. To help him think, he took a stick of gum from his shirt pocket and popped it in his mouth. Chewing it, he felt some measure of relief; its soothing spearmint powder melted over his tongue and made the world seem less threatening.

Just then, however, a car appeared from over a rise to his right, its headlamps like a pair of prison-yard searchlights, and Brian dove for the cover of a hedge, almost swallowing the gum—and leaving his suitcase sitting on the side of the road. The car passed, and he crept out.

He took his wallet from his back pocket and checked his supply of cash. He had enough to hail a cab to the airport, but where was he going to find one, in the middle of a residential district in the middle of the night? It was ironic that only this afternoon he'd boasted to Jerome that, being a seasoned city dweller, he could find a cab anywhere, whereas in reality he'd had to call a dispatcher to send him one for his trip to the U-Tote-Em. Was this God's way of getting back at him for lying? Nico was always saying the Almighty would have His revenge on Brian someday.

Well, even if he could find a cab, he knew he wouldn't have the nerve to take it—not now; not with the police out looking for him. What would he do if a squad car investigating Mrs. Kornacker's call happened to stop the cab? Would he bolt, make a run for it? He'd have to; he couldn't very well surrender—not to the police, and God, not looking like this . . .

He took out the handkerchief again and gave his face another rubbing.

A second car came over the rise, and Brian dove back behind the hedge. But instead of passing, it turned the corner and started down the gravel road. Brian dropped into a crouch and, chewing on his gum with a positive dementia, watched through the leaves as it passed. Just before it disappeared from sight, he got a split-second glimpse of its license plate: QQ 1281.

A heartbeat later, he was racing after it, his arms flailing. *"JEROOOOME! JEROOOOME!"*

The car stopped. Brian, however, had been running so hard that he couldn't bring *himself* to stop and so ended up plowing right into the trunk. Slightly dazed, he took a moment to straighten himself up, then lunged around the right side of the car, tore open the passenger door, and fell into the front seat. From the driver's side, Jerome leaned back and looked at him with eyes the size of tangerines.

"Hello, Jerome," Brian gasped. He let his head drop back onto the seat and gulped. "Guess what? Met your mother. Charming lady." He coughed, then realized with dismay that he'd lost his gum somewhere during his mad dash.

"Mother's home?" Jerome said, aghast.

"Yes," he replied, clearing his throat. "And she's set the police after me. Turn around, will you?"

"What happened to your face?"

"Max Factor. *Please* turn around. I left my luggage on the roadside."

Jerome dutifully attempted a three-point turnaround, but was so nervous he ended up felling a neighbor's mailbox.

"Whoops," he said sheepishly. He drove back to the intersection, where Brian ordered him to stop.

"Pop your trunk," Brian added as he leaped from the car and raced over to his luggage. He hauled both bags over to the car, threw them into the trunk, slammed it shut, then hurriedly returned to the front seat and locked himself in.

"Okay," he said. "Get me to the airport."

"But that's two hours away!"

"Then the sooner we get started, the better."

"I don't understand," said Jerome, a slight whine in his voice. "So *what* if my mother called the police? *I* can go back and tell them you're not a trespasser or a thief or anything. *I* can explain to them that you were in the house because I invited you there. After all, I live there, too! I have a right to have guests! Let's just go back and wait for them to—"

"*Jerome*," Brian barked, and he could feel panic distort his face into something like a fist, "for *Christ's* sake, will you just fucking *listen* to me? I want to go to the *fucking* AIRPORT!" He slammed his fist into the glove compartment in frustration. "I don't—I *won't*—go talking to any fucking cops no matter who—" He choked, pulled at his hair, then yanked out his wallet again. "What is it, you want me to *pay* you? Huh? Is *that* it?" He started snatching bills from the wallet and flinging them at Jerome. "Here, then! Twenty—forty—sixty—seventy—ninety—a hundred bucks! Okay, Jerome? Okay? A hundred *fucking* bucks for you to *fucking* take me to the *fucking* AIRPORT!"

He finished his tirade just as the bills were fluttering onto Jerome's shoulder and lap. And as he panted, quivering with rage and anxiety, he noticed tears streaming from Jerome's eyes, and Jerome's lips quivering like the earth above a sinkhole that's about to give way.

That was all it took. Brian dropped his head between his knees and locked his fingers behind his neck. "Oh, God, I'm *sorry*," he said. "Jerome, I'm sorry. Listen, I just *can't* risk talking to cops. You don't know what the police—I mean, *look* at me." He sat up, and his eyes were smeared with mascara.

"You look like the Masked Marauder," Jerome said, his voice wavering.

Brian let a laugh slip, then rolled his eyes. "I look like a *queer*, Jerome. And I'm not stupid; I *grew up* in a town like this. I know what that means here. When I was nineteen—" He shook his head. "Jesus H. Christ in a hair net, Jerome! I've never even told *Nico* about this!"

"Who's Nico?"

"My lover."

Jerome wrinkled his nose. "Oh. Got one of those, have you?"

Brian pivoted at the waist and leaned closer to Jerome. He was still breathing like a racehorse. "When I was nineteen, I went to this place near the aqueduct just outside our town, okay?

Because it was the local cruising spot for gay men. Don't ask how I knew; *everybody* knew. It was part of the town lore. Kids in *grade* school knew it. To be seen by the aqueduct was as good as—well, that's beside the point. Anyway, it was my first time there. It was around midnight, and I was terrified. I kept hearing stuff from the bushes, guys calling to me, but I didn't see anyone. I was scared, but I kept walking, and looking, and walking, and looking. And then I ran into some cops." He took a deep breath.

Jerome shrugged. "And?"

"And they beat the shit out of m—" A sob stopped up his throat, and he pivoted back, facing front, staring at the empty road ahead until he regained control of his voice. "They beat the *shit* out of me, Jerome. They *bashed* me. And no one helped. All those guys I knew were there, listening, and none of them—" He shook his head. "I was a teenager looking for love for the first time in my life, and what I found instead was—was—oh, *hell.*" He shut his eyes tight and bit his lip. "I know what cops are like in towns like this. Now, Jerome, for the love of Christ, or the love of whatever you want, for the love of goddamned Princess *Paragon*, if that's what it takes, will you *please* drive me to the airport?"

Jerome seemed about to say something, but apparently thought better of it. He put the car in gear and started driving. After a few minutes, he said, "You know, if you were Moonman or the Centipede or—"

"Jerome, *please*," Brian said in disgust.

"No, hear me out! This matters to me. Because you're one of the people who *writes* those stories, and I take what they say very seriously. If you were Moonman or the Centipede or Speed-Demon or Buster Brainpower or any of those heroes, you wouldn't let your fears fester like this for so many years, making you all hysterical. If you were the kind of hero you write about, you'd *face* your fears. That's what you'd do. Don't you even believe what you write?"

Brian was astonished that he actually had to explain it to him. "This is real life, Jerome," he said with as little sarcasm as possible.

They turned a corner, and all at once they were in the business district. College students were still hanging around the darkened streets, standing under streetlights talking, or smoking, or necking.

"No, it's bigger than that," Jerome said at last. "It means more than that."

Brian lost all patience with him. "So tell me, then, Mister Still-Lives-with-His-Mom," he said cruelly. "Tell me, with the fine example your heroes set for you, do you, in fact, face *your* fears?"

Jerome was quiet for a few moments more. Then, defiantly, he said, "I did tonight."

Brian clicked his tongue. "Yeah, with my help."

"Well, that's why I'm trying to return the favor."

Brian sat back and watched the streetlights fly by. "So, how'd it go, anyway? You get laid, or what?"

He couldn't see Jerome's face in the darkness; but the sudden, chilly silence was telling enough. Finally, Jerome said, "Why does it have to come down to that?"

"You didn't get laid," Brian said with a sigh.

"As if that's all there is—as if nothing else were impo—"

"What's that behind us?" Brian said, suddenly on alert.

"What? Where?" Jerome craned his neck and looked in the rearview mirror.

"Oh, God. Oh, Christ." In the distance, a mile or so back, Brian could see the red strobe lights of what must be a police car. "Listen to that," he said; he could faintly hear the accompanying siren. "Lose them, Jerome," he said tersely. "Don't let them find us. Don't let them get me."

"But where'll I go?" Jerome squealed, his voice growing shrill with fear, his steering becoming erratic and wild. "This is the only way I know to get to the highway that goes to the airport!"

"I don't *care*," Brian said, meaning it. "Go *anywhere*. Just turn. Get us out of here—get us off this road!"

And that's exactly what Jerome did.

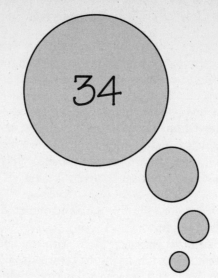

34

"Where the hell are we?" said Brian Parrish as Jerome pulled into the parking lot and stilled the car's motor.

"It's where I work," Jerome said. His voice was flat and exhausted, exactly matching how he felt. "I couldn't think of anywhere else to go."

"Can we get inside?"

"Yes." He displayed the key ring in his sweaty hand. "Technically, it's still my last night."

"*Great.*" The cartoonist hopped out of the car and fairly loped to the door. "There's a bathroom in here, too, I hope?" he called out as he ran. "I've *got* to get this crap off my face."

"There's one right off the lobby," puffed Jerome as he lumbered after him. He reached the glass door and unlocked it. Immediately, Brian Parrish slipped inside and disappeared behind the door marked Men. Jerome checked the clock on the wall. It was just past one in the morning. He looked around at all the familiar surroundings: the reception desk, the Naugahyde couch, the newspaper rack, the oil portrait of founder N. Booth Carter, the display stand featuring plastic replicas of the foods Carter produced. It suddenly struck him that this would be the last time he saw any of this. It already felt oddly different—as though he'd long since moved on. Here he was in a jacket and tie instead of his guard uniform; and instead of being here alone, he was accompanied by none other than the world's greatest comic-book artist.

He sat on the couch and waited for Brian Parrish to emerge from the men's room. When he did, his face was clear of makeup and his lingering bruises were shiny and bright. Jerome said, "Ready to go?"

The cartoonist buttoned his cuffs and shook his head. "No, Jerome. Sorry, but I just can't face that drive again. Not with patrol cars out looking for me. Can't I stay here while you go and clear things up with your mom?"

Jerome went pale. "But what if something happens here while I'm away? This is my job!"

Brian Parrish slicked back his damp hair. "You've already blown it off for half the night," he said. "Why not go for broke? I mean, hell—it's not like you've got a *future* here or anything." He grinned, and plopped down on the couch. "Seriously, I'll just sit tight here until you return with the all-clear. Then I'll even take a cab to the airport, how's that? Swear to God, Jerome. You'll be rid of me forever." He raised his eyebrows at him. "Okay, buddy? Good old Jerome, who never lets me down?"

That did the trick; for Jerome knew very well that he *had* let Brian Parrish down, in a very real and very unalterable way. Even as they sat here, Brian Parrish's script for *Princess Paragon* number three was disintegrating in a vat of grease not two hundred yards away. In view of that—and of all Brian Parrish had done to help pave his way with Amanda—how could Jerome possibly say no?

"All right," he said, relenting, with a sigh. "But you can't sit here, where anyone can see you."

"Fine. I'll go park it in one of the cubicles."

"*No*, no," Jerome said insistently. "I want you *well* out of the way. It'd be just my luck if something really did happen tonight and you were here. How would I explain it? And I do have to rely on getting a good reference from my boss here, you know. No, you have to hide. Come with me." He led him up the stairs and down the long, box-strewn corridor to the forgotten office that Jerome once used, about a million years ago it seemed, for his masturbation sessions on company time. He unlocked the door, swung it open, and flicked on the light.

"*Ugh*," said Brian Parrish as he entered. "What cramped little hell is *this*?"

"Nobody ever uses this office," Jerome said. "You can wait here."

"For Christ's sake, Jerome, it's not *healthy*. There's more dust than air!" He dragged the toe of his shoe along the floor. "And what's this crusty stuff all over?" He shook his head. "Sorry, it's just too creepy. Can't I wait outside, by the boxes or something?"

"I don't know how long I'll be," Jerome said with finality. "Will you *please* do me a favor and *just sit tight*?"

The various tensions of the evening must have finally taken their toll on Brian Parrish, because suddenly all the fight went out of him. He went visibly limp. "Fine, what the hell," he said, dropping into the chair by the desk. "I'll just sit here like a good little fugitive and won't move a muscle till I hear from you." He looked at the door. "You're not locking me in here, though, right? I mean, what if there's a fire or something?"

"I'm not locking the door," said Jerome as he headed out. "But stay in here, anyway."

"Oh," the cartoonist called out as Jerome was shutting him in, "make sure to tell your mom I'm sorry and I'll pay the cleaning bill for her kimono!"

Jerome nodded and closed the door, then stood with his hand on the knob for a moment, wondering what in the world Brian Parrish was talking about. He shook his head in confusion, then headed back down the stairs.

When he returned to the lobby, he found Mr. Pinkerton sitting primly on the couch.

The shock almost knocked him over. "Mr. P-P-Pinkerton," he yelped. "What a surp-p-p—"

"I imagine it *is* a surprise, Jerome," said Mr. Pinkerton grimly as he appraised Jerome's unwatchmanlike jacket and tie.

"What are you d-doing here so early?" Jerome asked.

"I'm here to pick up your keys." He got to his feet and extended his hand. "This is your farewell to our little family, you know."

"B-b-b-b-but my shift doesn't end till f-f-four o'clock."

"Your shift also *began* at *seven* o'clock, Jerome, yet when I checked here at nine-fifteen, and then again at eleven-thirty, there was no sign of you." He wiggled the fingers in his open hand. "I think you'd better hand over the keys and get out of here, Jerome. I don't want any explanations; just get out."

Jerome handed over the keys; he was trembling so much that they sounded like a wind chime in a hurricane until Mr. Pinkerton grabbed them and stuck them in his trench-coat pocket.

Then Jerome slunk out of the Carter Foods building—his erstwhile home-away-from-home, from which he was now banished forever.

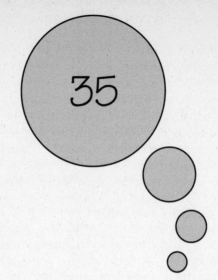

35

The dull hum of heavy machinery awakened Brian. For a moment, he didn't know where he was; then he took in his dingy, dusty surroundings and realized he was still in the unused office at Carter Foods. And it all came rushing back at him—the whole embarrassing and terrifying stream of events from the night before.

Reflecting on it now, with a cooler head and a few hours' sleep, he decided that he might possibly have overreacted. Could Jerome have been right? Might it have been better to face down Mrs. Kornacker and the police? Well, maybe he would've tried, had Mrs. Kornacker not happened on him at the worst possible moment, her kimono hitched up around his waist and his cock in his hand, pissing; there was just no recovering from that humiliation. Anyway, it was all beyond repairing now.

He'd spent the night slumped over the desk, his head resting on his arms. Now he sat up, stretched, and tried to work out a crick in his neck. Every muscle in his body felt stiff and sore. Well, he'd be in his own bed tonight, God willing.

But where was Jerome? He checked his watch: it was six in the morning. Surely it couldn't be taking him *this* long to straighten out the mess with his mother. If he didn't show up soon, it'd be too late for him to get Brian out of here unnoticed. It might *already* be too late; the noise of the machines could only mean that the workday was beginning. Still, there weren't likely to be many employees here as yet; Jerome had told Brian that the machines had to warm up for about an hour and a half before they could actually be operated.

He felt a knot of hunger tighten in his stomach. He recalled seeing a bay of vending machines last night, somewhere near the staircase, and a quick check of his pockets revealed a plethora of coins (Jerome had been very scrupulous about returning change after running errands for him). He got up and opened the office door; there didn't seem to be anyone milling about; in fact, the lights in the corridors hadn't even been switched on yet. Then he remembered that it was Saturday; the plant workers might be here, but the office workers would undoubtedly be off for the weekend.

Even so, he crept carefully down the long, box-strewn hallway, peeked into the connecting corridor, which was empty, and then shot over to the vending machines. The noise was much louder out here; the machinery must be right beyond these walls.

For a moment, he toyed with the idea of just continuing down the stairs and out of the building. Odds were he wouldn't run into anyone. But the mystery of Jerome's lateness made him think again; what if there *were* a problem with the police? What if they were grilling Jerome right now, trying to get him to tell them all he knew about Brian? What if Mrs. Kornacker had made some ridiculous charge against Brian (she had, after all, mentioned rape)—something that Jerome couldn't explain away?

He shuddered and decided to stick to his original plan. He bought a Diet Pepsi and a pair of granola bars for breakfast. Then he heard voices from somewhere below, and he froze. The voices faded quickly, but even so, he decided that rather than risk coming out in the hall again, he'd better just stock up on enough candy and soda pop to get him through the day. Alas, the machines offered no gum; since he'd finished his last piece the night before, he'd have to go cold turkey.

He then hightailed it back to the filthy little office, where he consumed a sticky, sugar-laden breakfast that made him feel dizzy and inert at the same time.

As long as he was stuck here for the day, he thought he might try to get a little more work done on *Princess Paragon* number four. He checked the desk for writing materials, but found only a stubby pencil and a pad of pink While You Were Out slips. Well, any port in a storm. He started scribbling away, and an hour and a half later he'd depleted the pad and had to stop. He tucked his notes into his shirt pocket and sighed. He was hungry again; writing always made him work up an appetite. He peeled open a Baby Ruth and almost swallowed it whole.

It was now eight in the morning, and there was still no sign of Jerome. He felt a flash of irritation. There was really no excuse for this. He ought to just get up and walk right out of here—bluff or bluster his way past anyone he happened to meet. He could walk to the nearest roadside phone booth and call a cab to take him to O'Hare. And that would be that.

Except that his luggage was still in the trunk of Jerome's car. And he was just enough of an aging queen to dread the idea of going anywhere without his wardrobe.

It was then that he saw the grimy beige telephone sitting forgotten on the floor in the dimmest corner of the office. The only reason he noticed it at all was that one of its extension buttons was now lit.

Why the *hell* isn't that sitting on the desk? he wondered, fuming. I could've used it last night!

He picked it up and placed it on the desk, then sat staring at it. It was a risk to use it now, of course; someone might notice. But he was getting a little stir crazy, so he decided to risk a call. He'd ring up Jerome and say, Where the hell are you? and then tell him he planned to leave the building on his own, and could he please meet him in the parking lot with his luggage?

He picked up the receiver (lighting up another extension button) and dialed Jerome's number. After three rings, he was greeted with, "Kornacker residence; Peachy Kornacker speaking."

He suppressed a shudder. "Oh—uh—hello," he said, trying to disguise his voice. "May I speak with Jerome, please?"

"I'm sorry, Jerome's busy sleeping. But if this is an emergency I can certainly disrobe him."

"Well, as a matter of fact, yes, it is an emergency."

"Oh, dear! Well, hold on, then." A slight pause. "Who might I tell him is calling him?"

"Umm . . . my name is Aaron Marks."

"Okay. Hold on, Officer Marks."

Brian hung up at once. *Officer* Marks? What was going on here? Why was Jerome *asleep*, of all things? And why would his mother just assume that Aaron Marks must be a policeman?

He got to his feet and started pacing the floor. Maybe Mrs. Kornacker *had* made some wild accusation against him, and Jerome couldn't talk her out of it. Maybe Jerome was under house arrest until he could be interrogated about Brian.

The more he thought about it, the wilder his suspicions became. He could sense himself reaching the verge of hysteria, and knew he was no longer able to think straight. The only way out of this was to call Nico right now and get his advice. It might be embarrassing, but if he couldn't turn to Nico, whom *could* he turn to?

He dialed home, and after the seventh ring he knew what he was going to hear. "Hi, this is Nico! Brian's off on business, and while the cat's away, the mouse will go to—"

"*Hell*," Brian barked, completing the sentence as he hung up. "Where the fuck *is* that tramp?"

He couldn't let Nico's gadding-about bother him right now; he had the Kornackers to deal with. He continued pacing for ten minutes more, suspicion turning to paranoia. Then he sat down again and commanded himself to remain calm. He hit on the idea of calling his studio answering machine and listening to his messages; he hadn't checked them in a week, and it would be a good way of getting his mind off his troubles until he could talk to Nico. He picked up the phone again and dialed.

After his answering machine picked up and started playing his greeting, Brian interrupted his taped self by punching in the code for retrieving messages. His greeting aborted, he waited while the message tape rewound itself.

The first message, as he'd expected, was from Perpetrial. "Brian, it was unforgivable—and, may I say, typically male—of you to leave me to handle the *Princess Paragon* panel alone, without even warning me. Fortunately, I did very well, better than I would've expected. Maybe you've already heard that. But that's not the point. You owe me a *big* apology, and I mean to have it. No one's seen you since before the panel; are you off sulking somewhere? You're not answering the phone in your room, so I'm calling your studio in Manhattan in case you check your messages. My extension at the hotel is eighteen-twenty. And I'm waiting."

Immediately following this was a beep, then a message from Nico. "Hi, hon, Monday morning here, don't know where else to reach you, you're not answering at the hotel. Sam's sick—nothing major—but he can't go to the Island this week, so at the last minute Larry invited me to come up and stay in the extra bed. I'm throwing together a suitcase right now. You have their number there, don't you? It's in your Filofax." Which is in Jerome's trunk, thought Brian glumly. "I'm taking off work, so don't try me there. I'll be back Sunday night. Lucy's minding the Leonards. Hope your tortured-artist thing is working out. Love ya."

Another beep, and another message from Perpetrial. "Brian, it's Monday afternoon; where are you? Regina and I thought something might be wrong, so we got a maid to let us into your room, and we found your closet empty and the first draft for issue three ripped in half and dumped in your wastebasket." Brian's heart skipped a beat. "Does that mean you no longer want to use it? Please call! You weren't on the flight back this morning, and we're getting worried."

Only one person could've torn up that draft, thought Brian,

a cold, bad feeling settling over him. Jerome. Jerome did it. And never even said a word, after everything I've done for him!

The next message was from Heloise. "Brian, it's Friday. Perpetrial says she hasn't spoken to you in days, and now suddenly this morning she comes in and finds a seventeen-page fax on her desk, from you. And it appears to be a script to replace the one she says you started but ripped up. Now, not only is this the worst script either of us has ever read, it's also a complete violation of everything we agreed on." A pause; she was obviously taking a few puffs off her cigarette. "I mean, what's going on here?" He heard pages flapping. "First, there's this business about Cosmique being an 'intergalactic lesbian slave trader' who's trying to make Princess Paragon her erotic thrall." More flapping. "And who the hell is this Jerome Kingsfield character who appears out of nowhere to rescue Princess Paragon and sweep her off her feet?" Another pause for puffing. "Perpetrial says you didn't discuss *any* of this with her, and she's deeply hurt. Me, I'm just mad as hell. First that disappearing stunt you pulled at the convention, and now this. Brian, you'd better get in touch with me *fast*."

The machine beeped three times, signaling that that had been the last message. Brian dropped the receiver back into its cradle and tried to stop his head from swimming.

It was all falling into place. Jerome had ripped up Brian's first-draft script in Chicago, then substituted his own finished script a few days later. And Brian had played right into his hands, hadn't he? Allowing—even *insisting*—that Jerome squirrel him away somewhere, so that he could have privacy to work on his final draft. And all he'd really done, of course, was give Jerome a free hand to proceed with *his* original plan to subvert the whole issue.

Brian was now trembling with fear and fury. The Bang offices were closed today, so he tried Perpetrial's home number, which he had no trouble recalling after having heard her leave it on his machine countless times. Even so, his fingers were shaking so much that he bungled it, and had to switch to another line and start over. Once he got through and Perpetrial picked up, he said, "Hi, it's Brian. I didn't send that script. It's a fake. Listen, I'm in some kind of trouble."

"Brian, where are you?" she said, sounding alarmed.

"You won't believe it. Remember that letter from the kid who was in love with Pr—"

"Excuse me," said a third voice, suddenly inserting itself into the conversation. "This is Mr. Pinkerton, and this is my private line. Who's using it?"

Brian went mute. Perpetrial said, "Brian? Hello? Are you there? Who's Mr. Pinkerton?"

"*Hang up!*" he rasped. "*Hang up!*" And he slammed down the receiver.

A moment later, the extension's light went out, so Brian knew that Perpetrial had obeyed him, and that whoever had discovered them had given up and gotten off the line. He didn't dare try another; the lines might be watched now, and he could get caught.

Brian was incinerating with anger. He could feel all of his fraternal affection for Jerome burning away, like a haze in harsh sunlight. Jerome would *pay* for this.

He spent the rest of the day like an alligator, lying in wait, barely moving, only occasionally checking his watch or downing a candy bar (and once, with great intrigue, sneaking off to a rest room). And when 7:00 came and the machines went silent and all the workers appeared to be gone from the building, Brian at last tiptoed to the door of the office, opened it quietly, and began making his way softly down the hall.

He had it in mind to derail Jerome's treachery with his own. Somehow, he'd get to a police station; he'd make up some story about having been beaten by Jerome at the hotel in Chicago and then abducted. If they doubted him, he'd point to the bruises on his face. He'd have them check the trunk of Jerome's car. Then he'd have Jerome arrested and thrown in jail. *That* would teach him, the lying, traitorous—

All at once he was physically knocked back by the deafening whoop of a shrill, sharp alarm siren. He stumbled back against the wall, clutching at his ears. It was impossible to think; the noise was *incredible*.

After a moment of being buffeted like a moth in a typhoon, he panicked.

He ran.

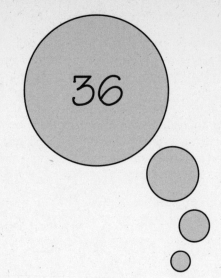

36

There had been no police cars in the Kornacker driveway when Jerome pulled up. Had they already come and gone, he wondered? Either way, he was in for an unpleasant scene with his mother. Not that there was any such thing as a *pleasant* scene with her, but this one promised to be worse than most.

He locked the car and headed into the house, where he found her sitting at her desk in the living room, a sheet of paper in her hands. She glared at him.

"I can explain everything," he said, shutting the door behind him.

"You don't have to. I understand now. Oh, what have I been harboring under these four walls?"

"What's that supposed to mean?" he asked, approaching her.

She leapt to her feet and scooted behind the chair. "You stay right there, young man!" she barked. "Not one foot closer!" She appeared to be genuinely frightened.

He sighed in exasperation and dropped his hands to his sides. "Mother, what on earth are you babbling about?"

"What do you *think*? Do you think I didn't somehow find him—that person you had enscotched upstairs with the bruised face? I let him get away, you know."

Jerome nodded. "I know."

"You *know*? A likely story! That was over an hour ago, Jerome. God knows where you were, running around at all hours of the night like some kind of hoodwink, but you sure weren't *here*."

"As it happens, I was. I found him on the street outside." She said nothing, but cowered behind the chair like a cornered animal. "Mother, for *God*'s sake. You're acting deranged."

"Hah! Look who's calling the kennel black!"

"That man was my guest here. You had no right to throw him out."

"Oh, your *guest*, was he? Come on, Jerome! Stop trying to pull the wolf over my eyes!"

He was growing impatient with her. "Look, just tell me whether you called the police," he said sternly.

She shook her head. "I didn't. I couldn't. Not even in spite of everything."

Well, *that* was a relief. "An uncharacteristically rational decision," he said. He couldn't quite bring himself to *thank* her. "He's really done nothing wrong, you know."

"Oh, I know *he* hasn't," she said, her voice almost breaking. "Is that what you were thinking I'd think?" She shook her head and gripped the back of the chair. "That poor soul! What he must have been through! It's a good thing for you I *didn't* call the police up, Jerome. But when that man goes and talks to them, it'll be like I may as well have."

"He won't do that, I promise you. What could he say, anyway?"

Her eyes clouded, and she fingered the buttons of her blouse. "I'll protect you as best I can," she moaned, and tears dotted her cheeks. "God knows you don't reserve it, but it's a mother's duty."

He shook his head in exasperation. "Protect me from *what*?"

Skittishly, she reached out and handed him the sheet of paper. "I found this up in Sandra's room, where I usually won't go except that man left the lights on," she said. Jerome fumbled and let the paper slip through his fingers. As he bent to retrieve it, she added, "It told me everything. Oh, Jerome, you've really gone and done it this time, haven't you?"

Jerome frowned at her, then looked at the paper. On it was written the following:

Again today, El Humongo denied me food and drink until I was weak with hunger; then, at the end of the day, he gave me moldy bread and brackish water. I ate and drank greedily, then threw up. El Humongo laughed at my discomfort. He never questions me, never asks for information, has not to my knowledge demanded a ransom for my release. He seems to want nothing from me but the perverse pleasure of watching me suffer. I dread hearing the floorboards outside the door creak beneath his appalling weight. If only I could find an opportunity to escape—if only there were some disguise I might don, and so slip away unnoticed when h

Jerome looked up at his mother. "What *is* this?"

"It's the note that man left," she said, her breathing raspy. She still refused to move from behind the chair. "He must have been busy writing it down just before you went out. Because look, he's writing about thinking of escaping in a disguise, and then when I found him he was trying my kimono on. It all *fits.*"

Jerome felt a chaotic fluttering in his breast. He didn't understand this. What was she implying? Was "El Humongo" supposed to be *him*? After everything Brian Parrish had said about weight not mattering? How could he *do* such a thing? And these absurd lies about the way he'd been treated! It was as if he were trying to set Jerome up or something—frame him as some kind of kidnapper! But why on earth would he do that, after all they'd been through together? Why would he want to do something as vengeful as—

His heart stopped. There was one possible reason. Maybe Brian Parrish had discovered Jerome's script-switch. But how? Maybe he'd called the Bang Comics offices during the day. (Jerome hadn't anticipated that; a tactical mistake on his part.) Of course, he'd have been angry—*very* angry. Which would explain why he'd hatched this ridiculous scheme to get revenge on Jerome—first to get him out of the house (hadn't the date with Amanda been his idea?), then to leave an incriminating journal at the scene of the "crime," then to show up at the police station in Jerome's mother's kimono, claiming to have been held captive. It was weird, and it almost certainly wouldn't work; but that was Brian Parrish for you.

Unfortunately for him, Jerome's mother had appeared and ruined the whole plan by kicking him out of the house. And then when he'd been out in the cold, with makeup on his face and nowhere to turn, he'd been so terrified of the police that he was only too glad to let Jerome rescue him—and he never said a word about his aborted plan. The lousy *hypocrite*.

Jerome looked at the scrawled message again. "I dread hearing the floorboards outside the door creak beneath his appalling weight," indeed! Rage swelled inside him, and he ripped the note into confetti and flung it into the air.

Through the swirl of shredded paper, his mother looked him in the eye and said, "Too late, Jerome. I already read it, and as you know I have a photogenic memory. Mostly I will never forget 'He seems to want nothing from me but the perverse pleasure of watching me suffer'! Was it *you* who did that to his face?"

He was about to deny it when he remembered that in fact he *had* done it. "Well, so what if it was?" he said defensively, and his mother blanched in horror. He immediately tried to console her by saying, "But that's not how it happened! The whole note is a filthy, disgusting lie!" His mother continued to regard him as she would a wild animal; and suddenly he could feel a razor slashing away at his brain. "Not a word of it is true!" he growled, his voice almost feral.

"If only I could believe that!" Mrs. Kornacker said with a sob. "I'm sorry, Jerome; once bitten, twice burned."

He sneered at her. Things were dancing around in his head now; snaky things, red-hot and hissing—things that hadn't been there since that day in the stairwell of the O'Hare Grifton Hotel.

He started up to his room. His mother called after him, "Whatever you did, you're still my son! Don't worry, Jerome; tomorrow morning I'm going to telephone up your father's old lawyer and he'll nip this thing in the butt." As he turned on the landing and climbed beyond her sight, she continued, "BUT I'M WARNING YOU, THIS HAD BETTER BE AN ISOLATED INCREMENT! IF THERE ARE OTHER BODIES BURIED IN THE BASEMENT OR CUT UP IN MASONITE JARS IN YOUR ROOM WHERE YOU NEVER LET ME GO, GETTING YOU OFF THE HOOK MAY NOT BE SUCH A PIECE OF PIE!"

He unclipped his tie and threw it into a chair, then lowered himself onto his bed without even removing his jacket or shoes. He lay there with clenched fists and let the madness taint his brain like a swarm of houseflies polluting a peach.

Somewhere in the recesses of his mind, he realized that Brian Parrish had been a kind of salvation for him. Essentially friendless, Jerome had lived out his life in a series of overlapping fantasies that had somehow managed to form a coherent, if wildly incomplete, reality. The appearance of Brian Parrish in his life had been too huge an event for that jerrybuilt reality to support; by his very presence, the cartoonist had dissipated it, and left Jerome foundering. But in its place, he gave Jerome his first taste of the world as it is: ungainly, rude, threatening, vulgar, fearsome—but, taken on its own terms, somehow invigorating. Jerome dimly realized that what he'd found with Brian Parrish was an intoxicating appreciation for the unexpected, for that exhilarating sensation of not knowing what happens next. Unlike Moonman or Acme-Man or the Quasar Quintet, Brian Parrish didn't live his life in the circumscribed world of a comic book, or in the safe, controllable realm of Jerome's imagination. He was unpredictable, like a garden hose on full blast—one minute benevolently watering the lawn for you; the next, rearing up to spray you in the face.

Jerome had only just begun to learn the risks of such an association, but he'd never thought those risks could be so great as to include hypocrisy and betrayal. Of course, he himself was guilty of betrayal; but that was different. He hadn't known what was at stake. People like Brian Parrish *grew up* knowing it.

He felt as though his skin had been stripped away and his nerve endings exposed. He lay on the bed, twitching and quivering; he wasn't aware that he had fallen asleep until his mother pounded on the door and he came to with a jolt, daylight dribbling across his face.

"*Wake up*, Jerome," she was pleading.

He rolled over. "What is it, Mother?"

"I'm afraid the gig is up," she called through the door. "There's a detective named Aaron Marks on the phone for you!"

Aaron Marks? Why would Aaron Marks be calling *him*?

Wait a minute. Aaron Marks was a fictional character. Wasn't he?

That meant—it could only be—

He picked up the extension in his room. "Hello?" he said. "Hello?"

Just a dial tone.

He hung up with a grunt. "Don't worry, Mother," he said, swinging his feet over the side of the bed and stretching. "That wasn't a lawman."

"Who else would've called up to tell me he had to speak to you about an emergency?"

"I don't know." He went over to the door and opened it. His mother stepped back, one hand over her heart. She was wearing a peach bathrobe and peach turban. She had only half applied her makeup. "And since you didn't think to ask," he continued, "I probably never will."

"Don't you go being ungrateful to me, young man," she said, wagging a finger at him. "I'm putting my ass on the lion for you!" She snorted and headed back to her bathroom.

Jerome ate a bowl of cereal for breakfast and then sat at the table before the remaining puddle of purple milk, staring into space, empty of thought. When he heard his mother make a phone call to her attorney ("We might need your help in the next day or so; Jerome's got himself into a pinch of trouble"), he couldn't bear it and went back to bed.

The thing to do now, obviously, was confront Brian Parrish. That is, if he hadn't left town. But the telephone call this morning made Jerome think he hadn't. If he'd managed to slip away from Carter Foods and get himself to the airport on his own, he'd scarcely call Jerome to say goodbye—not after what he knew about Jerome and the script. No, if he'd gotten out, he'd probably already have sicced the police on him, if for no other reason than to get his luggage back.

Jerome was betting instead that Brian Parrish was still holed up in the unused office at Carter Foods. His fear of the police would be enough to keep him there, anxiously awaiting Jerome's return with an all clear. In which case, Jerome could very well just let him sit there until he rotted; he was half tempted to just forget Brian Parrish ever existed. But the piping-hot, almost euphoric pulse of madness that had taken hold of Jerome the night before made it imperative that he go back and—what? This was just how he'd felt when he first learned that Brian Parrish would be appearing at the Grifton; he'd been compelled to go and confront him, but hadn't had any idea of what to say when he did so.

He slept on and off until early evening, when he showered and put on his guard uniform, just as though he were going to work (he hadn't yet told his mother he'd been fired).

He arrived at Carter Foods around 5:30. The building had thrown the entire parking lot into shadow. He drove to the far corner of the lot and then stilled the engine and watched. His dementia seemed to be manifesting itself in the form of paranormal clarity of thought; for although he knew that this was Saturday, and all the office workers should be off duty and the plant operated by a skeleton crew, he had the wit to deduce that Mr. Pinkerton might have come in anyway, just for the pleasure of being close to his adored new security system when it was officially switched on for its maiden run. And sure enough, at a quarter to six, after all the workers had departed, Mr. Pinkerton strolled out of the building in a snappy windbreaker and sky-blue golf pants, smiling like a man who's just had an especially satisfying visit with his mistress. He hopped into his Dodge Dart and drove off.

Jerome got out of the car and made his way around the perimeter of the parking lot to the side of the building. He knew of a first-floor window that had a weak, rusted latch; and thanks to Mr. Pinkerton having so proudly shown him the new security system's layout, he also knew that this window was not one of those that had been wired to the alarm. (It was, after all, merely the window to a small closet that was used by scarcely anyone but the cleaning lady and Ida the bookkeeper, who had been known to sneak naps there.)

He gave the window a couple of good tugs and the latch broke. He smiled at his own strength, then lifted the frame. But getting in through the opening was another matter—one that forced him to drastically re-evaluate his high opinion of his physical prowess. There was even one horrible moment, when he was more than halfway through, when his thighs became seemingly irrevocably jammed, and he had to consider the embarrassing possibility that he might have to stay that way till Monday morning and then holler for his former colleagues to come and help him. But after a few more minutes of maddening wriggling, he dropped through, hitting the floor like a sack of flour.

He got up and dusted himself off. Then he put his hand on his chin and thought for a moment. This closet might not be wired, but the hallway beyond it was; once he entered it, he calculated that he had roughly fifteen seconds' grace to get to the control panel in the lobby and prove he wasn't an intruder by punching in the correct code. If he ran, he could just make it. Then it'd be a simple thing to head up to where that lousy traitor Brian Parrish was hiding.

He opened the door and took a breath. Then he bolted.

On his second footfall, the alarm screamed to life.

He stopped, stunned; what had he done wrong?

Then he realized that it must be *Brian Parrish*, damn him, who had set the thing off. He must be wandering around loose upstairs!

Jerome resumed his flight to the lobby, but when he reached

the control panel, he found that his brain had been so rattled by the din that he couldn't recall the correct code. His fingers flew over the buttons: 3-3-4-4-5-6-Off! No, that didn't work. 3-4-4-3-5-6-Off! Still on, still *on*. 3-3-3-4-5-6-Off! God *damn* this thing!

He roared in frustration, then dashed through the maze of cubicles until he reached the president's office. He pried open the flimsy lock on the door of the rosewood cabinet and removed the pistol—the pistol he'd sworn never to use after having failed his training so badly. Well, desperate times . . .

He headed back to the lobby; running through this noise was like running through some kind of toxic radiation. He was just making his way up the first flight of stairs when something—someone—collided with him.

He fell back a few steps, almost dropping the pistol.

A voice cut through the shriek of the alarm: "ABOUT FUCKING TIME!"

He looked up into the eyes of Brian Parrish.

37

Brian looked beyond Jerome, half expecting to see a gaggle of policemen follow him into the stairwell; but no, he appeared to have come alone. Funny it should end like this, so like the way it had begun: the two of them squaring off on a staircase. Fate had its symmetry.

But not a perfect symmetry; this time they had a hideous, whooping alarm siren blaring in their ears, making it almost impossible to hear one another. They had to shout.

"I KNOW ABOUT THE SCRIPT," Brian yelled. "YOU'VE GOT A LOT OF GODDAMNED NERVE, COMING TO 'RESCUE' ME AFTER WHAT YOU DID!"

Jerome had stumbled when he and Brian collided, and was now pulling himself up with the handrail. When he again stood erect, Brian saw that he was holding a gun. Brian backed up the stairs.

"*YOU'VE* GOT A LOT OF NERVE FACING *ME*," Jerome screamed

at him. "I KNOW YOU WERE PLANNING TO TELL THE POLICE I KID-NAPPED YOU!"

How on earth did Jerome know *that?* Brian wondered. He'd only come up with the plan twenty minutes before!

"AND NO MATTER WHAT I'VE DONE," Jerome continued, trembling, "IT'S NOTHING TO WHAT *YOU* DID. YOU WERE THE GREATEST GENIUS IN COMICS, BUT YOU MISUSED YOUR POWER! THERE'S NO FORGIVING THAT!" He waved his hand in the air as if to accentuate the point; he appeared to have forgotten that he was holding a gun. Brian flinched as the barrel scanned his chest. "FIRST YOU TOOK OVER PRINCESS PARAGON AND TURNED HER INTO SOMETHING TOTALLY DEPRAVED!" He climbed two steps, and Brian backed up three. "THEN, WHEN SOMEONE LOYAL TO HER TRIED TO SAVE HER, YOU WERE GOING TO *FRAME* HIM! PUT HIM IN *JAIL!*"

At the word "depraved," Brian felt something inside him snap. In spite of everything they'd shared, this slob, this *nobody,* still clung to his ignorance and petty prejudices. Too angry now to care about the gun, he snarled, "YOU STUPID FUCKING HOMOPHOBIC MORON! WHAT I DO WITH PRINCESS PARAGON IS NONE OF YOUR BUSINESS! THAT'S BETWEEN ME AND BANG!"

"IT IS *TOO* MY BUSINESS," Jerome shrieked, and tears sprang from his eyes as if from lawn sprinklers. "SHE BELONGS TO ME, TOO—AND TO EVERYONE IN AMERICA! SHE'S PART OF OUR FOLK-LORE! YOU HAVE NO RIGHT TO TAMPER WITH HER!"

Brian laughed at Jerome's naiveté. "FOLKLORE MY ASS! FOLK-LORE IS PHENOMENAL, JEROME; IT JUST *HAPPENS.* IT COMES FROM THE *PEOPLE,* NOT FROM A FUCKING *PUBLISHING* COMPANY! PRIN-CESS PARAGON IS A COMMERCIAL PROPERTY ENTIRELY OWNED BY A MULTINATIONAL CORPORATION. SHE'S A *PRODUCT.* SHE DOESN'T BELONG TO YOU; SHE BELONGS TO *THEM*! AND SINCE I'M THE CUR-RENT LEASEHOLDER, BY RIGHTS SHE BELONGS TO *ME!*"

Jerome shook his head so hard that his cheeks flapped. He muttered something that Brian couldn't hear above the wails of the alarm.

"WHAT?" Brian shouted. "I CAN'T HEAR YOU!"

Jerome stood panting for a moment; all at once he seemed

to recall the gun in his hand. He looked at it for a moment, then raised it and pointed it at Brian.

Brian barked out a laugh and said, "I'D SAY YOU'RE BEING MELODRAMATIC, IF I THOUGHT FOR A MINUTE YOU HAD THE GUTS TO USE THAT THING." All the same, he backed up even more, giving away his nervousness by almost missing a stair and falling backward. He tried to cover his fumble with a show of bravado. "IN FACT, I *DARE* YOU TO USE IT, JEROME. GO ON, PULL THE TRIGGER. I DESERVE IT, AND DO YOU KNOW WHY? BECAUSE I'VE RUINED YOU! I'VE GIVEN YOU A PLACE TO HIDE, AND I'VE MADE IT SO MIND-NUMBINGLY BUSY THAT YOU'VE NEVER HAD A CHANCE TO LOOK AROUND AND REALIZE WHAT A SHALLOW, CHEAP-SHIT, SECOND-RATE PLACE IT IS." He crossed the landing and started backing up the next flight of stairs. Jerome followed, keeping the gun trained on him.

"CLIFFHANGERS! CROSSOVERS! COSTUME CHANGES!" he continued. "DASTARDLY PLOTS! MYSTERIOUS SUBPLOTS! ALL OF IT CHURNED OUT MONTH AFTER MONTH AFTER MONTH TILL THE CRACK OF FUCKING DOOM. BECAUSE IT KEEPS YOU COMING BACK. YOU'RE NEVER SATISFIED, BECAUSE WE NEVER GIVE YOU YOUR FILL—WE DON'T *WANT* TO. THAT'S THE BOTTOM LINE, JEROME. YOU START GETTING DISTRACTED, YOU START LOOKING AWAY TOWARD SOMETHING MORE SUBSTANTIAL, AND WHAT DO WE DO? WE DANGLE SOMETHING ELSE IN FRONT OF YOU, SOMETHING BRIGHT AND SHINY AND NEW, NEW, *NEW*. PRINCESS PARAGON A DYKE? YOU MAY NOT LIKE IT, BUT YOU'LL SURE AS HELL *BUY* IT. YOU WON'T BE ABLE TO HELP YOURSELF—YOU KNOW YOU WON'T! AND IF YOU SHOOT ME NOW, THE SYSTEM WILL JUST GO ON WITHOUT ME. THERE ARE TOO MANY PEOPLE LIKE YOU, TOO MANY JEROME T. KORNACKERS WHO CARE PASSIONATELY ABOUT THINGS CREATED WITHOUT PASSION, WHO THINK THAT PRODUCT IS FOLKLORE, WHO DON'T REALIZE THAT IF PRINCESS PARAGON ISN'T SELLING, SHE'S NOT AN AMERICAN ICON, SHE'S AN AMERICAN *FAILURE*. THAT'S THE NATURE OF COMMERCE, JEROME! FACE IT. YOU'RE DEFENDING THE HONOR OF A WOMAN WHO HASN'T *GOT* ANY. A WOMAN WHO'S NOT HETEROSEXUAL OR HOMOSEXUAL, OR EVEN A WOMAN, REALLY. SHE'S JUST A WHORE! I SHOULD KNOW; I'M HER

LATEST PIMP. AND YOU'RE THE POOR JOHN SHE NEVER HAD ANYTHING BUT CONTEMPT FOR!"

Jerome's face turned a color Brian had never seen before, and he began to suspect that he'd gone too far. Suddenly his anger was washed out of him by a wave of fear.

Jerome was shaking so hard, he looked like he might be dancing. He raised the gun and pointed it at Brian.

Well, I've done it now, Brian thought, his throat going dry; he was too terrified to move. Couldn't have kept my cool, could I? he scolded himself. Couldn't have just counted to ten!

The alarm was so loud it was making him feel faint; the noise actually seemed to have a texture now, a cold, sharp texture, like the Colorado rapids, rushing over him and slicing him to ribbons.

He suddenly realized that he was very likely going to die—right then, right there. A spasm of terror stopped up his throat for a moment. Then he saw how Jerome's gun hand was wobbling, and he knew that death was by far the least of his worries. He might instead end up with half his face blown away, or with his cock shot off, or with a hole in his spine that would leave him paralyzed for life. He started praying for death; and with the prayer came tears, unashamed and unabashed.

He looked at Jerome's wild eyes, at his quivering lips, and knew for certain that he would fire that gun. He had to. He was practically vibrating with uncontrollable fury. It would be impossible to suppress it much longer; either the gun would explode, or Jerome would.

"Oh, God," Brian said, his voice nothing more than a croak. He shut his eyes and tried to be at peace with himself, to meet the end, if it came, with a measure of self-possession; but everything within him roiled and boiled. He'd achieved no center, no tranquility, not in this life. And all at once he knew how tragic it would be to die this way.

Then he heard a crack and felt an explosion of blinding pain.

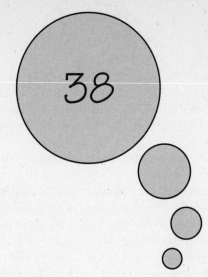

38

Princess Paragon spotted the museum from the air, and dove through the clouds toward its broad, emerald lawn. Once she'd touched down, she checked the name inscribed in marble above the lintel: The American Museum of Fine Art.

Yes, this is the place, she thought, nodding her head gravely.

She loped up the stairs three at a time, and when she arrived at the museum's enormous brass door, Aaron Marks was there to greet her.

"Glad you could make it, Princess," he said. "Your heightened Irian senses are our only hope of picking up the crooks' trail."

She wrapped her star-spangled cape around her shoulders and let him escort her into the cool, bright museum. "How much did they get away with?" she asked. Her footsteps sounded like gunshots in the cavernous main hall.

"More than a billion dollars in paintings," Agent Marks said as he trotted to keep pace with her.

"A *billion*?" she remarked, raising an eyebrow in surprise. "How is that possible?"

"You haven't heard?" he said. "No, of course not; you're too busy saving the galaxy to have time to notice a sideshow like this."

"Sideshow?" she said, not understanding the reference. "Explain."

They rounded a corner and found themselves in a long gallery filled from floor to ceiling with paintings. "The entire museum," said Agent Marks, "has been given over to a special exhibit, 'The Greatest Masterpieces in the History of the World.' This is one of the few galleries the thieves didn't have a chance to loot. Ah, here comes the curator; he'll explain."

Princess Paragon turned and saw a pudgy, balding little man in bifocals scurrying up to them. "What an honor to meet you, Princess," he said, eagerly shaking her hand. "Horton Xerxes at your service!"

Agent Marks said, "Perhaps you could explain the exhibit to Her Highness."

"Ah, yes!" said Xerxes. "Every museum in the world has lent us its greatest paintings, which we have arranged by theme. This gallery, for instance," he said, displaying its length with a grand sweep of his arm, "is devoted to classic portraits of women." He led them into the gallery, pointing out various canvases. "Here, for instance, is the Mona Lisa by Leonardo, one of the handful of indisputably immortal masterpieces of art."

"It's very beautiful," said Princess Paragon, gazing into the painting's inscrutable, timeless eyes.

"You've never seen it before?" asked Xerxes.

"No," she said, with a shake of her head that set her silken tresses tumbling. "I am somewhat new to your planet, Mr. Xerxes."

"Yes, of course. Silly of me to forget. Well, then, what a treat for you to see all these great works together! Here, for instance, is the famous serial portrait of Marilyn Monroe by Andy

Warhol. And over here, the glorious Armada portrait of Elizabeth the First. To the right, a brilliant picture of Jane Avril by Toulouse-Lautrec. And just below that, John Singer Sargent's decadent and gorgeous study of Madame X."

Princess Paragon was awestruck by such a concentrated dose of feminine splendor. "They're all magnificent," she said.

"Yes," Xerxes agreed happily. "I'm so glad the burglars didn't reach this gallery! It's my favorite. I think the only *true* aim of art is the veneration of women, don't you?"

"Perhaps," she said, trying not to smile at this gnomish little man's ardor for female perfection.

"In fact," he said, "it's a shame we don't have a portrait of *you* in this gallery! You seem to embody everything that's celebrated here."

She blushed at the compliment. "Alas, I've never been painted."

"Never? But that's a crime!" He clapped his hands. A bearded young man appeared, wearing a long white smock and a beret, and carrying an easel and a canvas. "This is my protégé, Thierry," he said. "Thierry is a promising young genius whose career I am guiding. If you're willing, Princess," he continued as Thierry set up his easel, "I'd like to have you sit for him, right now."

"Well," she said uneasily, "I really should begin the investigation. There are so many priceless masterpieces to be recovered! And I think I smell microscopic traces of Bad Barbara's perfume; she's probably the culprit. . . ."

"Oh, this won't take but an hour! Thierry is *very* fast." He turned and barked, "Thierry! Aren't you ready yet?"

"*Oui*, Monsieur Xerxes, I am," said the painter.

Xerxes clasped his hands beneath his chin. "With such a subject, this painting will be the crowning glory of the collection!"

Princess Paragon turned to Agent Marks. "Aaron, do you mind?"

"Of course not!" he said, grinning. "You can catch Bad Barbara later. You always do."

She shrugged her shoulders, then turned toward Thierry and adopted what she thought was a suitably heroic pose. "Very well, then. Whenever you're ready."

Thierry lifted his brush and looked at her for what seemed a very long time, first with his left eye, then with his right, then with both eyes open and his thumb at arm's length. Then, amazingly, he put down the brush and folded his arms.

"I cannot paint zees subject," he said.

"Why ever not?" asked Xerxes.

"Because eet ees not a woman."

Xerxes flushed scarlet. *"What?"*

"Look at heem," Thierry continued, tossing his nose dismissively toward the Princess. "He ees a man wearing cosmeteeks to try and fool us!"

They all looked at her, and when she tried to explain that Thierry was wrong, her voice came out deep and throaty. They started backing away from her in disgust, and when she reached out to beckon them back, she could see that her arms were coated with a swirl of thick, black hairs.

In desperation, she turned to Agent Marks, who now had two policemen standing beside him.

"Show this faggot what we think of goddamned queers," he said.

And for some reason she couldn't understand, Princess Paragon, the all-powerful daughter of the planet Iri, who had shattered mountains with her fists and carried ocean liners on her back, now found herself trembling in fear at the approach of two middle-aged policemen with clubs.

When the first club hit her in the face, her head snapped to the left, and she could see the spray of blood leap from her mouth and splatter against the wall behind her.

And then the second blow came, and the third, and as the fourth one descended, she screamed, "AAAAAAAAAAAAAAAAAA

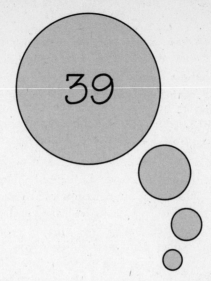

39

AAAAAAAAAAAAAAAAAAGH!"

Brian opened his eyes and panted in terror.

Regina DePadro was in a chair beside him, a black leather jacket over her shoulders and a magazine in her hand. "Don't try to talk," she said.

"Wh— wh—," he said, attempting to open his mouth; it seemed clamped shut.

"I told you not to try that," she said, shutting the magazine, which Brian saw was titled *On Our Backs*. She looked in vain for a place to put it, then gave up and stuck it under her thigh.

"Where am I?" he asked through clenched teeth.

"Hospital outside Chicago," she said, scooting the chair closer to the bed. "Perpetrial called me and asked if I'd keep an eye on you while you're here. Lucky thing I was still in town. After the convention I stayed on to visit some family—my old Aunt Debbie, who lives in Palatine with the world's fattest ferret. I was almost glad to hear you were hurt; gave me a chance to get away."

Brian was busy feeling his face. His entire head appeared to be bandaged, and his jaw seemed clamped to his skull. "What is this?" he asked.

"Well, your *jaw's* broken, silly," she said, as though he'd asked something monumentally stupid. "You're all wired shut. Liquid diet for you, for the next couple of weeks at least."

"I'm not dead?" he asked, staring at his hands.

"Jesus! You sound almost disappointed."

He was trying to sort through all the confusion in his head. "But Jerome shot me!"

"That his name? Guy who attacked you?" Brian nodded. "Well, he didn't *shoot* you, Brian." She crossed her legs and idly picked at the hole in the knee of her jeans. "Don't you remember? Apparently you were at some food plant with this guy, and he threw a gun at you and broke your jaw."

"He *threw* it at me?" he repeated, dumbfounded.

She nodded. "That's what he told the police. And there was no evidence the gun had been fired."

He shook his head. "*Threw* it. Goddamn! Fucker really *can't* do anything right."

Regina cocked her head at him. "Not to pressure you or anything—I mean, your jaw's still pretty fragile—but what the hell was going *on* there? How'd you end up in a food plant in the middle of some piddly little college town two hours outside Chicago?"

He was lying back on the pillow now; he knew he must be drugged, because it was so hard to think, and also because he could feel only slight pain in his jaw. Jerome had *thrown* the gun at him. He'd thought he was going to die or be maimed, and instead he'd ended up with a broken jaw. It was so ridiculous, he might have laughed; but however preferable to death, a broken jaw was still nothing to giggle about. Not to mention that between this and the previous bruises Jerome had inflicted on him, his looks might never be the same. Maybe he'd *rather* be dead.

"Where's Jerome now?" he said, moving his teeth as much as he dared.

"Well, I guess the police have him," she said, uncrossing her legs and stretching. "I'm not sure; I'm getting all this thirdhand from Perpetrial." She came out of her stretch and hung her arms behind the back of the chair. "Apparently, you called her at home and said you were in trouble, and then you had to hang up. She was pretty upset for most of the day; she felt so helpless. Then a brainstorm hit her: she went to the office and looked at the fax number on that script someone sent her with your name on it. Then she called the Chicago police and convinced them to trace that number, and when they called her back they told her that it was registered to a Carter Foods in a place called Park Woods, and that when they notified the Park Woods police of her call they were told there'd already been a disturbance there and that you were in a hospital and your assailant was in custody." She paused. "That's it, essentially. Sound credible?"

He nodded.

"Anyway, that's when Pet called me at Aunt Debbie's and asked me to come and check on you. Which, like I said, was the excuse I'd been looking for." She unhooked one arm and swept her hair behind her shoulders. "I hate that fucking ferret. Like a footstool with teeth. Anyway, I've been here a couple of hours, but you weren't great company till you woke up shrieking just now. Must've been one hell of a nightmare. What was it about?"

"I don't remember," he said, furrowing his brow.

She freed her other arm, leaned back in the chair, and hitched her thumbs in the pockets of her blue jeans. "You must've gotten pretty palsy-walsy with Perpetrial. She was almost hysterical when she called me. Never thought I'd see her so worked up over someone with a penis."

"That's still there, then?" he asked.

She cackled. "Didn't check; might've made me lose my lunch. You want to make sure, go feel around down there your-self." She nodded at the door. "Or I can fetch an orderly to do it. There's one on the floor who looks just like Marky Mark."

"I'm a married man, Regina."

She grunted. "Nothing more pathetic on the face of the earth than a monogamous faggot," she said. "Gay men are sexual *outlaws*, Brian—and for a reason. Without gay subversion, society would never progress. Civilization *depends* on the creative force generated by buggery. This goes back to Plato, to Alcibiades! My *God*. Why would you give up that heritage to become an ersatz Harriet Nelson? It's appalling!"

He sighed. "All right, all right. I give up. Fetch the orderly."

She shook her head and put one booted foot up on his bed. "You're not taking me seriously."

"I'm sorry. I can't really think straight." He looked at her. "It's nice of you to come and sit with me, though. I appreciate it."

She grinned. "I had an ulterior motive."

He immediately became alert. "What?"

She leaned over him and said, "All the time you've been unconscious, I've been whispering in your ear all my ideas about how you should be doing Princess Paragon. So now it's subliminal. You're not going to be able to help it. The minute you get back to your drawing board, you'll be overcome by an irresistible urge to turn her into a dominatrix for hire who wears stiletto heels and teaches humankind how to achieve spiritual transcendence through sadomasochistic rites."

He grunted. "Perpetrial would have a cow."

"Yes, wouldn't she!" She smiled brilliantly.

He grimaced. Was the entire *world* out to get its hands on his character? "How'd it go between you two, anyway?" he asked, changing the subject.

"Oh, hell," she said with a sigh. "Not good. All I wanted was for her to lose twenty-five pounds and wear a red silk teddy a few nights a week. I promised I wouldn't tell anyone. All she wanted from *me* was to give up leather and not eat meat in the house. I said okay. *She's* the one who balked."

He sighed. "I'm sorry."

"Don't be. My new letter carrier in Columbia, it turns out, is totally hot. Looks like Pat Benatar with a big nose. Never felt right about pursuing it before, but now that the book on me and

Perpetrial is officially closed, guess I can go ahead and ask her to come in and lick my envelope."

"She a dyke?"

"Must be. Every time I have to sign for something, I can hear the Indigo Girls coming from her personal stereo." She paused. "Course, I'll have to put a stop to *that.*"

He lolled his head to the right and shut his eyes. "I'm a little tired, Regina. This must be some megapainkiller they've got me on. I know I just woke up, but I honestly think I need a nap."

She got to her feet and slipped her arms into her jacket. "No big deal. I was supposed to go tell a nurse the minute you woke up, anyway."

"You were?" he said, yawning.

"Yeah," she replied, zipping the jacket. "The cops want to come by and ask you some questions." She grabbed her magazine from the chair.

His heart broke into a gallop. To have gone through all this and *still* have to face the police! "Hey, *I* didn't do anything wrong! I wasn't even—"

"I know, I know," she said, flapping a hand at him and heading toward the door. "From what I gather, they just want some dope on this Jerome character. Plus, they want to know if you want to press charges against him for assault with a deadly weapon. Be back later, okay?" She gave him a thumbs-up and headed into the hall.

Brian actually pushed himself up on his elbows and tried to yell after her through his clenched teeth. "WANT TO PRESS CHAR-GES?" he said. "YOU BET YOUR ASS I DO!"

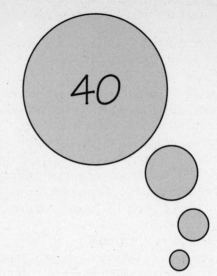

40

Mrs. Kornacker daubed at her eyes with her peach-bordered handkerchief and for the twelfth time in as many minutes emitted a ragged, stuttering sigh. "I blame only myself," she said, crumpling the handkerchief in her hands and then smoothing it out again over her knee. "For years you would lock yourself up behind that closed door of yours, but never did I let myself suspeculate a thing. What a *fool* I was! Behavior that abnormous should have been my first clue!"

Jerome sat in the holding cell with his hands on his thighs, palms up. He was looking at the floor of the cell, where a faint greenish splotch discolored the cement. He couldn't begin to guess what some previous felon had done to create such a stain. Maybe urinated chlorophyll?

His cousin Wilfred patted Mrs. Kornacker's hand and said, "There, there, Aunt Peachy. You mustn't take this so personally. I'm certain Cousin Jerome's derangement doesn't reflect on your merit as a mother. After all, look how well Cousin Sandra turned out!"

"Sandra! cried Mrs. Kornacker. "Don't mention that name to me! She's just as bad as Jerome is except for not being in prison. Do you know what she did to me? *Do you know what she did to me?*"

"What did she do to you?" asked Wilfred sympathetically.

"She asked me to please just leave," said Mrs. Kornacker, sitting back in her chair with a great show of wounded dignity. "She said I'd overstrayed my welcome and that besides I was scaring her kids. She said that whenever I was around them I made a face like a Hindu death god, and those are her extract words. Can you imagine? She said the kids were so terrorfied that they wouldn't even leave from their rooms while I was around. Even if that's the truth, no daughter should ever say a thing like that to the mother who gave her birth. Especially when she knows how touchy the mother who gave her birth is about that old plastic-surgery problem that makes her smile go down instead of up." She daubed her eyes again and gave forth with yet another near death-rattle of a sigh. "But *you*," she said to Jerome. "Your sister may be bad, but you bake the cake! All during my trip I kept wasting sleep wondering if you were safe from the muggers and kidnappers in Chicago, only to come home and find out that you were *one of* the muggers and kidnappers in Chicago. And if that wasn't bad enough, you go right out and heap attempted murderer on top of everything." She daubed at her eyes again. "Just my luck that the first time my Jerome shows a splint of ambition, it has to be for brute violence." She shook her finger at him. "I only wish your father was alive to see this! It would *kill* him."

Jerome continued staring at the green blotch. Someone could have eaten pea soup, he supposed, and then vomited it up after he was locked in here. Jerome could certainly understand that. He felt like vomiting himself. But if he did, Wilfred would mock him till the day the risen Christ returned for Armageddon. And probably a few days after.

He lightly touched the splotch with his foot, to see if it was sticky.

"Don't be *too* hard on Cousin Jerome, Aunt Peachy," said Wilfred with a syrupy lilt to his voice. "His intentions may have been the very worst, but we must take into account his complete incompetence in acting on them."

She sniffed. "You hit the nail on the target there, honey." She daubed her eyes again.

Wilfred turned and addressed Jerome directly. "In fact, I really must congratulate you, *Duh*-rome. This may be the first case of handgun violence in history to result from the assailant *throwing* the gun at his victim. I wonder what the NRA position will be on that?"

From across the station, Jerome heard the desk sergeant holler, "Kinison, you get ahold of that Pinkerton guy yet?"

"Yeah," came the reply, "he's on his way in. Said to give him ten minutes, tops."

Oh, thought Jerome, what a festival of humiliation this is turning out to be!

"Well," said Mrs. Kornacker with a sigh, "it's clear that my son is not going to open up his heart to his mother, so for all intensive purposes my staying here is listless." She got to her feet and slung her peach handbag over her shoulder. "Wilfred, darling, thank you for driving me today. Would you mind stopping on the way back at Jerome's lawyer's house, so I can keep him up-to-breast of this development?"

"Of course, Aunt Peachy. Anything for you, in your hour of need."

Jerome felt his forehead sting with anger, and his cheeks flushed hot. God, how he wished bone cancer on Wilfred!

After they'd gone, he sat quietly in the corner of the cell in the eerie, oddly hushed police station and ran through it all again in his mind: the buzzing, stinging madness overtaking him anew; his frightening urge to kill Brian Parrish; and the tiny, blinding glare of fear or reason or inadequacy that at the last second made him hurl the gun instead of shooting it. Then the sickening crack when it hit Brian Parrish's jaw; the astonished look on the cartoonist's face as he collapsed; and the subsequent arrival of the police, who treated him like he was some kind of Nazi war criminal. Handcuffs, for God's sake! He rubbed his wrists where they had bitten into him.

Worst of all, of course, was the sense of failure that clung to him like a particularly oily sweat. No matter what Bang Comics thought of his script, they'd never publish it now. And Princess Paragon would go on to become a lover of women. He'd failed her; she was beyond him, forever. He focused on the green splotch and tried to summon her up in it, so that he could apologize, explain to her; but there was nothing. He had been her last chance; now she was gone, transformed into something new—something alien to him and outside his realm of understanding. He felt a terrible ache, as though air were being slowly siphoned out of his cell, leaving him gasping for breath. The world he knew was dissipating, dissolving into mist. He had nothing to live for. Nothing.

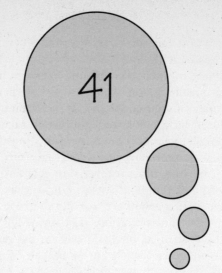

During the early days of their relationship, when Nico was going through his amateur psychologist phase, he would often accuse Brian of being oral-compulsive. And Brian, going through his ecstatically amorous phase, would reply, "Only about you, dear." But now it seemed as though Nico might have had a point; for with his jaw wired shut and thus barred to chewing gum, Brian found himself compelled to take up smoking ("Only temporarily," he assured Nico), just to have something to do with his mouth.

Heloise, for her part, had finally heard from her longtime boyfriend that the sole reason he hadn't given up his apartment and moved permanently into hers was that he just couldn't stomach her smoking. So as Brian sat before her desk trying out new methods of exhaling toxic fumes, she sat behind it chomping on a stick of gum with such fervor that she seemed to be trying to mulch it.

"The point is, Brian," she said, leaning back in her chair and flicking the gum from her left cheek to her right, "I had no idea where you were. I tried contacting you, I left you messages, and I got no reply. And given the torn-up script Perpetrial found in your hotel room and your simultaneous disappearance without a word—without even *checking out*, for God's sake—well, what were we supposed to think? The only explanation that made any sense was that you'd gotten pissed off after Bella Martinez raked you over the coals, and just walked off the book in a fit of wounded ego." She stretched out the gum with her tongue, then let it snap back into her mouth. "And given Perpetrial's close ties to the project, not to mention her handling of the slide show at the convention—well, I had a decision to make, and I made it."

Brian let a bubble of smoke escape his lips. "I'm not following you. What decision?"

She pushed her gum to the front of her mouth and sat there with pursed lips for a moment, looking for all the world as if she were waiting for Brian to kiss her. "This isn't easy to say," she admitted at last.

"Apparently not." He flicked his cigarette into her Moonman ashtray.

"Perpetrial is writing the dialogue for the third issue, based on your first-draft script, which she was loyal enough to tape back together."

He coughed, and for a second smoke obscured his vision. He fanned it away and said, "You can't do that. This is *my* book. I won't stand fo—"

"And *then*," she said, interrupting him, "she's going on to write the entirety of the fourth issue. And the fifth." She was now smacking her gum so frenziedly that Brian wondered if she might be sending a simultaneous message in Morse code. "And the sixth. And the seventh. And the—well, you get the picture." Smack, smack, smack, smack. "Of course, we'd love to have you stay on to *draw* the book."

Brian laughed derisively and blew smoke right at her face. She didn't even blink. "What an ingenious little palace revolution you've whipped up," he said with sugar-coated sarcasm.

"Unfortunately, this isn't czarist Russia, it's twentieth-century America. And I," he concluded grandly, "have a *contract*."

Heloise sighed. "Far as I'm concerned, you've already broken it."

"Bullshit." He stubbed out the cigarette and went immediately for another one. "Horseshit. *Whale*shit."

"It isn't, Brian. Your contract stipulates a weekly editorial conference, even if it's just by phone. You didn't live up to that." Smack, smack, smack.

The new cigarette hung from Brian's lips while he dug through his pockets, looking in vain for a book of matches. "That's a load of crap, Heloise," he said. "You never insisted I do that before."

"My prerogative," she said, handing him an enormous gold Acme-Man fluid lighter.

He considered refusing it, then decided the needs of his nervous system outweighed his pride. He took it, lit his cigarette, and set the lighter back on her desk with a thunk. He took in a lungful of nicotine and coughed it back out. "You can't get away with this," he said. "You may have found a flimsy little loophole, but that doesn't make this right, or honest, or ethical, or—"

"Look," she said, folding her hands on the desk and trying to sound reasonable, "I'm only thinking about what's best for the book. Perpetrial has interviews lined up with *Ms.*, *Mother Jones*, *Spin*, and about four other national rags. A male cartoonist writing about a lesbian superhero may be news. But a *lesbian* cartoonist writing about a lesbian superhero is a *milestone*."

He shook his head. "You just don't get it, Heloise. I've got a *contract*."

She smiled, and as she smiled she rolled the gum along her bottom row of teeth. "No, *you* don't get it, Brian. This isn't Enlightenment Amsterdam, it's twentieth-century America. You may have a contract, but *I've* got a battery of carnivorous lawyers at my beck and call who can keep you busy for years *proving* you've got a contract, all the while sapping every penny you've got. Bang can afford a nice, long lawsuit. You can't."

He snorted smoke through his nose and said, "But that

doesn't mean I couldn't hurt you in the meantime! I can get *my* attorney to slap a restraining order on you to prevent you from publishing any more *Princess Paragon* comics till the suit is settled. Easiest thing in the world." He grinned in triumph.

She cocked her head, as if disappointed by his ingenuousness. "Go ahead," she said, shrugging her shoulders. "See what your reputation is with comics fans, then. See what your reputation is in the gay community. Preventing a lesbian cartoonist from working on a lesbian character? Professional suicide, Brian."

They locked eyes for what seemed at least a month. Heloise gave up her chewing, and Brian's cigarette sat idle in his hand, smoke oozing lazily from its lengthening head. Brian fully expected Heloise to buckle beneath his scrutiny, to say, "Oh, all right, you can stay on the book, but never let this happen again!"

But Heloise was unmovable; she met his stare without a flinch. In fact, it was *she* who got to *him*. Her inflexibility spooked him, and he rose from his chair, thoroughly unsettled.

"You'll be hearing from my lawyer," he said, dropping the cigarette into her ashtray without bothering to snuff it. Let it tempt her!

He stormed out of her office, and when he was halfway down the hall he realized that she—that Heloise *Freitag*, for Christ's sake—had let him have the last word. *That* unnerved him more than anything. She must be supremely confident to pass up the opportunity. It was as though she considered him not worth the effort of one last jeer.

He had almost made it to the reception area when Perpetrial turned a corner, a pencil stuck carelessly through the left bank of her Afro and sporting a cartoon T-shirt showing Billie Jean King stepping on Bobby Riggs. At the sight of him, she erupted into a smile and raced up to him. "Goddess, Brian, it's so good to see you *safe*," she said. She tried to hug him.

He backed away. "Yeah, sure," he hissed, "safe so I could come back and have *you* stab me in the back."

Her face fell. "You've talked to Heloise," she said, her voice small. "Brian, this was *not* my idea. But you weren't around, so

I offered to step in, just for one issue, and afterward Heloise asked if I'd—oh, Brian, you *know* this has always been a dream of m—"

"Spare me, please," he said with as much scorn as he could muster (which was quite a bit). "You screwed me, and now you expect me to be happy about it. I must say, Perpetrial, that is an archetypally *male* thing to do."

No filthier words could he have hurled at her. She burst into tears and fled back the way she'd come.

Brian didn't remember his descent in the elevator, or the first five blocks of his walk. He wasn't even aware of his surroundings until a cabbie started cursing him for crossing the street against the light.

He shook himself out of devising death scenarios for Perpetrial and Heloise, then jumped back on the curb and found himself staring straight through the doorway of a dank, dark, dingy bar.

Providence, he thought.

The bar was nearly empty; it was, after all, only two in the afternoon. "Gypsies, Tramps and Thieves" was playing on the grime-encrusted jukebox. He took one of the cracked vinyl stools and ordered a Manhattan from a rubbery-faced woman bartender wearing enormous ankh earrings. "And bring a straw," he added.

"A *straw*?" she asked, perplexed.

He displayed his wired teeth. She nodded and went off to fix his drink.

After one sip, he felt fire burn in his veins, and he resolved to fight this gross injustice. Of *course* he'd fight it. Maybe it really was hopeless, but the way he felt right now, if it would annoy Heloise, he'd throw himself into a vat of acid. Anything, *anything* to get back at her. Lousy *bitch*. For decades, no one would touch her goddamned comic book; then he came along and made it hot again, and suddenly, even before his first issue hit the stands, everyone and his mother was trying to take it away from him. And Heloise was *allowing* it.

All at once he found himself wondering why he cared. What had he said to Jerome? Princess Paragon wasn't a character, she was a product; his handling of her amounted to nothing more than pimping. And hadn't he laughed at Nigel Cardew for taking Moonman and Comet so seriously, as though they were real people?

Why, then, despite continually telling himself that this was a matter of principle and nothing more, did he find himself taking each soggy sip of his Manhattan with the thought, *My princess . . . my princess . . .*

It was embarrassing. It was unprofessional. And yet he couldn't deny that when Heloise had told him he was off the book and Perpetrial was on, his first reaction had been something close to what he imagined a parent must feel when he hears his child has been abducted.

"So now you know how it feels," a voice said, and it took him a moment to realize that it wasn't in his head.

Alarmed, he turned and found an old man seated on the next stool. He had a bald, liver-spotted head, a salt-and-pepper goatee, and a potbelly the size of a honey-baked ham. Brian was fairly certain he'd never met him before. "How *what* feels?" he asked, a little warily.

"Having the Princess taken away from you," the old man said, incredibly. "What's your poison?"

Brian looked at his glass, as if he'd forgotten. "Manhattan," he mumbled.

The old man signaled the bartender. "Two Manhattans," he said. "In fact, make 'em doubles."

"Who are you?" Brian asked.

He extended his hand. "Roger Oaklyn," he replied, smiling sunnily. "We almost met once before. In Chicago. On the 'Bella' show."

Brian sighed and looked away. "Oh, *Christ,*" he muttered. "This day just keeps getting better and better." He turned back to Oaklyn and said, "You're exactly where all my troubles began, you know that?"

"Then you're a lucky man," Oaklyn replied. "Mine go back before you were born. You going to shake my hand, or what?"

Brian rolled his eyes heavenward, then shook his hand.

The bartender delivered their double Manhattans. The jukebox was now playing "Look What They Done to My Song, Ma."

Brian took the straw from his old drink and stuck it into the new, then sucked up a good mouthful. "How do *you* know they took her away from me?"

Oaklyn shrugged. "Still got a few friends up at Bang— secretaries, mailroom kids, even a couple old-timers like me, been there since God made Adam. They let me know what's up. One of 'em found out you were coming in today, then got wind of why, and called me. Said I should come down and enjoy the show."

Brian was too emotionally exhausted to be annoyed by this petty taunting. He felt a sort of detached, almost intellectual curiosity. "And how'd you find me here? In this bar, I mean."

Oaklyn chuckled and shook his head. "*Followed* you here. All the way from Bang. Rode down the goddamn elevator with you, matter of fact."

Brian squinted at him. "You're enjoying this, aren't you?"

Oaklyn took a large gulp from his drink, then suppressed a burp. "Truth to tell, yes I am. After what you did to me on that 'Bella' show—yes, indeed I am."

Brian sighed through his teeth, shook his head, and sucked up some more of his Manhattan.

"See," Oaklyn continued, leaning toward him, "this is about as close as I'll ever get to revenge. Hell! It's not even *that* close, 'cause your situation isn't any of my doing. Gloating is all it amounts to. But I'll take it."

His breath smelled like he'd eaten a live hamster the week before and not brushed his teeth since. "Go ahead and gloat," said Brian, sliding across the stool to get out of range. "Long as you're buying the drinks, I don't give a shit."

The old man sat back and his shoulders fell, as if he were somehow terribly let down. "You don't even care, do you? You don't even want to know why."

Brian laughed and shook his head. "No, I don't."

"I'll tell you anyway." He downed another swig, then leaned

into Brian again. "It's 'cause Bang Comics paid me four hundred bucks for all the rights to Princess Paragon, in perpetuity, and then spent the next fifty years making millions of dollars off her. And when I got a little too big for my britches and asked to see a part of that, they fired me, on the spot. Kicked me out and gave the series—*my* series—to some brain-damaged hack who almost buried it. I was on the book for exactly thirty-eight issues. That's it! That's my legacy. Then you come along, the latest in the line of gravediggers who've been churning me up for half a century, and you get some kind of million-dollar deal for turning my character into a pervert. I don't get consulted; I don't get any royalties; I don't even get any credit. What I get is kicked off the 'Bella' show. What I get is a fucking features reporter at my door once a fucking decade. What I get is to live with the memory that I was a twenty-three-year-old schmuck who sold his brain-child for four hundred pissant dollars to a bunch of fucking suits who used it to put their snob kids through college and join country clubs."

Brian refused to look at him. "Whine, whine, whine," he said between sips. "Why the hell didn't you just go out and create something new?"

Oaklyn bugged out his eyes and his forehead turned vermilion. "*Great* idea! Why didn't *I* think of that?" he said with violent sarcasm. Then he snarled, "You think I didn't *try*, you moronic little *runt*? I tried for twenty fucking *years*! You want the whole list—my whole fucking litany of failed features? Starting with *Chester Champion* and *Rootin'-Tootin' Rita* and running right through the *Polka-Dot Patrol* and *Betty Bikini*?" He consumed almost a third of his drink in one, herculean chug. "So now I work as a goddamned messenger, living in a two-room apartment in Jersey-fucking-City that I can't even afford, praying every night that my daughter someday convinces her rich proctologist husband to let me have the room above the garage of their house in New Rochelle, which he never will because he hates my fucking guts, and who can blame him? I'm a *loser*."

Brian was feeling the weight of the liquor pulling at him now, and Oaklyn's story wasn't helping. "Well, I hope it's made a difference, being able to gloat over me like this," he said, trying to seem unaffected.

Oaklyn got up. "Well, it was just gloating to *start*," he said. "Now I get to spend the rest of my life enjoying the knowledge of how you got screwed almost as bad as I did. Course, you didn't create Princess Paragon; you just made her *sell* again. Heard the advance orders are the highest the book's ever had. Funny thing is, in spite of the pervert stuff, I almost liked you for that. I was excited to meet you on 'Bella.' I was going to tell America that I thought you were pretty much okay. But you took that from me, and now they've taken her from *you*, and you can't do one goddamn thing about it, and I just think that's fucking *great*." He polished off his Manhattan, slammed the glass down on the bar, and walked out.

He was gone for three full minutes before Brian realized he hadn't left any money.

"Better and better," he mumbled, rubbing his forehead. "This day just keeps getting better and better and be—"

Something caught in his throat, surprising him. And he realized that Roger Oaklyn had had more of an impact on him than he'd thought. After all, what Jerome had tried to do to him, what Perpetrial *had* done to him, was nothing compared with what Bang had done to Oaklyn. In fact, Brian now realized that Jerome and Perpetrial had exactly as much right to Princess Paragon as he had—which was no right at all.

By any moral reckoning, she belonged to Roger Oaklyn. It was as plain as that. As plain, and as terrifying, as that.

It took two more Manhattans to make this sink in, in all its terrible complexity. Then, with the jukebox gurgling up "The Candy Man," he staggered to the pay phone and called Heloise.

"I'm nod going to fight choo," he told her.

"You're shit-faced," she said.

"Shud up and lissen, you stupid cow! I'm doing you a fugging *favor*! Now, like I said, I'm nod going to fight choo, Hel'weez, provided you do one thing: you gotta stard paying royalties to Roger Oaglyn."

"What?" A slight pause. "The guy you wouldn't even let

near you on 'Bella'?" He could hear her gum smacking. "Brian, are you all right?"

"Yes or no, Hel'weez? Jus' yes or no?"

Smack, smack, smack. "I want things to be right between us, Brian. I want you to do more work for Bang."

"YES OR NO, GODDAMMID?"

"*Christ.*" Smack, smack, smack, smack. "It can probably be arranged. I'm not promising anything." Smack, smack. "Call me about this tomorrow. *Sober.* I'll have more of an idea then."

"Okay, I will. I mean it. I'm nod gonna forget jus' coz I'm drung."

"I wasn't thinking that."

"Good. Lissen, conneck me wif Pepedrial, will ya?"

"Brian, no. You've upset her enough today. I won't have you—"

"Hel'weez, you dumb *fugg*, can you nod *see* I have had a change of heart?"

Smack, smack, smack, smack. "All right, then, Brian. But I'm warning you!"

"Yeah, yeah, yeah."

A moment later: "Perpetrial Cotton speaking." Her voice was barely there. Heloise must have warned her that it was him on the line.

"Pepedrial, it's Brine," he said grandly. "I jus' wan' to 'pologize and say I wish you all the luck in the worl' wif Princ'ss Paraglon."

An epic-length pause. "You mean it, Brian?" she said at last. "You're not being sarcastic?"

"I havvint god a sarcassic bone in my body!"

"And if you did, it'd be drowned in alcohol by now," she said gravely. He could almost see her shaking her head in disapproval. "Well, thank you, Brian. Apology accepted. I just hope this isn't the liquor talking."

"Silly bisch, liquor can'd talk!" He cackled.

"Right. Listen, why don't you go home and sleep this off?"

"Oh, no, ma'am! I've god one more phone call to make, thang you very much."

"Maybe you should put it off till you're sober, Brian. Who's it to?"

Brian told her.

And Perpetrial managed to convince him that it should *definitely* wait till he was sober.

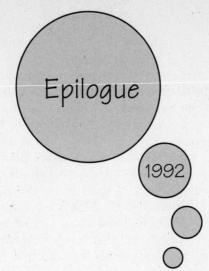

Epilogue

1992

Doug had been flipping through the new Comics Retailer Order Form for nearly twenty minutes when he called out, "Hey, Jerome, dig this: they're finally soliciting for the new Brian Parrish comic!"

Jerome was busy stacking the shelves with the day's new arrivals. He turned and asked, "What do they say about it?"

Doug held up the catalog-sized mailer and read, " '*Isabella, She-Wolf of France* number one, by Brian Parrish.' " He cleared his throat and continued. " 'A top comics creator returns after a too-long absence, this time under the imprint of Rage Comics, an independent publishing house he himself co-founded. His new ongoing series is a melodramatic, often campy Middle Ages serial based on the life of the ferocious "queen who married a queen": Isabella of France, whose husband was the first openly gay King of England, Edward the Second. In the debut issue, Isabella meets her fiancé for the first time, and is mortified to discover he has a boyfriend who's prettier than she is. She immediately hatches a plot to get the boyfriend sent off at the head of a Crusade—or, failing that, to have him drowned in the moat.' " Doug lowered the order form and raised an eyebrow. "*Bit* of a departure for your pal, I daresay."

Jerome dumped a stack of new *Sherman Tank* comics onto a shelf, then wiped his forehead with his sleeve and said, "Do me a favor and order a bunch of copies, okay? Brian Parrish could probably use it. Sounds like it'll be a tough sell."

Doug shook his head. "I don't know. Could turn out to be kind of Monty Python–ish. Maybe it'll take off."

"I hope so. Meantime, how about getting twenty or so?"

"*Twenty?* We barely sell that many of *Moonman*!"

Jerome put his hands on his hips and bent backward to relieve the stress of all the lifting he'd done. "I know, I know. But I'll *personally* pay for any copies that don't sell. You can even dock them from my paycheck." He came out of his stretch and cracked his knuckles. "After all, if Brian Parrish hadn't dropped those charges against me, I might've ended up in prison. I *owe* it to him." He stooped down to open the next cardboard shipping box. "Even volunteered to come back to town just to make a statement on my behalf, if need be. Which took some guts. Just *talking* to the police took guts, for him."

He opened the box, revealing the new issue of Perpetrial Cotton's *Princess Paragon*. It was issue number eleven—the first to bear the legend "Created by Roger Oaklyn" beneath the logo. He grabbed a handful of copies and started searching out their proper place on the shelves.

The bell above the door jangled to life. Jerome turned to inform the new arrival that the store wouldn't open for another ten minutes, then saw that it was Amanda, dressed in a frilly floral-print dress and carrying her tiny purse. "*Hi,*" she said brightly.

"H-hi," he said, instantly dropping his handful of comics. Even after months of dating, her appearance still flustered him.

She looked at her watch. "It's almost noon. You ready for lunch? Remember, your mother's meeting us today."

Jerome rolled his eyes. "I forgot. I promised her, didn't I?"

She nodded, biting her lower lip, as though trying not to giggle at his dread.

He looked pleadingly at Doug, who said, "What the hell, scoot. I can't stand between a man and his mother. I'll finish up here."

Jerome turned back to Amanda and said, "I'll be right out. Just let me clear up the mess here."

She agreed, winked at him, and then left the shop to wait outside, where she could bask her face in the white spring sunlight.

Jerome bent down to retrieve the comics he'd dropped. One of the copies had fallen open to the last page, and before he could pick it up, he found himself reading it—particularly the gorgeously rendered last panel, in which Princess Paragon and Cosmique stood hand in hand on an alien landscape, stars and comets whirling majestically above their heads.

"And what now, my love?" said Cosmique, the galaxy reflected in her iridescent eyes. "What next for us, now that the menace to my planet has at long last been quelled?"

Princess Paragon lifted her head high and said, "After a nightmare, there must be an awakening. Let us awaken. Let us begin a new day."